The Spanish Girl

Eugene Vesey

Published by Clink Street Publishing 2022

Copyright © 2022

First edition.

ISBNs:
978-1-914498-97-8 - paperback
978-1-914498-98-5 - ebook

For
La Senorita

CHAPTER ONE

In Dublin's fair city
Where the girls are so pretty

'My father is very bad-tempered,' Ana said. 'Once he didn't speak to me for two months.'

He laughed and took a quaff of the excellent stout. They were in the Stag's Head, one of his favourite hostelries in the centre of Dublin, close to the university, Trinity College, with its 'surly front' as Joyce described it, where he was teaching on an English language summer school for foreign students. Entering the Stag's Head was like stepping into a hundred-year time warp. It was all dark wood, tile and marble and high, ornately-plastered ceilings. They were in one of the cosy wood and cut-glass-panelled snugs. It probably hadn't changed much since Joyce's time.

She reminded him of the young waitress in the hotel in San Sebastian where he had stayed with his mother for a week on their way to Lourdes. How long ago was that? Eighteen years! He was twenty-one, still a seminarian, but sick in soul because, having lost his faith, he had lost his vocation to the priesthood too, but after nine years couldn't find the courage to leave and go back to the world he had left behind at the age of twelve, a world that was like another planet now.

At dinner in the hotel with his mother, who felt more like a chaperone than a companion, he had stolen surreptitious,

1

guilty glances at the young Spanish waitress with hopeless longing, crushed by the thought that if he stayed in this way of life he could never have a girlfriend like her, or *any* girlfriend, never have a wife, never have children, never be *normal* …

And now here he was, in a pub in central Dublin eighteen years later, chatting up a pretty young Spanish girl who looked not totally unlike that Spanish waitress all those years ago! A ripple of triumph went through him at the thought. He had escaped his fate, turned the tables on it, defied it! He had come through, to quote DH Lawrence, and come out the other side, though it had almost destroyed him.

Now he was in a different world, the *real* world, the world that, ironically, he had read about enviously in novels, the world of *real* people, of *real* men and women, *normal* people, not celibate sorcerers in black frocks who dealt in black magic and mumbo jumbo; the world where men and women met and mingled, fell in love, made love, had sex, made children, lived together, *lived*.

'What did you do to upset him so much?' he asked her with a wry smile, wondering if he should ask if it had been something to do with a boy, but refraining, because she seemed so innocent.

'I told him I wanted to go to England.'

'You mean, to live in England?'

'Yes. Just for a year. To study.'

'And he wouldn't let you? But you're twenty-one. He can't stop you, can he?'

'He stopped speaking to me.'

'For two months?'

'Yes. Until I agreed not to. That's why I've come here. It's a compromise with him.'

'It's not enough, three weeks.'

2

'I know. But I can't disobey him. I'm afraid of him.'

'You're afraid of your father?'

'He loves me.'

'He loves you too much then!'

'Yes, he's very possessive.'

'He has to let you go sooner or later.' He felt fraudulent saying it. What did he know, he who wasn't a father yet, might never be, if the doctors were right?

'Yes. But only when I get married.'

'I see. Will you get married?'

'I hope one day.'

This was his cue. 'Have you got a boyfriend?'

'Yes.' He was disappointed, though it was inevitable, she was so pretty.

'Tell me about him.' He could sense she wasn't happy with the relationship, which diluted his disappointment a little.

'His name is José.'

'Yes? Is he good-looking?'

'Yes. He's tall and thin like you, with long dark hair.' She pronounced 'you' like 'ju'.

'But better-looking than me?' he laughed, taking a swig of stout.

'You are good-looking.' *Ju are good-looking.*

'Gracias! And you are pretty.'

'You think so?' *Ju think so.*

'Yes, I do. Very pretty!' It was time to turn on the charm. He could see she was flattered, not used to being complimented, pretty though she was. 'So, tell me more.'

'About?'

'Your boyfriend.' Not that he really wanted to know. 'What does he do?'

'He's unemployed. Sometimes he helps my father.'

'What does your father do?'

'He's, how do you say, with wood?'

'Carpenter.'

'Si.'

'So, is that it?'

'What do you want to know?'

'How long have you been with him?'

'We met at school.'

'A few years then?'

'Si.'

'Is it serious?'

'I don't know.'

He interpreted that as a no, wondered if he dared ask the million-dollar question, took a slug of Guinness for courage.

'Do you – sleep with him? That's one way to tell if it's serious.'

'How dare you!' she expostulated, slapping his face, jumping up and running out of the pub.

To his relief, she didn't do that, but answered frankly. 'I've never made love with him.'

'I see. Doesn't he want to? Don't you want to?'

'He tries to have sex in the back of the car. He opens his trousers. It's embarrassing for me.'

'I'm sure it is.' He was shocked, but pleasantly surprised at her candour.

'You don't want to – have sex?' Again, to his relief, she didn't slap his face, but answered with surprising candour.

'I'm afraid.'

'You've never had – sex?'

'No.'

'So you're a – a virgin?'

'Si. Yes.'

'I see.' He was surprised, yet knew he shouldn't be, considering her background – Spanish, Catholic. At least, he supposed she was Catholic. He had had a female Spanish student who was a Jehovah's Witness, a convert from Catholicism, in his class once. Talk about out of the frying pan into the fire! 'What are you afraid of exactly?'

'I'm afraid of making love. I don't know anything about sex. I never read about sex.'

'Your mother didn't talk to you about sex?'

'No. She'd be too embarrassed.'

'You didn't have any sex education at school?'

'No. My teachers were nuns.'

'Ah, well, that explains that!' he laughed, taking another slug of the excellent Stag's Head stout.

So she must be Catholic. It wasn't completely different from his own case – educated for the most part by celibate brothers and priests who hadn't a clue about such matters, indeed had warped views about them. Some of whom were warped themselves. He didn't tell her that though. That would be for later – if there was a later. Time for a little pep talk. A little homily.

'There's nothing wrong with sex, you know, Ana. It's healthy and natural. You don't have to suppress it. It's not a sin, despite what the Catholic church says. As long as you're careful, of course. I mean, careful not to get pregnant. Unless you want to get pregnant. Careful not to catch a disease. And preferably do it with someone you love. Or at least someone who means something to you. Someone special.'

He was amused to hear himself giving sex education to a pretty young Spanish girl. He'd certainly come a long way since that time eighteen years ago in San Sebastian! The Spanish waitress hovered sad-eyed on the periphery of his vision. *Sad-Eyed Lady of the Lowlands.*

'I'm sorry,' she said.

'What are you sorry about?' he smiled, taking another swig of stout.

'I'm boring.'

'You're not boring!' he laughed. 'I like you.'

'You like me?'

'Yes! That's why I invited you for a drink.'

'Why do you like me?'

'I don't know,' he laughed. 'There's just something about you I like. I mean, apart from the fact you're pretty. And intelligent.' *And you're Spanish.*

'I like you.' *I like ju.*

'Come here.' He put his arm around her fragile shoulders and pulled her towards him. To his relief, she didn't resist. He put a finger under her chin, tilted her head upwards and gave her a quick kiss on her lips. 'There, that didn't hurt, did it?' he grinned, gazing into her brown eyes. God, she was pretty!

'I like you so much,' she sighed, resting her head on his chest.

'You don't sound very happy.'

'I'm jealous.' She pronounced it 'jelloos'.

'Jealous? Of who?'

'The other girls. I know they like you.'

He laughed, flattered. 'You're the only one I like. That's why I'm here with *you*.' This was only half true – there were a couple of other girls on the course he liked, but not as much as her. There really was something about her ...

'I'm jealous of your girlfriend.'

'How do you know I have a girlfriend?'

'Have you got?' *Hab ju got.*

'Yes, but it's not good.'

'Do you live with her?'

'Yes, but.' He shrugged.

'I hate her.'

'You don't need to hate her,' he said, shocked, taking his arm from her shoulders, and added glumly: 'I don't think it'll last very much longer.'

A stab of guilt went through him at the thought of Rania back home in London. She loved him and he loved her – or did he? – but it was impossible. She was impossible. It was a massive mistake. They were incompatible. Two very different people, from two very different cultures and with an almost twenty-year age gap between them. He had to leave her, for her sake and his. Yet until now he hadn't been able to find the guts to do so. Maybe if he found another girl first, he surmised, it would give him the motivation he needed. Maybe this girl beside him now could be the one. He picked up her hand, held it tenderly in his. It was like a child's.

'Can I ask you something, Ana?' he said, lifting her chin, tilting her head towards him and gazing into her brown eyes again, a snatch of Van Morrison's 'Brown Eyed Girl' playing on his mental jukebox.

'You can ask,' she replied. *Ju can ask.*

'Will you be my girl?' *My brown-eyed girl.*

It only took her a second to reply, but it felt like minutes, during which his heart seemed to stop beating and he braced himself for her to say no, snatch her hand away indignantly, slap his face, flee …

'Yes,' she said, gazing back into his eyes. 'But can I ask you something?'

'Sure.'

'You won't hurt me, will you?'

'I won't hurt you.'

'You promise? Because I'm very easy to hurt.'

'I promise.' He meant it, though he wasn't totally sure he'd be able to keep it. After all, he'd been here before with Danielle, his French girlfriend. He'd lost her, but this time he'd do better, he told himself. He'd learned from his mistake.

'OK?' he asked.

'OK,' she said.

'Can I give you a kiss?'

'If you want.' *If ju want.*

He put his hand on the back of her slender neck, pulled her gently towards him and kissed her lightly on the lips.

'Te quiero,' she murmured.

'What does that mean?' he asked, though he knew.

'I love you.' *I love ju.*

'Te quiero,' he said, pulling her close and giving her another kiss on the lips. Somehow, it sounded better in Spanish.

That was how it had started. They spent the rest of the evening in the pub, cuddling and exchanging life stories. She told him she loved animals, because as she charmingly put it, they were 'innocent'. She had a dog called Dama, who slept on her bed. She had two sisters, both younger. (Are they as pretty as you, he asked, teasing?) Her father had a glass of whisky every night after work. She said she was self-conscious about being so small, especially having small breasts. (He told her that didn't matter to him, which it didn't, and that what mattered was what was inside, which was largely true.) She believed in God and went to Mass every Sunday, but her boyfriend didn't believe in God or go to church – it was a problem between them. (He kept his counsel on that one.) Her boyfriend didn't want to mix with her friends – that was another problem between them. She was going to leave him when she went home.

He told her about growing up in an Irish Catholic family in Manchester, about childhood holidays in Ireland, about his time in the seminary (though not about the sexual, physical and psychological abuse), about losing his faith and his vocation, about the breakdown of his relationship with his parents as a result, about how he knew Charles, the director of the summer school, from seminary days, about the college in London where he taught, about how his girl-friend had been one of his students there, about how he now realised their relationship was a mistake, they were incompatible, he was going to leave her when he went home ...

'I don't know if I should,' she said primly, when he suggested sleeping with her that night.

They were sitting on the metal-framed sofa in the living-room of her flat in Trinity – like all the student flats spacious but somewhat spartan: a couple of functional, metal-framed, black-cushioned armchairs to go with the sofa, a threadbare carpet over ancient floorboards, a bookcase built into the thick stone wall, a gas fire, a large wooden table-cum-desk, faded wallpaper, tatty curtains on the tall sash windows also set deep into the old, grey-black, granite walls.

After leaving the pub at closing time, they had gone for a romantic walk hand in hand along the Liffey quays – his favourite part of Dublin – not talking much, just happy to be in each other's company. When they arrived back at the college, having been allowed in by the porter through the fortress-like wooden front gate, he had to persuade her to invite him into her flat. She tried to use her flatmate, Maria José, as an excuse to deter him, but he argued that as it was after midnight MJ would almost certainly be tucked up in bed asleep. Besides, he knew MJ wasn't the problem. *She* was the problem.

'Why not?' he asked, his arm around her on the sofa. 'Just for a while. An hour or two. I can't stay all night. We don't have to do anything. Just to be together a bit longer.'

'I'm afraid,' she said.

'What are you afraid of?'

'I'm afraid of my father.'

'But your father can't see you!' He had to stop himself laughing. God, she was really hung up about her father!

'I need time.'

'We don't need to do anything. We can just lie on the bed together. We don't even have to get undressed.'

'Promise you won't do anything. I know you're more experienced than me.'

'Of course I won't do anything. We've only just met. I'm not going to take advantage of you. I just want to be with you. Te quiero.' He pulled her towards him and gave her a kiss on the lips.

'Te quiero,' she murmured shyly.

'Let's go then.'

He stood up, took hold of her hand and pulled her up from the sofa. She let him lead her by the hand to her bedroom, one of the two in the flat, and they lay on her bed fully clothed except for shoes. It was a single bed, so they were forced to be close together, which suited him. He took her in his arms.

They kissed properly, French kissed, though he had to teach her, and he tried to fondle her breasts, but she stopped him. 'Stop! You're exciting me!' she remonstrated, pulling his hand away.

'I'm sorry,' he said, silly as it sounded.

'Tell me something,' she said.

'Yes?'

'What do you feel?'

'You mean, right now?'

'Si.'

'Frustrated, I suppose.' He might as well be honest, he decided.

'Everyone is frustrated round me,' she sighed and to his shock he saw tears welling in her big brown eyes.

'Hey,' he said guiltily, kissing her and giving her a hug. 'It doesn't matter. We don't have to have sex. I'm happy to be here with you. I love you.'

'I'm sorry,' she said. 'You're disappointed.'

'There's nothing to be sorry about,' he insisted, tenderly wiping the tears from her cheeks with a finger and wishing he hadn't been so honest. 'And I'm not disappointed. I'm happy. Happy to be with you. You're lovely. I love you.' The waitress in San Sebastian eighteen years ago, who had been following him phantom-like all evening, was standing in the corner, watching anxiously.

'I love you,' she whispered. 'Promise you won't hurt me.'

'I promise,' he said and meant it.

The waitress smiled a Mona Lisa smile and disappeared.

CHAPTER TWO

The sea oh the sea

On the ferry home across Joyce's scrotum-tightening Irish Sea, he told himself he'd forget her and try to make a go of it with his girlfriend, Rania, despite their differences. He told himself it had just been a holiday romance – fun while it lasted, but not serious, it couldn't last, he loved her but they were too far apart, she had a boyfriend, he had a girlfriend, it was too complicated …

He wrote a long letter telling her so during the crossing, sitting on the top deck in the sunshine and supping a pint of Guinness, enjoying the sensation of being on the wide, empty sea under an equally empty, cloudless, blue sky, as if in a state of suspension from ordinary everyday life. Enjoying too the rhythmic throb of the ship's engines as it ploughed imperiously through the choppy waves, escorted by a squadron of screeching gulls like avian mini-fighter jets. When he finished, he folded up the sheet of A4 and slipped it into his inside pocket. He'd post it tomorrow.

'Let's treasure this time as just a happy memory,' he wrote. 'Think of it like a delicious dream, but no more than a dream, a dream that came miraculously true for a while, but that could not last, could not survive in the real, material world of daily life and work, because dreams by definition are ephemeral, as ephemeral as comets, butterflies, gossamer …'

Sitting and supping his pint, though, as the ship churned relentlessly on towards Holyhead, surrounded by 'the lonely sea and the sky', he wondered if it was really true, if it *was* only a dream, if he was doing the right thing, if he shouldn't try to keep it going. During the three weeks of the summer school he had become more and more fond of her. In fact he had fallen in love with her – even though she hadn't let him make love with her, even though their relationship was still only semi-platonic. God, he missed her already!

He took out from his inside pocket the envelope containing the birthday card she had given him before leaving Dublin a few days ago, with strict instructions to open it only on his birthday, which had now passed. He opened it and read again the message she had written inside in her elongated, upright handwriting:

Thank you for your love and friendship. I'll never be able to forget you and these three happy weeks in Dublin.

With love,

Ana x

August 1986

So simple, so sweet! It brought tears to his eyes. Or was that just the salt-spiced wind whipping off the water? 'The wind like a whetted knife,' to quote one of his favourite poems again.

The fact that it was a jokey card rather than a romantic one made the message all the more touching to him. On the front were three pictures of a dopey-looking Basset hound doing tricks with a ball, such as balancing it on its nose, with the caption:

... FOR YOUR BIRTHDAY ... I thought I would teach you something new and exciting to do! ... something fun

& different, something satisfying and trendy ... and then I remembered ...

Inside, it said:

... you can't teach an old dog new tricks!!!

It wasn't Oscar Wilde, but it made him smile, remembering how they used to joke about him being old enough to be her father. But she said she liked the idea of having a second 'daddy', an older boyfriend, because it made her feel doubly secure.

She was so insecure, so shy, so timid! Especially when it came to sex. They had fallen out once or twice because of her refusal to have sex. He had even accused her of being 'frigid' once, making her cry. The memory pierced him painfully, even though he had apologised immediately. He had sent her to Coventry once, too, for over a day. That made him writhe even more with remorse, though he had made up with her. It also made him realise what he felt for her wasn't just lust, but something more, something deeper. Something like love.

And even though she wouldn't let him have sex with her, she was very jealous, had quite a temper, became really angry with him once because he sat next to Encarnita, another Spanish girl, on the coach to Glendalough. *She* gave *him* the silent treatment that day, refused to go near him or speak to him for the whole day, moved away if he tried to approach her. Later that evening, when he confronted her in her flat about her behaviour, she accused him of fancying Encarnita and they had a big row, which ended up with him storming out and going to the pub on his own.

He went to Bartley Dunne's, their secret rendezvous, to sink his sorrows in a few pints of stout, knowing there was no chance of any of the other students wandering in there. It was cutting off his nose to spite his face, because he felt lonely, wanted company, always enjoyed the company of the students, especially at the end of a day out, but he hoped she'd follow him in and apologise. Which she did. And he apologised, too, though he felt he had won the moral victory and the power struggle. So they kissed and made up. Now, sitting alone on the windy top deck of the ferry as it churned inexorably towards Holyhead, away from Dublin, away from the dream, the memory filled him with a mixture of sweetest pleasure and sharpest pain.

'You don't talk much, don't show yourself,' she said to him in the heart to heart that followed, which even in memory still shocked – and needled – him.

'I have to make love with a girl before I can reveal myself fully,' he replied. 'Break down all the physical and emotional barriers.'

'Why didn't you tell me this before?' she demanded.

'I never realised it before myself,' he shrugged.

It was at least half true. She wasn't the first girl to say something like that to him and it always disconcerted him. He was starting to realise he was a bit reserved, a bit buttoned up emotionally – probably because of his background as a seminarian – and it was only through sex he was really able to open the floodgates and reveal himself fully. And it was only that evening he realised that, because she wouldn't let him have sex with her, he was unconsciously holding himself back from her …

'Are you telling that because you want to make love with me?' she asked.

'Of course not!' he denied, offended but not taking offence, because he didn't want to imperil their reconciliation. 'I don't want to make love with you.'

'You don't want to make love with me?' she demanded, as if offended herself. *God, sometimes you can't win!*

'Of course I want to make love with you,' he protested, 'but I know you're not ready. I can wait.'

'Si,' she said. 'I'm not ready.'

'I know, you need time,' he laughed, giving her a hug. It had become a joke between them, a kind of secret catch-phrase. *I need time.*

'I'm sorry,' she said.

'You don't need to be sorry,' he soothed her. 'I understand. As I said, I can wait.'

'Te quiero mucho,' she replied.

'Te quiero,' he said, pulling her close and kissing her on the lips.

One of the gulls landed on the rail and fixed him with a beady stare for a while, then flew off to rejoin his fellow aviators around the stern of the vessel, squawking and soaring and swooping with them. Oh, to be a seagull, he chuckled to himself, with not a care in the world, except maybe where your next crumb of food was coming from! Chevaliers of the skies indeed.

He had tried to teach the advanced group Hopkins's 'The Windhover', partly because it was one of his own favourite poems and partly because of Hopkins's connection with Dublin. He had even taken them to see Hopkins's grave in Glasnevin Cemetery. The poem had been hard work and not all of them had appreciated it, because not all of them were literary-minded, but most of them had and in teaching it he had gained a better understanding of it himself. To his relief, Ana had been *very* appreciative. He was relieved, because – strange thought perhaps – he didn't think he could like any girl who didn't have some appreciation of poetry. It would be like trying to relate to someone who said they didn't like music! Or sunsets. Or flowers. Or paintings.

There were such people, he knew. People who were tone-deaf in one way or another. Philistines.

It pained him to think Ana was everything Rania was not. She was sweet, soft, meek, submissive, deferential. She openly admired him and looked up to him. She was intelligent, not that Rania wasn't intelligent, but more in the sciences. Ana loved literature – novels, poetry, theatre – was eager to learn about it, encouraged him in his own aspirations to write. She loved the Irish music he introduced her to. She never disagreed or argued with him. The only problem between them, apart from the geographical distance, was sex. But that wasn't really a problem. He was prepared to wait for her. To give her *time*.

It didn't matter now, though, he told himself. It was over. It had to end. He had tried to tell her so the night before she left Dublin to fly back to Madrid, but she refused to accept it. 'No, no, no!' she cried, throwing her arms around him and clinging to him. 'Please don't tell me that! Ju promised ju wouldn't hurt me! Ju said ju loved me! Ju were lying!' Tears welled in her beautiful big brown eyes.

'Oh, Ana,' he said, hugging her, his heart breaking. 'I do love you. I haven't lied to you. I've been honest and truthful with you from the start. We both know it had to end.'

'No, no, no!' she wept. 'I love ju! Please don't leave me! If ju leave me, I'll die.'

He was shocked. Did she mean if he left her, she would …? He didn't dare ask. He took back what he had said about ending it and agreed to continue the relationship, at least as friends, even to go and see her in Madrid. Well, he thought, they were really only friends anyway. Loving friends. What they had was something like what the French called an 'amitié amoureuse'. (There was no good English equivalent he could think of. Loving friendship?) He regretted it now though. It was better to end it cleanly, as he had tried to.

Otherwise, it was only dragging out the agony. It would end in even worse tears. Hence the letter nestled in his inside jacket pocket. He'd post it first thing tomorrow.

When he got home, among the mail – most of it junk and bills – Rania had collected in a large bundle for him, was a letter from Spain. It was postmarked from Valencia, rather than Madrid, but he knew it had to be from Ana, recognised her handwriting on the front. In spite of himself, he felt a ripple of excitement, but deliberately waited to open it until Rania was out of the way. He took out and unfolded a sheet of unlined A4 covered from top to bottom on both sides in the same upright, spidery handwriting, each side numbered in the top right-hand corner, with a little circle round the number, as if it were a piece of homework:

Gandia, 27 August 86

Dear Francis,

As I promised to you, I'm writing on Tuesday. You have to forgive my mistakes and correct them if you want, because I left my dictionary in Madrid. The travel was very sad and the arrival even worse: José was waiting for me at the airport. We went to have dinner together and for a drink after dinner. As you can imagine the situation was extremely annoying for me. After being without seeing him almost a month, I was supposed to have a "close" meeting/appointment with him. (Can you understand me?)

That type of appointment was impossible for me because of my depressive mood. He was in a bad mood as usual, very sentimental and he couldn't avoid crying. I'm not strong enough yet to speak to him, but I was preparing the way for the next serious conversation. I asked him to think about our relationship, how we've changed and how we're hurting each other and so on. I didn't want him to be waiting for me, but if he had to be there, I'd like to have met a happy man. But I met a man who seemed to be doing a routine, who kissed my cheek as if yesterday were the last time I'd seen him. My dog was even more emotional and passionate than my boyfriend. Don't be jealous (I don't remember the spelling. Something like /dzeləs/. Translation: celoso.) Read about myself now.

I'm not exactly O.K. I miss you very much and I remember you at any time. I'm very sad. I can't find a solution: If I try not to remember you, my mood becomes melancholic, upset. On the other hand, I'd like to talk to somebody about you so that perhaps I could express my feelings and perhaps my remembrance about you could dissappear little by little. In fact I can't forget you. I can't recognize myself. Where are you? I dream with you every night. I need you, your help, your friendship, your love. Why aren't you with me? Why happiness is such a short period of life? Maybe nothing ever happened! I was only imagining happiness.

My imagination created a happy situation because I need someone like you. I often read what you've written to me. I almost know your letter by heart. I can't avoid telling about you and my mother has realised it at once. DON'T BE AFRAID OF RINGING ME UP OR WRITING. There's no problem about it.

I'm afraid of losing you. I'm afraid I can never see you again. As a young girl – silly me – I fell in love with my teacher. I'm in love with you. Please, don't think you had better not to write to me so that I would be able to forget you. That would be wrong because I do love you and because you're my <u>friend</u>. I hope you won't be offended when I tell you I'm frightened of losing (to lose?) you.

I'm frightened because I love you. I'd like not to love you. I wish I'd never met you. Geography is a great barrier for love.

I try thinking of you like a friend. I mean not like a man whom I like, I love, I'd like to be with for ever. I'm fighting against my feelings. I'm trying to be strong i.e. when I'm getting melancholic because I miss you. I remember what happy persons we've been together. Then, despite my eyes are full with tears, I can smile. I trust a happy future for both of us.

I must stop. I don't want you to be tired of reading my awful English. I'm surprised to see how long letters I can write to you. I'd like to know you wouldn't mind my writing to you as often as I need it. Writing to you helps me relax. I'm looking forward to receiving some news from you by letter, telephone or a shocking visit to me.

My last message for you: I do love you, although you think I don't love you enough because … I want you to be with me in Ireland, Spain or wherever. I don't want to share you with anybody or anything. I'm sorry for being so honest.

Thank you for reading my letter.

Con cariño,

Ana

¡¡Te quiero mucho!!

CHAPTER THREE

London Bridge is falling down

'Shut up, you fool!' Rania shouted at him. At *him*!

They were in a restaurant, where they were belatedly celebrating his birthday with her family and his friends a couple of days after he returned from Ireland. He was so angry he didn't speak to her for the rest of the evening and slept in the study that night.

Ana would *never* say something like that to him, he kept thinking, which only made the knife twist.

He continued to freeze her out all the next day, Sunday, until she came and apologised. He accepted her apology and gave her a hug, but also gave her a talking to about her rudeness. She was suitably penitent, but he knew it was partly because she was nervous about the new job she was starting as a maths teacher in a comprehensive school the next day and wanted his support.

'Will you still give me a lift in the morning?' she supplicated.

'Of course I will,' he said. 'Just make sure you never tell me to shut up again, especially in public.'

'I won't, I promise,' she said, contrite.

'Good,' he said. 'We'll have to leave at eight, so I can get to work on time myself. Make sure you have everything ready tonight. You don't want to be late on your first day!'

'Oh, thank you, darling!' she exclaimed, throwing her arms around him. 'I love you! I don't know what I'd do without you! You'll never leave me, will you?'

'Of course I won't leave you,' he laughed ironically. This was emotional blackmail! 'Why should I leave you?'

He could think of at least one good reason. He had received another letter from her only yesterday. It was locked in the drawer of his desk upstairs. He had read it so many times he almost knew it off by heart. Words and phrases from it kept coming back to him, each time making the knife twist again. Before going to bed, he couldn't resist unlocking his desk, taking it out and reading it yet again:

Madrid, 3th September 86

Dear Francis,

"I want to know what you're doing every minute," or something like that you told me once. Do you remember? I want to tell you everything every minute.

Although you aren't with me, I often speak to you. If I think about you, I speak to you loudly. Not only this happens to me. I can't forget you even while sleeping! I'm very happy my family can't understand English, because I talk to you in English while I'm dreaming and it happens very often.

Whenever I'm alone, I remember our appointments at the Main Gate of Trinity College, the places where we were together, our conversations. I miss you very much. Now I find myself "funny", strange, sad, lonely, depressed because I don't go with my boyfriend. And because you're not with me of course. This situation is new for me. Don't laugh at me, but I don't know what to do when I enter a pub alone. I don't want to meet my friends, because all of them want to know what has happened and so on.

And another point is my family. I thought they could understand my decision to leave my boyfriend and they could, but I can't stand that they're embarrassed when they meet José's relatives, especially my mother. They think we'd better not to come back to my village during all winter. They don't want me to introduce them any other boyfriend. I think my life at home has become worse. As I don't go with my boyfriend, I'm supposed to stay at home at night and as I'm not in a hurry to go out at any other time during the day, I always have to help my mother.

My mother's first advice was not to destroy families and be careful with married men, apart from her command about new possible boyfriends. In fact my father seems to be happier than my mother. He seems not have "difficult" situations with José's relatives, although he's worried about gossip.

Again I need your experience and help. I need your advice to finish my loneliness. (Does this word exist? I'm looking for the noun of alone. I'm sorry but I left my dictionary in Madrid and now I'm in Soto.) I'm afraid I'm not strong enough to bear this situation. I know it's difficult to him too, because he came at my home on Monday night and Tuesday afternoon to pick me up for a drink or something. I'm sure if I go on seeing him, I'll go with him again. I'm very lazy and I find myself very bad, but I don't want to go with him again.

Would you mind ringing me up sometimes? I've tried to ring you up twice, but I couldn't. The first time I was so frightened and nervous that my knees weren't able to bear my weight, I lost my voice and I decided not to ring you up. The second time you weren't at home. I'll try again, perhaps on 15th September, our wedding day. I hope I don't bother you with my letters and my "future" call if I dare. I don't want to destroy your life with your girlfriend, if you're "happy" with her. (A little bit of irony.) I'm writing to you because you are a "special" friend of mine. But I don't want to cause you problems. If I caused you them, tell it to me, please.

I haven't received your letter yet. I haven't known anything about you for two weeks. And I need to know that someone looks after me or loves me in any way. I have decided to write the second letter for you because it helps me relax. Can you believe me?

May I give you a suggestion for your next letter? Thank you. Your theme could be:

a. How could you manage when you get divorced? How could you fight against such a depressive situation?
b. Who is Francis? Tell me something about yourself. You told me that you were going to try it.

I hope your first letter arrives here soon. I need to have some news about you.

With love,

Ana (Te quiero mucho)

Note: The following weekend (6th – 7th September) I'm going to Madrid and I'll be there for the whole year until summer. Write to that address. In fact, you should write to my address in Madrid because letters arrive there quicker than here and my father can always take them.

I'm sending you some leaves of a pink rose. Your favourite flower and favourite colour. Don't forget me!!

The next morning he drove Rania to the school to start her first job as a maths teacher, as promised. She was very nervous, so he spent the whole journey reassuring her. She was so nervous that when they arrived at the school, he almost had to force her to get out of the car and go in. It was nerve-racking though, he understood that. He still felt nervous himself sometimes before entering the classroom, despite his experience. The trick was to be well-prepared, as he kept telling her.

It was a sunny September day and he wasn't back at work himself yet, so in the afternoon, after doing some writing, he went to the Marshes for a walk and some lunch at one of the pubs on the river. Apparently, the Marshes had once been common land, used for growing crops and grazing cattle. You still sometimes saw cattle grazing in enclosures, as today, presumably to keep the grass down.

The Marshes were like a slice of countryside, only ten miles or less from Piccadilly Circus, a long ribbon of meadows, river and reservoirs stretching out into rural Hertfordshire, a virtual nature reserve teeming with wildlife feathered and furred, lush with a motley variety of wildflowers, grasses and reeds and dotted with bushes such as hawthorn and elderberry that blossomed showily and fragrantly in spring. It was a fantastic resource to have on his doorstep, he always thought gratefully, grateful especially that it hadn't been concreted over.

Joni Mitchell sang 'Big Yellow Taxi' in his head as he strolled down Coppermill Lane, past the waterworks with their filter beds and the reservoirs with their wooded islets, over the level crossing, past the marina with its cruisers and houseboats, over the metal footbridge – Horseshoe Bridge, as it was quaintly named on the maps – and along the towpath downriver on the other side to the Robin Hood. He preferred the Robin Hood to the Anchor and Hope farther along, because he knew he would get a good ploughman's there and, more importantly, a decent pint of Guinness, probably served by the Irish landlord, who always said 'Now!' in his baritone brogue after he had topped it up expertly, knifed off the excess cream and passed it to you with priestlike piety over the battered bar as if it were a chalice of nectar.

He also preferred the Robin Hood because there was a spacious patio at the front overlooking the river, where he liked to sit with his pint, even if it was chilly, and gaze reflectively at the river, with its houseboats and waterfowl, and the grasslands opposite, stretching away almost as far as the eye could see, with hardly a manmade object in sight apart from the railway viaduct and electricity pylons.

Today was an Indian summer's day, so he sat at his favourite wooden table and took a first delicious sup of the black nectar. A butterfly fluttered around the buddleia nearby, a bumble bee buzzed about some ragged dahlias, pigeons swooped down to forage for scraps of food, a few people strolled by on the towpath below, a racing skiff swept past on the ink-black water, oars whirling, a pair of swans glided by regally in its wake, a few Canada geese doddled about on the banks, a man added a few more dabs of paint to his gaily-coloured houseboat, a train rattled over the viaduct towards Cambridge, the cows grazed peacefully in the meadow opposite, a heron lifted off and flapped across to the island in the middle of the reservoir, a silver jet sliced silently through the azure sky high above and, to complete the serenity of the scene, there was an evocative smell of woodsmoke, which always reminded him nostalgically of turfsmoke and childhood summer holidays in Ireland …

Rania was such a strange mixture. So feisty yet so timid. So innocent in some ways too. They went to Clissold Park in Stoke Newington earlier in the year and there were deer there. She said she'd never seen deer before! Not all that surprising maybe. There probably weren't any deer in Guyana. She had such mood swings. One minute she was like a kid squealing with delight over the deer, the next minute, because he happened to say she was part-British, Guyana having been a British colony, she went into a big sulk, stamping her foot and pouting, 'I'm not British!' He couldn't help laughing at her, which made her even more angry: 'Don't come near me! I don't want to be with you! I'll go home on my own! You're horrible and stupid!' He bought her an ice cream to pacify her, a Cornetto, and instantly she flipped back into a delighted, adulatory little girl, telling him how much she loved him and how wonderful he was. That Spanish girl Beatriz at the college. He was quite smitten by her. She was so damned attractive! He always remembered her in the tight red sweater that accentuated her shapely breasts so beautifully. He was glad she'd resisted his advances though. If she hadn't, he wouldn't've been able to have a relationship with Ana. Another lovely Spanish girl, though in a much quieter, less obvious, more unassuming sort of way. Which he preferred really. He had her letter in his pocket and was tempted to take it out and read it for the umpteenth time, but resisted. He'd try to reply to her tonight. God, she was so lovely! It made his heart twist to think of her. The feelings he had for Ana were the feelings he should have for Rania but didn't. But how could he leave Rania? He didn't love her, but knew she loved him in her own peculiar, contradictory way. Did it take two to tango, as they said? He was only staying with her out of loyalty. And stubbornness. And pity. And pusillanimity. Ana's wasn't the only letter in his pocket. There was another one. From William Heinemann. Last week. Yet another letter rejecting his novel. Another dagger in the guts. But at least it was a proper letter, not just a slip with the usual platitude scrawled on it: 'Thank you for letting us read your manuscript. However, we do not think it will fit into our list at the present time. Good luck elsewhere.'

God, he had quite a collection of those now! But this morning's letter was a long one, full of positive, constructive comments, asking him to change the ending, then resubmit it, and they would probably publish it. He wasn't going to change the ending though. There was his stubbornness coming out again. To hell with them! Even if he was cutting off his nose. Rania's response when he'd showed it to her was both cringeworthy and touching: 'Well done! You're going to be successful! You're going to be rich! You're on the way. When you're rich, I won't have to work, will I? The book you're writing now is a bestseller, isn't it?' 'Not exactly.' 'Why did you say so?' 'I was joking. Anyway, it could be. Who knows?' 'Be serious. You're not serious. Every night when I go to bed, I pray to Allah that your book will be successful and you will be successful. I know your writing is important to you, isn't it? When you're rich, you'll send me to college. I want to become a teacher of maths.' He smiled at the memory. She was such a bundle of contradictions. Well, now she *was* a teacher of maths. He'd encouraged her to apply and helped her with her application. He hoped she was getting on all right, not that she was doing any actual teaching today. It was induction, as they called it. Sounded like some sort of electric shock therapy. Geoff Walker obviously fancied Beatriz too. What was the comment he'd made about her? 'She's a little cutie!' He added glumly that he was wasting his time though, being married. 'Even half-married like me,' he'd quipped. He was a randy so-and-so, Geoff. Even randier than he was. It was hard not to be, with all those sexy foreign au pairs around. The air in the college was full of female pheromones. That French girl Valerie was a case in point. A real charmer. Long black curly hair, red lippy, tight sweater, tight black skirt, red leggings. He had to smile – he gave her a kiss on the cheek once when she came into the Bell, but she insisted on a second one on her other cheek by tapping it. It was enough to test a monk's vow of chastity. It was a pleasure just to be in her company. Chambermaid-cum-waitress in a hotel in Earl's Court. Told him she'd had to go back to France in February, because her father was seriously ill, and she'd just come back. Blood clot or something in his abdomen. Had to have a big operation. They took out the blocked artery and replaced it with plastic. It was 'touch and go' for a few weeks, but he 'pulled through'. It made you realise these girls weren't just sex objects, but real people, with real problems, real emotions. Not that he thought of them as sex objects. He gave her a hug and told her he was sorry, but glad her father was OK, congratulating her on her use of idiom and phrasal verb. Of course, ironically, the fact that she'd had such a difficult experience only made her all the more attractive to him, aroused his protective instincts. He hadn't taken advantage of her though, even when she told him she wanted to take the Proficiency exam in December and asked him to mark some compositions for her, which he agreed to happily. In fact, he didn't fancy her. Just liked her. It was pleasant, liking a girl without any conscious sexual or erotic element. That was a terrible row with Rania the other day. She found a letter from Cinzia, his Italian ex, and unleashed a tirade of abuse at him. He retaliated by pretending to be angry with her for snooping and spying on him and gave her a good telling off. Well, he was angry, but he hammed it up a bit. He'd learned that was the best way to deal with her temper. Fight fire with fire. Eventually she said sorry and they made up. 'It's just a letter,' he said, putting an arm round her. 'We're penfriends now, that's all. It's actions that count, isn't it? I'm here with you, aren't I, not there with her?' He resisted adding, 'I could be there with her if I wanted.' 'I don't want you to get letters from ex-girlfriends though,' she pouted. 'I don't want anyone else to have you. You're mine. I don't want to share you. I love you.' That took the wind out of his sails! It was typical of her, swinging from one extreme to the other. One minute screaming abuse, the next minute all lovey-dovey. He didn't know where he was up to!

His colleague Keith Johnson had gone up in his estimation since that day he'd given him a lift home from college. Keith was one of the leather jacket and jeans brigade and somewhat full of himself, had even dared to criticise his teaching once. Not that he'd ever actually seen him teach. And not that he really cared what Keith Johnson thought. He only cared what his students thought and they all liked him. As they drove, Keith asked him about his writing and he gave the usual evasive, vague answer, since he didn't like talking about it. He said it took a lot of discipline to get up in the morning and do it, then go to work in the afternoon. Keith admitted he couldn't get up in the morning if he didn't have to, which amused him. Maybe that was because he hadn't been in a monastery or the army or prison for nine years! He told him about the encouraging letter of rejection he'd received from Heinemann and to his surprise Keith was very complimentary, encouraged him to carry on, don't give up. Not such a bad lad after all. He was back in his good books. Last time he was here was with Rania and they bumped into Adrian from the London Rubber Company, i.e. the London Condom and Surgical Glove Company, where Rania worked. Adrian was a keen birdwatcher, always appropriately attired in anorak and wellies with binoculars round his neck. Actually he suspected Adrian fancied Rania and sometimes wondered if he was stalking her. He and Rania used to joke about it. It was May, with that heady perfume of hawthorn blossom in the air. Swifts swooping about all over the place like mini jets. Swifts only landed for nesting, Adrian informed them. They mated and fed and even slept on the wing. Didn't land at all for the first three years of life. Well, you live and learn! His friend, Rob, in Yorkshire, who was at junior seminary with him, amused him because he never stopped talking about it. He was even more deeply scarred by the experience than he was himself.

Rob remembered details he'd forgotten completely about. For example the sign language they had to use for things like bread, salt and milk in the ref, because meals were usually in silence, while they listened to some dreary religious tract such as *The Imitation of Christ* read out from the 'rostrum'. Though some of the stuff wasn't so bad, such as HV Morton's *In Search of the Holy Land*. There always had to be a religious dimension of course. There was no let-up in the brainwashing and indoctrination. Father Director would tinkle his little bell on the small dining table he ate at to correct you if you made a mistake. It was good training in a way, he supposed. He couldn't help chuckling when Rob told him how he hated the hardboiled eggs they were given for supper sometimes, said they literally made him sick, and Father Director gave him the strap once for trying to hide one behind a radiator. Apparently poor old Rob got the strap regularly, unlike himself. Well, he was a bit of a goodygoody, as well as being Father Director's pet and plaything. Rob claimed he never wanked, because he didn't know about it. He could believe that, because it was the same for him. Rob said he went to Confession before Mass in the morning once and Father Phelan dismissed him, because he had nothing to confess. Apparently it was a special Confession in case you were guilty of 'toggle tugging', as they called it, the night before, so you could receive Holy Communion without committing a mortal sin and being damned to roast in Hell for all eternity if you suddenly died. That was something else he'd forgotten about himself, maybe because he'd never needed to avail of it. God, the sheer madness of it all, when he looked back! Sex was always on Rob's mind, as it was on his. 'I didn't know what women looked like till I left senior seminary when I was twenty-one and saw a kids' programme on BBC 2 about sex!' he confessed. 'I didn't know the facts of life. I didn't have sisters like you, you see. I thought women were smooth all the way round. I didn't know about pubic hair. I thought anal intercourse was the normal method! I had a crush on a cousin in Ireland. We used to kiss and cuddle. I didn't know what else to do. I was so innocent! I used to be embarrassed when I saw snoggers. I didn't know what I was doing when I took my vow of chastity. I couldn't deny my sexuality. I would've gone off the rails sooner or later, so I'm glad I left when I did. I can't live without women. I love chasing them.' Well, they had the last bit in common. They had a lot in common of course. Rob always apologised for 'talking shop'. 'We have to talk it out,' he said. 'Get it out of our systems.' He couldn't help being amused by that. Rob had been getting it out of his system for almost twenty years! Somewhat to his surprise, Rob confessed to fancying Rania's younger seventeen-year-old sister, whom he'd met, not that she was unfanciable, quite the reverse. Rania had thrown cold water on it though. 'Dream on, Rob,' she'd said to him in her sharp-tongued, sarcastic way. 'You're much too old for her. She's just a kid.' He could tell Rob was offended, though she probably couldn't. Well, she wouldn't – she had a habit of saying offensive things to people, himself included, seemingly oblivious of the offence they might cause. If he ever complained about some comment, she'd just scoff and tell him he was a wimp. She had some sort of social deficiency disorder. He could tell Rob liked her though. She could be very charming. And very generous. She was this funny mixture of rough and smooth. Swift and slow, sweet and sour, adazzle, dim … What a poem that was! But what a tragic case Hopkins himself was. Imagine converting to Catholicism from Anglicanism in your early twenties and, even more crazily, becoming a Jesuit. A *Jesuit*! The very name gave him the heebie-jeebies. Turning your back on the world, on life. Throwing it all away. All in the deluded belief there was another life after this one! Giving up love, romance, sex, marriage, children, family, career … Giving up *poetry,* for God's sake! Yes, literally for God's sake. What a waste! All for some imaginary, fictitious god. So deluded. And then to die at forty-four. Just a few years older than he was himself. Funny, Hopkins had taken exactly the opposite road to him. That was partly what made him so morbidly fascinating. Well, he found all the Catholic writers fascinating, because they were Catholic or ex-Catholic, especially if they were Irish too: Joyce, Greene, Waugh, Burgess, O'Brien, Lodge, Brian Moore … That was a funny little exchange with Eva, the German student. 'How's your wife?' she asked. 'Which wife?' he joked. 'I don't know,' she replied. 'Have you got more than one?' Back to college next week. He was looking forward to it. He missed the students. A few of his colleagues too. What a pompous prat that premises superintendent, Patterson, was. 'Pratnose' as he had dubbed him himself. Left a note in his pigeon-hole refusing permission to hold a party again, because he claimed they didn't clear up properly last time. Battle-axe Bertha, the head of the English as a Foreign Language department, soon sorted him out and put him back in his box! She was a pain, but she had her uses. And Ken Cameron, the Head of Faculty, backing Pratnose up! Spineless so-and-so. No wonder he was called 'Grey Ken'. Rania won't stop buying stuff. On credit! Had to tell her off for buying a set of silver cutlery by mail order. 'Haven't you got enough debts?' Went into a big sulk. God, it was like dealing with a three-year-old sometimes. Better go and pick her up. Ah, nectar of the gods indeed!

CHAPTER FOUR

London

Fri. 6.6.86

Meeting at college with Ken Cameron, Head of the General Education faculty. Present were Bertha, colleagues Geoff Walker, Harriet Jenkins, Keith Johnson and myself. Ken Cameron, or 'Grey Ken' as we call him, is a rather dour, grey-haired, grey-faced, grey-suited Edinburgher. The meeting was about Pratnose's, the so-called Premises Superintendent's, refusal to allow us to have our traditional end-of-year party, of which I'm the organiser, supposedly because the head cleaner had complained about the classrooms not being cleaned up properly afterwards last time. Bertha was in feisty mode, but KC was having none of it, just blankly refused to countenance it. 'Look, Bertha,' he said after some toing and froing across his spacious but suspiciously tidy desk, in that irritatingly mild-mannered, soft Edinburgh burr of his, 'I'm not arguing about this any further. I don't see why I should be held responsible for something I have no control over. Go and speak to the cleaner.' Geoff spoke up well: 'This is a function that is enjoyed by all, students and staff. It helps to make the college a more welcoming and friendly place. Frankly, I'm not happy with the way the college is going and this is just another symptom.' Well said, Geoff! 'The cleaner is exaggerating,' Bertha protested. 'Are you saying the cleaner is not telling the truth?' KC inquired. Bertha's hackles went right up: 'Are you saying *we* are not telling the truth?' she demanded, crimson-faced with indignation. 'There are three senior members of staff, plus Frank Walsh and Keith Johnson here, all saying the same thing, that the cleaner is exaggerating.' But Grey Ken wouldn't budge. It was like talking to granite. 'What a pathetic, weak man!' Bertha expostulated outside the office afterwards and wanted to storm off to see the Vice-Principal about it, but we stopped her. Bertha can be a very useful ally, but she can also make matters worse, pour petrol on the flames. We agreed to take it to the student union instead. 'Premises Superintendent,' I laughed. 'He's just a bloody caretaker, but thinks he's the Principal!' They all laughed in agreement. This so-called Premises Superintendent has put a lot of backs up since he arrived, marching about the college in his dark-blue uniform and peaked cap, telling everyone what they can and can't do. Well, he is an ex-military policeman apparently. And he's another Scotty. Maybe it's a conspiracy. Revenge for the clearing of the glens. On my way out of college, Spanish Bea, who I can't help fancying, stopped me in the foyer to give me one of the extra compositions I've agreed to mark for her. She looked very sexy in a red dress and red mac. I couldn't resist chatting her up, even though she's made it clear she doesn't want an intimate relationship of any sort, seems a bit straitlaced in fact. 'I can tell you're a man of experience,' she remarked in the course of the conversation. I wasn't sure whether to be flattered or not. There was a hint of irony in her voice when she said it. It's certainly ironic to be called that by a gorgeous Spanish girl, in view of my background! I noticed Geoff chatting up Margarita, a trainee teacher, in the foyer, too. I think he was offering her a lift home, because she followed him out to his car. I reckon he's even more of a player than me. Not that I think of myself as a player really.

Sun. 8.6.86

Went to an Eid celebration with Rania. I go to these things out of curiosity rather than any sort of piety, since I'm a total nonbeliever in all religion. Anyway, I certainly wouldn't go from Catholicism to Islam. That really would be out of the frying pan into the fire ha ha. Besides, from what I've seen so far, Catholicism is much superior as religions go, certainly in terms of liturgy and ceremonial, which seem to be virtually non-existent in Islam. From what I've read of the Koran, too, it seems to be a very strident, dogmatic, even fanatical book, though it has its good bits. Anyway, there were lots of prayers and speeches, the speeches mostly pretty boring by men – always men, never women, who are strictly segregated and have to remain respectfully quiet in purdah – who obviously like the sound of their own voices. 'We must thank Allah for sending Mr Geldof to us, but we shouldn't need him,' one of them opined, making my ears prick up. Little did they know that Mr Geldof and I were educated by the same freaks in frocks viz. the Holy Ghost Fathers, whose ideas on education were indeed as vague as their name, as Mr Geldof commented in his autobiography, though he went to their school in Blackrock, near Dublin, rather than Castlehead in the English Lake District like me. According to his autobiography, we did share one teacher though, a mad, leprechaun-like, little Irish priest called Father Egan, who was our Dean of Studies, who went around in a state of almost permanent apoplexy, given to fits of rage in which he might hurl a liber – a book of Gregorian chant as big as a missal – at you for singing a wrong note in singing class or a board duster or whatever else was to hand if you mispronounced something in French class, so that his classes were like a war zone and indeed you dreaded them. He was also a fanatical Irish nationalist, apt to launch into anti-English tirades at any moment, even in the middle of French or singing class. He kept a 'pandybat' in the pocket of his habit, a sort of lead-weighted cosh made of leather reinforced with whalebone, which he would take out at the drop of a hat and whack you on the hands with and it really hurt, reduced some boys to tears sometimes. Like a few of the other priests there, he shouldn't have been allowed within a million miles of children of course. In fact, I suspect he was mentally ill, bipolar perhaps, needed help, probably should have been on medication. Though, as far as I know, at least he didn't interfere with little boys, unlike some of the other priests. Anyway, after the prayers and speeches in the mosque, we went to the cemetery to visit Rania's grandmother's grave. It was a warm, breezy summer's day with a mixture of cloud and sun. The grave was very overgrown, but the stone showed that she was born in 1904 and died in 1981. 'May her soul rest in peace' was engraved underneath. As always it made me reflect on how pathetically brief and meaningless life is, any of our lives, on this tiny, insignificant speck of dust we call Earth, in one unimaginably immense galaxy in the middle of billions of other such galaxies, each with their billions of stars and planets. 'Spirits follow you if you look back when you go in or out,' Rania informed me. She's full of such superstitious beliefs, which I usually just laugh away, to her annoyance. I actually cracked a few jokes about how people were dying to get in here and how it was operating on a skeleton staff, which one or two of her sisters giggled at, but she didn't. 'I was there when Nan passed away,' she said. 'I saw her die. She was groaning. She had a bad cold in her throat. Then suddenly she stopped and her eyes rolled up. Zabir couldn't believe she was dead. She was travelling on her journey home. The doctor came to certify her dead.' 'She was travelling on her journey home.' I must admit that moved me, it was such a poetic way of expressing what had happened. We cleared the grave as best we could without any tools, though one of the family had brought a knife, which helped. Then we stood around the grave in a circle with our hands cupped while prayers were said in both Arabic and English by one of the imams: 'Almighty and merciful Allah, we are gathered here today, sons, daughters and grandchildren, to pray for the soul of Grandmother. Grant her rest we beg you. Bring her to your arms safely.' Those were touching words too. After the prayers they planted incense sticks in the soil on the grave, placed a sprig of parsley in a pot in the middle and sprinkled water on it. It was rather a moving little ceremony, I had to admit, though it still didn't compare with a Requiem Mass, especially one sung. 'Dies irae, dies illa ...' Hard to beat that for sublime mournfulness! It was kind of silly to be comparing, but how could I help it? After these obsequies I went for a little meander around the cemetery, reading some of the other gravestones and contemplating the brevity of life again. While doing so I bumped into Zabir. (Zabir is a relation of the family, as well as one of the imams at the mosque, a gent in his seventies.) 'Looking for a nice plot, Frank?' he joked. 'Well, we're all in the waiting room, aren't we?' I joked back morbidly, wincing inside at the thought even as I said it. They do have a sense of humour, these Guyanese, I must give them that. Though some of them are too sanctimonious for my taste. 'Death follows you around like a panther, waiting to pounce.' Was that a quote or did I make it up myself? God, cemeteries were such morbid places! I was dying for a drink – ha ha – but there was no chance of that, no chance of sloping off to the pub.

Mon. 9.6.86
Unbelievable! Got a note of apology in my pigeonhole from Grey Ken, granting permission for the party. The complaint

was about another party! It makes sense, though, because we are always ultra-scrupulous about clearing up afterwards. I make sure of that. And there are always a few students who are happy to muck in and help.

Tues. 10.6.86
Lloyd Park. I was feeding ducks in the lake when a gnomish little bloke sidled up beside me. 'Go on, give em a bit more. Someone come with a rifle and shot em two years ago. Must be sick. Like this man who assaults children. Mind you, it's not always their fault. Sometimes the kids ask for it. I woz in the toilet at Central the other day. A bloke went into a cubicle. A Paki kid about fourteen went in after im. They locked the door, but of course we know what was going on in there, don't we? They come up next to you in the gents sometimes. Push up close. Got any money on you? We know what they're after, don't we? Sometimes if you're feeling randy enough, you'll let them, won't you? I woz in the Tatler cinema once. I used to go in there when the pub was closed till opening time again. Just to pass the time, kill a couple of hours. I woz watching this pornographic film, yer know. Must've been bored coz I fell asleep. I must've been dreaming. I woke up with a hard-on up to here! This Paki kid had it in his mouth. Sucking me off e woz! Well, I woz too far gone by then, weren't I? I let him get on with it. I couldn't stop it. Funny thing is these blokes have wives at home if they want it. Human nature's funny, ennit? Mind you, animals do it. I seen a dog go up another dog. Not a bitch, a dog. Can't be all that unnatural then, can it? We're only a species of animal, ain't we? Dirty, ain't we? I'm not working at the minute. I usually go to a mate's house in the afternoon and watch a couple of blue films. Starting a new job next week. Gardening. Three days per week. Fifty-seven quid. Forty quid after stoppages. On the dole for the other

two days. Can't be bad.' I'd had enough by that point, so made my excuses and sloped off. He was a revolting little man, but I felt sorry for him. Later I went shopping with Rania, then for a drink in the Coach and Horses and we ended up having a row about the budget for our holiday in Ireland. She expects me to pay for everything, even though she's earning. All I asked her for was a contribution. She went into a tantrum. 'I won't go then. I can't afford it. I'll stay at home and visit my friends. It'll be just as good. You never do anything for me. You're always chopping and changing. Take someone else! You've got plenty of women to choose from! You never keep your promises. You promised to buy me a casserole dish in Sainsbury's, but you broke it.' I was angry, but I had to laugh. She's so irrational sometimes. And so childish. I sometimes wonder if I've married a child.

Sat. 14.6.86
Took a few students (Eva, André, Ann, Nicole) to the Victoria on Holloway Road to hear some Irish music. Crannog were playing. They're very good, with a great traditional singer from Galway. Nicole, who is French-Canadian, in her thirties and partnered, was flirting with me as usual. 'I don't want to go to bed with you,' she told me. 'I don't know you well enough yet. I just want to have a good time.' Fortunately, or unfortunately, I like her, but don't fancy her, but she keeps coming on to me. 'We're having a good time, aren't we?' I riposted, taking another swig of Guinness. We did have a good time, too, except that German Eva, in khaki mac with black and white striped trousers and orange hair, who's only about eighteen, got drunk, probably because she was drinking Guinness for the first time and smoking roll-ups too, and vomited outside the pub, so I had to take her home. Luckily, she's an au pair

in Woodford, so it wasn't too far out of my way. En route, she told me her father left just before she was born, while she was still in her mother's womb. I think she's looking for a replacement father. It must leave a deep psychological wound, to think your father abandoned you before you were even born.

Sun. 15.6.86
Went for a walk on the Marshes with Rania. Purple, white and yellow wildflowers everywhere. Had a funny conversation. She still thinks I'm going to write a bestseller, even though I told her I got my novel back from yet another publisher yesterday. Another rejection, another crushing blow. She still thinks I'm going to be successful, rich and famous though. I can't help being touched by her somewhat naïve belief in me – even though at other times she can be very scathing about my writing, which is one of the aspects of her personality that most disappoints me. Unlike Danielle, my French girlfriend, who was always admiring, almost adulatory, and supportive of me. Danielle, who I still miss acutely, who I was a fool to lose. But it was better not to think about Danielle, I told myself sternly. Besides, I had Ana now. Maybe she would be my road to freedom and happiness …
R: If you write a bestseller and become rich, I'll enjoy it all and I'm only twenty-four! I'm lucky, aren't I?
Me: What if I don't though? (Wincing inside at the thought of my latest rejection, knowing how unlikely it seemed.)
R: I'll still be happy.
Me: I should hope so!
R: I know I'm lucky too.
Me: Why? Because you met me?
R: Yes. You're educated and intelligent. That's what attracted me most to you.

Me (laughing): What about handsome and charming?

R: I must admit you are quite handsome too. I know a lot of your students are attracted to you. But you chose me.

Me: Well, you chose me too. It wasn't all one way!

R: This path reminds me of a road in Guyana. (We were on the towpath by the River Lea, potholed and gravelly.) You remind me of my father in some ways. He was highly intelligent, even though he was poor and had no education like you. He left school when he was seven. He wanted education for his kids though. That's why he sent us to England. He read a lot of Moslem books. He knew all about Islam. He was Hindu, but converted to Islam to marry my mum. He was very religious, but wanted to enjoy life too. He ate himself to death. He didn't understand the dangers. Nobody did then. I miss him. I think he would've liked you.

Me (putting an arm round her): Well, you've got me now. I'm nearly old enough to be your dad!

R: I do love you. Even though I know you don't love me and no one can replace my dad anyway.

Me (annoyed): Why do you always have to spoil things with that sharp tongue of yours?

R: It's true, isn't it? You don't really love me, do you?

Me: How do you know I don't love you?

R: I can just feel it.

Me: Well, if you think I don't love you, you should leave me, shouldn't you? (And go back to your mum, I was going to add, but bit my tongue. She had run away from her mum and bullying brothers to be with me. It would have been below the belt …)

R: Maybe you do love me, but not enough. Not in the way you should.

Me: I'm here with you, aren't I? I'm doing my best. I'm sorry if it's not good enough for you. (I said this with a mixture of annoyance and guilt, because while it was true I was doing my best, I felt guilty because I knew I didn't really love her enough or in the way she wanted, but that was at least partly her fault, there are two sides to every story …)

R (contrite): I'm sorry. I know you do love me. And I love you too. I never want to lose you. Do you want to go inside for a drink?

We had arrived at one of my favourite hostelries, the Robin Hood, overlooking the river. 'That's the nicest thing you've said to me all day!' I laughed. I was going to ask her if the Pope was a Catholic, but it would probably have gone past her, since being Muslim and Guyanese she scarcely knew who the Pope was, lucky her. 'Are you going to buy me a pint?' 'I will if you want,' she said. 'I know you love your pint. You're a typical Irishman.' I couldn't help being needled but at the same time pleased at being called an Irishman in that way, since I'm happy to call myself one, even if I wasn't brought up in Ireland the country. Later, sitting on the patio, chatting and supping my pint and gazing out across the river, the green meadows and the pink sky opposite, I suddenly noticed on a table nearby a girl who reminded me of my first ever girlfriend in London, an eighteen-year-old Yugoslav girl called Marina, who was a student in the very first class I ever taught, in Soho. She was the spitting image of Marina, in a low-cut summer dress, with short, bobbed, blond hair, a cherubic face and beautiful breasts. The likeness was so striking that for a second or two I wondered if it actually was Marina and my heart seemed to stop. The illusion was shattered when I heard her speak though, in a strong Cockney accent full of glottal stops, stretched vowels and dropped aitches. Rania told me to stop staring at her, even though I thought I was doing so discreetly. 'I wasn't staring at her,' I protested, pretending to be offended. 'It's just that she reminded me of someone.' 'Yes, one of your many girlfriends, I suppose,' Rania riposted sarcastically.

God, she has a razor-sharp tongue! By then, though, the Guinness, combined with the almost Constable-like view and the memory of Marina, poignant as it was, had put me in such a good mood I ignored the remark and we managed to have a pleasant time together without arguing for once. I only wish that could happen more often.

Mon. 16.6.86

Finished my Proficiency class early and went for the last drink of term with some of my students in the Bell, just down the road from the college. Before leaving the classroom we shared two bottles of Bordeaux, kindly brought by Martine to celebrate the end of the course. I bought her and a few of the others a drink in the pub. Nicole chatted me up again. I don't fancy her, mainly because she's too tall and too thin, but she's a good sort. 'Finally, at the end of the year I get to know you,' she said. 'Do you believe in friendship between men and women?' 'Yes, but …' 'I'd like to be friends with you, get to know you better. Would you like to have a drink with me some time?' 'Sure,' I agreed and exchanged phone numbers with her, though I wasn't really keen. 'I think you're soft underneath,' she observed, in her somewhat blunt way, 'but on the surface you're cold.' 'Really?' I said, feigning surprise, rattled – it wasn't the first time a girl had said something similar to me and it always shocked me, though I half-understood why. I knew I could appear reserved, if not cold. 'Yes,' she affirmed. 'Well,' I said, trying to make a joke of it, 'the top layer is hard, the next layer is soft and the core is as hard as rock ha ha.' 'I just want to know your second layer then,' she rejoined wittily. Geoff, giraffe-tall and ginger, came in with a few of his students and sat at the table next to us, but came over to have a few words. 'I hear you've been taking some of your lot to Irish pubs on Holloway Road,' he observed jovially. 'They seem to have enjoyed it!' 'I think some of them enjoyed it too much!' I laughed, thinking of Eva, who at that moment, funnily enough, came over. 'I haven't exchanged a word with you all night,' she said. 'Exchange one now – sit down,' I said, making a space for her and she did. 'I want to go to the Victoria again,' she said, pronouncing the 'w' as a 'v' and the 'V' as a 'W' in her Teutonic way. Somehow it sounded charmingly childish. 'We'll go again, don't worry,' I said, pleased. 'I'll organise something.' She looks a bit punk-ish with her orange hair and zany clothes, but she seems to really like the Irish music and craic, which puts her straight into my good books. Beatriz left early, I noticed, and without really talking properly to me, to my annoyance. The few students Geoff had brought in left soon and he came over to join us, which at first I wasn't too happy about, because I don't like competition when I'm holding court with my students. But I told myself not to be so petty-minded, especially since I get on well with Geoff, regard him as a friend, as well an ally, and he's always very supportive towards me. We have lots of enjoyable chats in the staffroom, mostly about women and football – though only when female members of staff are not present of course. He's always unfailingly polite too. 'Mind if I join you?' he asked, coming over. 'Not at all,' I said, though I could hardly refuse, and joked: 'You can help me chat up some of these women.' The company was nearly all female as usual and the ones nearby who heard it laughed, enjoying the joke. 'Oh, I don't think you need help with that,' he laughed, finding a seat. 'You're not called "the au pairs' delight" for nothing!' 'Oh, dear,' I laughed, as always both flattered and embarrassed by this sobriquet conferred on me by Tony Holloway, another colleague. 'I'm not so sure about that!' In the end, a good night was had by all, including me, though I had one or two over the odds. It was one of those nights when I couldn't help thinking I had the best job in the world.

Tues. 17.6.86

Had to invigilate the Cambridge First Certificate exam in
the main hall with a hangover, then go for my 'staff development interview' with Grey Ken. I find these interviews a
waste of time and even a bit embarrassing, mainly because
I don't want to be developed. I'm happy as I am, happy
to plough the same old furrow for the foreseeable future.
I'm not a career lecturer in that sense, don't want to climb
any greasy poles or rubber ladders. I just want to teach and
write. That's why I only teach part time. I think Ken used to
find my lack of ambition disconcerting, but seems to have
accepted it now. 'I haven't got much to say to you really,'
he shrugged, after a few complimentary remarks about me.
'How's the writing going?' he inquired, as always, which
is decent enough of him, but it's a question I hate, though
I know he means well. 'I've had one or two encouraging
letters from publishers, but that's about all,' I said evasively,
eager to get out of his office and carry on with my life. He
was gracious enough to apologise about the party fiasco,
too, so he's gone back up a notch or two in my estimation,
though admittedly from a rather low base. On my way out
of the office I got nobbled by Roy Bunting in the corridor,
balding and hunched, in a white cotton jacket and baggy
grey flannels and puffing on a cigarette in a cigarette holder
as always. Roy used to teach French and German in the
college, but retired a few years ago and comes back to 'visit'
once a year. Sadly, when he does, most people try to avoid
him, or scarcely give him the time of day, as they always
did, because he's possibly the most boring man in the world,
but for those very reasons I've always tried to be friendly to
him, which I know he appreciates. He seems to be a lonely
old soul, too, having no wife or children or friends, as far as
anyone knows. I tend to feel sorry for lonely people, maybe
because I've had periods of soul-destroying loneliness in my

own life, especially after leaving the seminary. Well, aren't we all lonely deep down? Anyway, besides all that, I tend to share his somewhat jaundiced view of college politics, not to mention world politics. When I told him I'd just had my staff development interview with Grey Ken, he exhaled a cloud of Gauloise and replied mordantly in his broad estuary accent: 'Staff development interviews? There are no new ideas in education. If anyone needs developing, it's KC! He's in a rut. A well-paid rut. The only development he's interested in is his salary! You know, Frank, I can't believe I've been retired three years. It's amazing how time …' As always I had to struggle to listen to him, because he does chunner on and you don't get much of a word in edgeways. As I did so I noticed one or two colleagues approach in the corridor and turn back when they saw him or rush past as if they had important business. Which made me feel even more sorry for him than I already felt. I remembered one colleague, who taught drama, saying to me once in his waspish, theatrically gay way, 'You know, Frank, I think Roy was sent as a warning to me. I might be like that in ten years. I do admire the way you handle him though.' A backhanded compliment if ever there was one. Anyway, I felt so sorry for Roy that I offered him a lift home, somewhat against my better judgement, and he accepted eagerly. On the way he told me he'd worked in Coleraine for two years in his very first job. 'I went to Dublin for four days during the coronation, to avoid all that royalist rubbish,' he said. 'I like Dublin. It's a beautiful city. I enjoyed myself. The troubles hadn't started then. Did you know some of Southern Ireland is in the north? Well, you do because you're Irish, I know. Rubbish that, isn't it?' Of course, I was both surprised and pleased to hear this and decided he wasn't all that boring after all. Still, I was relieved to drop him off at his semi-detached house in Chingford, because by then I'd had enough. 'It was very nice of you to give me a lift,' he said, before getting out of the car. 'I'm a scrounger, aren't I?' 'No, Roy,' I said, 'I offered.' 'Well, very decent of you, anyway. Nice car you've got. Sorry about refusing to wear the seat belt. I hate seatbelts.' Afterwards I went for a walk by the river before picking Rania up from work. I needed some space and air, what with my hangover and having my ears chewed off by Roy. The Marshes looked positively bucolic, with horses and cows grazing in the meadows, the whole scene rife with greenery and wildflowers. I sat on the riverbank for a while, avoiding the anglers, gazing at the water and the boats and wildfowl, trying not to think about Roy, or Rania, or Ana, or college, or publishers, or the past, or life, or death …

Wed. 18.6.86
Had a picnic with students in Lloyd Park to celebrate the end of exams. Luckily it was sunny and warm though breezy. Bea lay on the grass provocatively, sunning herself, in khaki shorts and pink blouse, so I struggled to keep my eyes off her. I wish I could stop fancying her! Nicole and Eva were arm wrestling. We ate bread, cheese, tomatoes, nuts and crisps with beer, wine and soft drinks. Afterwards we went to the Bell. 'I'm very slow to fall in love, but I couldn't go to bed with someone just for sex,' Eva, in her stripey trousers, confided to me. I told her it was the same for me, though I'm not sure about the first part or the second part for that matter. I think I could go to bed with Bea just for sex, even though I probably wouldn't. 'But sex can lead to love can't it, just as love leads to sex?' I said to her, playing devil's advocate. 'I don't know,' she shrugged. I think she's very innocent and probably a virgin. I like her, feel fatherly towards her, which I think is what she's looking for, a surrogate father.

Thurs. 19.6.86
Bertha told us in a meeting that the Royal Society of Arts (one of our accrediting bodies) inspector had given us a bad report. Like the rest of my colleagues, at first I was indignant. Some trouser-suited hag who probably can't hack it in the classroom herself had nosed around a few weeks ago. 'Fucking cheek!' Mark, my South African colleague, swore behind his hand to me. However, we were mollified when Bertha went on to explain that the main criticism was the lack of a resources room, rather than actual teaching. From what I see and know of my colleagues and myself, I reckon our teaching is pretty good. So we've applied for a room to be used for resources and I was volunteered to be 'resources manager'. 'Let Frank do it,' Harriet Jenkins proposed, to unanimous approval. 'He's a methodical type.' I felt flattered, of course, though I'm always a bit wary of any sort of praise from Harriet, since it often has a sting in the tail. In the end it's a good thing, because it means the college will probably have to give us a room for resources, since we bring in a lot of money. In the afternoon Geoff and I organised a football match with the students on the playing fields behind the college. A few of the girls joined in, one or two of them, such as Bea, very sexily if ineffectually. I played in goals as usual, because of my gammy knee, though it's my preferred position anyway. Geoff, who knows quite a bit about football, is always very laudatory of my goalkeeping and sometimes I wish I could have extended my career. It's another reason for me to like Geoff. Afterwards a few of us went to the Bell to say some goodbyes. Polish Andrew said he wanted to come back to Britain and I joked that he must be a Communist spy. To my relief he laughed heartily. He's a good lad and I'm sorry to see him go. But then I like most of my students and am nearly always sorry to see them go. At the same time I always enjoy the thought that I've helped

them on their path a little bit and not necessarily always just linguistically, but by being kind and friendly to them too. I know how difficult it can be for them, surviving in a foreign country, even if it's their own choice to be here. Sometimes I imagine one of my own as yet unborn children being in a similar situation at some point in the future and that helps me to be empathetic. I wonder if I'll ever be a father? Rania wants a baby and so do I, but I've been stalling because our relationship is so rocky. She was delighted because I got home early, i.e. earlier than my usual 11.30 pm on a Thursday night, since teaching has finished. 'Oh, darling, I'm so happy to see you!' she exclaimed when I opened the door, and threw her arms around me. 'You've made my day! I love you!' I was touched, gave her a hug, but wish she behaved more like that all the time, instead of being so Jekyll and Hyde.

Mon. 23.6.86
Went for a drink with French-Canadian Nicole in the Bell. She fancies me, but I don't fancy her. I quite like her though. She admitted to being 'nervous' about our tryst, even though it wasn't really a tryst. We talked about friend-ship between men and women, love, sex, religion, intuition, writing, holidays etc. She's going to the Lake District for a holiday with her boyfriend, so I gave her some information. 'You're nice,' she said, after a glass of wine or two. 'Can I kiss you?' 'Sure,' I shrugged, trying not to be embarrassed, and she gave me a quick kiss on the lips. 'There you are,' she said. 'I told you I was going to kiss you!' It served me right, I thought, remembering how I'd asked Spanish Beatriz if I could kiss her in the pub once, but she declined, to my chagrin. At least I had the grace to let Nicole kiss me. I can't help feeling guilty about her though. She's a good sort, but I just don't feel any sexual attraction to her. It's how a lot of

women feel when men chase them, I suppose. Anyway, she has a boyfriend, so it wouldn't be right.

Wed. 25.6.86

Had a silly row with Rania in the Coach and Horses, just because I said I didn't want to go shopping with her. 'I'll leave you. I'll leave and take half!' she blazed. 'What, and go back to the family that kicked you out?' I laughed, quaffing some Guinness. 'Leave my family out of it!' she fired back. 'What about *your* family? They don't even know where you live! They never come to visit you! They don't care about you!' I laughed, but was secretly stung. Not so much because of what she said, which was at least half true, but the fact that she could be so bitchy as to say such a thing to me. I who after all had taken her in and given her refuge. Later, she did apologise, but all these arrows she shoots at me leave wounds that never fully heal.

Thurs. 26.6.86

Big Ed told one of his risqué jokes in the staffroom. I didn't quite catch it, but caught enough of it to sense a certain froideur on the part of the female members of staff present. Something about fluorescent condoms and lead kindly light. He's a card! We call him 'Big Ed' because he's about six foot six and as broad as a barn door. He told me that in the inner-city comp where he used to teach the kids called him 'Frankenstein', which he seemed to find very amusing. He does look a bit like Boris Karloff in the film, except he always wears a tweed jacket and cord trousers – as I do myself. He also considers himself Irish, like me, though he was born and brought up in Surrey and speaks with an RP accent, unlike me with my northern vowels. He also smokes a pipe, unlike Frankenstein, I think, and certainly unlike me.

Sat. 28.6.86

Went to the wedding of Godfrey, Rania's boss at the London Rubber Company. I felt a bit uncomfortable, because I knew Godfrey fancied Rania and she liked him. 'If I wasn't with you, I'd be with Godfrey,' she'd told me more than once, to try and make me jealous. Godfrey is from Goa and Catholic, so the wedding was in a Catholic church with a nuptial Mass. I think it was the first time Rania had been in a Catholic church. She asked me what the tabernacle was, so I explained how Catholics believed Jesus was God and the priest changed the host, i.e. a biscuit, into the body of Jesus, in other words into God, by saying special prayers over it during the ceremony of the Mass and that it was kept in the tabernacle, so the tabernacle was where God was kept … Even as I was explaining this, I realised how bizarre such a belief must sound to her ears, how barmy it was. I even felt vaguely foolish to think I'd once believed it myself, believed it absolutely, blindly, unthinkingly, just like all the other bizarre doctrines of Catholicism. I have the same feeling when I try to explain these things for my non-Catholic students in class, as I sometimes do. The excuse I always make to myself is that I was young and I'd been brainwashed from birth into believing these fictions. And at least I'd had the good sense to liberate myself from them as soon as I was able to think for myself. At the reception, another colleague of Rania's, Adrian, the 'twitcher', told us how he'd come across a couple 'hard at it' in the reeds by the reservoir, when he was out birding the other day. I was a bit embarrassed for Rania's sake, but she giggled like a schoolgirl. She may be from a somewhat sheltered background, but she's not particularly prudish. In fact, she seems to enjoy salacious jokes. I must introduce her to Big Ed.

Sat, 5.7.86

Had a big row with Rania, because I refused to go to her mother's (the begum's as I call her) after an even more boring korantrif or koranic reading than usual at her brother's. A couple of students from the Moslem University of Saudi Arabia were present and chanted away in a monotonous drone in Arabic (give me Gregorian chant any day) for what seemed like an eternity and this was followed by a pompous, boring fifteen-minute sermon by one of the imams present. By the time it was over, I was so paralysed with boredom and stiffness, sitting cross-legged on the floor, that I just wanted to go home and watch telly or read, but I went to the begum's anyway, just for the sake of peace.

Mon. 7.7.86

Went for a drink in the Bell after my Advanced evening class with students as usual. I got buttonholed by Andrew from Poland, to my annoyance, because I wanted to chat up one or two of the girls. Andrew's a likeable enough lad, but a bit of a bore, likes the sound of his own voice. He insisted on telling me about the system in Poland. He's very anti-communist. 'There's no individual freedom there,' he asserted. 'It's a dictatorship. A tyranny. The people are mindless, like sheep. You can't say, write, paint the picture you want. You only go up if you comply with the state. The USA lent Russia arms and technology in World War Two. It was the only way Russia could win. Russia lost over twenty million people, but Poland lost six million, one sixth of its population. In Poland the state forces craftsmen to produce bad work, because the state supplies only bad materials. My friends went to the USA, made money, came back and opened a chicken farm. They had a contract with the state to supply eggs. The food supply for the chickens stopped, so the eggs stopped. The state said, 'Where are our eggs?' My friends were forced to sign false papers, do a fiddle as you say. People are forced to become corrupt. Russia puts their own people in control in Poland. The Poles hate the Russians. There are plenty of the old guard left. In the West people tend to think Eastern bloc countries are all one, but not so. There are divisions, differences. In Poland you can only buy alcohol from 12 to 10 pm. After 10 pm you have to go to a restaurant, but it's very expensive. Polish is a very inflected language. English is very badly taught there. Young teachers who want change leave. Competition is necessary. It's human nature ...' I wanted to argue the last point, if only to be argumentative, and tell him 'human nature' wasn't something fixed or engraved on tablets of stone, but was malleable, changeable, could evolve etc., otherwise what was the purpose of education and law and society and, if he was right, we'd still be savages in the jungle blah blah, but I held my tongue, because I didn't want to get into a debate with him, I was more interested in Beatriz, who is considerably prettier than Andrew, and I could see was trying to attract my attention with her beautiful Spanish eyes ...

Tues. 8.7.86
Took Rania and her friend Rabina, or Ribena as I call her, to see the hadji in Ilford. Rabina wanted her hand read to know if she should marry a chap in Pakistan arranged by her father. I tried to tell them this was all superstitious nonsense (I didn't bother to comment on the arranged marriage aspect, which I find rebarbative) but Rania insisted. Their gullibility astonishes me. They are both university-educated, Westernised young women, yet they believe in such mumbo-jumbo. The white-haired hadji is in a long, alb-like frock or nightgown and embroidered pantomime slippers. There are Islamic religious pictures all over the walls of the shabby room he does his 'consultations' in. He held Rabina's hand

and spoke in a thick Pakistani accent: 'What's your name? What's your mummy's name? What's the boy's name? Someone did something to hurt you two years ago. You're a good girl. You're not thief, not kill, not lie, not do no wrong. The boy's not good. He low-class boy, you high-class girl. No balance. I didn't let my nephew make married for same reason. You will live long time. Maybe ninety, ninety-two. Unnerstan?' 'So she has another ten years then?' I couldn't resist joking, somewhat facetiously, but my little joke was ignored. The hadji wrote or made a pretence of writing on a clipboard with a biro as he read her hand. 'You not make married for long time,' he told Rabina. 'Maybe two or three years. You will have eleven children. Nine boys and two girls. But you will have bad health after five years.' Rabina told him, as she had told us, that at night she heard strange tapping noises under her bed. 'I must come to room where you sleep. Make ceremony on bed. Burn. Chase bad spirits away. We must believe, we Muslim.' 'I believe,' Rania said, too eagerly for my liking. 'You are good girl,' the old shaman said to her. 'Your husband is good boy. Nice boy. He never say or do bad to anyone. His book will publish. I publish four books in Pakistan. In Urdu.' He addressed me directly. 'Your book will publish, inshallah.' 'Thank you,' I said, embarrassed, deciding maybe he wasn't such an old fraud after all. In the car Rania told me she'd given him twenty pounds for Rabina's consultation, which took about half an hour. 'Twenty quid for that? I'm in the wrong job!' I joked. 'I know you think it's a load of rubbish,' Rania protested huffily, 'but he told you your book will publish, so you have to believe it.' 'I believe,' I laughed, not completely kidding. 'Where are we going?' Rabina asked. 'We're going to the pub for a drink,' I said. 'I need a beer.' 'I don't drink,' Rabina said. 'I know,' I said, 'but I do, and you're going to buy me a pint of Guinness for taking you to see the hadji, aren't you?' 'He's an alcoholic, don't encourage him,' Rania scoffed. 'It's all right,' Rabina said. 'I'll give you the money for a drink, but you have to buy it. I'm grateful.' 'Spoken like a true Moslem girl,' I said, laughing to myself at the incongruous thought that I was taking two young Moslem women to the pub with me. In the pub Rania and I ended up having a minor row in front of Rabina, because between sups of Guinness I kept insisting that Islam like all religion was just fantasy and fiction and the Koran like the Bible just a book of fairytales. 'He's entitled to his opinion,' Ribena remonstrated with Rania, when she started getting angry with me. She's not such a bad sort, Ribena. 'I think I've married the wrong one!' I joked, encouraged by the Guinness. 'Huh, she's welcome to you!' Rania hit back in her combative way. Actually Ribena is much more my type – amenable, meek, submissive. I found myself starting to fancy her. I had to keep reminding myself that she was seriously depressive, gloomy and glum, as well as from an even more narrow-minded Moslem background than Rania, despite her having entered the den of iniquity of the pub and even paid for my pint as promised. She stayed the night and slept with Rania in our double bed, while I slept in the single bed in the study, even though, fortified by a few slugs of Jameson's to chase the Guinness, I jokingly suggested we could all three share the double bed. But even Ribena wasn't liberal enough to go for that.

Wed. 9.7.86

'Have you finished your book yet?' Rania asked me. 'You will tell me when you do, won't you? I want to buy you a drink, just like I did last time. I think you're very clever really, to be able to write a book. Not anybody can. Think of the population of the world, billions, how many out of them could write a book. I couldn't.' She can be so charming, so sweet, when she wants to be. It depends on her moods. I'm starting to get used to the mood swings. Pratnose's car went on fire in the college car park. A fire engine had to attend, presumably from the fire station just down the road. Everyone was gleeful at the sight. I almost felt sorry for him, but he brings it on himself, being so officious, marching around as if he owns the place. 'Pity he wasn't in it,' Mark commented viciously later in the staffroom. 'I quite fancy some roast pratnose.' I laughed but cringed at the same time. I wouldn't want to get into Mark's bad books. Geoff drew a cruel but funny cartoon of the incident and stuck it on the notice board outside the staffroom. Everyone wondered if it was arson. It's not beyond the bounds.

Thurs. 10.7.86

Pratnose himself came into the reprographics room and saw me struggling with one of the photocopiers. 'Don't look so serious, Frank,' he remarked. 'Life's no' that bad.' 'I know, it's worse,' I laughed mirthlessly. 'These bloody machines are so damn useless.' I was stressed out about being late for my class – I who was never late – but unable to get the copier to function and annoyed with myself for leaving it till the last minute. 'Sorry about your car,' I forced myself to say, wondering if he might suspect me of being the one who torched it, since we had a history of clashes over the EFL party. 'Ach, it was near the end o' the road anyway,' he said, in his broad Scottish accent. 'Worse things happen at sea.' Sometimes I think he might be almost human! He reminds me of Mr Mackay, the prison warden in *Porridge*. At the end of my class, German Eva told me she was leaving next week and gave me a blank cassette to record some Irish music on for her, as I'd agreed. She's really into it! You'd think she'd be more into the Stranglers and the Clash the way she looks, with her spiky orange hair and punky clothes, including safety pins. She's a really sweet girl behind all that. She told me she's going back to Germany to study law and thanked me both for my lessons and introducing her to Irish music. That made me feel a whole lot better about life. I agreed to join her and a few others for a farewell drink next Friday.

Sun. 13.7.86
Went for dinner with my private Egyptian student, Jimmy. He's married to an English girl – who converted to Islam for the purpose – and has two young kids, a son and a daughter called Halah. 'I'd like a little daughter like Halah,' Rania said to me in the car on the way home. 'Can we have one?' 'Sure,' I joked. 'We'll go to the supermarket tomorrow.' 'I hate you,' she shot back. 'You're never serious.' The joke was to hide the painful thought that I might never be able to have kids, because according to the doctors I'm infertile, or 'subfertile', as they call it, based on 'sperm count'. The pain was sharpened by the thought that I'd secretly love to have a daughter, but I didn't tell Rania that, because now wasn't the time for us to have a baby. Apart from anything else, I'm not sure I want to stay with her and I definitely couldn't leave her if I had a child with her. I'm well and truly trapped. Between the devil and the deep blue sea.

Wed. 16.7.86
Rania took a day off work from testing condoms at the London Rubber Company to go to a teaching job interview in the local comp. They offered her a one-year contract teaching maths plus teacher training. 'I'm over the moon!' she exclaimed, throwing her arms around me when she got home. All the teachers were nice, she said. However, they told her there was a problem with racism in the school and the parents were very demanding, as well as racist. One of the teachers, Mr Singh, gave her a lift home. 'It's a long time

since we had a charming young lady in this school,' she told me he said to her on the way and added teasingly: 'I think he fancies me.' I laughed and kept my thoughts to myself.

Fri. 18.7.86
Went to the Bell for a farewell drink with Eva and a few others. Nicole was there, in white blouse and jeans, wearing sunglasses because she had a black eye. Apparently some lout punched her in the park, because she tried to stop him shooting birds with an air-rifle. She said she'd reported it to the police. Eva looked less punkish than usual, in a green T-shirt and black leotards/leggings. I gave her back the cassette she gave me to record Irish music on for her and she kissed me. 'Ven I play it, I'll sink of ze Wictoria,' she said. 'I thought you were going to say you'd think of me!' I pretended to be offended. 'Vell,' she riposted. 'You are connected wiz ze Wictoria!' I laughed and gave her a hug. Nicole said: 'Don't ever change, Eva.' Two such lovely ladies, lovely people. They reminded me why I have the best job in the world. I felt quite choked when I gave Eva a hug and said my final goodbye to her at the end of the night. She gave me her address in Germany, to add to my collection, but I knew I'd probably never see her again. I walked home on a strange high fuelled by a potent mixture of happiness, sadness and alcohol ...

CHAPTER FIVE

London

'Days pass,' as my cynical South African colleague Mark once commented, when I asked him how he was. Weeks pass. Months pass. All things must pass, to quote George Harrison. There's something depressingly Catholic about that thought. What's that branch of theology called, eschatology? God, they know how to suck the joy out of life! I studied it for a while at the senior seminary – not that I took theology seriously. It was all moonshine to me. I was more interested in reading novels, finding out a bit about the *real* world.

And here I am in the real world. I go to see my solicitor, Veronica, in Holborn, to finalise my divorce from Mary, my first wife. 'Veronica'. Must be Catholic but I don't ask. I wonder if she would wipe my face for me? She doesn't look anything like the Veronica in the Stations of the Cross, whom I always rather fancied. This one is short and plump and doesn't wear a veil. Not in the office anyway. Ah, sweet, lovely, honest Mary. It's still dragging on, over three years after the break-up. You don't get much more real than divorce. The memory still provokes a stab of pain deep in my guts. A sense of failure. A sense of guilt. It's a kind of death. Death of a dream. Tread softly. Discussing the sordid details with Veronica and dealing with the paperwork

– consent orders, forms, letters to the court – doesn't help. Nor does the thought that my second marriage, to Rania, is no better. Not that it's a legal marriage. Afterwards I go to the nearest decent hostelry to drown my sorrows in several pints of Guinness. I write to Ana too. Ana! She is the light in the darkness. The light at the end of the tunnel. My possible escape route. Escape to victory. Well, freedom maybe.

As I write, I read and reread her letter to me, received only this morning, trying not to spill beer or tears on it:

Madrid, 5 September 86

Dear Francis,

I could write to you every hour. The way in which your letters are written tears my heart. Although you don't want me to cry, I cry but also smile at the same time when I'm reading them. It's true I had doubts in my mind when I came here. But now after reading your letter, I assure you there is not the slightest doubt in my mind. I don't know how to express my feelings about you in English. In fact I'm ashamed to write English. I know you're a teacher, but I wonder if you can understand me when you're reading my letters.

The first time I saw you, I felt attracted to you only physically, but with a different intention from yours. I wanted to practise my English with a native. Little by little I like you more and more. I was fed up about Joseph's jokes on you and me. I didn't want to talk to you, see you, be with you. I was afraid you played with me, so I pretended not to be interested in you. At the beginning I only wanted to prove myself that I'm just like the other girls who can have 'adventures' with boys or men without feeling themselves emotionally involved with them. I'm very unlucky on this point as you can see.

I fell in love with you and I am in love. At the beginning I could become angry with you easily. You were always joking at me and I didn't understand your sense of humour. Your jokes sometimes seemed to me offensive i.e. do you remember when we were visiting the church where you could find the saint's head? Do you remember what you told me? I think your jokes hurt me because I was in love with you and I found myself ridiculous of being in love with my teacher.

I can remember my first appointment with you: I was so nervous that I dropped the soap-box and it was broken. I couldn't paint my nails by myself. I couldn't believe I was going to see you alone. I remember your first "quick" kiss, when you asked me to sit down on the bed, to lie down, to take my shoes off and so on. Everything was a new experience for me. Even your kisses are different, as I've already told you. I remember everything about you except your face. When I try to remember it, I can't. THAT'S MY LIMITATION. I need a good photo of you!

This letter is being written in two different days. I began it when I received your letter. And today I continue it when I've just found another message from you. I'm in Madrid. I've played the record you gave me. I've found a message written on it. I've not listened to it before, because I've not got a record player in my village. Of course, the record gives me good memories but also sadness. Instead of thinking on you less, my feelings, thoughts, I myself, are always with you.

I thought this would be easier. You're very far but we can write to each other. It's unbearable, letters are very slow, every minute I'm asking myself what you're doing, if you'll have forgotten me, how your feelings about me are, if they'll have changed from the 25th August. But I didn't want to complain about anything now. What I wanted to tell you is that you needn't thank me anything now. I mean, when

I read what you've written to me, you usually finish saying "thank you". We were happy together and perhaps I have to thank you more than you have to thank me.

I was fully happy. (Is it right?) You're a lovely man. And I love you because of your good humour, your friendship, your optimistic position about life ("optimistic" in the following sense: you pretend to laugh at any situation of life. But your real feelings are the same as mine. There's a word which describes mine perfectly: BITTERNESS). Because, I think I can see behind your mask (you have got a mask, haven't you?) what you are. Perhaps a shy person who needs to love and to be loved, who is afraid of people and doesn't want to be known by them not to be hurt. Life has been very hard to you and you're frightened. Both of us are frightened but our reasons are different. Because I don't know the world around me is my reason. Yours is you think you know the world quite well. Maybe I'm wrong with you, you must tell me if I am or not. Perhaps I have to look for a mask myself, have I?

I stop now. Next letter more ideas.

Little messages:

Are you tired of receiving my letters? Don't worry. I hope I'll write few letters when I begin my studies. Writing letters in English takes me a long time. (A little bit of joke. Don't be angry.)

I like your record very much. Not only it gets me melancholic. <u>Send me the cassette</u>. I'll send you photos when I develop them. I've no money at the moment. I need a good photo of you.

THIS IS MY FIRST LETTER TO YOU. It speaks of my feelings about you. I think I've been selfish. (Writing to you only about my problems wasn't what you were waiting for. It's my opinion. But my mood wasn't OK. It's not OK now, but it's better.)

How is our plant? Is it growing?

I've got the biography of James Joyce by Richard Ellmann. About 700 pages in English!

Regards to you from Maria José.

I haven't sent kisses (xxx) to you before, because I didn't believe it. I couldn't believe xxx were true. I mean, people put them on letters. (We haven't got such a custom. But it's lovely, isn't it?) Now I send <u>one thousand</u> kisses to you.

With love,

Ana (xxx)

TE QUIERO MUCHO

Days pass. I go to the airport with Rania and other members of the tribe to see off Rafeeqah, one of Rania's sisters, or 'Radio' as I call her, since she is such a blabbermouth. She's going to see her 'boyfriend' in Guyana, much to her mother's snobbish disapproval, because the boyfriend isn't a brain surgeon or barrister, so they're at war. Her mother – the begum – has stayed at home sulking. 'I feel so guilty,' Radio keeps saying in the car over and over again, threatening not to board the flight, but she does. I feel sorry for both of them, because they're both so hot-blooded, fiery, proud – and I can see the same features in Rania. I can't help feeling amused too – there's something childish about them, all of them. 'Your family are better than EastEnders,' I joke to Rania, but she doesn't see the funny side and goes into a huff.

When we get back from the airport, I carry on helping Rania prepare her first lessons as a teacher for tomorrow, even though I'm jet-lagged and even though I go back to work myself tomorrow, though only to enrol students, not to teach. But helping her helps to distract me from the end-of-holiday, back-to-work blues. Rania is teaching maths, health and hygiene, biology and botany. I don't know much about these subjects, but the principles of teaching are the same, so I'm able to help. She needs reassurance as much as anything. 'Thank you for all your support,' she says at midnight, when we finish, giving me a big hug. 'I couldn't have done it otherwise.' Sometimes I remember why I fell for her in the first place.

I'm half-glad to go back to work, even though it's something of a shock to the system after almost two months' holiday. I like my colleagues and I like the students even more. It's interesting meeting people from all over the world and being in a position to help them. I enjoy the sensation of being able to give them the benefit of the education I've been lucky enough to receive. It makes me feel I'm sharing my good fortune with them. And most of them are so appreciative, so grateful. Well, they are all adults and there because they want to be, want to learn, see learning English as a way of developing themselves, furthering their careers.

'Mother causes all the problems in the family,' Rania moans to me in the pub, as we're talking about her sister Rafeeqah, who has gone to Guyana to meet some boy she wants to marry against her mother's wishes. 'She didn't want you to marry me only because you're white. My dad wouldn't have objected. He admired teachers. He'd be proud of me today, being a teacher. I wish he hadn't died when I was thirteen. I miss him. I'm very unfortunate really. Radio says that's why I've married an older man, because I need fatherly love. Maybe it's true.'

I'm touched. She talks about her father quite often. Probably sees me as a sort of surrogate. It must be a terrible blow, losing a parent at thirteen. When I was that age I was in the junior seminary, a hundred miles from home, and I always remember how terrified I was of being called to

Father Director's office to be told my mum or dad had died. Of course, in a sense I'd already lost them …

I get yet another rejection letter from a publisher, but I don't tell Rania. It's like a knife in the guts. 'Maybe you should try doing something else,' she commented last time, sticking another knife in my guts, and twisted it by adding: 'You don't seem to be getting anywhere.' She just doesn't understand. Unlike Ana. From whom I also receive a letter the same day. It doesn't do much to alleviate the pain though.

Madrid, 16th September 1986

Dear Francis,

Thank you for your third letter. I'm not exactly upset, but I was disappointed by reading your second letter. By the way, have you received another letter of mine? I posted them in my village and the mail is slower, I'm afraid. I'll try to be honest, but before reading the letter you must promise me not to be angry. IF YOU DON'T WANT TO READ IT, I'll tell you where you can read. Consider that I sometimes express myself strongly in your language and that I never lie.

WARNING! LEAVE NEXT PARA OUT IF YOU WANT

I know that you want me to know that "you are already committed to someone" whom you love. I know it but I knew it too. You needn't repeat it to me in every letter. That makes me unhappy – that you stay with her and that I can't forget it. That's one of your complications and I think the most insuperable one. Have a look at the taxonomy you have used: committed to, love, dramatic change, and so on. I'm confused about it. And perhaps you are confused too so that your letters are written ambiguously. I can't forget her, but if you continue telling me about her, I will think what you want is to finish our relationship in any sense. Yet you don't want to directly, when you write to me about her. I feel myself as if what I'm doing is to destroy your sentimental life with her. I love you and I respect your life. I would hate to hurt you in any way. But I can't avoid that this fact bothers me. After reading your second letter I understand that what you meant was the same as what you told me when we went to the theatre – to be <u>special</u> friends. You do explain yourself very well, but I don't know if it can exist. I wish I could believe that it can exist. I'm not asking you to do anything. I'm only telling my feelings. I'd hate to hear you telling me good-bye. I'd love to stay with you forever, but I know our limitation and your special complication. Money and geography are my barriers. But listen, they're not insuperable. I need only two hours by plane to see you again, and some money. It's not impossible for me to stay with you again. I don't need a great change in my life to get it. To work hard to get the money, to sleep less, to study at nights, some quarrels with my family and to take the plane to London. But when I arrived at London, in which mood would I find you? Could you stay with me every hour even if you weren't working? You know what I'm referring to. ****

Whenever we try to be realistic our letters become sad. Don't worry, Francis. I do only my best to understand you – it's quite difficult though. Please, don't take any decision. I'm not asking you to take any decision. Besides, my spirits aren't high enough to bear another displeasure, sorrow – I don't know the right word. You are my teacher, so you can tell me.

Now, finished. I don't want to think more about barriers, complications, limitations. I'm sorry. Maybe I will some time do it.

Next subject: Platonic love. Before you talked about it.

I've already thought that our love was becoming in such a love. Perhaps it's the most perfect way of love. I'm not sure. There is a danger that you can idealise the other person. Idealisation is not allowed to any of us. They're only ideas. I have to think more deeply about it.

Answer to your third letter: You'll be welcome whenever you want to come to Madrid. I'm looking forward to your visiting.

Thank you again for your third letter. It was very nice and I needed it. There are no words to express my feelings about you, but I hope that by choosing the simplest one you can "catch" all that I mean: I love you. Come to me as soon as possible. (Is it enough for you?)

Kisses and love,

Ana xxxxx

P.S. I didn't ring you up because you are right, it's better to write to each other.

My father likes the whiskey you recommended me very much. (Jameson.)

It's more difficult to find flowers in Madrid. Do you remember what a flower simbolises to me? If I don't find any to send you, I hope at least you remember me whenever you look at a flower (especially roses).

Today I am your boss. You are not allowed to be dissappointed or angry after reading my letter.

Te quiero mucho, muchisimo,

Ana

Despite what she says about flowers in Madrid, the letter includes three rose petals. I hold them in the palm of my hand. They are as light as feathers, but weigh like stones on my heart.

Radio returns from Guyana, having arranged to marry her boyfriend there so she can bring him to the UK. The begum is in high dudgeon about it and uses me as her release valve, sitting in the kitchen having a cup of tea – strong, sweet and dark, 'just like my women', as I joke to Rania's younger sisters, who giggle like naughty schoolgirls. Begum: 'Mister Francis, let me tell you, after my first husband pass away, I got remarried but gave up my husband for my children. My children are scamps! They don't know all the sacrifices I made. My first husband didn't leave me a rich woman. I had to pay for my own passage to UK! Excuse me telling you this, Mister Francis, but I have to tell someone. I have no husband to tell or help me. Rafeeqah has always been a nice girl with me. Why couldn't she just be a little bit more nice? I'm not against her boyfriend. I just want the marriage done in the Indian way, according to Indian custom. She went to Guyana on her own to get legal married. It makes me shame, makes me embarrass. I was only opposed to you because you were English, not Indian. Not because I don't respect you. You are lecturer, educated man. I will go back to Guyana and remarry! I'll leave the children to look after themselves! Old and ugly as I am, I'll find someone to take me. I done my duty by my kids. I fed, clothed and educated them. I don't want no one to curse me. The pressure of all these problems is too much for me.' By now she's almost in tears and I'm feeling genuinely sorry for her. 'Oh, mother, I haven't come here to argue or to listen to this and I'm sure Francis doesn't want to either!' Radio exclaims angrily and grabbing her handbag flounces out of the kitchen. The begum follows and shouts after her: 'Why have you come here? Go away if you don't want to listen! Francis is one of the family now. Why shouldn't he hear? I will tell him the truth. I have nothing to hide. You will know what it's like when you have kids of your own.' 'I don't want to have kids,' Radio flings back at her. 'It's too much trouble. You see the trouble you say we cause for you! I'm going.' 'Then you'll be known as a barren woman, ha!' the begum shoots her in the back as she rushes down the hallway to the door, making me wince. 'Go and pray to Allah for guidance!' she shouts. 'He will guide you! He will put you on right path! No one of us can survive without God! We all need God!' But Radio rushes out, slamming the front door behind her. I sit silently, shocked, not knowing what to say. I still feel I'm an outsider, despite what the begum says about me being 'one of the family'. There's a turnup for the books! Rania's younger brother, Tubby as they call him, though he isn't tubby at all, has been sitting at the kitchen table throughout the performance, studying his accountancy, but suddenly he stands up, collects his books and papers together and leaves the room. 'I give up,' he says angrily. 'I can't study in this environment! I'm going to find a place of my own!' The begum bursts into tears and wails: 'You see, Mister Francis, what scamps my children are! They all want to leave me! They all want to desert me! What have I done so wrong to them?' Well, you are a bit of a tyrant, with special expertise in emotional blackmail, I think to myself, but don't answer, deciding it's a rhetorical question, and after uttering a few soothing platitudes, excuse myself by saying I have to go and pick Rania up. She's visiting some neighbour nearby and has left me there on my own, for the first time ever. Never again, I tell myself! Of course, I don't go and pick Rania up straightaway. I nip off to have a crafty pint of Guinness in the Black Boy and read Ana's latest letter for the umpteenth time.

Madrid, 25th September 1986

Dear Francis,

A week without hearing from you. I was getting used to receive a letter from you every few days. It's not a complain. I know you're working and you haven't so much time to write to me. I hope you're not angry with me because of my last letter. I hope you will have been able to understand me – it was like a "burst of energy". I needed to say it. But now I regret of having done it. I hope again you have not changed your feelings about me. I have not about you.

Today is 25th September. I did not see you since a month ago. Summer has just finished. We're in Autumn. It rains a lot. There are few flowers in the fields. I still miss you. I foresee a terribly sad day, today Thursday. I could hardly sleep yesterday night. I was thinking and crying. Why I haven't received another letter from Francis? Perhaps he's angry with me. Perhaps I love him in a different way he loves me. Why he hasn't telephoned me yet? Perhaps it's difficult for him/you to write about yourself to an "unknown" person. You don't trust me enough. Perhaps you're trying to forget me or you want me to forget you. I'm causing you to be in troubles. I can do it easily I'm afraid: my boyfriend doesn't understand me and feels himself alone, sad, since we don't see each other.

My family, as it seems, only has got problems when I'm at home (our problem nowadays is my car which I have to share with my sister). Yesterday night I was thinking about my friends. My best friend is Maria José now, but I like living in contact with nature. I hate going to discos. I like going out early in the afternoon when the sun still shines, going for a walk while you're looking at trees, flowers, animals. I can go with her for a play or a lecture. Do you understand me? I mean, going to discos is the commonest activity among the Spanish youth during their free time. Even my boyfriend goes to discos now and dances. I don't want to go. I don't enjoy myself there.

By writing this letter I try to share my thoughts with you to increase our friendship. (You know I love you very, very much, but I haven't got words to say it. You express this feeling a lot better than I can as I have checked it so that I wouldn't want to say how much I love you, but to show you what kind of friend you are to me.) I'm not referring to the thoughts I've just written, but the thoughts which can be suggested by the following. My melancholy has got me to read "memories", I mean books which I hadn't read for ages in which I used to write small commentaries on the margins. Among these books I chose Tagore, Hesse and a Spanish poet whom I don't like so much now but whom I loved when I was 14. His name is Pedro Salinas. He writes very long love poems. I've included some verses belonging to Salinas' poetry (in Spanish) on a separate sheet for you. (I don't dare to translate Spanish poetry into English. Anyway, practise your Spanish!) Here is the excerpt from Tagore, which I will translate for you, though you can try it first:

> "¡No me escondas tu el secreto de tu corazón!
> ¡Dímelo a mi, que soy tu amigo, solo a mi! …
> Dímelo tan dulce como te sonríes, que no te oirán
> mis oidos, sino mi corazón!" (Tagore)

> (Don't hide the secret of your heart. Say it to me, because I am your friend, only to me … Say it to me as sweetly as you smile, so that my ears will not hear you, but my heart will.)

I've written a passage from Herman Hesse on another separate sheet of paper for you. It's from Lektüre für Minuten. I've included the original German and a Spanish translation (not mine). You can translate it into English from the German or the Spanish or both. (I think your Spanish is better than your German though.) Anyway, that's your homework! You can return it with your next letter to me and I will mark it for you. Am I a good teacher? It's good practice for me!

Of course, you are the person chosen to be the receiver of both these messages. Writing this I try to speak with you without saying words. You will be always in my mind as you are now. I think I can wait for what the future holds in store for both of us (your own words, I think) in this way. Perhaps also in this way we can be special friends.

I'm looking forward to receiving news from you. Be in a hurry! I'm dying for hearing from you.

Love and many kisses,

Ana (xxxx)

P.S. Tuesdays at (3.30 pm English time) 5.30 pm in Spain from next week is almost impossible for me to ring you up. I have my German lessons on Tuesdays and Thursdays from 4.00 pm to 6.00 pm. I could leave out a little bit of my German lesson. What about another day at the same time or any day in the evening?

Our pink plant will have flowers. I've found it out.

Forgive my horrible "bursts of energy", please. I love you, and write even only a few words to me.

Te quiero mucho.

He had a quick look at the Hesse passage and was able to get the gist of it with his limited Spanish. Something about the sadness and misery of human life, but life also being beautiful and delicious. Why had she sent such a pessimistic passage, he wondered? Why something from Hesse, the world champion of weltschmerz? Well, she was a bit of a pessimist herself, he was starting to realise, putting her letter and Hesse back in the envelope, not sure he would do his homework, even if it meant getting a nought out of ten.

'I just gave this wow of a lecture. Someone asked me what 'coitus interruptus' meant. I told them in graphic detail.' Thus Mark in the staffroom. I laugh but am secretly horrified. I can just imagine! Knowing him he probably drew pictures on the board to illustrate. He's a hard nut. Ex-South African paratrooper. Though he likes to describe himself as a 'teddy bear'. He's teaching A-level psychology now, having got himself a first-class degree in the subject, as well as EFL, which he calls 'effel' and regards as 'vacuous' because lacking in 'content'. About which I'll grant he's half right. Though he says he'll stay in it for the time being – till he can get a university post – because of the 'crumpet'. He's right about the crumpet, even if the word isn't part of my idiolect. I love being around the foreign girls too, though the only one I'm *really* interested in now is Ana. I don't tell him that though. He regards me as a fellow 'player', so I play the game with him. As I do with Geoff. Though I'm a bit peeved with Geoff, because he's chasing Spanish Beatriz, who's one of my students, not his, and who I still fancy, though she's rejected me. But all is fair in love and war, I remind myself. It's one of my favourite apothegms. And anyway, I'm in love with Ana, aren't I? Or amn't I, as the Irish would say – more logically. Yes, I tell myself, but with a certain sense of hopelessness and angst, because I'm trapped, and I don't have the balls to escape. That word isn't in my idiolect either. I don't even know why I've used it. I must have been talking to Mark too much! Days pass.

Bea tells me during the break in class that her mother is ill, so she has to fly to Spain tomorrow. It sounds serious. I tell her I'm sorry, which I am, genuinely sorry. It's a reminder that she's a real person, with real emotions, and not just some sort of fantasy sex object. Not that I really need such a reminder. I invite her for a drink, thinking she may need some tea and sympathy, but she tells me she's already been invited by Geoff. In spite of myself, my sympathy for her suddenly evaporates. Not completely, but considerably. I feel annoyed with her. She declined my advances months ago, supposedly because I was married, but Geoff is married too, so why is she going out with him? Unless he's told her he isn't. But that's unlikely, since everyone knows he is. I feel annoyed with Geoff, unfairly. I'm even more annoyed with myself for still fancying her, for caring, for being bothered, especially as I now have Ana. Thank goodness I still have Ana. I end up going for a drink on my own instead of with the students, most unusually, so that I can lick my wounds and read Ana's latest letter again. That and a couple of pints of Guinness soothe the pain considerably.

Madrid, 6th October, 1986

Dear Francis,

Thanks a lot for the cassette. I received it on Wednesday and your letter on Monday. This time you didn't surprise me with your brief note written on it. After opening the parcel, reading the piece of paper, I opened the cassette quickly and read your lovely words on it. I didn't see your words on the record till I played it, do you remember? I'm very glad you've done the cassette for me. It means you think of me and when I'm listening to it I try to imagine which kind of thoughts you had in mind when you were doing it. I'd love to listen to it with you helping me to understand the words of the songs.

By the way, I need your help with your special song for me. I can't understand the words. Could you translate it into understandable English, please? The cassette brings me many happy memories as you hoped to, but I wanted them not to be memories but suddenly to become into realities, you and me/I together again, without 'complications', enjoying the life, being happy.

Maybe you'd like to know the effect of your last letter on me. Well, that letter has been the first one I've received until now, as regard its content. I read it quickly the first time and I didn't notice exactly what you meant, but with my second reading I felt how I was blushing – neither do you laugh, neither do you be angry. I'm a shy girl, you know. When I finished reading it, I understood how much you trust me if you dare say me your feelings honestly. I don't mind you admitting it to me and my blushing is natural in/of me. But I have to clarify you something you misunderstood in Dublin perhaps, because I didn't express myself clearly enough or I don't know what happened. The misunderstanding is that I don't relieve myself sexually, nevertheless I'm usually frustrated. But you can tell me all your feelings and I'll listen to them with pleasure. You're right when you say that it's important to tell each other about our feelings (and especially for each other).

There's another misunderstanding, when I told you that our relationship was becoming platonic I referred to our relationship through letters and this was my impression after your first two letters. Talking about our relationship, I don't know if I'm wrong, but I think you feel yourself more optimistic about our future. If you feel yourself so, why do you feel so? Answer my question. I've noticed that you don't answer all my questions and perhaps the reason is that I don't insist on your answer, as a "stubborn" girl, like I am to your mind, should insist. (If you don't agree, I need your reason, too.)

As regards your possible stay in Madrid, I'd like to stay with you every hour (day & night) too. But if we wanted to do so, we'd have to invent something. (What a pity, isn't it?) If you told me when you're coming exactly, I could study the possibilities of spending a weekend together. Of course Ma José has to come with me and she's asked me to tell you that she wouldn't bother/mind if Rob comes with you. (I think she likes him.) I believe she's talking seriously. Anyway, Francis, come as soon as possible and when you can. I'd like to see you again and possibly you'll be able to come before I can go to England.

Now I have to finish. My dog is becoming jealous of you. She's on my table trying to draw my attention to play with her. When I finish my letters, I wonder if Dama should put her "legprint" on them. If she could speak English, she could explain you my feelings about you as well as I could if I spoke it well.

No, I'm not helping my father with his whiskey! I don't drink alcohol except Martini and not at home. Flowers symbolize my love to you. YOU SHOULDN'T HAVE FORGOTTEN IT. I'd like to do something for you in return for your cassette and everything you are doing for me. Can I do something?

With all my love, kisses (long and quick) and caresses.

Ana (xxxx)

P.S: Tomorrow I begin my classes at University. I think the difference in time between your country and mine is only of one hour more in Spain than in England. (I wrote it badly wrongly in my previous letter.)

CHAPTER SIX

London

'Take me home. I knew it would be a disaster. I'll never go shopping with you again.'

A red mist descended on him. Furious, biting his tongue, he stomped out of the shop, marched to the car, got in and started the engine. He was in half a mind to drive off and leave her there, but didn't, waited for her, his mind a storm of black thoughts. *I can't take this any more. I have to leave her. It's hopeless. No matter how I try, no matter what I do, it's not good enough. We're two different people. I don't need this. I could be with Ana. Or Danielle. Or Cinzia. Or …*

She suddenly appeared, yanked the back door of the car open, threw herself in the back seat and slammed the door shut, making the whole car shake, which annoyed him even more. In the mirror he could see her scowling thunderously. It was like being out with a three-year-old, he told himself, not for the first time. And all because he had refused to buy a chandelier, for hundreds of pounds, on credit, adding even more to their debts.

He gunned the accelerator, not realising he was in third gear, shot out of the parking bay, almost colliding with a car coming in, and drove out of the car park, warning himself to calm down, an accident would make his day a whole lot worse. She didn't make it easy though, because she immediately embarked on a tirade of abuse from behind, telling him he was useless, he was mean, he was arrogant, he was a swine, she was going to leave him. 'Don't think I'm going to stay with you for the rest of my life, you arrogant pig!' He bit his tongue, knowing it would be futile to retaliate, just tried to ignore her insults and concentrate on getting home without having an accident.

As soon as they arrived she opened the car door even before he had stopped properly and jumped out, slammed the door shut, making the car shake again, and stormed off towards the house. Teeth gritted, he sped off, hoping she had her key with her, but not really caring. He had to get away from her as fast as possible, before he said or did something he'd regret. He was the least violent man in the world, had never laid a finger on anyone in anger, especially a woman, but there were times when he felt like throttling her, started to understand how crimes of passion occurred. Her tirade of abuse had been so continuous and relentless that he had been tempted to stop the car on the main road, drag her out and dump her there, but somehow he had managed not to lose it.

He drove to the Marshes, parked, pushed open the gate of the level crossing and almost stepped in front of the train that came whooshing past, stepping back just in time. He waited for a few moments after it had thundered away into the distance, telling himself to calm down and breathing a sigh of relief, remembering how he had once seen a woman struck by a train at this very spot, though miraculously not killed. When he had collected himself, he checked carefully twice in both directions and walked quickly across the tracks, through the gate on the other side and along the footpath towards the river, passing the reservoir on one side and one of the many meadows that made up the Marshes on the other side, a great expanse of wild, long, wind-ruffled grass bordered by bushes, railway embankment, river and, in the far distance, Lea Bridge Road, along which he could see the toylike traffic sliding silently.

At the marina he crossed the river by the metal footbridge to the other side, then made his way along the towpath towards the Robin Hood, the river with its moored-up narrowboats and motor cruisers to his left, to his right the steep upward slopes of Springfield Park, with its lawns and trees. The sky was a cold, clear, October blue, but he was so angry and depressed it might as well have been black. The river looked ink-black and the macabre thought flitted through his mind of how easy it would be to end it all and escape this vale of tears by jumping in, if he hadn't already jumped in front of a train. But no, he thought, that wasn't the way to do it. The way to do it was by swallowing a few pints of the other black stuff in the Robin Hood, so in he went and ordered one, professionally served as always by the Irish landlord with the proper invocation after he had topped it up: 'Now.'

He took his pint and, even though it was chilly, sat at one of the picnic tables on the patio outside overlooking the river and meadows of the Marshes. The vegetation still looked surprisingly green, though tinted with the palette of autumn – browns, russets, gingers, yellows. The usual wildfowl – swans, geese, ducks, coots, moorhens – paddled and dabbled about on the river, disturbed only by an occasional sculler from the boating club just upriver beyond the footbridge. There was a smell of woodsmoke from the gaily-painted houseboats that lined the banks, reminding him as always of the scent of turfsmoke and childhood holidays in Ireland. Another train rattled across the multi-arched viaduct on its way to Cambridge, disturbing only briefly the serenity of the scene. The sound always reminded him incongruously of Wilfred Owen's 'stuttering rifles' rapid rattle', made him think gratefully that it wasn't the sound of rifles or machine-guns he was hearing. There was little other evidence of man in the scene, apart from the pylons that stretched out into the distance. It probably hadn't changed much in hundreds of years or at least he liked to think so. It was a thought that helped to put his problems into some perspective and soothe his troubled soul, like the scene itself.

His soul was further soothed by his first sup of the Guinness, which he imbibed with a gasp of pleasure. If only this moment could last for ever, he thought! If only life were so pleasant, so peaceful, so simple, so idyllic! Instead of full of worry, struggle, stress, pain, confusion, mystery, perplexity, disappointment. The disappointment of another publisher's rejection letter, for example, received this very morning and sitting like a slab of stone on his heart in the inside pocket of his jacket. Or rather, stuck like a dagger in his heart. He thought of taking it out to read it again, but didn't. That would be sheer masochism. Would only twist the blade and reopen the wound. Anyway, he more or less knew the plati- tudinous, formulaic words off by heart: '… we don't feel that your ms. would fit into our list at this time…' blah blah. Fuck them! But luckily there was another letter in his pocket, one that acted as a kind of antidote to that one, and that he couldn't resist taking out and reading yet again, true balm for his troubled spirit:

Madrid, 24th October 86

Dear Francis,

Now I'm lazy to write letters. Well, not exactly lazy, as you know I've begun my studies at University and I'm busy too.

I don't think I am a wonderful letter writer as you affirm, but, on the other hand, I think your letters are wonderful.

They sometimes amuse me so much. I mean, they are highly romantic. Romanticism is one of my favourite cultural movements for many reasons e.g. because it deals with Nature, because it's misterious in some way and life, which becomes unknown for us regards fate, destiny or future turns into a mistery too, because of people's feelings which stand upon freedom and so on.

But I have difficulties to identify myself as the girl whom you write to. I like your letters so much, I could be in love with anyone who writes as you do, but I don't know if they're written to me in fact. Perhaps it happens to me because your letters are the first ones I have received as regards their content, letters of love. Nobody has ever told me his feelings about me as you're doing. Anyway, I love your letters and I love you. TE QUIERO.

When you rang me up I'd written as far as what you've read. From now on I've got a new point of view to continue writing.

A good beginning could be I love you, I still love you. When writing these words, I feel myself dissapointed because I don't know how to express such a feeling writing. I envy your ability to describe this feeling and perhaps my problems of identifying myself with "your lover" are due to my inability to describe this feeling through words. As you can see there is a contradiction in myself. I consider myself as a person who loves everybody and likes to be loved in return, but I can't write letters of love. I can only say "te quiero" in the simplest way.

As you can't forbid me to ask whatever I want in my letters – you can on the telephone of course – I'm going to ask you something again, after my frustrated attempt on last Friday. I'm curious and another reason for doing it is that I don't want any "taboo" theme between us: How is your girlfriend? Why don't you say anything about her in your last letters? Do you have problems with her? And, please, don't be dissappointed, angry or something because of my following criticism about something you told me in your last letter, that is you love me one hundred per cent. You told me in Dublin and in some of your first letters that you love your girlfriend too, so you should say you love me 50% but not 100%. (Try to understand, I'm not ironic, this is only my not serious way of telling it.)

By the way, thank you very much for telephoning me. It was very kind of you. Again you make me happy. Let me explain everything about your telephone call briefly (I have to post the letter tomorrow):

Situation: I was watching T.V. Sleepy. Bored. All the evening in bed with headache. At last it disappeared.

Telephone call: Surprising. You're like a child because you always do exactly the opposite you're asked to. I mean, when I asked you to ring me up, you didn't and when I agreed you didn't telephone, then you telephoned.

Your voice is so sweet and nice. I was very pleased to listen to it.

Happiness and pleasure by hearing your laugh. I had forgotten your face, laugh and voice already. It's horrible, isn't it?

I know the conversation was not very interesting but it was my fault. I can't speak on the telephone. I don't know what to say. Nevertheless I'd like to repeat that experience.

I have remorse: it was very expensive. Although it's very nice to think that the purpose of your calling was only to say, 'I love you'.

Regards from Maria José. I'm very sorry to hear of Rob's illness. I hope he'll be totally recovered by this time. Please tell him to take care of himself. Maybe I write him a letter.

Now to finish my letter a quotation from J. Joyce's biography. Interpret why I thought of you when I read it:

"… I spoke to you satirically tonight but I was speaking of the world not of you. I am an enemy of the ignobleness and slavishness of people but not of you. Can you not see the simplicity which is at the back of all my disguises? We all wear masks …"

(It's a piece of a letter to Nora, p. 170)

With love,

Ana (xx)

P.S. Photographs in the next letter. Katherine haven't seen them yet. I've seen José again. I've often seen him.

(Many kisses.)

He read the letter several times while he drank several more pints of Guinness and a few whiskey chasers. Every time he read it, he felt more and more certain of what he needed to do, what he wanted to do, what he *would* do. He'd go home and tell Rania that their relationship had to end, they weren't right for each other, they should go their separate ways. Being with her was a terrible mistake. They were on completely different wavelengths, from very different backgrounds and cultures. And that was on top of the gender gap, he laughed wryly to himself. She said she loved him and maybe she did in her own way, but she didn't *respect* him. That was what hurt him the most. Whereas Ana did. Ana loved *and* respected him. Ana was in love with him, as he was in love with her! He was a fool to stay with someone who didn't respect him. Why had he stayed so long? Yes, he'd go home and tell her he was leaving. He'd go to Madrid, teach English there, learn Spanish, live with Ana …

He knocked back the dregs of his fifth pint, stood up unsteadily and walked on rubbery legs back along the tow-path towards the car park. He had to warn himself not to stumble into the water, especially as by now it was dusk

– he was so drunk he probably wouldn't be able to swim, wouldn't know what had happened, would drown like a dog in a ditch. What an undignified, inglorious end to his life that would be, he laughed bitterly to himself! He imagined the headline in the local *Guardian*:

DRUNK TEACHER DROWNS IN RIVER LEA

And to add insult to injury, it might not even make the front page. No, that was no way to go, he admonished himself. *Be careful, for God's sake!* He didn't want to die. He certainly didn't want to drown. Besides, he was going to start a new life, so had every reason to live. Leave her! As he should have done long ago. Turn over a new page. Move to Madrid. Live with Ana. Ana. Sweet, lovely, loving, sensitive, adoring, adorable Ana! *Te quiero, Ana! Te quiero mucho!*

By the time he reached his car, which was the only one in the tiny car park, fumbled the keys from his pocket and tried to unlock the door, he knew he was unfit to drive. He could hardly even stand. That would be another stupid way to die, he reflected ruefully – in a car crash while drunk. Even worse, kill someone else. He really was – what was the expression? – 'legless'. He laughed emptily. It was so apposite. Described his condition perfectly. He gave up trying to unlock the car door, pushed the keys back into his pocket, staggered into the field behind and sank onto his back in the grass, arms outstretched.

There were a few stars in the dim blue sky, he noticed, glimmering like tiny diamonds, millions or billions of light years away no doubt. God, what a mysterious place the universe was! What a *puzzle* life was! But at least now he had Ana to face it with. Ah, Ana! 'Te quiero!' he shouted up at the stars. Then he passed out.

When he finally got home, it was past midnight. She opened the door before he could open it himself and threw her arms around him, crying. 'Thank God you're safe! I was afraid something had happened to you! I'm sorry! Please forgive me! You're right, darling. These things are only materialistic. I've been thinking about it. I can do without them. I've got *you*! I love you. You're the only important thing. I couldn't live without you. I was worried about you. Where were you? You must be tired and hungry. I've made some food for you. Cassava and two eggs. Take your coat off. I'll hang it up. Don't start that stupid talk again about living separately. I'm sorry. Forgive me, please.'

After that, how could he tell her he wanted to leave her? The speech he had been rehearsing all afternoon, even as he drove home still half drunk, suddenly sounded absurdly melodramatic. It was always the same, he realised. It was becoming a pattern: she insulted him, he resolved to leave her, she was contrite, his resolve collapsed. It was like some sort of game, a silly, stupid, childish game. Maybe she enjoyed it, he suddenly suspected. It was a thought that only added to his annoyance at himself for his weakness, for allowing himself to be manipulated in this way, to be blackmailed.

'I don't want anything to eat,' he said impatiently, breaking free from her clasp. 'I just want to go to bed.'

'You're not going to sleep in the study, are you?' she called after him as he climbed the stairs clinging to the banister.

It was what he usually did when they had had a row and he didn't want to sleep with her. He might not have been able to leave her tonight, but he didn't want to sleep with her. She'd probably want to have sex to make up with him and he definitely didn't want that. Anyway, he was too tired and too drunk.

'Please don't sleep in the study, darling,' she called up the stairs, weepily. 'I'm sorry. I love you. Please stay with me tonight. Please don't leave me alone.'

He had already opened the door of the study to go in, but paused, shaking his head, turned and went into the bedroom instead. It was emotional blackmail, he told himself, collapsing onto the bed without undressing, but he didn't have the heart or the stomach to fight back. She won again.

'I'm sorry, Ana,' he thought, as blackness descended. 'I still love you though. Te quiero …'

CHAPTER SEVEN

Ireland

'Bad news I'm afraid. Dad died about half an hour ago.'

It was his younger brother, Kevin. When the phone rang at eight o'clock on a Monday morning, he had a presentiment that something was wrong. It was a shock, but he wasn't shocked. Shock – and horror – would come later, when it had sunk in. Kevin had sounded almost matter-of-fact. *Dad died about half an hour ago.* There was something almost banal about the words. As if it was something that happened regularly. Nothing out of the ordinary. Just a bit of news among all the other news. *Just thought I'd let you know. Anyway, how's yourself?* Kevin liked an Irish turn of phrase. Not that he actually said that of course.

Apparently his father had died in his sleep. Heart attack. *About half an hour ago.* Just as he himself was getting up to face a new day. First day of the Christmas holiday fortunately. He had been perfectly normal the day before. Got up. Had breakfast. Went to the shop in his car. Read the paper from front to back. Pottered about the house and garden. Went for a toddle up the lane. Nattered with a neighbour or two no doubt. Read his cowboy or detective book. Had dinner. Watched telly. Went to bed. Just like a thousand times before. Well, to be precise, like 365 multiplied by seventy-one times before, whatever that was.

Seventy-one. Three score years and eleven. One bonus year for being a good lad maybe. Not old really. It gave *him* about another thirty years. Not long. Not as long as he'd already had. Already over half way through possibly. Life was short. And it got shorter every day. Carpe diem!

The funeral was already arranged for Thursday. (It was the custom in Ireland to bury the body quickly, Kevin told him, though it seemed somehow unceremonious and yet, well, when you were dead, you were dead, let the dead bury the dead ...) However, the 'removal' – when the body was removed from the house to the church in its coffin – was arranged for the next day, so he booked a train and ferry there and then, while Rania packed a bag and made some sandwiches for him. This was the sort of situation where Rania came into her own, the other Rania – the affectionate, sympathetic, supportive, practical, wifely Rania. There were tears in her eyes when she kissed him as he was waiting for his taxi. If only she could be like that all the time, he thought, as it took him to the underground station. And yet, what did it matter? In the face of death, nothing mattered. It made everything meaningless.

He had plenty of time to think about the meaning of life and death on the train from Euston to Holyhead, then the ferry from Holyhead to Dun Laoghaire. Especially his father's life and death. The father he felt he didn't really know, certainly didn't feel close to. Having left home at twelve to enter the seminary. *Leave all and follow me.* Jesus! Such arrogance! Such stupidity! The words of a megalomaniac, a crackpot, a crank. If Jesus had ever even existed. If he suddenly appeared in the train carriage and started spouting such nonsense, you'd change carriages sharpish. Or call the guard. Yes, the father whose religious beliefs he had rejected. Religious beliefs that he now considered nonsensical, childish, potty. And yet a fundamentally decent man who lived a good life. Born in Manchester to working-class Irish immigrant parents. Went to the same Catholic grammar school, Xaverian College, as himself. Probably around the same time as Anthony Burgess, funnily enough, another Irish Mancunian. Met and married Mum just before the outbreak of the Second World War. Was conscripted and sent off to fight in North Africa, Malta, Italy – not that he did much fighting, as far as anyone could work out. Probably did more singing to entertain the troops than fighting, since he had such a fine voice. Was demobbed. Became a primary school teacher. Had five kids. Retired to Ireland. Died in his sleep. End of story. A whole life summed up right there in about a hundred words! God, it didn't really amount to much, did it? It didn't amount to a hill of beans, to quote Ernie. Or was it *Casablanca*?

He was touched and impressed by what Rania had said to him while they were waiting for the taxi: 'Isn't it terrible? Your mum and dad bring you up, you learn, you struggle to achieve something, then you start to grow old, crack up and die. Life has nothing to offer in the end except death.'

'It's a game you can't win,' he had laughed sourly and couldn't resist a dig at Islam – though the same question could be asked of all the gods. 'Why did Allah design it like that?'

'I don't know,' she said defensively, being a Muslim. 'I'll ask him when I see him. But I don't want you to die before me. I'll go with you. I'd prefer to go before you though. I'll die of grief. My mum grieved for six months when my dad died. She cried every day. She had to suddenly do everything on her own, take care of everything.'

'Yeah, life's a bitch,' he said morosely and was glad the taxi came just then, because he didn't want to get into a theological or philosophical debate with her at that particular juncture in human history.

The funny thing about people like Rania, people who 'believed', was that no matter how bad life was, or got, they still believed. Whatever happened, no matter how bad, or tragic, it was 'God's will'. 'Inshallah', as they were always saying. It was the same servile attitude as Catholics had, especially Irish Catholics. It was an attitude that both annoyed and perplexed him. He would be hearing such sentiments expressed repeatedly over the next day or two by family and friends, especially his mother, and the thought depressed him, as did the thought of his father's obsequies.

He wasn't depressed so much by the fact that his father had gone, as by the thought of all the religious mumbo-jumbo that would surround the funeral. All the nonsense about Jesus and heaven and angels and saints and forgiveness of sins and eternal life. The sheer superstitious crassness of it all. But you have to go along with it obviously. Act your part. Play along. After all, what did it matter? There had to be a ceremony of some sort. It made no difference to him really. Except that he found it such a strain pretending. Especially being an ex-priest. Or ex-almost priest. In their eyes the odour of sanctity still hung about him. Aargh! The thought made him cringe.

He had been tempted to make up some excuse not to go, but when he had tentatively voiced the idea, Rania had insisted he must, virtually forced him to. It was another aspect of her personality where he knew her instincts were right, better than his own. He didn't even have the excuse of work, since it was Christmas holidays. Of course, deep down he knew he had to go and would have gone. You couldn't not go to your own father's funeral, could you? No matter how disconnected or under duress you felt.

It was funny, he liked trains and train journeys, but they always reminded him of going back to the seminary after vacations at home, which happened twice a year, Christmas and summer. It was like going back to prison. And yet at the same time he was always secretly glad to be going back. He didn't feel 'at home' at home any more. He felt like a stranger there. He felt more at home in the seminary. He remembered how his dad had taken him to look at the place the year before he went, when he was only eleven years old. Just to look at the place, not to go in. Well, it was worth looking at, a secluded mansion at the foot of a woody hill in the middle of a plain of velvet-green fields, surrounded by picture-postcard mountains on the edge of the Lake District.

What age had his dad been then? About his own age now, forty, he reckoned. He pictured him, as they walked together along the winding country road from the train station to the college gates, tree-clad fell on one side, drystone wall and level fields reclaimed from the sea on the other, the college itself half hidden by trees at the foot of the hill. The memory brought a lump to his throat and tears to his eyes. How could that man, photographically clear in his memory, now be no more? Was it possible he'd never again hear that sublime tenor voice singing 'I'll Take You Home Again, Kathleen' or 'Believe Me If All Those Endearing Young Charms'? What a cruel, vicious, merciless, tyrannical, egotistical god he was, if he existed!

He had to stop thinking about it. At least he had Ana's recent letters to distract him, he reminded himself, taking one out to read, even though it wasn't all good news:

Madrid, 7th November 1986

Dear Francis,

Now I'm confused. I can't decide anything. Everything seems to be problems around me. I'm cross, angry with everybody. Very disappointed just like a young girl when she feels that nobody can understand her. I only enjoy going to university. There I feel myself free.

Francis, I'm very afraid of your coming here. Nevertheless I'm looking forward to it. Here, at home I don't feel myself as Ana, at least at the moment. I can be either my parent's daughter or a neighbour who lives on the 3rd floor or the girl who goes/went with José – the last point for more people than those whom I had never desired. I'm afraid you will find me different, but I assure you I am as I (myself) showed you in Dublin. (Can you understand this sentence? I mean, as you knew me in Dublin.)

I want to see you because I was happy with you and I'd love to be happy being with you again. I don't know what to write, because perhaps you don't trust me now, you think I've betrayed our love. No. To my mind, I'd betray our love if I stopped loving you. Yo te quiero mucho. (I still love you very much.) You must believe it, please. If you were with me, I wouldn't see him ever. (I don't think the problem is your fault, of course not.)

Are you coming, then? I'd like our love were special and it didn't allow you to doubt about your coming. By the way, you can come as an "special" friend.

Regarding those days (15 – 19 Dec.) they are O.K. I'll get my holidays from 16th Dec to 7th January. The week you suggest me it's not exactly holidays – we've got a Congress in Zaragoza dealing with English Language and Literature. It's not compulsory to assist, but it could be interesting. Perhaps we could go, it's only a suggestion. If you agree, I need your answer before 30th Nov because I have to pay our "enrolment" before that date (about 2.500 pts). I need another details such as if you're coming to Madrid first and then we're traveling together to Zaragoza, about your hotel, etc. If not, I'll stay in Madrid.

I'd like to comment you something about your

"worshipped" J. Joyce. In fact I need your advice. When I finish my studies at University, I'd like to prepare what we call "tesina" (less than a thesis). Last year I decided to work on a literary subject, but I couldn't choose well (as my tutor told me. I wanted to study how some medieval themes of Eng. Literature had influence in Tolkien's work). As I'm so fascinated with J. Joyce's biography, I'd like to investigate an aspect of his literary work or perhaps an easy book of his. (I prefer the former because I could be more original.) Please, can you suggest me some themes? My tutor's suggestion is 'Women in Ulysses'. What do you think?

I hope you aren't depressed, sad, unhappy or something because of my other letter. I don't want to cheat you. I don't lie when I say Te quiero, it's very true, but my boyfriend needs a support and it's fair I help him, at least I want to think so. (I'm a complete stupid, I know.) Anyway, you are my support, I could be his. (I don't understand it, so you don't worry if you don't either.) Until now my relationship with him is a close friendship. I'm in a complete mess and this situation makes me sad and depressed. My duty is to tell you the truth (because our relationship should be based on it). I hope you keep writing to me.

My letter should show my "entangled" mind (can you say it?). If not, please imagine my situation, you know me a little bit, don't you?

With all my love,

Ana (xxxx)

P.S. I'm sending one photograph because I don't like photographs and if I send you many I could be annoyed. So I'll send you little by little. (Kisses. Sorry for mistakes but I'm in a hurry.)

She had written the 'other' letter she referred to before this one, but put it in the same envelope. He had been tempted to destroy it, but hadn't. It had made him *very* 'depressed, sad and unhappy or *something*' to use her words – 'something' meaning 'angry'. He knew he shouldn't, because it would only reopen the wound, plus he was feeling morose enough already, but masochistically he took it out and read it again anyway:

Dear Francis,

Perhaps you'll be surprised when you receive this letter. I have to speak with you. It's like something inside me had exploded suddenly. Something terrible has appeared and as usual between us. I'm crying. Let me explain some dreams to you. I'd have liked to live with you, to be with you for ever, to love you for ever, to feel myself loved by you. I won't ever forget you. I won't be able to stop loving you. You must believe me. I insist on it because you could misunderstand me.

I go with José again. Reasons: I've found smth to support our relationship, our intimacy which I broke in Dublin and because he needs me so much. He's so miserable being without me. Since I'm not with him, he's stopped going to school where he was learning informatics and today he told me he gave the sack to himself – I don't know how to say it in E. – that life without me hadn't got any sense. That it wasn't worthy to live without me.

Once you told me you'd hate to hurt your girlfriend. I can't stand to see him so unhappy. I told him about you (not today but before) with 2 different purposes: to give him no hope to be with me again and to be honest with him. But today after saying to me, "Me he despedido/I've quit my job" and lots of other things, he asked me to go with him again. I asked him for time to answer. But there would have been no time.

I wrote this when this event happened, nearly a week now. Notwithstanding I was optimistic, now I feel myself defeated by anyone who depends on me entirely. (It's a horrible experience.) Nor can I understand why I'm telling it to you. I hope you understand. (You understand I'm silly, I know, but I couldn't stand his crying, his sadness.) Do you think I've betrayed our love? No, please don't think so. I wish I could get rid of all my links to here and I were with you. Also, I'm defeated because I'm not allowed to think of our future together. I'm afraid of you, I don't know you well and I don't know how this fact could affect you. May I change the subject?

Now I'm asking myself if you still want to come here. I'd like it very much, I'd like to see you again and to clear up our relationship – now I'm confused. You can come as a special friend if you like. I'd only ask you, do you want to come because you want? I think you should come if you love me so much. I've made up my mind and I need your support, please.

He felt a stab of pain in his guts almost as bad as the first time he had read it. He folded it up and replaced it in the envelope, wished he hadn't reread it. So she was back with Joe! It seemed Joey Boy had won. But only because he had used emotional blackmail on her. Still, all was fair in love and war. That was his own motto. Hoist with his own petard! So he'd lost both his father and his girlfriend. What a cruel juxtaposition! Not that they were comparable of course. Or maybe they were. People died for love. And killed. What a powerful emotion it was! Even more powerful than the instinct for self-preservation sometimes. There was a certain madness about it. I love you madly. I'm madly in love with you. Come back, Ana!

The only ray of hope was that she said she still wanted

him to go to Madrid. What was the point though, if she was back with José? He knew he could get her back, but only if he told her he was leaving Rania, and he couldn't do that. It would mean kicking her out. Especially not after what she'd said to him this morning. *I don't want you to die before me. I'll go with you. I'll die of grief.* It summed up his dilemma. She had a devil inside her – a jinn maybe – that made her behave like a spoilt brat and an insolent hussy, but she loved him, in her own weird way. But he didn't love her. Not as he should. Not as he loved Ana. Had loved Danielle. Had loved and lost Danielle. Cinzia, too. He didn't want it to happen again with Ana. Twice was tragic. Three times would be tragicomic! Was that the part he was scripted to play, a fool for love? No no no! He was nobody's fool. And yet …

To go or not to go to Madrid, that was the question. God, how he wished he was on his way to Madrid now, rather than Ireland. Much as he loved Ireland. He had hoped to go to Madrid at Christmas, but that was out of the question now. Lucky he hadn't booked anything. Maybe he could go at New Year. No, it would have to be at half-term in February. Or Easter. If he went at all. Maybe this was his cue to end it. With a ready-made excuse. He started drafting the letter in his head as the darkening, snow-caked, wintry landscape flickered by the carriage window.

Dearest Ana,

I was shocked by your 'other' letter telling me you were back with José … It was like a dagger in my heart … I feel betrayed … How can I go to Madrid if you are back with him? … I'd feel like what we call in English a 'gooseberry' … How could you go back to him, when you don't love him? … You are letting him blackmail you! … You are letting him use you … I don't want to go to Madrid as your 'friend', 'special' or otherwise! … I have enough friends of one sort or another … I want to go as your lover … I don't want to go to Madrid to 'clear up' our relationship … I want to go so we can try to cement it, work out how to be together, make some sort of plan for the future … I thought that was the point! … Here am I trying to work out how I can detach myself from her so I can be with you and you go back to your ex! … How do you expect me to feel? … You've completely pulled the rug from under my feet! … You've made it impossible for me … You say in your letter something has 'exploded' inside you … It's the same for me … I feel as if something has exploded inside me … Your letter was like a bomb … a letter-bomb … Now my heart is shattered … The dream is in ruins … I'm sorry … I still love you but I think our love is fated to fail … There seem to be too many obstacles … Let's try to keep it as a precious memory though … I'll always remember you with affection … And pleasure … Pleasure mixed with pain perhaps but more pleasure than pain … I hope you can find happiness … with José or someone else … I'm sorry … Te quiero …

He'd write the letter on the ferry, he decided. Maybe with a pint or two of Guinness to bolster his courage. As long as the sea wasn't too rough. In which case he'd just have to concentrate on not being sick. Normally he looked forward to the ferry crossing. Even a night crossing. But not tonight. Not in the middle of winter. Not with the weather like this. Not on the way to bury his father.

He wouldn't post it from Ireland though. He'd wait till he got back home. Should he tell her about his father? He'd have to, he supposed. He glanced out of the carriage window. Night had fallen on the white fields zipping past. It was snowing. No doubt snowflakes were falling too on the bog behind his parents' house. On the little lough. Falling silently and softly through the darkness. Falling upon the lonely churchyard in Loughduff where soon his father would lie. Drifting on the crooked crosses and headstones. On the barren bushes. On the spears of the little silver gate. Silently, softly, sweetly falling. Upon all the living and the dead. Cold and white. Like a shroud upon the earth. A shroud upon his soul.

CHAPTER EIGHT

Ireland

When he boarded the ferry home, he stood on deck to watch it cast off from the small harbour in Dun Laoghaire and stayed there for a while as it powered out into the darkness and emptiness of the Irish Sea. The sea always filled him with a certain excitement, especially at night, it was so vast, so empty, so silent and so mysterious, beautiful yet scary, like space, like the space that hung above it, a seeming infinity of darkness and emptiness beyond some scudding black clouds. If nothing else, he reflected wryly, being on the deck of a ship in the middle of the sea, in the middle of the night, reminded you how small, fragile and insignificant you were in this vast, hostile universe, at least if it were godless, as he believed.

He stayed on deck until the Wicklow Mountains merged into the general blackness, then went inside. He settled himself in the bar with a pint of Guinness and took a first delicious sup of the bitter black liquid with a gasp of pleasure. A wave of relief rolled over him, washing all the tension of the last few days from his system, leaving him feeling light, weightless, floaty ... Well, he was *afloat*, both literally and figuratively, he smiled to himself, taking a second sup of the black stuff, enjoying the rhythmic, almost hypnotic, monodic hum of the ship's engines and its small, shuddering movements, letting the wave of relief sweep him along with it …

There was a sense of guilt in its wake though – guilt for feeling relieved to be leaving his beloved Ireland, guilt for feeling relieved that his father's funeral was over, guilt for not getting to know his father better while he was alive, guilt for not feeling enough grief, guilt about Rania, guilt about Ana, guilt about Danielle, guilt about – 'STOP!' he commanded himself. It was pointless, all this guilt. It was the by-product of having been brought up a Catholic. As his friend Terry, a fellow lapsed Catholic of Irish pedigree, joked in his sardonic way, you had a first-class honours degree in guilt if you were brought up a Catholic. It started at the age of seven, with your first Confession. *Bless me Father for I have sinned.* Seven! Child abuse.

He wanted to write the letter he had been mulling over since travelling to Ireland, but for some reason couldn't bring himself to put pen to paper, even though several times he took both out to do so. It was because of the emotional drama of his father's funeral, he supposed, as well as the strain of meeting and greeting people and, partly at least, pretending to be somebody he wasn't any more. It was the same now. He had placed his writing pad and biro on the table next to his pint, but instead of picking up the pen continued to pick up the glass and take another slug, waiting for the moment of inspiration that never came.

Memories of his father's funeral kept intruding, especially the memory of his first view of his father's corpse lying on the bed in his parents' bedroom, curtains symbolically closed. What shocked him most was the sheer, absolute, total immobility of the body, like the immobility of a statue or waxwork – like one of those figures you saw lying on the top of tombs in churches. It might as well have been made of stone or plastic or some other inorganic material. It was hard to believe that it would never move again, that it really was *lifeless*, as lifeless as a piece of furniture, that his father was no more. It was hard to believe that until a day or two ago it had been a living, breathing, moving person with feelings, thoughts, emotions, needs, wants.

The 'thing' on the bed looked like his father, yet it wasn't any more. The eyes were shut and those eyelids would *never* flicker open or blink again. The nose, like the lips, had turned slightly purplish and looked bigger than in real life somehow, bigger than he remembered it anyway. (Though his brothers did sometimes make fun of their dad's 'hooter', he remembered afterwards, wincing at the memory.) The cheeks still had a pale-pink flush to them, but there was some purplish discoloration around the ears and neck too, he noticed. The narrow ribbon of remaining hair around the sides of the otherwise bald, slightly ovoid, skull was as white as snow, as white as the snow lying thinly on the fields outside and no doubt on the graveyard where his grave was waiting for him …

Most of the body was covered by a white candlewick bed-spread, except for the head and arms. The mottled hands, with a rosary wrapped around them and clutching a cruci-fix, were clasped together on the chest – that once powerful chest that could propel out an Irish song as impressively as any singer, professional or otherwise, he had ever heard. A candle was lit on each side of the bed and chairs had been placed around the room for people to come and sit and watch and reminisce and ponder, perhaps about their own demise.

'Poor John!' his mother sighed, in her Cavan brogue, an utterance he found immensely poignant, that somehow seemed to sum up the situation perfectly. An utterance made all the more poignant by the fact that his mother had never been particularly demonstrative towards his father or indeed any of them, except towards himself when he was a little boy. But that was another story.

That evening the body was removed to the local church by the undertakers, who struggled to manoeuvre the coffin out of the front door of the bungalow, but not before a decade of the Rosary had been recited by a room filled with mourners on their knees, including himself. Not that he uttered any of the words, which he now found silly, himself. *Our Father, who art in Heaven, hallowed be thy name; Thy kingdom come; Thy will be done on Earth, as it is in Heaven* … 'Thy will be done' – it summed up everything he disliked about Catholicism, Christianity in general, most religions: the docility, the servility, the abjection, the self-abasement. He remembered it better in Latin from his seminary days: *Pater noster, qui es in coelis, sanctificetur nomen tuum. Adveniat regnum tuum. Fiat voluntas tua, sicut in coelo et in terra* … Somehow it sounded better in Latin, maybe because the meaning was less immediately clear, though he suspected most people parroted the prayer without actually thinking about the meaning anyway.

The ten Hail Marys recited after the Our Father he found even sillier. *Hail Mary, full of grace. The Lord is with thee. Blessed art thou amongst women and blessed is the fruit of thy womb, Jesus* … 'The fruit of thy womb.' What a grotesque expression! Over and over again, ten times! How ridiculous to idealise and elevate this woman, who probably never even actually existed, to the status of 'mother of God'! *Mother of God!* And to believe that because of her status as 'mother' of God she was 'immaculate', had been conceived without 'original sin', unlike the rest of the human race, managed to produce Jesus, the 'fruit' of her womb, without having sexual intercourse like all other humans and when she died was whisked up to Heaven on a cloud – or was it a flying saucer? – rather than dying and decomposing like other mortals, like his poor old dad. It was obviously no more than a fairytale, but people believed it, including no doubt most of the mourners at his father's funeral.

He recited it to himself in Latin instead. Like the Our Father, it somehow sounded better in Latin. *Ave Maria, gratia plena, Dominus tecum, benedicta tu in mulieribus et benedictus fructus ventris tui, Iesus.* In Latin, you could ignore the actual meaning of the words and just enjoy the sound, the music, the poetry. Mind you, he reflected, it would have sounded even better sung by his dad, lying dead on the bed in front of him, and the thought crossed his mind of how funny, not to say miraculous, it would be if he suddenly sat up and burst into song à la Finnegans Wake …

He carried the coffin from the hearse into the church with his two brothers and a cousin and placed it on the trestles waiting in front of the altar. It was like a beautiful piece of furniture – polished pale wood, beech he surmised, with four shiny, ornate brass handles, on the lid a crucifix and a brass plate with his father's name. The lid was removed for a few minutes for a last view by mourners, condolences were offered to the family with a handshake – 'Sorry for your loss' – the lid was replaced, prayers were recited, led by the parish priest, and then his father was left alone in his box in the church for the night, while they went home for yet more cups of tea and cake and beer and whiskey and chat. It seemed cruel somehow to leave him alone there in the cold, dark, empty church, but of course his father would never feel lonely again or pain of any kind. 'It's one advantage of being dead, I suppose,' as he remarked wryly to his brother after a Jameson's or two.

The Requiem Mass was held the next afternoon. He had to admit that it was a beautiful ceremony, but then the Catholic liturgy *was* beautiful. After all, they had had 2000 years to rehearse it and get it spot on! For him the most beautiful part had been the saddest part, when the priest in his vestments walked around the coffin after the Mass, incensing it and asperging it with holy water. But for him there were always false notes to spoil the effect, like the prayer that was said, the 'Libera Me':

Deliver me, O Lord, from death eternal on that fearful day,
When the heavens and the earth shall be moved,
When thou shalt come to judge the world by fire.

I am made to tremble, and I fear, till the judgment be upon us, and the coming wrath,
When the heavens and the earth shall be moved.
That day, day of wrath, calamity and misery, day of great and exceeding bitterness …

'Fearful'. 'Tremble'. 'Fear'. 'Wrath'. 'Calamity'. 'Misery'. 'Bitterness'. What a litany of terror! It made him feel angry and insulted, standing in his pew in the cold and draughty church, to hear such sentiments expressed over the body of his father, even though he had been a practising Catholic. But then again, he wondered how seriously or literally most Catholics took such words. About as seriously as they took the Church's commandments against contraception, abortion or divorce, he suspected. In other words, not very.

To his relief, the prayer spoken by the priest as he led the procession out of the church, with himself and his brothers carrying the coffin behind him, was considerably more upbeat:

May the angels lead you into paradise; may the martyrs
receive you at your arrival and lead you to the holy city
Jerusalem. May choirs of angels receive you and with Lazarus,
once a poor man, may you have eternal rest.

That was more like it, he thought, as he followed the priest and servers out of the church with his father on his shoulder – silly as the sentiments were. 'Angels'? 'Paradise'? 'Martyrs'? 'Lazarus'? 'The holy city Jerusalem'? Personally, he'd never particularly fancied going to Jerusalem. It was a bit like Northern Ireland. Too much religious bigotry there. He certainly wasn't dying to go there ha ha. The only Jerusalem he fancied going to was the Trip to Jerusalem pub – supposedly the oldest in England – in Nottingham, where his brother lived, his brother now in front of him and struggling slightly like himself to keep the box on his shoulder.

Suddenly, he felt like laughing out loud at the surreality of it all, felt like patting the side of the coffin and saying to his dad inside, 'You see, Dad, nothing to worry about, you'll be OK – you've got choirs of angels waiting for you. They'll probably want you to join the choir! And it sounds as if there might be a pub up there too!' It must be a reaction to all the stress and tension and melodrama, he supposed, warning himself to behave, reminding himself it was almost over, though the worst part was about to come.

They had to carry the coffin, containing all fourteen or fifteen stone of his father, from the church to the grave-yard several hundred yards farther down the road, through a mini-blizzard. Well, it was rural Ireland in the middle of December. He stumbled and almost fell a few times going through the graveyard itself, because of the uneven ground, hillocks and hummocks camouflaged by snow, a freezing sleet lashing his eyes. By the time they reached the open grave, he lowered the coffin to the ground with a gasp of relief, his clavicle in an agony of pain. 'Fuck, now I know how Jesus felt!' he was tempted to crack to his brother, but refrained. Apart from anything else, his father, who had never uttered the f-word in his life, who had a bit of the puritan about him, would be appalled to hear him use it and he would certainly never have used it in front of him in life. *Behave yourself, Frank!*

More prayers were said and they lowered the coffin on straps into the 'hole', as his mother grimly referred to the grave. It looked well over six foot deep, he reckoned, imagining himself at six foot two inches tall standing in it, though not dwelling on the image. His time would come, he knew, but for now he had more important matters on his mind than eschatological ones – the letter he still hadn't written to Ana telling her it was over, for example. The thought sent a knife of regret through him, regret mixed with anger that she should have gone back to José. She must have known that would mean curtains for them! Maybe that was what she wanted. That thought made the knife twist. He shouldn't be too angry with her, though, he told himself. It was his fault as much as hers. He had had his chance, but he had prevaricated. Just like with Danielle, his French girlfriend. Just like with Cinzia, his Italian girlfriend. Oh God, his father was being buried and he was thinking about girlfriends! It was disgraceful. Stop it, he told himself! And yet it was life. *Let the dead bury the dead.*

After the priest had sprinkled yet more holy water on the coffin as it lay at the bottom of the 'hole', they took turns to chuck on a handful of the wet, muddy earth that waited in a heap beside it. It seemed almost a desecration, he thought, seeing and hearing the clods of dirt land with a percussive clunk on the polished wooden lid of the coffin, a desecration of both the coffin itself and his father lying inside. They then took turns to shovel on the rest of the earth. It didn't take long to fill the hole up. Well, most of the male mourners were local farmers who were used to handling spades and shovels, so they made short work of it.

'Your father was one of nature's gentlemen,' one of them remarked to him, as they stood by the freshly filled-in grave, cap respectfully off his mottled head, though it was swirling with sleet, and for the first time during the obsequies tears came to his eyes – tears that because of the sleet, he hoped, nobody would notice.

CHAPTER NINE

London

'Where are you?'

When he arrived at London Euston at seven in the morning two days later, tired, hungry and depressed, Rania wasn't there to meet him, as she had promised, so he phoned her. She told him she had overslept, would get up and leave now. He told her not to bother and put the phone down angrily. On top of everything else he seemed to have caught a cold.

It wasn't that he needed her to meet him. It was just that it would have been nice to see her, would have lifted his mood. She had 'overslept'! It sounded so childish, so immature. Well, it only confirmed what he already knew. It made his already bad mood even worse.

She redeemed herself somewhat by giving him a hug and apologising profusely when he arrived home, then making him a fry-up – vegetarian of course. That raised his spirits considerably. She did have her good points. While he ate she asked him about his trip, wanted to know everything, but he didn't want to talk about it, so replied vaguely and evasively.

Afterwards he wondered why he had been so taciturn, excusing himself that it had been depressing, that he was tired, that he had a cold, so reasonably enough didn't feel like talking. But he also knew it was his way of punishing her for not meeting him, for not being the girl he thought she was, for not being the wife he wanted ...

'Thanks,' he said, when he had finished eating, standing up and giving her a peck on the cheek as she stood at the sink washing dishes. 'I'm shattered. I'm going for a kip.'

'There's some mail on your desk,' she said.

'Oh, thanks,' he said, going upstairs with his bag.

He went into his study, picked up the bundle of letters and sorted through them quickly. To his surprise, among the junk there was one from Spain, a familiar blue-and-red-bordered airmail envelope with a pretty stamp showing a picture of a handsome ram standing proudly in a bucolic landscape of grass and trees and distant mountains. 'Conferencia Mundial del Merino' it said, which for some reason made him smile.

It could only be from Ana, he knew, especially seeing his name and address in her familiar perpendicular handwriting. He checked to make sure the envelope hadn't been tampered with and she hadn't put her name and address on the back, as he had instructed her. He wondered if he should open it, afraid it would contain more bad news, telling him she was now officially engaged to José perhaps, was going to marry him. In his present mood he didn't feel up to dealing with bad news. He'd put it in his desk and read it when he woke up, he decided, sitting on the chair, taking out his key and opening one of the drawers.

But he knew he wouldn't be able to sleep properly, tired as he was and rough as he felt, if he didn't read the letter now. Nervously, he picked up the letter-opener from the desk and slit open the envelope carefully. He held it for a few moments, wondering whether to take the letter out, then slowly did so. It was her usual stiff, unlined paper, a single sheet folded twice to fit the envelope. He opened it out and saw that it was written on both sides from top to bottom. Was that a good sign or a bad sign, he wondered? There was only one way to find out. It was dated the very day his father had died.

Madrid, 15th December 1986

Dear Francis,

This morning I telephoned you, perhaps you know it at this time. A woman answered me and said you were not at home. Instead of calling you later, I decided to write. I could not have borne a woman's voice again. I would have prefered your answer instead of hers. I needed to listen to you and not face myself with your/our "insuperable barrier". (I suppose she was.) Sorry for being ironic. Being ironic – only a little bit – releases my jealousy.

I'm worried about my last letter. I'm afraid you won't write to me any more. I need you so much. I'm longing to see you again. They are reasons why I rang you up. Also I wanted to know if your feelings towards me had changed and what kind of feelings they are.

This morning, after my frustrated attempt to hear you yesterday, I thought of my feelings towards you. What do you mean to me? Why do I remember you so much? Why are you inside me all the time? Why do I become melancholic in Geography class and Language one – those teachers are English and their accent sounds me like yours. Why can't I read either Joyce or Yeats or D. H. Lawrence without thinking of you? Why do I see you everywhere? Even if I can't imagine you in a certain place, I dream I'll bring you there. I know exactly the effects which are produced by a reason – feeling. Will it be <u>love</u>? Do you know what love means? Tell me. Say the meaning.

I feel you are far from me in all senses. In every letter I hope to know you better. I need to know everything about you, but I can't because you keep yourself to yourself, don't you? Writing these questions I'm trying to describe my feelings. This morning I thought it was unfair to ask about your feelings without analysing mine. Francis, te quiero.

So far so good, he thought. Well, bad and good. *Te quiero.* More good than bad. Or was it? Maybe it was all just a preamble to telling him they were finished, it was over, she was softening him up for the blow, she was going to marry José, *gracias por los recuerdos* … He steeled himself to read on, braced himself for the bullet:

There is no solution for José and me. Again broken our relationship.

He read it several times to make sure he had understood it correctly. 'Again broken our relationship.' Her usually good English was 'broken', but if he understood correctly, she was saying her relationship with José was broken again. 'Yes!' he couldn't resist exclaiming triumphantly to himself. But was that what she meant? And was it final? Did she want to end it with him, too, anyway? He read on with a mixture of excitement and apprehension, half wishing now he'd left the letter until later:

Today is Saturday. As usually I'm in my village, at home and in front of the fire place where I've just put a piece of wood to be burnt. Have you any fire place in your living-room? The only noise I can hear is the one produced by the fire – crackling, do you say it? This atmosphere is very nice for me and makes me relax and enjoy myself.

I was reading 'The Purple Colour' by Alice Walker just before going on writing – I'm writing little by little. You should read it. I wanted to share this peaceful moment with you. Don't think I'm always angry. No. I try my best to enjoy myself. Perhaps later I dare go out for a drink facing people's "cheeky" looks when they see me alone without male company.

Everything is not bad. I affirm I love you and we can discuss which type of love is ours when you come here. I hope you will come. Don't you think our love is a "special friendship" in the same terms you said it when we were in Dublin?

Only one more objection: your girlfriend. I can't forget her. There's a funny colloquial expression in Spanish, "me esta comiendo el coco". (Literally, "it's eating my brain".) Francis, perhaps when I clear myself up – my spiritual, moral, interior situation – I can't stand it any longer. Forget it, it's not a good moment to say what I'm thinking.

Please, come! Don't doubt. Perhaps we'd better stay in Madrid. I don't want to hide myself away. I'd like to say about your coming to my parents. I know there are many advantages if we go to Zaragoza, but I'm not sure. What do you prefer? Maria José won't come with us to Zaragoza if we go on our own. But I would have to say I'm coming with her. Can you understand me?

If I hurt you with my last letter, can you forgive me? I love you. I assure you my love will last for ever, at least as friendship if not as the other kind of love. Do you believe me? You must believe me. Write me another letter, please. You didn't write since about 3 weeks ago.

I've got a "cheeky" question for you. May I ask it? How do you imagine me making love with you! (Don't blush!)

Te quiero mucho,

Ana (xxxx)

Besitos (kisses)

Hasta pronto! (See you soon.)

P.D. I won't send another photograph until you write.

P.D. Your advice about what I asked you about J. Joyce is very important. Give me your suitable themes as soon as you can.

(Love.)

Wow! Well, that was good news, he supposed. Was it? Had he missed anything? Misread anything? Misunderstood? She said she loved him, needed him, wanted him to go to Madrid to see her. What could be clearer? He read the letter again, but was too tired to take it in properly. He folded it, put it back in the envelope, slipped it into the drawer, locked the drawer, hid the key and headed to bed. Thank goodness he hadn't written his letter to her.

He fell asleep almost as soon as his head hit the pillow, but not before another, more unpleasant thought, had suddenly insinuated itself into his head – the thought that maybe he should tell her no, he wouldn't go to Madrid to see her, it was finished, finito, over, he didn't love her any more, she had killed his love ...

CHAPTER TEN

London

The very next day, before he had chance to write back to her, another letter from Spain arrived. He deliberately waited until later in the morning to open it, trying to suppress any excitement, having decided that after all he wouldn't go to Spain to see her, that by going back to José, even though she had broken up with him again, she had broken his trust, shaken his faith, destroyed the dream.

Anyway, he kept telling himself, they were too far apart, it couldn't work, it was hopeless. After reading the very first line, though, his anger, despair and disillusionment were swept away and with a smile he fell in love with her all over again:

Madrid, 19th Dec. 86

Hello, my dear boss!

I'm glad you weren't bad, but as you seem to be a good diplomat, you should have said: "I wasn't bad but now I'm well because you've rang me up."

On the phone I forgot to tell you about my Christmas present. I'd like to read <u>your novel</u> – send it, if not all at least four pages and the 'secret' title. Oh, don't worry for my work at university. I can find time for whatever I like.

Now, speaking seriously, I'm not getting on with my papers very well, but it's not my fault. Do you remember my teacher of English History, that horrible old man who didn't allow me to pass the course in English History? O.K., he's giving me American History this year and as usually he's disturbing "my rhythm of work". (I wanted to say it with a colloquial expression similar to one which is inside my head, in Spanish of course.) I mean, my lovely attractive handsome teacher of American literature, Johnny, gave me the paper with time enough – I've already read Jonathan Edwards, B. Franklin and some bibliography on Emerson. Now I have to read the three essays by Emerson, think, compose and write my paper. But now I'm in a hurry because I have to read a book for my History subject, study my horrible teacher's notes and write his paper about something so mysterious that even the title is ununderstandable and of course impossible to translate (a four-line title, full of philosophical terms). On the other hand, I'm supposed to hand in another paper in February which I hope your help with. I have to compare a 200-word piece of a book written in a dialect of English with standard English. I'm thinking of choosing it from 'The Playboy of the Western World.' I know you're expert in that, because you told me you acted in it once. (Though not as the "playboy"!)

As you can see Joyce is postponed, nevertheless Maria José is urging me to work on it, because if I wrote my "tesina", I wouldn't be a 'normal' graduate, what means I would have more possibilities to get a job. And of course I'll want your help with Joyce too. I'm sorry if I'm keeping you busy!

I don't know why I told you I was fine. The opposite is true. I was looking forward to seeing you so much, for many reasons and to begin with my health worries me. I've lost weight again, am very pale, tired, not hungry at all (I eat less than before). All these things are my mother's opinion.

I hoped to see your face when you looked at me. I don't believe her so much. I'll go to the doctor anyway.

Uncertainty shatters me (can you say it?). You're the reason for my uncertainty. Also I can't stand knowing that anyone hates me and José does: he's told me that I'm dead, I'm the past time which doesn't exist. (The latter isn't true because the only time which doesn't exist is the present, to my mind.) This is what happens to me. I can't know the future. I hate weekends and from now on holidays too. I don't feel like going out, doing anything (example: I haven't bought any Christmas present yet). There's something worse: I don't know what I have to live for. I've been looking for reasons, but all deal with other people, not with me. Perhaps I ought not to tell it to you. Don't be afraid. I'm not brave enough to commit suicide.

I was afraid of your coming here, but now I'm sad, depressed, dissappointed. LIFE IS HORRIBLE. La vida es horrible. We had to speak about many things, especially your girlfriend. You must write what you feel towards her, I mean "write to me". I know you like living with her, you're so much attached to her etc. Could you stop living with her? I'm not sure if I want to know the answer. Now again I feel the heavy load of our geographical barrier on my shoulders (land, sea, kilometres, miles …).

When will I see you again? Do you feel like seeing me as much as I do? Can I go to London or will I be well-come whenever I go? While she's there, I won't go. (That's what I think now, it's not absolute/definitive. I myself don't believe it. My common sense is writing now. Not my heart.) I understand your relation with her in one sense, Francis. I'm dying to kiss anyone. Kisses are the effect of loving and love is similar to energy. Can you imagine a volcano when it's ready to burst? Maybe I'm a little bit exaggerated comparing my interior energy with a volcano.

What's true is that I'm passionate, although I wasn't so much with you. I need to know a person to love him and then to kiss him. I can't kiss anyone. So you are a privileged man.

Thank you very much for your Christmas card. It's very nice and beautiful. Did you know that Impressionism is my favourite painting movement? Now I feel myself ashamed because I haven't sent you any.

I could only continue writing my plans about your staying in Madrid, but I don't want you to get tired by reading my awful written English.

Thank you for calling me. It was very nice of you.

Enjoy yourself as much as possible in Paris. I love Paris. I think it's the nicest town I know. Will you remember me when new year arrives? I will remember you.

What would you like me to give you as my Christmas present?

I'm sorry for your father's death. How did you get on with him? Tell me things that you remember in your next letter.

Merry Christmas. My best wishes for the New Year.

Hasta la vista. As many kisses as you may desire from my endless interior energy are yours.

Ana (xxx)

How could his heart not be softened by such a letter? By such sweetness, such charm, such sensitivity, such intelligence? How could he think even for a moment of refusing such a gift from the gods? What a fool he'd be! It was as if the gods were recompensing him for that time twenty years ago in San Sebastian, when he had gazed with adoring, dumb despair at the young Spanish waitress in the hotel, in love with her but knowing she would never, could never, be his …

And Ana even looked like her, with her doll-like figure and face and jet-black curls! How could he forget? What a fool he was! The gods were giving him a second chance, a chance to heal the wound, a second bite of the cherry, and he was going to turn it down? He'd be mad to do so.

Of course he would go to Madrid!

CHAPTER ELEVEN

Paris, London

Mon. 29.12.86

To Paris with Rania to see Charles, who organises the summer schools in Trinity College, Dublin. He teaches English at the British Institute in Paris. He's an old seminary colleague, very opinionated and somewhat pompous, rather right-wing too, but I like him and we get on well enough. We went by hovercraft. En route the rubber skirt on the vessel suddenly started whipping up with deafeningly loud smacks against the very window next to which Rania and I were sitting, making the craft roll crazily on the already choppy sea. I thought we were going to capsize and drown like rats, because there seemed to be no lifebelts or lifeboats and no way out of the cabin anyway. I was so alarmed that for a split second I was tempted to make an Act of Contrition, but resisted the temptation. The power of conditioning! Rania clung to me hysterical with terror: 'Don't leave me! Don't leave me! I want to die with you!' After a few minutes the vessel slowed and an officer came in to calm the panicking passengers down, saying the skirt had broken, but it wasn't dangerous. And so we limped to Calais, though the skirt continued to flap up against the window alarmingly all the way. We had a good time in Paris, did some of the sights and saw in the new year with

Charles and his French wife – but I'll never go on a hover-craft again. No, nae, never no more!

Mon. 5.1.87

Back to work. Had the usual Sunday evening blues yesterday, but as always it's the waiting that's worst. Once I got into the staffroom at 8.30 and made myself a coffee, it was almost as if I'd never been away. My colleagues were all very sympathetic about my father, even battle-axe Bertha, the Head of Department. 'I heard about your sad news,' she said, stopping me in the corridor, even though I'd been trying to avoid her as usual, so that afterwards I felt guilty. I'm not quite sure how they found out, but I obviously mentioned it at some point. I was very touched anyway. They're a decent crew I must say. Even one or two of the students expressed their condolences. Naim, a Syrian student in my Proficiency class, said: 'Sorry about your father, but we all have to go under the ground.' Cheerful sod! The Proficiency class didn't go very well. I felt dull, sluggish, uninspired, as if I was just going through the motions, but they seemed happy. I suppose I'm experienced enough after doing it for fifteen years to get away with it. Bea, the Spanish girl I fancy, was there, but we didn't speak. It doesn't matter. I have Ana. Or do I?

Thurs. 8.1.87

'Ah, the bon viveur!' Tony Holloway exclaimed, seeing me in the corridor. 'Swinging down the boulevard in your boater with a stick!' He'd obviously heard about my jolly to Paris on the grapevine. I was amused, flattered and slightly embarrassed all at once. But at least he didn't come out with his usual announcement for all to hear when he sees me: 'Ah, the au pairs' delight!' He's a very amiable chap, short and bespectacled, wears safari suits, very jovial, teaches history, like me has little time for the higher- ups or powers that be, not just in the college but the world at large. 'Apparently the correct expression is "bon vivant", Tony,' I corrected him, laughing. (I knew because Charles had corrected me only a few days ago.) 'I bow to your superior linguistic knowledge, O wise one!' he chortled heartily, actually bowing. 'Arise,' I signalled with an upward sweep of my hand, 'and go on thy way.' We have these little comic interactions, usually in the middle of the corridor for all to witness, which can be a bit embarrassing. I can't help but like him though.

Fri. 9.1.87

Got another letter from Ana. 'How are you? Better than the last time you spoke with me?' she wrote. I'm not sure what she means by that. She's also been to Paris, I don't know why or who with. I'm not sure I want to know. I wonder if she was there while I was there? I don't want to know that either. She says she was depressed over Christmas, but feels better now. 'I was very busy on getting my spirits down and depressing myself. But now things are changing. I've given up my usual sadness and I'm almost happy.' She's a funny girl. Apparently, things began to 'change' on New Year's Eve. She went to a pub in her village on her own and started chatting with a group of boys. Very unlike her. I was worried till I read, 'Oh, I'm sorry if you dislike my new acquaintances, who are only boys. Imagine my face: a wink and a tender smile.' She knocks me out! She says she wants to try and go out and enjoy herself more, but has to wear a 'mask' in order to do so. I've realised she's naturally somewhat depressive; melancholic anyway. As I am myself maybe. I wear a mask too. Doesn't everyone? The last para-graph made me fall in love with her again. She says she has examinations coming next month, so won't be able to write much from now on. 'Nevertheless, I'd like you to continue writing as often as possible. Your letters are so beautifully written. And I love to read them. Sometimes I answer what you've written writing my sudden thoughts on your letter's margins. I can't forget you. I do still miss you so much. Te quiero.' With the usual three kisses in brackets. That always makes me smile. She's so prim!

Thurs. 15.1.87

'As a fully paid-up agnostic, I object to her interfering with my religion,' Angela, a German student, complained to me after class about one of the other girls in the group, who apparently is a Pentecostal and was always spouting about her religious beliefs. 'I'll speak to her,' I told Angela, relieved she wasn't complaining about me or my teaching. As a teacher, especially of adults, you're always on show, on trial, in a sense. And if anyone's going to complain, it'll be a German! I like the Germans, but then I like everyone or try to. My colleague, Geoff, doesn't like them and makes no secret of it, not with me anyway. 'Krauts' he calls them, to my amusement. Not that that would stop him shagging one, as he admits himself. He's a randy bugger.

Sun. 18.1.87

Rania keeps saying she wants a baby. Today she gave me a lecture on ovulation. (She knows more about these things than I do, having studied science – absurdly enough there was no science on the seminary curriculum.) But I don't think this is a good idea, in view of the fragility of our relationship. I do want to be a father, though, even if not in the sacerdotal sense. After all, I'm nearly forty. The clock is ticking. I keep making excuses. I want to <u>leave</u> her, not have a child with her. Then I really would be trapped. What a dilemma!

Wed. 21.1.87

Apparently two students fell down the college stairwell from the third-floor landing yesterday. They'd been larking about. Thankfully they weren't killed, but broke a few bones. Today they were installing wire mesh guards to prevent it happening again. The rail is a bit low, though not dangerously so. 'That'd be one way to get rid of Bertha,' quipped my South African colleague, Mark, who hates her guts. To which Geoff riposted: 'But can you imagine the crater she'd leave in the foyer?' He hates Bertha too, though maybe not quite as virulently as Mark. I laughed dutifully – Bertha gets on my nerves and I go out of my way to avoid her, but I can't say I harbour any homicidal thoughts about her.

Thurs. 22.1.87

'Apparently, Jane Dawson doesn't believe in evolution,' I told Mark, having heard it from another colleague. Jane Dawson is a middle-aged colleague who belongs to some fundamentalist Protestant sect, the Jehovah's Witnesses, I suspect. 'What does she believe?' Mark inquired. 'I don't know,' I replied. 'The Book of Genesis, I suppose.' 'She must have the brains of a cuckoo then,' Mark riposted in his usual uncompromising way. I had to laugh. He's a sarcastic bastard, but I have to agree with him. I can't understand any intelligent person believing literally in such stories – any of the stories in the Bible for that matter. Jane Dawson is the colleague who commented on the reading list I gave the Advanced class I shared with her once: 'Oh, they're all Irish!' as if it somehow invalidated it. 'I just happen to be into Irish writers mostly,' I shrugged, walking away, not wanting to get into a petty discussion of the relative merits of Irish versus British writers. Not that they were ALL Irish, anyway. DHL was on there, as were Hemingway and

Steinbeck. Anyway, JD has now gone down another notch in my esteem.

Thurs. 29.1.87

Pratnose, the premises superintendent, has been suspended for corruption! There's been no wailing and weeping and gnashing of teeth. He's obviously rubbed too many people up the wrong way and trod on too many toes. Including mine. Geoff told me, to my horror, Bertha wants to stop us having breaks during class. 'Over my dead body,' I said. 'Mine too,' Geoff said. 'She's the one who's always bloody late for her lessons too. Has a break before she even starts! She's a nasty piece of work. You've got to watch her.' Sometimes I think I should be more like Geoff and Mark when it comes to Bertha, take a harder line like them. I certainly will if she takes our breaks off us. A ten-minute break in a two-hour class is good for both teacher and students. It certainly gives teachers ten merciful minutes of respite, because language teaching is so intense. Not that you always get a break as such. Often you find yourself dealing with students' questions about some linguistic point or even with their personal problems. Anyway, if she tries it, as union rep I'll take it to the union. I'll certainly give her an even wider 'berth' from now on ha ha.

Sat. 7.2.87

Went by train to visit my mother, who since my father's death has moved back to Manchester from Ireland to live with my sister. It was Rania who pushed me to go. My relationship with my mother is very strained, because I was once her blue-eyed boy, but am now something of a black sheep, having not only left the seminary, but also the church. Plus, I'm considered to be living in sin. I could see the pain in her eyes when I said I was going for a walk on Sunday morning instead of going to Mass. I just couldn't bring myself to attend what I now consider to be little better than a séance, full of hocus pocus and mumbo jumbo. When I got home on Sunday evening, Rania had cooked a candlelit dinner for me. 'What's this all about?' I laughed. 'It's because I love you,' she said, a trifle offended I think. 'I missed you. I don't like it when you go away and leave me.' 'It was only one night,' I laughed. 'And it was you who made me go!' I was touched, of course, but suspected there was more to it and was proved right after we went to bed. She's been talking more and more lately about wanting a baby and insisted on trying. I complied reluctantly, because I was tired, emotionally and physically, after my trip, but also because I'm really not sure we should be bringing another life into the world, considering the state of our relationship. Not to mention the state of the world.

Thurs. 12.2.87

The word on the corridor is that the college principal, Jack Fullerton, or Jack Fullofhimself as I call him, is applying for a new job as principal of some private college in Regents Park. 'He's getting out before they catch up with him,' some wag commented, to general amusement. It'll be good riddance as far as I'm concerned, as I find him a pompous, rude, arrogant bully, as I think most people do. Now it seems he's a bit of a crook too. A spiv anyway.

Sat. 14.2.87

I took Rania to buy a shalwar kameez, but it ended up in an argument as usual, because she expected me to pay for it. I'd've been happy to pay for it, but I pay all the bills and don't have that much left over at the end of the month. All she will pay for is the food. She accuses me of being 'mean'. I tell her she's spoilt, which she is. She sulked and I was in a bad mood for the rest of the day, ignored her. I hate this constant, almost daily, quarrelling. I consoled myself with thoughts of Ana. And I had the evening to look forward to. I took a few of my students to the Boulevard Theatre to see *Hancock's Finest Hour*, followed by a drink in the pub. It proved a very convivial evening as usual – especially as three of the six who turned up were Spanish girls and I enjoyed flirting with them, thinking of Ana all the time. I really do enjoy socialising with my students, introducing them to British – and Irish, pace Jane Dawson – culture in the process and of course they enjoy and appreciate it too. I've always regarded my students not just as customers or clients, but as friends. I think a few of them, like Saeid from Iran, who was 'best man' at my 'wedding' to Rania, will be lifelong friends. It was the kind of evening that makes me think I have the best job in the world. When I got home Rania was in bed and asked me to join her. I was still angry with her as well as a bit drunk though, so I slept in the study.

Wed. 18.2.87
I took a few of my students to the Victoria on Holloway Road for a drink and to hear the Connolly Folk and Saoirse, two great Irish groups. I enjoyed telling them a bit about Irish history as well as the Irish language, especially the meaning and pronunciation of Saoirse. Admittedly I had to check the latter with my friend Rob, who knows more than I do about the Irish language. Anyway, good craic was had by all.

Wed. 25.2.87
'I'm a leader of Islamic jihad! I'm a friend of Ayatollah Khomeini! I'm a revolutionary terrorist!' Thus ranted some crazy relative of Rania's when I went to pick her up from

her mother's. I didn't bother to argue with him. Sometimes I wonder what sort of people I've 'married' into. Not that Rania or her immediate family, though Muslim, are at all fanatical, except for one of her brothers maybe. (Like Jane Dawson, he doesn't believe in evolution.) In fact they were laughing at the jihadist. But the more I see and hear of Islam, the less I like it. There's a certain built-in arrogance and arrogance is only a step or two away from fanaticism. Not that arrogance is peculiar to Islam. It's a feature of almost all religions, as far as I can see. They all think or believe they are right; they have the truth; they are the Lord's anointed. That's one reason why I'm no longer a Catholic. Though it still saddens me sometimes that I can no longer believe. It was such a pervasive part of my childhood and youth. I spent nine years studying to be a priest, for God's sake! Still, the feeling of liberation outweighs any feeling of sadness or regret. I'm all for liberation theology ha ha. As far as I can tell, Ana is still a practising Catholic. It could be an issue between us. Even a deal-breaker. Which is why I'm avoiding the topic for now. If we fall out terminally, I don't want it to be because of religion. I got another letter from her. Her letters are like shafts of sunlight. Not that my life is all darkness by any means. Just a bit foggy in parts. I just don't quite feel I've reached the sunny uplands yet.

Madrid, Sunday, 22 Feb. 87

Dear Francis,

How much time without writing! Can you forgive me? I love you.

I've made up my mind to post this letter tomorrow, so I'll write so many things as it will be possible. I've got a great number of questions to answer and I can't answer all of them tonight. But I promise I'll write again soon.

How are you? I hope you will be fine. I received your letter with the first chapter of your novel and everything, and also your second letter – I liked it very much – with your notes on Molly Bloom. Thanks a lot. Until now I haven't worked on my "tesina", but I intend to begin reading 'Ulysses' (first reading in Spanish) next week, when I'll be having more free time. What I've already done is all the papers which are involved in it. I'm supposed to hand it in by October. As for my reference books, there are lots of books on J. Joyce but books which deal with my subject exclusively, not really. I've found two of this type: BROWN, Richard, J. J. and Sexuality; BONNIE KIME SCOTT, Joyce and Feminism. I haven't found the book by Anthony Burgess you recommended me. I'm very interested in it though. I must try to find it in the British Institute, even they could borrow it from England if they hadn't it and if I needed it. Please continue writing your ideas about Molly, they are very interesting and helpful for me. If you want to be more expansive, you can, I don't mind. I hope I'll be able to write my ideas about her very soon.

Re your novel: I liked your few pages very much, although I must recognize I need a second reading, but unfortunately I haven't found any available time for it yet. My re-reading will be necessary to discover the author, who must be hidden behind the words. Doesn't being called "author" sound to you funny? The word "author" has got connotations of respectability, superiority, he/she can create and play with his/her creatures-characters, nevertheless his/her creatures can behave themselves in a different way of what the author hoped. How does the author feel himself when one of his fictitious characters rebels against him? In the end is its fatum or destiny predetermined by the author or not? If 'yes', then would the author be considered a semi-god? I think not. The sub-consciousness's influence. On the other hand, to what extent are the characters fictitious? Stop, Ana! It doesn't deal with your book, it deals with my perception of a writer. Anyway, I'll read your pages carefully again, so that I'll see you "behind the words" there. I wish to read the whole novel. Could you bring it (the complete novel) with you in April?

Regarding Easter holidays, I'd like to comment you something. I'll be very dissapointed if you go to America instead of seeing me in Madrid. That would mean that you always find something more important or interesting to delay our so promised and hoped meeting. I'll begin to doubt if we'll meet each other again.

However, I love you and the crucial message of my letter consists on reassuring you that my love still lasts and maybe it will last for ever. As usual you describe your feelings much better than I could ever do. You're right, I feel, too, those opposed feelings and a different one: I know you're with me, even if you're not in body, and I trust you and I hope that if not our love, at least our friendship, will last for ever.

A possible good piece of news: I've applied for a job as assistant for Spanish Conversation in any Secondary School in Great Britain for the academic year 87–88. Maybe I could be lucky enough to work near you next year. In fact, my curriculum vitae is quite good and to my surprise one of my teachers has recommended me insistently. Also I have applied to some universities in EEUU, where I have the opportunity of studying an M.A. at the same time (while I'm working, I mean).

Regards from Maria José, who has just rung me up. By the way, she told me a few days ago you looked like any male character of O'Neill's books. I disagree entirely. Very funny, isn't it?

My paper on 'Synge, The Playboy of the Western World', was a complete success. Now pay attention, please.

Anglo-Irish must sound something like the following: "…and I writin this letter, the way you'll not be forgettin I love you. I do be finishin my letter, I'm thinkin." Doesn't it sound like that?

I'm sending my special, long, loving kiss as your Christmas present and as many of the same quality as you may desire.

With love,
Ana (xxxx)

Francis, I don't understand when you say B.V.M., jotting down a few points about Molly. What does it mean, please?

Muchos besos.

I'll try to find out what could be involved in opening a school in Madrid. From now onwards, I'll have more time.

Te quiero.

Fri. 27.2.87

Received a shocking phone call from Yoko, the Japanese wife of my colleague and friend, Roger. (Yes, Yoko, as in Yoko Ono, or Ono Not Yoko, as I've been known to refer to her.) Roger is one of the few real intellectuals in the college, possibly the only one. He's extremely erudite and has published several books, mostly biographies of obscure writers, as well as poetry. To my surprised delight, delight tinged with envy I must admit, a few years ago he married Yoko, one of his students, a rather sexy Japanese girl in her twenties, though he was in his late forties then, with long grey locks, a bald pate, disastrous teeth and an ample belly. Now though, Yoko tells me she wants to divorce him and go back to Japan, even though she's always said she hates Japan. I agree to go and talk to them on Sunday, though I hardly feel qualified to give marriage counselling, having one failed marriage behind me and one potentially failed marriage in front of me. I'm dismayed, because I know if she leaves him, Roger will be devastated. Until he met Yoko and somehow attracted her, he was very lonely. It's ironic, because I know he used to envy me, since I was never without female company. Now I'm the lonely one, because I'm with someone I don't want to be with, which is possibly the worst form of loneliness. I'd be a lot more lonely if it weren't for Ana. Her last letter really buoyed me up. She's still in love with me. She still wants me to visit her in Madrid. And, cherry on the cake, she likes the first chapter of my novel. What more could I ask for?

Sun. 1.3.87

I went to see Roger. He lives in a gloomy bedsit cluttered with old-fashioned furniture and crammed with books in Shepherd's Bush. Yoko lives in the bedsit next door. He told me how intelligent she was, but also depressive, was incapable of enjoying herself. Said she'd had a mental breakdown. When I heard that, I really felt out of my depth. Yoko herself came in during the course of the conversation, dressed all in black as usual, looking pale and wan, almost wraith-like. She said she couldn't stand 'this country, this way of life, Roger, any longer'. I was shocked. She said she hadn't slept for five nights, because she had nightmares when she did, and wanted to go back to Japan as soon as possible. She claimed Roger wasn't 'interested in married life', couldn't support her, because he made little or no money from his writing and only worked part-time. I could well believe Roger wasn't interested in 'married life', because he lives a Bohemian lifestyle, traipsing around the country researching his books and then spending hours in libraries writing them, but I wondered why she expects him to support her. That's not how the capitalist system works any more, is it?

Meanwhile Yoko complained she was left at home all day, not knowing what to do with herself. When I suggested she get a job, Roger declared, somewhat proudly, that she was 'too intelligent to work with other people or in a team', which struck me as delusional. He seems to have a rather inflated idea of her 'intelligence', oddly since he's such an intelligent bloke himself, but then I know he's besotted with her, feels incredibly lucky to have found her. 'I should've gone back to Japan years ago,' Yoko kept saying, all the time refusing to speak to Roger or even look at him. I soon realised it was hopeless, because Roger was never going to change his life-style and she was obviously mentally ill. When I suggested she see a doctor, I could tell she was offended. Nevertheless, she sweetly gave me a present of a set of Wedgewood cups and saucers when, with relief, I left. I fear for Roger if she leaves him, but I think it's a lost cause and in the end he'll be better off without her – not that I dared to tell him that.

Sun. 8.3.8
I went with Roger to see my solicitor friend, Malachy, for advice about his divorce from Yoko, which now seems to be inevitable. Afterwards Roger and I went for a drink, not that he's a drinker. He was effusively grateful for my support, including my visit last week. He confirmed that Yoko had been 'insulted' by my suggestion she see a doctor. 'It was the only false step you made,' he told me, which I regard as something of a double-edged compliment. Anyway it's a disaster for him. And for her, I suppose. But then, 193 people died in a ferry disaster the other day. That's several hundred families devastated. Where was God then? Where is God now? Where is the all-powerful, all-merciful, all-loving God ever?

Madrid, Monday, 16th March 1987

Dear Francis,

How are you? I hope you will be perfectly well. I am surviving.

As I have plenty of free time because of the teachers and students going on strike, I've made up my mind to write to you a long letter. As I long to receive a very long letter from you, in which you'll be saying everything you do, see, think, feel, imagine, dream, fear, I'm trying to do the same.

First of all, I've begun to read 'Ulysses'. It was an attempt to change my routine of every day – going to university, studying, eating, sleeping … Wonderful, exciting, fascinating, funny – its humour is special, in the sense that you can't avoid smiling but you can't laugh i.e. I've read only the first six chapters but I notice as if life lacked of any serious sense at all – a ridiculous life – but anyway, we're living such an absurd life.

Before beginning the book itself, I read the prologue and a short summary of the plot. I was so nervous while reading it that my heart beat fiercely. I wanted to begin the book without any preamble. I felt that my inner feelings were in harmony with what I was pretending to do. Then, I began it. Yes, my dear. Do you remember when we were visiting the Martello Tower and you told me that Ulysses began there and what our chat was about? Then, only for a few minutes that seemed to be hours, we were both looking at the sea from the wall, after a lovely walk near the shore. It was a warm day, wasn't it? I could listen to your voice, see your gestures, feel how you held me in your arms. I could smell of the salty weather. I felt how my face was getting wet. I could hear the "clicks" of your camera like an echo filling the great hall of remembrance. Suddenly, though, my dreams, visions, faded away and I was alone.

You're very far. I can hardly remember your physical characteristics. However, you're very special for me. Imagine a little glow in Ana's heart which is never put out and sometimes, when something makes Ana feel nearer you, the little glow becomes a flame. Example: while reading 'Ulysses' I'm sharing those beautiful moments with you.

Regarding sharing some minutes with me, Francis, I hope you won't forget that my birthday is next Friday. What about sharing some minutes with me? We may share the peace that sunset may give us on that Friday and after that we could drink something – you could drink some Guinness and I, I don't know yet – and at the same time we're drinking we could remember some of the happy moments we had together. Do you agree?

I realise this is not a long letter, but I want to post it on Monday without any delay. Because of two reasons: firstly, I don't want you to believe I don't remember/love you. Secondly, I want you to receive it by the time of my birthday, in case you've forgot it.

As to my new friends: Not becoming more friendly with any. I don't go out with any <u>single</u> young but with <u>many</u>.

I promise to write more frequently from now onwards. Don't get angry because I didn't write to you so often as both could have wanted. Can you forgive me?

"Te quiero mucho." "Muchos, muchos besos" as much as you desire I'm sending you.

Ana (xxxxx)

P.S. Are you coming at Easter? Of course I want to see you. Is there the slightest doubt in your mind about it?

<u>Kisses</u>

By the time of finishing this letter, I'm reading the 7th chapter. (Aeolus, I think. I know, J.J. didn't separate his novel in chapters.)

By the way, we're already in Spring and there are many flowers. Can you buy a red rose on my behalf for my birthday and put it in front of you on the place where you usually write, please?

All my love,

Ana

Monday, 23.3.87

Another letter from Ana this morning. It made me realise what a gem she is! As if I didn't already know. I was so charmed by it I went to the travel agent's this afternoon and booked a flight to Madrid, with hotel, during the Easter holidays. Then I wrote to tell her. How could I doubt her after a letter like that? Pratnose has been sacked. I almost feel sorry for him. Maybe that's just because with my Madrid trip to look forward to, I suddenly feel so pleased with life. My good mood was punctured slightly in the evening by my private student, Egyptian Jimmy. He used to be a bit of a 'lad', but he's turning into a born-again Muslim with disgusting views: 'Islam will conquer the world. It says so in the Koran.' 'Thieves should have their hands chopped off.' 'Prostitutes should be stoned to death.' Such views revolt me, but I just tried to laugh them off. I don't want to get into an argument with him. I wonder if I should find an excuse not to teach him any more? I've started to find his company highly unpleasant. Mind you, Rania comes out with similar stupidly reactionary opinions too. The other day, in the Three Blackbirds, she insisted that if we ever have a kid, it will be brought up as a Muslim. I told her I'd just tell any child of mine what I believe, namely that the idea of God is superstitious nonsense. 'God exists because I feel it around me,' she asserted. 'I can't argue with that,' I took a swig of Guinness and laughed, 'since it's emotional, not rational or logical.' I also insisted that any child of mine will be brought up vegetarian. I know she daren't contradict me on that one. She doesn't believe in evolution either. And she teaches science! 'I don't believe we came from lizards. We were created. All the world will be Muslim eventually.' I had to laugh, especially at the 'lizards'. I really can't be bothered arguing with such ignorance and stupidity any more. But underneath I'm disgusted, especially by the arrogance. Just another reason to break free from her. Thank god for Ana! I can hardly wait to see her. I'll tell her I'll leave Rania. I know I can't keep her on a string any longer.

Madrid, Wednesday, 1st April 1987

Dear Francis,

Surprised and delighted with your letter. But I have to comment you some things.

Firstly, my father will be on holidays, exactly the same days that you will stay here. The problem is that we usually spend the holidays in the village. I could stay in Madrid with you from Sunday until Thursday, no longer, I'm afraid. On the other hand, my mother is going to have an operation, we hope next week, but as you probably may know by this time, everybody is going on strike in Spain (even hospitals). It means her operation could be postponed. Moreover on 18th April will be my mother's birthday. I must be present, help her and make her feel happy, which means I don't have to discuss with my father – so I'd better share my holidays between both of you/or among all of you.

There's something more I'd like to comment. I don't intend you to get angry or jealous. I'm trying to be sincere – to tell the truth. Of course I want to see you again, I long to speak with you again. However, you must know how I feel myself. I feel myself perfectly well, tranquil, quiet, non-excited. The reason is that I can identify myself with my new friends, especially with one of them – it doesn't mean I'm going out with him, definitely not. "Identify" means I'm O.K. with them and with him. I don't hasten to go with him or whatever you can imagine. No, I need time. I don't want to fail again and again. He had suffered from the same sad experiences I had, so although I have never spoken with him about anything having to do with love, I think neither of us wants to hasten. I wanted you to know it. I insist that I don't know anything about his feelings. I know I'm not the girl who is going to hurt him again. He is so kind. Francis, I'm trying to describe my feelings. I must say it to you. Angry? Disappointed? Jealous? I know you can understand. I hope you're still coming, despite all those "obstacles". I'm looking forward to seeing you. I love you in any way. I hope you don't doubt it. You're a very special friend of mine and for me. If you think I've offended you in some way, forgive me. I hope not. Our special friendship should be based on the truth and love – whatever kind of love it's based on, don't you agree?

If you don't answer this letter or telephone me before the 6th, I'll assume you're coming on Sunday. Then I'll try to buy your tickets to Barcelona for Thursday and Saturday. Advice: Travel by plane – there's flights which cost as inexpensive as by train. (It could be a transport strike for the holidays, I have no idea about it.) I'll be meeting you at the airport.

I don't want to oblige you to come. Make up your mind carefully. In any case, I'll continue keeping in touch with you.

Love,

Ana (xxx)

P.D. In case I went with him, you should know that I would be totally faithful to him. He's worthy of my loyalty, respect and love. (Don't get angry. Forgive me as you love me. Try to understand.)

Besos.

Mon. 6.4.87

First day of the Easter holiday, spoiled by a letter from Ana. I'm shellshocked. Shocked and disgusted. I'm so shocked, I feel like cancelling my flight. How could she write a letter like that to me after I've gone to the trouble and expense of booking flights and a hotel just to go and see her? So many 'obstacles', as she calls them! Excuses more like. A new 'boy-friend' too. That's the killer. And all this silly talk about 'friendship'. I don't want 'friendship'! Reading between the lines, she doesn't want me to go. So I won't go. I'll cancel. She's ruined it. Angry? You bet! Disappointed? You bet! Jealous! You bet! Depressed, too. Rania being extra bitchy, just to round things off. Got drunk listening to Leonard Cohen.

CHAPTER TWELVE

Madrid

When he arrived at Madrid-Barajas airport, Ana and, to his annoyance, her friend Maria José, were waiting for him in arrivals. Despite his annoyance, he holaed and hugged and kissed them both warmly on the cheeks, Spanish style. Ana was wearing a yellow sweater and blue jeans. He was disappointed to see she had cut her hair shorter, though she still looked pretty.

'Eres hermosa. You look pretty,' he said, practising both his Spanish and his charm immediately.

MJ drove them to his hotel, the Los Angeles, out in the suburbs. When they arrived, Ana declined to go to his room with him. 'Why not?' he asked. 'We're not allowed,' she said. 'Why not?' he asked, annoyed. 'Because people use it to make love,' she said. 'I see,' he said, though he didn't, and went upstairs to his room on his own, even more annoyed. This wasn't a good start!

Later, MJ drove them to Ana's flat. Her family were away in their holiday place in the village. Was MJ going to chaperone Ana for the rest of his stay, he wondered? Thankfully, when he told Ana he had something for her, she was sensitive enough to leave the room for a few minutes. He gave Ana a present of duty-free perfume and the books about Joyce he had bought for her. She said gracias and gave him a shy kiss on the cheek in return.

Then MJ drove them to her house, though he didn't want to go there. He hadn't come to Madrid to see MJ! However, he decided to go with the flow and not rock the boat. He had a whole week in Madrid, so he could be patient. MJ insisted on showing him pictures of her family, though he wasn't really interested, including an oil painting of her grandfather, who was apparently a famous right-wing, Francoist journalist. He thought of mentioning the article he had read on the flight, about how during Franco's time the authorities had stolen babies from their republican mothers and given them to Franco supporters, but he decided to save it for later. MJ herself came across as middle-class and conservative, as well as prim and proper, though not particularly right-wing, but knowing she had a Francoist grandfather made him feel even more resentful of her presence, even though he knew that was unfair. *The sins of the fathers …*

Later they went for a sightseeing stroll around the centre of the city and then to a restaurant for dinner. Ana had changed into a dress, put on some make-up and looked even prettier, which made him resent MJ all the more, because he wanted to be alone with her. However, he forced himself to remain friendly and cheerful. A couple of beers and a few glasses of rioja helped, though the menu didn't, because there was nothing vegetarian on it, so he had to order a Spanish omelette.

That would probably have to be his diet for the rest of the week, MJ joked, explaining that Spain was very much a carnivorous country, as he already knew, having read a guidebook, as well as Hemingway, and topped up his limited knowledge of the language before going. He laughed and thought of riposting, 'Well, Spain is the land of bull-fighting,' but bit his tongue. Maybe he would have that conversation later, too. Anyway, the omelette was good, as was the mushrooms and garlic he had as a starter, so he wasn't too disgruntled.

After dinner MJ drove Ana home and then drove him to his hotel. It was made clear there was no question of Ana joining him at his hotel and of course there was no question of him spending the night with her in her family home. He was starting to feel they were playing some sort of prank on him, had lured him to Madrid under false pretences. He felt like going back to the airport and getting the first flight home.

His mood wasn't improved when MJ bluntly asked him, as she drove, 'Why have you come to Madrid?'

'Why do you think?' he asked, biting his tongue again.

'It sounds horrible to say it, but to seduce Ana?'

He didn't know whether to be insulted or amused. It was insulting, but he decided not to be insulted, because this was Ana's best friend and he didn't want to fall out with her, not on his first evening in Madrid. So he decided to be amused. Amused privately, anyway. He replied seriously, 'No, she's too nice, too good, too vulnerable, too sensitive. I like her too much. I respect her too much. I'm very fond of her. I won't take advantage of her.'

'Lo siento, I'm sorry,' MJ said, realising maybe she had misjudged him and overstepped the mark. 'I always put my – what do you say, foot? elbow? – in it.'

'Foot. It's OK,' he said, forcing himself to be conciliatory. 'I know you're her friend and you're just trying to protect her.' He didn't feel it was necessary to add: 'You don't need to protect her from me.'

'Thank you,' she said.

To his relief they had reached his hotel, because he didn't want to discuss the matter any further with her or even be with her any longer. He resented her, because he saw her as a barrier between himself and Ana and she made him feel guilty for coming.

'Gracias,' he said, jumping out of the car quickly and added through the open door before closing it: 'Hasta luego. See you tomorrow.'

Why did he have to say that, he wondered, hurrying to the hotel entrance? He didn't want to see her tomorrow! He didn't want to see her again this week. She was the enemy. She was keeping him from Ana. He'd come all this way, at considerable expense and trouble, and he was going to spend the night on his own in a cheap hotel out here in the sticks!

When he entered his room – comfortable but functional, basic, impersonal – a wave of loneliness swept over him. He sat in the armchair in the semi-darkness, trying not to look at the bed, trying not to look at the picture of a matador impaling a bull on one of the walls, trying not to feel as angry, frustrated and disappointed as he felt, trying not to sink into a slough of despond.

It was hopeless, he told himself. He'd made a mistake coming here. He shouldn't be here. He didn't belong here. Ana was stringing him along, playing with him, making a fool of him, not the other way round. She wasn't as sweet and innocent and naive as she seemed. She'd already found a new 'boyfriend', for God's sake, though she denied he was a 'boyfriend'. What a mug he was! He'd go home tomorrow. Go back to the airport on his own and take the first flight back to London.

That would teach her, the little minx! That would teach that bitch MJ too!

When he eventually, reluctantly, went to bed, he couldn't sleep, though he was tired out, emotionally and physically. It was always the same in a strange place, but tonight was exacerbated by his foul mood. He tossed and turned for several hours before finally slipping into a series of fitful dozes and bad dreams.

The next morning Ana came to his hotel at eleven, though she insisted on meeting him in the foyer, refused to go to his room. But at least she was alone. She was wearing a green sweater and jeans. She was so pretty! He wanted to hug her, but all she would allow was a demure kiss on both cheeks. They took a bus to the city centre to do some more sightseeing.

She insisted on telling him about both her old boyfriend and her new 'friend', as she coyly referred to him, named Chema. She said she didn't understand why her old boyfriend hated her. He understood very well, but didn't bother to explain to her. She told him her old boyfriend had a new girlfriend, though she had a 'bad reputation'. That at least was good news, he thought.

'Now speak to me about your girlfriend,' she ordered, as they walked about.

'I don't want to speak about her,' he said, not falling into the trap.

'You have to speak about her sooner or later,' she insisted.

'Later,' he refused. 'Not now.'

He told her about his 'girlfriend' over a coffee. About how they met, how she was a student in one of his classes at the college, how he was attracted to her because she seemed 'exotic', how he found her, having run away from her bullying family, in his bed one night when he came home from the pub after his evening class, how he took her in …

'But it's no good,' he heard himself saying. 'We're too different. I mean, apart from being male and female! We might as well be from different planets. Different backgrounds, different cultures, different personalities. I can't talk about certain things with her, such as books, literature, history, politics, current affairs, even music. She never reads anything, not even a newspaper. She's not unintelligent, but she's ignorant, except about science. I'm ignorant about science, I admit, but I'm not proud of it. I'm ashamed of it! She's proud of her ignorance though. She thinks she's very clever, because she knows a bit about science and mathematics. Actually I'm not sure how much she even knows about those subjects, though she's teaching them now. There's a touch of arrogance about her. Especially when it comes to religion. She's Muslim, so she thinks she knows the truth about the world, brags that Islam will conquer the world one day! That's a big problem between us, because I don't believe in any god or gods any more, as you know. I regard all religion as childish, superstitious nonsense.' Even as he said these words, he wondered if he was saying too much, digging a hole for himself, because he knew she was a practising Catholic, so he hurried on quickly. 'She's also very childish. If she doesn't get what she wants, she throws a strop or/and goes into a big sulk. Sometimes it's like living with a three-year-old.' He had to explain 'strop' and she made a note of it, as was her studious way.

'You must leave her,' Ana stated.

'I want to leave her,' he said. 'That's why I'm here. It's difficult though. I can't just throw her out. She'd have to go back to her family and they'd make her life hell, even worse than before.' This wasn't what he should be saying to her, he thought. It must sound to her as if he was getting his excuses in early. 'I will leave her. I just need – time. And – ' How to put this? 'And I need to be certain.'

'Certain about what?'

'Certain about you.'

'Certain how?'

'Certain that you – love me.'

'You think I don't love you?'

'I know you love me but – '

'Pero?'

'Last night – '

'Last night?'

'Last night I was disappointed.' That was putting it mildly!

'Por qué?'

'Because – because you didn't stay with me.'

'It was difficult.'

'Why?'

'Because of Maria José.' Damn that girl! Thank goodness she wasn't around today. So far, anyway.

'What about tonight?'

'Do you want I stay with you?'

'Of course! We don't have to have sex. I just want to be with you, close to you.' Damn, why did he say that? It gave her a readymade excuse!

'OK,' she said.

'You'll stay with me tonight?'

'Si. But what will the woman think of me?'

'What woman?'

'The woman on the desk.'

God, now she was worried about what some anonymous woman on the reception desk would think of her! But he had to remember, this was still Catholic Spain, not permissive, promiscuous, swinging London. And she *was* a practising Catholic, of sorts. It was only ten or so years since they were under Franco's jackboot. Crushed between Franco and church. He remembered a cop telling off a young couple just for holding hands as they walked along the beach at San Sebastian all those years ago …

'Don't worry about her,' he smiled, taking her hand and holding it, surprised and relieved that she let him. 'Come on, let's go. Vamos.'

They continued their sightseeing tour: town hall, cathedral, old city … She let him hold her hand as they did so, which was a small victory for him and one in the eye for

Franco, he thought with satisfaction. And most satisfying of all, it was revenge for San Sebastian. *No pasarán!*

Ana turned into quite the chatterbox. She told him her father was angry with her mother because of her, Ana. He was refusing to speak to either of them. They didn't get on, but would never divorce, because they were Catholic. Her mother was too soft. They still didn't know the date of her operation. She was upset because he didn't accompany her to the hospital for her tests …

They had lunch in a bar – for him, vegetable soup, fried eggs with chips, and his first Spanish beer. *Una cerveza, por favour.* After lunch she took him to see her university. She seemed to relax even more there, as if it were a separate world from the city, as in a way it was, he supposed – an ivory tower. It was warm and sunny, so they sat on a bench on the campus and she let him kiss her properly for the first time since he'd arrived – kiss her on the lips, not just the cheeks.

For some reason, they started talking about death and she shocked him by saying she didn't care if she died tomorrow. She definitely had a depressive streak, he thought, telling her he had no wish at all to die, he enjoyed life, life was good. Besides, he told her, for him death meant extinction, and he didn't fancy being extinct, not yet. He asked her if she believed in an afterlife and she said she wasn't sure.

'But you're a Catholic, aren't you?'

'Yes, but I'm not sure about the afterlife. I don't mind to be extinct. Perhaps it's better that way.'

'In a way, yes, it probably is better. In my case anyway, because I'd probably be destined for Hell ha ha!' She didn't seem to find this funny, so he added: 'I thought the whole point of being religious, Catholic anyway, was that you believe in the possibility of a better life after this one. Heaven. Paradise.'

'I think it's just a dream,' she shrugged.

This was music to his ears. It suggested she wasn't such a traditional Catholic after all. In fact it suggested she wasn't even a Catholic. Could you be a Catholic and not believe in Heaven and Hell? Maybe these days. It wasn't the way he had been brought up, having to believe everything literally and absolutely. It seemed to be pick'n'mix now. Still, he couldn't see any point in religion if it didn't offer an afterlife.

'I think you're right, it's just a dream,' he agreed.

'Dreams can come true,' she replied, impishly.

'Yes, perhaps,' he laughed. 'You don't believe in an afterlife, but you still go to Mass.'

'Is it strange?'

'Well, it's a bit – paradoxical.'

'I think I go from habit. And because my parents. And because I like it. It's like an escape. From daily life. Daily reality.'

'I see.' He did see. She made it sound like going to the theatre or cinema, but he didn't risk saying that. He was glad to think she wasn't such a dyed-in-the-wool Catholic. More of a woolly Catholic ha ha. He'd work on her. Maybe he'd already had some influence on her. She was intelligent. She would see the light, he was sure. He definitely didn't want religion to come between them. But he wasn't going to change his mind.

'What about God?' he asked her. Surely you couldn't not believe in God and be a Catholic? Maybe you could! Maybe that applied to him. *Once a Catholic, always a Catholic.*

'Yes, I believe in God.' This was bad news, though he already knew it, just hoped she might have changed her mind. 'I know you don't.'

'No, I don't,' he said bluntly, tempted to go on an anti-God riff, but resisting – he was afraid of alienating her. Maybe he had already alienated her, though she already knew his views about religion, more or less.

'There must be somebody or something,' she said. It was such a banal observation, but he didn't say so.

'Maybe,' he agreed for the sake of humouring her. 'But there's no evidence. He or she or it is unknowable. Saying that doesn't get us very far. It doesn't get us anywhere. Yes, there may be something above and beyond us, beyond our powers of understanding or imagination, but it could be anything. It could be a super computer! Like the computer in the film, *2001: A Space Odyssey.* And even if it's a person of some sort, it doesn't mean it's a benevolent person, a loving god. In fact, if anything, it seems to me the opposite. If god exists, he's a cruel god. She's a cruel god.'

'Why do you think so?'

'I think life is cruel.'

'Por qué? I thought you said life was good.'

'Yes, life is good for me right now. But I've had my bad times, my struggles, my disappointments, my problems. Like everyone. But in the end life's cruel, because it ends in death. Death negates everything. Which is precisely why people believe in an afterlife. It negates the negation of death. But it's a delusion. A fantasy.'

'Te quiero.'

Wow! That was a relief. He thought he might have gone too far, been too direct, too honest. 'Te quiero,' he said and they kissed again.

'I love you,' she said. 'I'm not sure how or why, but I love you.'

This didn't sound so good. 'What do you mean?' he asked.

'I'm afraid,' she said.

'What are you afraid of?' He knew she was a virgin, was afraid of sex, but waited for her to say it, so he could tell her it didn't matter, sex wasn't that important, it wasn't the most important thing …

'I'm afraid to give my heart.' That caught him by surprise.

'Don't be afraid, Ana,' he said, taking hold of her hand. 'I know it's a risk and you're afraid, but life's a risk. If you give me your heart, I'll take good care of it, I promise.'

'You don't love me.' She might as well have stabbed him in the chest.

'Why do you say that?' he demanded, letting go of her hand. What a cruel thing to say to him! After all that had already passed between them. She was making it so difficult, such hard work! He was angry. He was so angry he felt like standing up and leaving her on the bench there and then, just walking away. But he didn't. He couldn't do that to her. He wouldn't do that to her. He loved her, in spite of himself, even if she didn't believe it.

'You only like me,' she said. It made the knife twist.

'I do like you,' he said, ignoring the pain her remark had caused him. 'But I don't just like you, Ana, I love you. I mean, I love you as a woman. My feelings for you aren't just platonic.'

'Promise you won't hurt me, Francis,' she said.

'I promise,' he said, taking her in his arms.

'Te quiero,' she said into his chest, clinging to him tightly.

'Te quiero,' he said, kissing her head and stroking it tenderly.

'Do you want to look inside?' she asked after a while, lifting her head.

'Yes, I want to look inside this,' he laughed, tapping the side of her head gently.

'Te quiero,' she said, offering him her lips.

'Te quiero,' he said, giving them a quick kiss, taking her hand and pulling her up. 'Vamos!'

The buildings – which were mainly grey, graffiti-defaced, concrete blocks and scruffy-looking – were locked up, so they continued to stroll hand in hand around the pleasant, park-like grounds.

'I can ask you something, Francis?' she said, stopping suddenly.

'Yes?' he said, on alert, keeping hold of her hand.

'If I have a boyfriend here, will you leave me?'

That put him on the spot! He had a 'girlfriend', so how could he object to her having a 'boyfriend'? But the circumstances were different.

'Yes,' he said, letting go of her hand.

'Por qué?'

'Because I want to be your boyfriend. I don't want to be just your friend.'

'Pero, but you are not free.'

'I know I'm not free. But I will be free. I will leave her. I just need time.' He tried not to sound as exasperated as he felt. It seemed they kept having the same conversation over and over again. 'I want you. That's why I'm here. I want you to be my girlfriend. I want you to be my wife one day.'

'Te quiero,' she said, throwing her arms around him.

'Te quiero,' he said, hugging her, knowing she wouldn't do this if they hadn't been alone. The campus was virtually deserted.

'Please don't leave me, Francis,' she pleaded, looking up at him, her big brown eyes moist with tears.

'OK, I won't leave you,' he said, giving her a kiss on the forehead.

'Promise.'

'Promise,' he said, though he wasn't sure he would be able to keep it. Not if she went with Chema. No way!

'I need you,' she said.

'Why do you need me?'

'I need your letters.'

'Is that all you need me for?' he smiled, pulling away slightly, but keeping his hands clasped behind her back.

'I learn a lot from them.'

'So we're just going to be penpals, are we?' he laughed, though he was worried that was what she meant, that was all she wanted.

'No, I want to be with you.'

'That's what I want too.'

He pulled her close again, cradling her head in his hands, and they stood like that for a while in the middle of the tree-lined, sun-dappled path. Hopkins's poem suddenly came to his mind, so on a whim he recited the first few lines out loud:

'Glory be to God for dappled things –
For skies of couple-colour as a brinded cow;
For rose-moles all in stipple upon trout that swim;
Fresh fire-coal chestnut-falls; finches' wings;
Landscape plotted and pieced – fold, fallow and plough;
And all trades, their gear and tackle and trim.'

'It's a famous poem,' he explained. 'I was just looking at the path here, how the sunlight falls in patches on it, what a pretty pattern it makes.'

'Did you write it?'

'I wish,' he laughed and told her it was by Gerard Manley Hopkins.

'I remember, you told us about him in Dublin.'

'Yes,' he said. 'He's my favourite poet. Though I think he was a very sad case.'

'Te quiero,' she said, gazing up at him and offering him her lips for the second time that morning, her hands on his shoulders. She was so short – like a child!

'Te quiero,' he said, pulling her towards him and kissing them.

'Will you write a poem for me?' she asked. 'Before you leave?'

'Yes, sure,' he agreed, wondering why he hadn't thought of doing it before. *Thank you, Gerard!* 'Vamos? I think it's time for lunch.'

He took her hand and she let him lead her along the sun-dappled path back towards the main road to catch the bus into the city centre. She even let him put his arm around her on the bus and, though a few glances were passed, the Guardia Civil weren't called to arrest them.

Spain had moved on, he reflected wryly to himself – and so had she. Or, at least, so he hoped.

CHAPTER THIRTEEN

Madrid

The next morning, they met in the street outside his hotel – she was too timid even to enter the reception area – and took a bus to the centre. She looked prettier than ever, in a white blouse, pink cardigan and stonewashed jeans. He didn't compliment her though and gave her the briefest of kisses on each cheek. He was angry with her, because last night she had refused to stay in the hotel with him as she had promised. Because 'that woman' was on the desk. 'That woman' did resemble a fire-breathing dragon, but …

They visited the Cortes Ingles, the Athenaeum, Plaza Major (again) and the Botin, a restaurant that had apparently been Hemingway's favourite, though they didn't lunch there. They had lunch in more of a workingman's bar, which was the sort of place he preferred. He deliberately refrained from holding her hand as they strolled around or showing her any physical affection and hardly even spoke to her. This was her punishment. Not for the first time he found himself wondering why he had come here to Madrid, what he was doing here. He just didn't know where he was up to with her.

After lunch, which they had in virtual silence, they took a bus to the Retiro Park and after a short stroll sat on a bench opposite some children playing in a sandpit. The sun was fire-hot, but there was a pleasant breeze blowing through the plane trees, which lent some shade. God, he thought morosely, here he was in a beautiful park in Madrid on a lovely spring day with a pretty Spanish girl – he should be happy, but instead he was miserable, fed up, disappointed, frustrated, confused. Coming here was a terrible mistake!

'Are you angry with me?' she asked, after a few minutes sitting in silence.

He declined to answer for a few seconds, then said: 'What do you think?' without looking at her, keeping his eyes on the kids playing in the sand, envying them their childish innocence and fun.

'I think ju are angry.'

'I think I am angry too.'

'Why are ju angry?'

'You really don't know?' he laughed bitterly, still refusing to look at her.

'Because I didn't stay with you?'

'Yes,' he said roughly, swinging round to glare at her. 'Yes!' For a split second, he wanted to hurt her, release all his pent-up anger and frustration, tell her she was frigid, a prude, a cockteaser …

However, seeing tears in her eyes, he regretted it immediately. He'd never spoken to her so angrily before. It broke his heart to see her cry. 'I'm sorry,' he said, stricken with remorse. He wanted to take her in his arms, but stopped himself. He needed to sort this out with her once and for all, no matter how painful. Otherwise he was liable to end up leaving her in a fit of frustration.

'I'm afraid of that woman.'

'I think that's just an excuse.'

'An excuse?'

'Yes. What you're afraid of is sex.'

'Yes,' she agreed. 'You're right. Are you running out of patience with me? Do you want to leave me?'

'No, I don't want to leave you,' he said, choking. 'I love you. I just want to be with you. I mean, spend the night with you. We don't have to have sex. It's not about sex. I've told you that.' This wasn't entirely true. He wanted to have sex with her, yes, of course, but he was willing to wait until she was ready.

'We can go to the hotel now if you want.'

'Now?'

'Si.'

'You're sure?'

'I want to go.'

'What about that woman?'

'I think she's not there now.'

'Te quiero,' he said, giving her a quick hug – he knew she would be too embarrassed to let him hug her properly.

'Vamos,' she said, standing up.

Fortunately, dragon woman wasn't on the desk when they arrived at the hotel, just a waistcoated boy who barely glanced up at them and said 'Hola'. As soon as they entered his room, he threw his arms around her and held her tight.

'Shall we go to bed?' he asked after a while, releasing her.

'Si, for siesta,' she smiled.

'If you want,' he laughed, though it wasn't what he had in mind and he wasn't sure if she was joking.

He took her by the hand, led her to the bed and pulled the covers back. Before he had finished, though, she threw herself down on her front, her head sideways on her arms. Smiling he lay down beside her and resting on his elbow put his hand on her back.

'Aren't you going to turn over?' he asked.

'I always sleep like this,' she said, half into the pillow.

'I see,' he smiled. 'You want to sleep?'

'We can talk if you want,' she said.

'What do you want to talk about?' he asked to humour her, though as far as he was concerned they had done enough talking.

'You decide,' she said.

'Do you want to get married?' he asked.

'Yes, one day,' she said.

'Do you think it's a good idea to live together first?'

'Yes,' she said. He was pleasantly surprised. 'But it's difficult in Spain,' she added.

'Is it?' he asked, though this didn't surprise him. He had to remember this was a very different world from London, though it was only 800 miles away and on roughly the same longitude. He knew, because he had checked during his flight.

'Do you want to get married to me?' he asked.

'If we get married, we'll disagree about religion, food and children.' This wasn't the answer he had hoped for.

'Well, then we'd have to get divorced,' he laughed. 'But I suppose you don't believe in divorce, do you?'

'I would divorce if necessary and go to Confession,' she said.

'That's cheating!' he laughed.

'Why?'

'If you want to be forgiven, you have to be genuinely sorry, genuinely contrite.'

'I will be sorry.'

'You can't just choose the rules you want to keep,' he grinned – not that she could see.

'Why not?' she said.

'Well, maybe now you can,' he laughed. 'It's not the way it used to be though.'

Would he have stayed in the church, remained a Catholic, if things had been so relaxed when he was being brought up, he wondered whimsically? Hardly, he told himself, since he disbelieved in more or less the whole caboodle, from the virgin birth to the resurrection. Doubted the very existence of Jesus. Certainly doubted the existence of God. That was something of a dealbreaker, he supposed. In a way it was a shame though – it would have simplified his relationship with *her*, if he was still a Catholic …

'Don't you want to turn over?' he asked, deciding they had discussed Catholic doctrine and dogma enough.

'Why?' she asked.

'I want to see you.'

'You can see me.'

'I can't see your face.'

To his surprise she turned over. God, she was pretty! As pretty as a doll. He pushed her hair back, stroked her face tenderly with his fingertips, leaned down and kissed her softly on the forehead, the nose, the lips … She remained impassive, however, so he stopped.

'What's wrong?' she asked.

'I just wish you would give yourself a bit more,' he said. 'Physically, I mean.'

'I'm sorry,' she said. 'What do you want to do?'

'I just want to touch you,' he said. 'Your skin. The real you.'

'You can touch me.'

He took this as permission to fondle her breasts. 'Te quiero,' he murmured, kissing her face as he did so and she kissed him back. He took this as permission to go further and she let him unbutton her blouse but wouldn't let him take her bra off, so he didn't insist, just squeezed her breasts softly. Eventually she let him take her jeans off, but not her knickers, which like her bra were white. He took his own clothes off, crossed a leg over hers, pulled her close, kissed and caressed the length of her body, eased himself on top of her, rubbed himself against her …

To his delight she slowly became more and more excited, emitting little whimpers like a kitten. She even let him take her breasts out and kiss them, putting her arms around his neck and pulling him down to her, whimpering more and more loudly. This was it, he thought, this was the big break-through, she was going to let him make love properly with her, she'd finally overcome her fear of sex. But suddenly she stopped and froze, took her arms from around his neck, pushed him up and away from her.

'What's wrong?' he inquired, gazing down into her fear-ful eyes.

'I'm ashamed,' she said.

'Ashamed?' he asked, his heart sinking. 'Why?'

'I lost control. I can't control myself.'

'That's not something to be ashamed of! It's OK to lose control sometimes!'

'What would you do if my father came in now?'

His head dropped. His whole body sagged with disbe-lief. *I give up.* He rolled away from her onto his back and pulled the duvet up. He lay there in shocked silence, star-ing up at the ceiling with its electric fan whirring slowly, wondering what to say, wondering what to do, wondering if he should just get up and pack his bags now …

'Please don't leave me,' she said to the ceiling, as if read-ing his thoughts. 'I need your friendship at least.'

'I want more than friendship,' he said to the ceiling.

'I'm sorry,' she said.

'There's no need to be sorry,' he replied. 'It's not your fault. It's because of your Catholic upbringing. You've been brainwashed, programmed, into thinking sex is sinful. Even in marriage, if you're not doing it for procreation. But you can de-programme yourself. I had to. If you don't, you'll have trouble even when you're married. You should make love as often as possible. It's normal and natural. Make love with your new boyfriend, if you can't make love with me.' He immediately regretted the last remark – it was like telling her he had given up on her, was admitting defeat, was resigned to losing her.

'Impossible,' she said.

'Make love with someone, anyone,' he insisted, digging an even deeper hole for himself, he supposed. 'As long as it's someone you love. Or like at least. And as long as it's safe.'

'I can't,' she said. 'I feel guilty. I'm a bad girl.'

'You're not a bad girl!' he contradicted her, annoyed. It seemed as if he might as well have been *literally* talking to the ceiling! 'You're a good girl! "I'm a good girl." That's what you should be telling yourself, like a mantra! There's nothing wrong with you. I've told you, you feel guilty because of your Catholic upbringing. And because of your father. You're afraid of your father! You have some sort of complex about him. I'm sure psychiatrists must have a word for it. You need to get away from him. You're twenty-three, not thirteen! He's a repressive influence on you. You need to break free.'

'Will you help me?' she asked, turning towards him.

'I'm trying, Ana,' he sighed wearily, turning towards her and propping himself up on his elbow. 'That's why I'm here. But you're making it difficult for me.' He immediately regretted the last remark again.

'I'm sorry,' she said.

'No, I'm sorry,' he shook his head, putting an arm around her and pulling her close. 'It's not your fault. It's the Catholic church's fault. It's society's fault. It's your parents' fault. But it's not *your* fault. You've been damaged. We're all damaged to some extent, some of us more than others maybe. I'll help you if I can. We can work through it together. I love you.' He kissed her on the forehead.

'Thank you,' she said. 'I'm so glad you came. Are you glad you came?'

'Yes,' he said, though he wasn't a hundred per cent sure.

'Can I visit you in London?'

'Yes, of course.'

'Will you still write to me? I need your letters.'

'Yes, sure,' he said and added with a grin: 'As long as you write back.'

'Shall we sleep?'

'You want to sleep?'

'Si. What do you want to do?'

I want to make mad, passionate love with you.

'OK, let's sleep.'

She turned onto her front again, her head on her arms, and seemed to fall asleep immediately, like a child, to his amusement. He remained propped on his elbow for a while, gazing down at her, doodling on her back with a finger, wondering why he loved her and wishing – or almost wishing – he didn't.

Luckily, when they left a couple of hours later to go out for dinner, waistcoat boy was still on duty, not dragon woman. He looked up and smiled briefly as they passed, Ana hurrying ahead of him, making sure they were separate. Waistcoat boy looked exactly the same age as he had been the first time he came to Spain, all those years ago. He probably thought they were lovers and had enjoyed an afternoon of passionate lovemaking. He might even be envious. *If only he knew.*

CHAPTER FOURTEEN

Madrid

'Did ju sleep on my question?'

It was late morning and the sun blazed down from a blindingly blue Madrid sky. They were sitting on a bench in the Parque del Oeste, having had breakfast – coffee and croissants in the café she told him she went to with her mother, Café Antonio – and visited the Temple of Debod. They were sitting on benches in parks a lot, he realised, but he liked parks: parks and pubs. Some future anthropologist would probably label them the 'Park People' or maybe the 'Bench People', he chuckled to himself.

'Sorry?' he said, though he had heard her question – it was just that he didn't want to answer it, didn't want to discuss it, was hoping she would have forgotten about it. The question she was referring to was the one she had asked him last night over dinner: 'Am I free to go with another boy after you leave?'

'I thought we'd already discussed that,' he had said and evasively offered to 'sleep on it'.

'You said you'd think about it again,' she reminded him now. 'You said you'd sleep on it.' God, she was persistent!

'Yes, you're free,' he shrugged, not so much because it was what he really felt as to avoid an argument or falling out.

Anyway, what did it matter, he told himself? She was here

and he was there. He wouldn't see and what the eye doesn't see … Though no doubt she would spill all out in letters in her usual candid, heart-on-her-sleeve way. He loved her, but had more or less resigned himself to not being able to have a proper relationship with her. There were just too many barriers, too many complications – not least her seeming inability to give herself to him sexually. Not that that mattered to him really. He was prepared to wait for her, work on it with her, but the thought had crossed his mind: What if she was *never* able to overcome her hang-up about sex, even if they were married? How ironic that would be! Maybe it would be better to be just friends, as she kept suggesting, he had started to think, though the thought didn't fill his soul with joy.

'You won't be jeloos?'

'"Jealous",' he corrected her pronunciation. 'The stress is on the first syllable. The second syllable is weak.' This would be the point in class where he might play John Lennon's 'Jealous Guy' to them.

'"Jealous",' she repeated more or less correctly, reached into her bag and produced a pen and notebook. 'Can you write in phonetic, please?'

'Sorry, I didn't mean to make it a pronunciation lesson,' he laughed, doing what she asked: /ˈdʒeləs/. 'There you are.'

'Gracias.'

'And to answer your question, yes, I *would* be jealous. But it doesn't matter. You are free, as I am free.'

He said it with the tiniest twist of spite, for which he was ashamed, because he didn't really want to be free and didn't want her to be free. He wanted commitment. But she seemed to be unwilling to give the commitment he wanted, so she could have it her way.

'Ju are sure?' she asked, which wasn't quite the response he had hoped for. He wasn't sure what he had hoped for.

Perhaps something like, 'I don't want to be free' or 'I only speak theoretically'.

'Yes, I'm sure,' he shrugged.

They sat in silence for a while. It was a resonant silence though. Like the silence of a deep, bottomless well. A well without water perhaps. His words were like stones. They seemed to fall into the silence. Be swallowed up by the silence. He felt a poem coming on. Well, she had asked him for one, but it might not be the one she wanted.

'Shall we carry on?' he suggested, not wanting to discuss it further, feeling it was futile, not wanting to cloud such a beautiful spring day. He jumped up, took her hand and pulled her up. 'Vamos.'

They took the Teleférico cable car to yet another park, Casa de Campo, where they had lunch in a restaurant by the lake, then sat on the skimpy grass under a scraggy oak on the lake shore – surrounded by other 'day trippers' doing the same, including a few young couples canoodling horizontally. Spain had certainly changed, he thought, observing them with a twinge of envy. She would never behave like that in public. It was hard enough to get her to behave like that in private! Not that he was one for such public displays of affection himself, if he was honest. Maybe the pendulum had swung too far the other way. Some of the women wandering by looked half dressed and when he commented that they looked like prostitutes, she told him they probably were, it was a problem here in the park. The pendulum had definitely swung too far the other way.

Somehow they started talking about suicide and to his shock she told him she had thought about it. 'My mother was afraid, because she knew I might do it.' He was even more shocked when she told him she had tried to do it once. 'How?' he asked, frowning. 'When?'

'When I was fourteen. I walked across the road without looking.'

'That's a terrible thing to do,' he said, with a shake of his head. It broke his heart to hear her say it.

'No, it's just an end,' she replied. 'You said so yourself.'

'Yes, I believe death is an end, but to take your own life. At such a young age. That's truly tragic.' He shook his head again. This was a side of her that he hadn't realised. A dark side. It shocked him, but didn't stop him loving her. She wasn't the first girl who had told him something similar. 'I was suicidal myself once,' he added, regretting it immediately.

'You were?' It was her turn to be shocked.

'Yes,' he shrugged, not wanting to make it sound too much of a drama. 'Before I left the seminary. And for a few years afterwards.' He had told her about his past life in a religious order, but not about this

'You didn't – ?'

'I took some sleeping pills once, but they didn't work, I'm glad to say. Or I wouldn't be here with you today.' He laughed, trying to make a joke of it, though it had been no joke at the time. 'I was in a very dark place, as they say, for a while.'

'I'm sorry,' she said.

'It's OK,' he said, wishing he hadn't mentioned it, not wanting to discuss the topic at all, wondering why they were doing so. 'It's a long time ago now. Another time, another place.' Sitting here beside a pretty Spanish girl, by a lake in a beautiful park in Madrid on a brilliant spring day, it did indeed seem like another time, another world, another incarnation ...

'My grandfather committed suicide,' she informed him.

'Really?' he said. It seemed he wasn't going to be allowed to evade the topic. 'How? Why?'

'By hanging himself from a bridge. I can't remember why. It was during the Civil War. He was a republican. He had to flee to France.'

'That is tragic,' he said, shaking his head. It was worrying, because he knew suicide was supposed to run in families. He could only hope her grandfather's suicide was caused by the Civil War, rather than any mental illness that might have a genetic dimension. 'The Civil War was one big tragedy though,' he added, hoping to steer away from the subject of suicide. He had read a bit about it before coming, as well as having read Hemingway and Orwell, and had been shocked by the apparent savagery on both sides. Though he knew which side he would have been on – and it wouldn't have been Franco's.

'The war is not finished,' she said.

'What do you mean?'

'The fighting is finished, but people are still very divided. It's a very deep division here between republican and nationalist.'

'I see,' he said, surprised.

It was hard to believe, looking at the peaceful, pleasant, idyllic scene in front of him. It was hard to believe these people were capable of killing, murdering, torturing and raping each other, had been doing so only fifty years ago, within the lifetimes of some of them. Some of the old men shuffling about or sitting on benches smoking their Ducados had probably been involved, maybe done terrible things. It was hard to believe, because all the Spanish people he met here or in his work in London were so charming and likeable. It was hard to believe, looking at the pretty, sweet young Spanish girl sitting beside him right now. But then, he supposed, most societies were riven by deep divisions of one sort or another, political, ethnic, religious. Catholic versus Protestant in the UK for example. That was a civil war that was still going on! British and Irish people were murdering each other today because of religion, albeit religion mixed up with politics and power, as religion usually was …

'What are you thinking about?' she asked, so he told her and again it was her turn to be shocked, although she must have known something about the topic from his classes in Dublin.

'So your family are republican, are they?' he asked, not wanting to get too bogged down in Irish history – or any history for that matter.

'Yes,' she said. 'We're republicans. But we're disillusioned with the present government, because they're not true socialist. They're not helping the working man. The next government will be right-wing. I'm a socialist like you. My father calls himself a socialist, but he doesn't do anything. He never reads, except the newspaper. He has no hobbies or interests. He used to go out with my mother after work, but no more.'

Well, that didn't seem all that unusual – his own mother and father didn't go out together, as far he knew, except to church perhaps. He didn't say so though. He was tired of serious talk. He lay back on the grass and half-closed his eyes against the blinding sun.

'What are you doing?' she asked.

'Relaxing,' he said. 'Lie down.'

To his surprise she obeyed, though she was careful not to get too close to him, unlike some of the other young couples nearby. He wanted to reach out and hold her hand, but didn't even dare to do that. He turned his head to look at her. Her arms were folded modestly across her chest. It wasn't as if her breasts, being small, were noticeable. He couldn't help smiling at her, though his heart was pierced with a sudden stab of almost paternal affection for her.

'Why are ju laughing at me?' she demanded.

167

'I'm not,' he lied, turning on his side towards her and propping himself on an elbow. He wanted to put a hand on her stomach, kiss her, take her in his arms and pull her close to him, kiss her some more, but he knew she wouldn't let him. 'Shall we go to the hotel?' he suggested.

'I'm not sure if I should. To do what?'

'I want to make mad, passionate love with you.'

'Ju see, ju are laughing at me, making fun of me.'

'Yes, because you're so predictable!'

'Why am I predictable?'

'As soon as I suggest any sort of intimacy, you have a conditioned response. You immediately become tense, anxious, nervous, defensive. That's precisely why you should do it. You need to overcome your fear.'

'Maybe you should ask one of these ladies.' She was referring to the prostitutes who sashayed past occasionally.

'I'd much prefer to go with you,' he laughed. 'Just for a siesta, that's all,' he added as a sop.

'We can go if ju want,' she agreed, to his surprise.

'Really?' he said. 'Let's go then. Vamos.'

To his relief, when they arrived at the hotel, waistcoat boy was on the desk, so she had no excuse to chicken out, though she kept a judicious distance from him as they passed. Waistcoat boy merely glanced up and nodded. He'd have to give him a tip before he left, he told himself.

When they entered his room, he went to use the bathroom and when he came back she was sitting on the chair, reading his book, *For Whom the Bell Tolls*. He was annoyed, but didn't show it. He pulled the covers down, flopped onto the bed and put his hands under his head with a sigh of relief – they had done a lot of walking.

'Don't you want to lie down?' he asked, patting the bed beside him.

'I prefer to read,' she said.

'That's *my* book,' he joked, though he wasn't really in the mood for a silly game.

'Do ju like?'

'Yes. It's Hemingway. It's not Joyce or Lawrence or Fitzgerald. It's a very particular prism to look at the world through. Very limited in some ways, in both style and substance. Very exterior, man of action, tough guy, macho. Though the hero, Robert Jordan, is supposed to be a university professor, I think. It certainly paints a vivid picture of the Spanish Civil War, what it must have been like during that time, especially to be involved in the fighting. Very good at describing the landscape and terrain too.' He didn't really want to talk literature. He didn't really want to talk at all. They really had done too much talking! But he couldn't resist adding: 'The sex scenes are not very good though.'

'Por qué?'

'Hemingway isn't very good at writing about sex,' he smiled. 'I think he was limited by his background, as well as the times he wrote in. Though that didn't stop Joyce or Lawrence. Are you coming here? Or are you going to read *For Whom the Bell Tolls*?' How ironic, he thought – Hemingway was one of his favourite writers, partly because he envied the swashbuckling, adventurous, picaresque, romantic life he seemed to have led, and now here he was, having his own Spanish adventure with his own 'Maria', but she was hiding behind one of the aforesaid Hemingway's books, hiding behind Hemingway. *Hiding Behind Hemingway* – it'd make a good title for a short story …

'Ju want me to come over there?' she asked, closing the book and replacing it on the desk.

'Yes,' he said. 'Come and lie down.'

'I'm afraid.' *Oh, God!*

'What are you afraid of? I don't bite!' Apart from love-bites, he was tempted to joke, but refrained.

'I'm afraid of getting my skirt creased.'

For a moment he thought she was joking and almost burst out laughing, but realised she was serious.

'Take it off,' he suggested, with a hint of impatience.

To his surprise she stood up to do so.

'Ju mustn't look,' she said.

'OK,' he laughed, shutting his eyes.

'Face the wall!' she ordered.

'Yes, boss,' he laughed, doing so.

When he turned back and looked, she was lying face down in her bra and knickers again, like yesterday. Not very encouraging, he thought. *Stay away from me.* Or did she *want* him to seduce her? Even rape her? He wasn't really in the business of seduction though, despite MJ's insinuation, and he definitely wasn't a rapist.

'Can you put out that horrible light?' she asked and he turned to switch off the bedside lamp.

'Do you want to sleep?' he asked, turning to her again and laying a hand on her naked back.

'We can talk,' she said. She was facing away from him.

'Aren't you fed up with talking?'

'It relaxes me to listen to your voice.'

'What do you want to talk about?' he asked, trailing his fingertips up and down her spine.

'Talk to me about Dublin,' she said. 'They were happy days. Life didn't seem so complicated then.'

'Well, yes, we were on holiday in a sense,' he said.

'I found you interesting in Dublin, because you wore a mask.'

'What do you mean?' he asked, vaguely offended. It wasn't the first time she had accused him of this. If it was an accusation.

'You were playing a role.'

'Maybe, but don't we all play roles most of the time? I could say you were playing a role too.'

'Si. Unconsciously I think I was.'

'I don't think it matters anyway. Even if I was playing a role, it was still me. I was expressing myself as I felt then. In that particular context. At that particular time. I meant everything I said to you. I hope you don't think I was just pretending. If I was, I wouldn't be here now. I'm still basically the same. I haven't changed. I mean, I may be playing a slightly different role now, because this is Act Two, but it's still me, saying what I really think and feel. I do think life is like a play sometimes. But without a script. You have to learn your lines or make them up as you go along. It does seem unreal. I mean, here I am in this hotel room in Madrid with *you*. There is something unreal, even surreal, about it. Almost dreamlike. Maybe that's a better analogy. Life is like a dream rather than a play. Sometimes I feel as if I'm acting in my own dream. Or in a play within a dream maybe. Or maybe the other way round, a dream within a play. Don't you have the same feeling sometimes? Don't you have that feeling now, about us, here in this hotel room?' Stop rabbiting, he told himself, the expression *Methinks he doth protest too much* flashing up on his mental screen.

There was no answer to his question though. He leaned over her and realised she was sleeping like a baby, snoring almost inaudibly. She had missed his little lecture! He smiled, bent down and planted kisses along the length of her back from her neck downwards, then pulled the duvet up to cover her lower half, though the room was hot and stuffy, despite the whirring ceiling fan.

Lying on his side, propped on his elbow, he gazed down at her semi-naked body for a while. He should be angry with her, he supposed, because he had hoped she would have sex with him at last, but he wasn't. Well, he was, but any anger was swept away by a sudden rush of paternal affection for her again. If he wasn't careful, he thought, he'd start calling her 'daughter', like Hem with his women!

He definitely didn't want her to call him Papa though, he smiled wryly to himself, lying back to stare up at the whorls on the ceiling and hypnotically, somniferously whirring fan ...

When they left the hotel, she suddenly suggested going for a drink, even though she had said she wanted to go home. It was still early evening and he didn't want to spend it alone, so he agreed eagerly, glad of company. They took a bus to the city centre, found a bar in what she said was a fashionable district – though a 'druggy' district too, she said – and went in. *Una cerveza por favor.* She had a glass of wine. He had a cheese sandwich too. It would do for his dinner, he told himself.

'Are ju still my friend?' she asked.

'Of course,' he laughed. 'Why shouldn't I be?' *Because you wouldn't have sex with me?*

In fact, when she woke up, she had become quite excited, let him fondle her breasts, even get on top of her, but wouldn't let him go any further, had stopped him when he tried to do so.

'I'm sorry,' she said.

'Sorry about what?' he asked, thinking she meant because she wouldn't have sex with him.

'I almost lost control again.'

'I've told you,' he laughed, 'there's nothing wrong with losing control sometimes! When you're having sex, for example. In fact, you have to lose control.'

'You never seem to lose control. I want to be cold like you.'

'You think I'm cold?' he asked, offended. 'I don't think I'm cold. I just know how to control myself.'

'That's what I mean. You know how to control yourself. You control yourself very well.'

'Well, sometimes, to be honest, I think I'm too self-controlled.'

'Will you help me?'

'Help you to learn self-control?'

'Si.'

'I'm trying.' This was so ironic! If anything, he wanted to help her do the opposite, lose control and have sex with him. But here he was agreeing to help her control herself. His head was spinning like that fan ...

'Are you fed up with me?'

'Yes, I am.'

'Please don't do what my ex-boyfriend did, leave me.'

God, he wished she wasn't so pretty! Heartbreakingly pretty. That was what had attracted him to her in the first place. But – there was something wrong with her. She was messed up. She looked so fragile too, because she was so small. Perversely it made her all the more attractive to him. His heart went out to her. This must be what it was like to have a daughter. What a weird thought! Was it the Hemingway effect? Oh, God, he didn't want her to be his daughter though! He wanted her to be his girlfriend, his lover, his wife ...

'Are you going to leave me?'

'No.'

'But you're fed up with me?'

'I may be fed up with you, but I'm not going to leave you. I don't leave people, unless they give me good reason to. Besides, I love you.' She let him take her hand and hold it.

'I'm sorry for being so –'

'So what?'

'Not like other girls.'

'You don't have to be like other girls. I don't want you to

173

be like other girls. I probably wouldn't love you if you were. I love you because you're you. Ana. If you have a problem, I'll help you.'

'Ju will be my friend?'

'I am your friend.' *Though I want to be more than your friend.*

'Will you be my friend for life?'

'Yes, for life.'

'Do you promise?'

'I promise.'

'And you will write to me? I need your letters. I need your friendship.'

'I'll write to you.'

'Do you promise?'

'Yes, I promise.'

'Te quiero.'

'Te quiero.'

CHAPTER FIFTEEN

Madrid

The next day they had a late breakfast in Café Antonio again. They spent most of the time talking about mundanities such as varieties of coffee and what he should do for the rest of the day. He was going to spend it solo, because she was going to the village to stay with her family in their holiday house. It felt strange, he thought, as if they were just two old friends who hadn't met for a while, rather than would-be lovers. Strange and unreal.

After she left, he took a bus to the Prado, but it was about to close for the afternoon, so he didn't go in. He didn't really want to go in anyway. He felt lonely. The last thing he wanted to do was traipse around an art gallery gawping at paintings with a herd of other tourists – especially Picasso's blue paintings, if they were there. He was blue enough already.

Instead he went to the Botanical Gardens next door, ambled around for a while and sat on some grass out of the blazing Spanish sun, as far away from other visitors as he could get. Most of them were in groups, which only accentuated his loneliness. Some of them were young couples. It gave him a mixture of pleasure and pain to see them, holding hands or with arms around each other, chatting with easy familiarity, occasionally even stealing a quick lovers' kiss.

He couldn't even have the luxury of feeling sorry for himself. He had got himself into this situation, silly as it was. He had come all the way to Madrid to see a girl he thought he loved and who he thought loved him, but she wasn't playing ball, wouldn't have sex with him, seemed to want to be just friends not lovers, even seemed to want him to be some sort of father figure to her rather than a lover – and he definitely didn't want to play that part. He wasn't that much of a Hemingway aficionado.

He wished he hadn't come to Madrid now. He wished he could just go home, but his flight wasn't till Sunday and it was only Thursday. He thought of telling her there was some emergency at home and he had to leave suddenly, but knew she wouldn't believe him and would be terribly hurt. He couldn't do that to her – in spite of everything, he loved her. He couldn't go home early anyway, because of Rania. Rania, whom ironically he didn't want to be with any more. He'd have to go and stay in a hotel somewhere in London for three nights. What a ludicrous, depressing prospect that was!

He lay back on the grass, hands behind his head, and half-shut his eyes against the blindingly-bright blue above. He half-wished he could be subsumed into that blue, his being dispersed back into the unconscious atoms it had been assembled from by whatever mysterious, miraculous force. Not a divine or supernatural force of any kind, he believed now, though gazing up into that infinite empyrean above, what did he know? He knew next to nothing. There was a certain comfort in knowing you knew nothing, in knowing it was ultimately unknowable, in knowing it was futile trying to understand what it was all about, how it had all come into being, why there was anything rather than nothing. There was even a certain excitement in feeling so helpless in front of the mystery, a sense of liberation, a lightness of being. There was nothing unbearable about it, though, pace Milan Kundera. Quite the opposite. If only he could float off into the mystic, he thought. The words of a poem started forming in his mind: *blue sky in my eye why oh why must we die but I'd die without a sigh if to die meant that I could simply fly up to that sky this earth defy dissolve on high.* Was that some sort of quasi-Keatsian death wish, he wondered? He didn't want to die. And yet the thought of not existing, of going back to the oblivion you came from, had a certain appeal to it. At least the authorities couldn't get to you then. There'd be no more bills to pay. No anxiety, no illness, no disease, no disappointment, no pain, no problems, no stress, no nothing ... No perplexity! You really would be free. That was why people committed suicide, he supposed. Which was another reason not to do anything to upset her too much. What she had told him about almost committing suicide had shocked him. Made him realise how fragile and vulnerable she was. And yet there was a certain hardness about her too. Something almost steely. Maybe it was just stubbornness. She admitted she had a stubborn streak. As he did himself. In her case it was probably just a defensive weapon, he surmised. Because she was so small physically. Almost childishly small. A bit childlike too. People probably tried to take advantage of her. Including men. He wouldn't do that. He wanted to help her. She made it difficult though. By not letting him have sex with her. Not letting him through. Keeping the wall up. Just another brick in the wall. Not that sex was important in and of itself. He could manage without sex. He had plenty of self-control – coldness, as she had called it yesterday, to his offence. He had once taken a vow of chastity for god's sake! He wanted to have sex with her, yes, but more for her sake than his own. She was so hung up. So locked up. Sex was the key, he was sure. If they had sex, if she would only let him have sex with her, as well as letting him in, it would imply commitment too. Some level of commitment anyway. It didn't even have to be sex as such. She would hardly even let him touch her though. She was so scared of any physical intimacy. She claimed she was just scared of losing control, but he wasn't too sure about that. It went deeper than that. She was damaged. Which was tragic, because she was so lovely, so sincere, so sweet, so genuine, so sensitive, so honest, so real. If only she'd give herself, he'd give himself back. But instead she kept talking about going with other men. Especially this Chema fellow. It was like throwing sand in his face! Maybe he was deluding himself about her. Maybe she wasn't as innocent and sweet as he thought. He should probably talk to MJ more about her. She probably knew her as well as anyone. He didn't like MJ much, saw her as the enemy, had been avoiding her, but maybe he should give her a call, meet her, tonight if possible, since he was going to be on his own. Ana herself had suggested it. It'd be company too. Any company was better than no company. He was dreading having to spend the evening alone. Yes, he'd swallow his pride and do that, he thought. Kill two birds. Meanwhile he still had most of the afternoon to kill. He'd walk back to the hotel, he decided, getting up and taking his map out, see whatever there was to see and have something to eat on the way. That would kill an hour or two. Then he could have a siesta. Or a lie down at least. Stare at the ceiling for a couple of hours. Maybe read a bit more of *FWTBT*. That would kill another couple of hours. Then he could go out. Call MJ. Invite her for a drink. Dinner too, if she wanted. That would just about get him through to bedtime. God, what a ridiculous, depressing situation he'd got himself into, he thought. 'I bet ol' Papa Hemingway never had this problem,' he laughed sourly to himself, setting off.

He left the hotel again at seven, found a phone kiosk and after a struggle got through to MJ, but she said she wasn't free. However, she agreed to give him a lift to Ana's village tomorrow, pick Ana up and go to the mountains with them. 'Gracias,' he said, but felt as if he had been jilted, jilted twice over. Well, here he was, alone again, naturally, as the song said. There was only one way to kill the evening. Do a bar crawl and have a few beers. Who knows, he might even meet a pretty Spanish girl! It would serve her right for inviting him to Madrid and abandoning him like this. Yes, he said to himself, go out and enjoy yourself! Get drunk! Get laid! Get even!

The next morning he had breakfast in Café Antonio. Alone again naturally. Afterwards, MJ picked him up at his hotel as promised and drove him to Ana's village, which took about an hour. The atmosphere between them was strained. It seemed as if neither of them wanted to talk about Ana, so they made small talk, in a mixture of her uncertain English and his rudimentary Spanish. He'd have to talk to her at some point though, he told himself. Maybe this evening, on the way home or over a drink …

They picked Ana up on the outskirts of the village and decided to visit El Escorial before going to the mountains, since it was en route. Ana was in a pink cardigan, pink cords and, it seemed, a good mood – maybe because she was with MJ or because she had her dog, Dama, with her. It was a Corgi, tiny like Ana herself, but MJ referred to it as the 'monster' and didn't seem too happy about having it in her car – a red and black Citroen 2CV – though it sat on Ana's lap most of the time and only gave the occasional excited, irritating yap. She was very affectionate to it and, absurdly, he found himself feeling a twinge or two of jealousy.

After queuing for ages and visiting the palace, they had

lunch in a bar in the town, for him a cerveza and cheese sandwich as usual. Ana was friendly enough to him, but studiously avoided any physical contact, apart from letting him kiss her on the cheeks at first meeting. This was partly, he supposed, because of MJ's presence, which was under-standable, but it frustrated him. For heaven's sake, he didn't want to make love with her, just hold her hand or put an arm around her occasionally! He found himself resenting MJ's presence, which he knew was unfair, since she was taxiing them around as well as giving of her time. He man-aged to remain friendly and good-humoured, but it was an effort. And anyway it was better than being on his own, he told himself.

After lunch they drove up into the Guadarrama Mountains north-west of Madrid, about which two things surprised him – first, that they were there at all, within an hour of the city, second, that they had snow on the peaks. They parked high up, got out and walked, Dama running about excitedly. It was such a dramatically different world from busy, bustling, built-up, traffic-congested Madrid – magnificent, rugged, snow-capped mountain scenery and fresh, clean air spiced with the resiny tang of the ubiqui-tous pine trees. The fact that these were the very mountains that Hemingway described in *FWTBT*, where most of the action took place, gave them an added attraction for him, an almost mythical dimension, as if he had stepped out of the real world and into the novel. He kept his thoughts to himself on that score though, kept the conversation light, easy, playful.

After a couple of hours rambling in the mountains, they drove back down to the village and, because the girls wanted one, went into a hamburger bar. There, to his horror, there were not only bits of dead cow in the form of hamburgers, but also some of Ana's friends, including, horror of horrors,

Chema, her prospective 'boyfriend'. If he was jealous of Ana's dog, which they had left in the car, he now found himself not only jealous, but embarrassed and angry, angry with himself for falling into this trap and angry with Ana for letting him. He even wondered if she had done it deliberately. He could hardly believe that, but she must have known there was a chance he might be there, since the village was such a one-horse place.

Not that Chema himself looked much to be jealous of – a short, skinny, bespectacled, geeky-looking young lad in a grey T-shirt and jeans. Ana insisted on introducing them and he reluctantly let her, not wanting to appear discourteous or unfriendly. She introduced him as 'mi profesor', which niggled him, and he shook hands with the briefest of holas. Fortunately, Chema couldn't speak any English, so wasn't interested in making conversation and quickly returned to his coterie of pals, while he went outside to wait for the girls. He found the presence of not only Chema, but also dead cow, extremely uncomfortable.

When they came out, Ana apologised. 'I'm sorry. Are ju angry? Forgive me. I couldn't help it.'

'It's OK,' he said, having had time to cool down while waiting for them, but impatient now to leave the place and get back to Madrid. 'Go home. Go to bed. Sleep tight. Relax. Be calm. Thanks for a nice day. See you Sunday.'

She allowed him to kiss her on the cheeks, but neither of them said 'te quiero', even though MJ had discreetly left them alone. Ana then went off with Dama under her arm and he got in the car with MJ to drive back to Madrid. He felt fed up, didn't want to talk, but after a while, out of the blue, MJ suddenly volunteered her thoughts. *Out of the blue …*

'Chema is a good boy,' she observed. 'He would suit Ana. She was happy with him before you came. Now she tells me she begins to fall in love with you again. Chema is shy, but he's after her. She's confused. You impress her. You're an older man. She never went with an older man before. José was twenty. Chema is younger than her. You speak in a special way. You're good with words. You're a writer. She tells me you write beautiful letters to her. She tells me she's learned a lot from you, pero …'

'But?'

'You're not fair.'

'I'm not fair?' He didn't really want this conversation, but he was trapped. It had to be had anyway, he knew. 'Why am I not fair?'

'You're married, aren't you?'

'Actually, no. I'm not legally married in fact. I live with someone, but I don't want to continue living with her. We're completely incompatible. I can't just leave her though. She loves me even if I don't love her.'

'What are you going to do then?'

'I'm going to try and do what's best for all three people involved. Four people if you include him. I love Ana. I'm very fond of her. I don't want to hurt her. If necessary though, I'll let her go to Chema or someone else. I want her to be happy.'

'If you love her, I don't know how you can do that.'

'Because, with respect, you don't know me. I know you think I just want to use her, then toss her aside. It's not like that though. I'm not like that. I don't treat people like that, especially women. I try to treat people the way I like to be treated myself. With respect. I love her, but I know I probably can't have her, so if necessary I'll let her go. No matter how much it hurts me.'

'I admire you.'

'Well, it'll be my loss,' he said, taken aback by the compliment. 'I just hope she'll have gained something from me. I've certainly gained a lot from her. A lot of happiness, pleasure, nice feelings. I hope we can at least remain friends, though I know that's very difficult between a man and a woman. Sex always gets in the way, that's the problem.'

'She's very afraid of sex. That's the main reason why her relationship with José broke up. Because she wouldn't make love with him. It's because of her father. She's afraid of her father. She's twenty-three! He's a monster. She needs to escape from him.'

'That's what I thought,' he said. 'That's what I've told her.'

'She needs you to teach her many things about life.'

'So what do you think I should do?'

'I don't tell you that. I don't want to put my foot in it again. It's between your heart and hers.'

That was a good way to put it, even if it didn't help him much, he thought, glancing at her as she drove. Maybe she wasn't such a bad old stick! She was even quite fanciable, behind that somewhat starchy, schoolmistressy, librarian-like exterior. *Between your heart and hers.* It wasn't just about hearts though, was it? His heart said one thing, but his head said another – and in the end he usually listened to his head. His heart said he loved her, fight to keep her, but his head said leave her, let her go …

Luckily they were near his hotel and to his relief she seemed happy to let the subject drop and finish the journey more or less in silence, apart from arranging to meet tomorrow and some desultory small talk.

'Muchas gracias,' he said, when she finally pulled up outside the hotel, giving her the regulation kisses on the cheeks and opening the car door. 'Buenas noches. Hasta luego.'

'So what will you do?' she inquired. He wasn't going to get off scot-free!

'I don't know yet,' he replied, getting out, but holding the car door open. 'I have to think about it. I'll tell you.'

Deep down in his heart of hearts, though, he already

knew, but he was afraid to say the words, even to himself. They could become a fait accompli, a self-fulfilling prophecy.

'Buenas noches,' he said again, shutting the car door quickly, turning and hurrying into the hotel, where dragon woman was waiting for him with a steely stare. He gave only a cursory nod and avoided looking at her as he passed, not so much because he was scared of her – though she was scary – as because he suddenly realised to his embarrassment there were tears in his eyes …

CHAPTER SIXTEEN

Madrid

The next day was his last full day in Madrid, for which he was now grateful, dismal thought though that was. After breakfast at Café Antonio, he finally visited the Prado, despite the usual horrendous queues – mostly of American tourists it seemed – and his heart not being in it. He was lonely, missed Ana and looked at the paintings without seeing them. He was bored by them, bored by the place, bored by everything. He just wanted to go home!

When he came to the El Grecos, with their grotesquely elongated figures, he was not just bored, but hit by a sudden wave of revulsion, because they reminded him of the junior seminary, where some prints of his paintings hung on the corridor walls. He felt a sudden sense of claustrophobia too, since the place was so crowded. Or was it agoraphobia? Anyway, he couldn't stand the atmosphere any longer, so turned and hurried out, even though he had only been there less than an hour, less than the time for which he had queued.

He walked to the Retiro Park, relieved to escape the city and the crowds, though the park was busy too and blast furnace-hot under another high, early-afternoon sun. He found the bench he had sat on with Ana the other day and sat there for a while, wishing she was beside him, even though their relationship seemed to have reached an impasse. At the same time, he told himself, it was probably better that she wasn't with him. He wasn't going to see her at all today. He wouldn't see her again until he was leaving tomorrow. It would probably be better if he didn't see her again at all. Better if he left the Spanish dream behind.

It was funny, he reflected wryly – in his younger days, this was the sort of romantic situation he had so often read about in novels, seen in films, listened to in songs, the sort of situation he had yearned enviously to find himself in, but now that he was here, actually in his own real-life romantic mini-drama, it didn't seem quite so much fun. In fact it wasn't any fun at all. It was depressing and – dare he think it? – *boring*. He was as bored with the situation as he had been with the paintings in the museum. He shook his head and let out a sudden ironic laugh. The birdlike old dear who had perched on the bench next to him, where Ana should have been, got up and left hastily, as if he might be some sort of mental case. Maybe between the situation and the fiery Spanish sun he was going a trifle doolally, he laughed again, but this time to himself.

Still, it was all grist to the writing mill, he supposed. That was some consolation. Maybe you had to suffer for your art. Not that he really believed that or wanted to believe it. It smacked too much of the Catholicism he had rejected, where suffering was elevated to something valuable, some-thing desirable, clocking you up credit in Heaven. You had to suffer for your sins, even if you hadn't committed any! You had to suffer for the sins of your ancestors going right back to Adam and Eve! You had to suffer whether you were good or bad. Suffering was good for you! Jesus suffered for the sins of the world. Died on the cross for us. Except he didn't really die of course. God almighty, what a mad, sick, stupid, psychotic idea! What a load of codswallop! To think he had been brainwashed with such nonsense from birth. Thank God he had managed to de-programme himself. Yet so many people still believed such nonsense. Indeed, it was all around him here in Spain, with its cathedrals, churches, shrines, statues, crucifixes, priests in their black frocks …

These were dark thoughts, he told himself. Better not to think them. Better not to think at all! He would only sink deeper into despondency. Better to move, keep moving, look outwards, not inwards. He jumped up and walked out of the park to Puerta del Sol, the square in the centre of the city. He had some lunch in a backstreet bar, wandered around for a while just to kill some time, then took a bus to his hotel for a siesta to kill some more time before going out for the evening. He had arranged to meet MJ for a drink and, somewhat pathetically, felt so lonely he found himself looking forward to it.

To his relief, waistcoat boy was on the desk – not that it mattered, since he was alone. Alone again. Waistcoat boy gave him a friendly 'Hola' and he returned it, but hurried past. Ironically, he felt embarrassed about being on his own. Waistcoat boy was probably wondering why the pretty senorita wasn't with him, he supposed. It was something he was wondering himself …

A couple of hours later he left the hotel and took a bus back to the city centre, where he wandered about aimlessly until he met MJ at eight o'clock in Plaza España. She was wearing a dress and make-up for the first time, a dress that revealed a sexy figure and make-up that transformed her face from plain to almost pretty behind the studious glasses. She was actually quite fanciable, he thought guiltily, kissing her on the cheeks, and he probably *would* fancy her if he wasn't in love with Ana.

He had invited her to dinner as a way of saying thank

you for her services, so she took him to a restaurant called El Molinero, which he guessed correctly meant 'the miller', impressing her. After a glass or two of vino, she became loquacious, almost garrulous. 'I was against you at first, but not now,' she told him. 'Now I can see that you're sincero. You know, Ana has a rebellious streak. You must thank God for it! Why? Because it's another reason for you to fight for her! If you love her. Her father's a monster. He wants to keep her locked up. Like his pet. But her mother's more liberal. My mother was a monster. She walked out on the family when I was eleven. She had a job in TV. She was too fond of money and the things it can buy. She's living with another woman now! No, I never see her. My father? My father's the best person in the world to me. I'm his favourite girl. He says he prefers me to his sons! We play tennis together. I'm not sure about Chema any more. I'm afraid that if Ana married him, she'd become bad. I mean, now she's a nice mixture of liberal socialist and conservative. But Chema's parents are very well-off, very conservative, and so is he. That's why Ana's father likes him, even though he's supposed to be a socialist. Strangely enough, Chema gets on well with him. They play cards together. Her father wants her to marry him. She's confused though, because she likes Chema, but doesn't want to do what her father says. She always rebels against him. And now she says she's falling in love with you again. I think you should fight for her, if you love her. Si, I know. I've changed my mind. I didn't know you before. As I say, I always put my foot in it. I think Ana loves you. You know, don't tell Ana, but her father invited me out to a disco in Madrid in front of her mother, because he was angry with her. Si, shocking. Her mother's fed up with him, but they won't divorce, because they're Catholic. Spain's still a very Catholic country. A very conservative country. Nothing has changed.

Only on the surface. It's the same as in Franco's time. There was censorship then – even my grandfather was prevented from publishing certain things – and there's still censorship. No, I'm not like my grandfather. I admire him, but I'm in the middle. I'm not reactionary. I'm Catholic, but not very Catholic. No, I don't go to Mass every week. I don't believe everything. I'm like Ana. I think it's why we like each other. We have the same general view. Yes, we met in Dublin. She enjoyed Dublin because of you. I was depressed though. Because my boyfriend had left me. Not because of Dublin. That's why I flew back early for the first time in my life. No, it's finished. I think I'll never marry. I'm happy now. I'll find somebody if I want to. I don't love easily. I don't trust people any more. My mother left me, my boyfriend left me. I have to survive alone if necessary. May I ask you something? If you love her, please don't leave her. I know she loves you. At least, don't stop writing to her. She loves your letters. She becomes very down when you don't write. When she thinks you don't want her any more. I see her. I see how she is. She's confused, but I know she loves you. If you leave her, she'll die. I don't mean physically. I mean inside. Her heart will die. My heart died. She's a good person. I think you're a good person too. I believe you love her. I believe she can be happy with you. I know you make her happy. She's always happy when she gets a letter from you! Will you at least promise to write to her?'

Wow! What a turnup for the books! How could he refuse an entreaty like that? From someone he thought was the opposition! It made things complicated again though. He thought he'd made his decision. Now it seemed he'd have to unmake it. He had to hedge his bets though. He didn't want to make any promises he couldn't keep.

'I'll think about it,' he said, softened up by the wine, as well as her heartfelt words.

'Gracias,' she said. 'Will you do something else for me?'

'Yes, I suppose so!' he laughed, taking another slug of red, though he had probably had enough.

'Call her.'

'Call her? Now?'

'After dinner. Outside. I'll help you.'

'Why?'

'She misses you.'

'OK,' he shrugged. He wasn't sure he wanted to, still felt a prick of resentment that she wasn't here with him, no matter how illogical or unfair that was. 'Sure,' he added brightly, the alcohol suddenly lifting his spirits.

'You're a good person,' MJ said, and coming from her, on top of the wine, that made him feel really high.

'So are you!' he laughed, draining his glass.

'Gracias,' she said. 'Vamos?'

'Si,' he said, calling for the bill.

'Como estas?' he asked her, when he got through.

'Estoy – I'm down,' she said dully.

'Por que?'

'I miss you.'

'I miss you.'

'Is it true?'

'Yes. Why don't you jump in your car and come to Madrid?'

'I would if I could.'

'Have you been out?'

'No, not really.'

'Why not?'

'I didn't feel like it.'

'What did you do?'

'I tried to read.'

'What were you trying to read?'

'Ulysses.'

'That's heavy going, I know. But worth it.'

'I'm in Proteus. I need your help with it.'

'I'm here.'

'Not now. I'll write my questions to you.'

'OK. I won't charge you.'

'How's MJ?' She ignored the joke.

'She's OK. We just had dinner. I treated her.'

'That was kind of you.'

'Do you want to speak to her?'

'Just say hola to her. I'm not in a good mood and I'm tired. I'm sorry.'

Suddenly he was tired himself, tired of this non-conversation.

'You should go to bed then. Sleep well. Sweet dreams. See you tomorrow for our last coffee.'

'No. Not last. In Spain there's an expression, "Last before last". Can you understand?'

'Yes, I think so,' he half-laughed. 'Nice one. Buenas noches. Te quiero.'

'Buenas noches.'

He kept the receiver to his ear, wondering if that was it, waiting for her to say the words he wanted to hear, telling himself if she didn't say them, he'd put the phone down and never speak to her again.

'Te quiero,' she said at last, almost inaudibly, and only then did he replace the receiver.

They met the next morning at Café Antonio, after he had checked out of the hotel, for their 'last before last' coffee. She was wearing a pale-yellow blouse and pink cord skirt, looked as pretty as a daffodil or rose. She told him she would try to obtain an assistantship teaching Spanish in a UK school for September. He told her to try and get something in London, but she said it wasn't up to her, she had to take whatever they offered her.

'Will you come to see me?' she asked.

'Do you want me to?' he returned the ball to her.

'If you want to,' she batted it back.

'I want to, but I'm not sure you want me to.'

'I want you to, but I'm not sure about you. I'm not sure you love me. I have doubts about you.'

'I do love you,' he said, trying not to sound exasperated. 'That's why I'm here.'

'But you don't love me enough to leave your girlfriend.'

'I've told you, I do. I just need time. And I need to be sure about you. I'm not sure about you.'

He felt mean, throwing it back at her. He didn't want to have this conversation at all, but it was necessary, he supposed, unavoidable. He certainly didn't want to have an argument with her at this, their last meeting. At what could be their last meeting ever …

'Why are you not sure?'

'Well, you have this boyfriend here,' he shrugged.

'He's not my boyfriend. Just my friend.'

'Yes, but – ' He wasn't sure how to put it. 'Promise you won't get too close to him.'

'I can't promise that.'

It wasn't the answer he wanted. It felt like a slap in the face. Or a punch in the stomach. Sometimes he wondered if she realised how hurtful she could be. Or was she doing it on purpose, playing a game, using Chema to make him go to her? No, she wasn't that cunning or manipulative! Or was she?

'In that case, it's over,' he felt like saying, felt like standing up and walking out of the café, leaving her there, leaving her for good. But she looked so sweet, so childlike, so pretty, sitting opposite him with her big brown eyes in that innocent face, that he couldn't. He couldn't because, he realised, he loved her, even if she didn't love him. He could never deliberately hurt her. Hoist with his own petard again!

'OK,' he said instead, taking her hand and holding it. 'Let's not make any decisions now. Let's see how things go. We're both free. What's meant to be, will be. Que sera, sera, as the Italians say.' He glanced at his watch. 'It's time to go.'

He stood up. He didn't want her to reply, to say anything he didn't want to hear. He didn't want her to agree with him. *What's meant to be, will be.* He didn't believe it himself. It sounded phony, even in his own ears. It was just something to say. Filler. Bullshit, as Papa might have said. A sticking plaster. Philosophaster! 'Are you ready? I'll pay the bill. Vamos.'

At the airport he went for a beer and sandwich before checking in, but she had nothing, said she was too nervous. 'I'm the one who should be nervous!' he laughed. He tried to engage her in small talk, wanting to avoid any serious conversation, but she was reserved. After a while he gave up and they sat in virtual silence while he finished eating and drinking. What an anticlimax, he thought sadly.

After checking in, he still had plenty of time to spare before his flight, but she told him to go through. He was secretly impatient to leave, so agreed – waiting with her was just prolonging the agony. He gave her a kiss on each cheek, accompanied by a quick hug. This wasn't how it was meant to be, he reflected wryly, even as he did so – usually in films the romantic lovers embraced and clung to each other for as long as possible before the gate was closed! Perhaps even longer …

As soon the plane took off, a wave of relief swept over him. That wasn't in the script either! It wasn't that he didn't love her. She wouldn't *let* him love her. That was the problem!

She seemed to have built a wall against him. Whenever he tried to break through, she put up another brick. *Another brick in the wall.*

It was no good, he decided. He'd tried his best, but it hadn't worked. It couldn't work. It wasn't all her fault. It was as much his fault. Either way, it hadn't worked. Better to end it now. It would only be more painful later. Let it go. Let her go. Try to keep a few happy memories. Memories of what had been. Memories of what might have been …

When he got home, he'd write and tell her, he decided, as the plane jetted higher and higher into the seemingly infinite blue emptiness, flying faster and faster, farther and farther, away from Spain, away from her, as if it had all been just a film, a play, a fairytale, a dream.

CHAPTER SEVENTEEN

London

Madrid, 20th – 22nd April '87

Dear Francis,

Today is Monday. It's 4.45. Sitting on a bench, in the sun, waiting for Maria José. I can't believe you're only two hours by plane away from me. I feel as if you were going to telephone me or visit me in a few minutes.

Yesterday, I was very sad too. I asked you to jump into your plane quickly to make the "good-bye" easy. I wanted to say to you "good-bye" with a smile. O.K., I mean, to say "Hasta luego". Whenever I'm with you, I'm happy. Have you noticed it? My mama has noticed it as well. She hopes I won't loose my appetite and won't become pale again – I'm a bit more hungry than I used to be. I hope both last for a while.

Wednesday's setting: I'm writing in my car. At university. Under the tree I showed you. A warm day. The sun shining. Between my English language class and American literature.

I miss you. Now I'm wondering why I didn't jump towards your arms in the airport, why I didn't kiss you, why I didn't stop you leaving me. I was a bit cold, but don't worry, it was the effect of having been living a dream and being just about to wake up.

Thinking about how long we were together in Madrid is ambiguous. The very first moment when I met you in the airport seems to be a long time ago, however we were together a whole week.

I noticed a complete change in you and in me, of course. As you said, we'd been writing letters to images that became alive on Sunday, 12th. They were reborn. Happiness stretches its limbs towards us, offering a new choice.

I hope you won't be examining carefully why I have some doubts about the meaning of love. I owe you an explanation and here it is: Perhaps you noticed I was a bit cold at the beginning of our "second choice" – in fact, I can't understand why I was a bit passionate the day and the time you are thinking. What I mean is that I offered myself in body and soul to my ex-boyfriend, I gave him everything. I trusted him thoroughly, I loved him completely. When we broke our relationship, as I'd offered him not only love but also friendship, confidence, help, understanding … I hoped a different 'answer' to our new situation. I hoped he went on keeping contact with me and if we were unable to understand each other as a man and a woman, at least we could be friends. Now I believe he was interested in me only as a woman, not as a person – at least in the end of our relationship.

Afterwards you appeared in my life. We had a very good time in Dublin, were happy and so on. However, you are emotionally involved with your girlfriend. O.K. that's the point. This is not a reproach. Again I'm not able to be sufficient by myself – this is not exactly what I mean, but it's close. On the other hand, I can't ask you to leave her, because I'm not absolutely sure of what I want. I need time and thank God I have it. I foresee that if we become more and more emotionally involved, one day you'll say to me: "Ana, this is the end." And again I'll loose a friend. That's why I don't understand the meaning of love and I'm afraid of it. What I know is that love is something uncontrollable and selfish (they are not quite positive characteristics, what do you think?).

I feel saying what I think it's easier by letters than by words. You're right. I can write more fluently than speak.

Sorry for sending this on Thursday but I'm working like mad writing my paper for history, reading Mark Twain etc.

Things to be reminded to Francis:

Send the application form from your college.

Write soon, please – a ten-page letter.

I'll try my best to write soon again. Many "besos" and love, and more kisses and "amor",

Ana (xxx)

SORRY FOR MISTAKES (DON'T LOOK AT THEM)

He folded the letter up, put it back in the red and blue-bordered airmail envelope, slipped it back into his inside jacket pocket and took another sup of Guinness. He didn't know what to make of the letter. It was full of mixed messages. Not mixed metaphors ha ha. She seemed to have somewhat different memories of their week in Madrid. Which in fact was less than a week, since she wasn't with me the whole week. 'Whenever I'm with you, I'm happy.' You could have fooled me! 'I have some doubts about the meaning of love.' Why? Stop cerebrating! It's a feeling! An emotion. You know if you have it! Embrace it! Go with it! 'I offered myself in body and soul to my ex-boyfriend, I gave him everything.' Yet you refused to have sex with him. Just as you refused to have sex with me. 'At least we could be friends.' Of course he didn't want to be just friends with you! Just as I don't! This is your get-out-of-jail card, the one you always play, because you're afraid of *sex*. You've done it to me too. You've led me on, then shut the door in my face. If only you knew how frustrating that is. Oh, I know you don't do it deliberately or maliciously. You're not a cockteaser like one or two other women I've met. (What's the Spanish expression, I wonder?) You only do it because you have such a phobia about sex. 'I'm not absolutely sure of what I want.' But I thought you wanted to be with me? I thought you loved me. That's what you keep telling me! Many "besos" and love, and more kisses and "amor". You sound so romantic, so sexy, so passionate, in your letters, yet when it comes to it, you go cold, freeze, run away like a frightened rabbit. No, maybe not a rabbit. That's the wrong word in the context. Maybe it was true what Julia, another Spanish student, told me once. 'Spanish girls are repressed. Some go a bit loco when they come to England on freedom. Others just stay very quiet and shy.' You're definitely in the latter category! You're the living, walking, breathing epitome and personification! General Franco has a lot to answer for. And the Catholic church. What a toxic, lethal combination! Still, no one was more repressed than me, with my history, and I've managed to liberate myself. Thrown off the 'mind-forged manacles'. It can be done! Not that even I am completely free. The indoctrination goes so deep. The brainwashing. Your very soul is steeped in it, dyed in it. Indelibly dyed. Dyed in the wool. The wool is pulled over your eyes too. Till you wake up and see the light. Or smell the coffee. Dulce, my previous Spanish girlfriend, was in the first category. She couldn't get enough sex! She was mad for it. Mind you, I think she was the same in Spain. She had a boyfriend there. A Jesuit priest no less! She must have smelled the incense on me. More or less threw herself at me. She was good fun though. In a way Ana isn't. And yet in spite of everything I love Ana. Or I'm in love with her anyway. That's the irony. The other irony is that I don't really care about the sex angle. I'm not a sex maniac. I can control myself. All too well. I'm prepared to wait for her. Chastity has something to be said for it, if not poverty and obedience. It's just that after flying all the way to Madrid, I was hoping for some romance, some passion. Some fireworks. Some fun and games. I didn't just want sex either. I wanted to *make love* with her. There's a subtle difference. Or not so subtle. Show her that I loved her. I just couldn't break through though. God, there's something almost *nunnish* about her! I feel sorry for her. She's trapped. Emotionally stunted. Blocked. And yet she has the sweetest, loveliest nature. Which only makes it worse. She won't, can't, *give* herself. She won't let me help her. She won't let me in. Damaged. Psychologically damaged. By the system. The real tragedy is she'll always have problems. Even if she ever gets married. If she doesn't manage to free herself. So she'll always be unhappy. That's what worries me. That's what really makes me sad. She's not the only one of course. Christianity, especially Catholicism, has inflicted similar damage on millions of victims throughout the centuries. Not just psychological damage either. You were tortured or burned at the stake in days gone by if you didn't bow down, conform and comply! Evil masquerading as good. Popes and priests in their fancy dress, frocks and pointy hats. Like druids, wizards, sorcerers. Telling us what to do. Threatening us with eternal hellfire if we don't! Bribing us with promises of paradise if we do! Fiendishly cunning indeed. Infernally clever ha ha. Thank god they don't have the same power any more. I'd be in serious trouble if they did. To think a bunch of religious fanatics have exerted so much power over men's minds for nigh on 2000 years. Infiltrated society. Infected it. Until only thirty years ago in Spain. And relatively recently in Ireland too. As I know to my own cost. Poor Ana! I can't leave you. I can't leave you because I love you. I can't leave you, because if I did it would mean the forces of evil had prevailed. I'm not going to give up on you. When I go home, I'll tear up the letter I've started writing to you. Telling you it's over. How could I be so foolish, so stupid, so weak, so dim? MJ was right. *If you love her, you'll fight for her.* Thank god I haven't sent it! I'll be your saviour, Ana. I'll be your knight in shining armour. I'll extricate you from the cult. Free you from your tower. I'll make it my mission. Whether you want to be saved or not! Me against the forces of evil. I'll write a new letter tonight. Must remember to tell her about that mistake she keeps making too, confusing 'loose' and 'lose'. Yes MJ, I'll fight for her. I'll show you too how serious I am. You thought I was just a playboy, didn't you? Well, I think you've already glimpsed the real me. I'll prove it to you once and for all. How serious I am about her. God what a fool I nearly was! Never send a letter straightaway. *Scripta manent.* That's the moral of the story. Always sleep on it. Maybe have a drink on it too ha ha. Phew that was close! I'm sorry, Ana. Te quiero. I'll come back for you! How could I think of leaving you? Besides, Rania, the woman who calls herself my wife, gets worse and worse. That's why I'm sitting here in the pub getting drunk on my own and talking to myself after work on a Wednesday evening, instead of going home. I don't want to see her. I can hardly bear the sight of her. She has a tongue like a razor blade. Like a scalpel. What was it she said earlier? *You're nearly forty and you're nothing. You've got nothing. You only earn 7000! You brag about having ten babies but you can't even support one. It's ridiculous!* I pretend not to be bothered by her verbal assaults, but I am. Words can be worse than sticks and stones. Not just because they hurt my feelings or wound my pride, but because it shows how little respect she has for me, how little love. And yet. What was it she said to me the other day? We went for a walk along the river. She was in a playful mood, I remember. We were throwing flowers at each other. After our walk we went for a drink in the Ferry Boat Inn on the river. 'How much would it cost to transport a dead body across the Atlantic?' she suddenly asks. 'What a weird question!' I laughed. 'Why on earth do you ask that?' 'Mum said she wants to be buried in Guyana when she dies,' she said. 'Not before she dies, I hope,' I was tempted to quip, but refrained. 'Why?' I asked instead. 'To be next to her husband,' she replied. 'It doesn't really matter, when you're dead, does it?' I said, in my usual slightly cynical way, partly just to wind her up. 'Yes, it does,' she replied. 'I want to be buried next to you. I hope you'll reserve a place for me.' *I want to be buried next to you.* That put a dent in my world-weary cynicism! She meant it too. That's a declaration of love if ever there was one! She comes out with stuff like that. The trouble is she comes out with the other stuff too, the vicious, insulting, nasty, abusive, sarcastic stuff. She's definitely schizoid. Angel and devil in one. That's the problem. That's what I can't cope with. That's why I want to get away. Why I need to get away. For both our sakes. I may not love her or be able to live with her, but I know she loves me, even if it's like being loved by a monster. Or a devil. What a trap to find yourself in! Still, it's my own fault. I got myself into it. It's up to me to get out of it. She disappoints me in other ways, too. The other day she said she'd vote for Margaret Thatcher in the forthcoming general election. Shock, horror, disgust, revulsion. Though she may have just been winding me up. If she does, I'll have no compunction. I couldn't live with a Tory. Not that she knows much about politics. I detest Thatcher. Apart from her politics, she seems to be a philistine. No soul. No hinterland. Doesn't read. Doubt she listens to music. Certainly not Celtic soul music anyway. Not the Furey Brothers or Moving Hearts. That's enough for me not to vote for her. Not that I'd ever vote Tory anyway. Not my tribe. They're the party of the rich and they'll always put the interests of the rich first. That was a blow, my book rejected by Hamish Hamilton and having to collect it from the post office. Talk about rubbing salt in the wound. Still maybe

Wolfhound will take it. Glimmer of hope there. Geoff Walker's a funny bugger. In one of our little man-to-man chats in the college bogs, he tells me he went away for a week-end with Corinne, the French student he's been having a fling with. 'She was dying for it. I'm shagged out! But life is short. I'm forty. Forty out of seventy. You have to grab all you can.' Funnily enough, an image of my father lying dead on the bed flashed through my mind. Or not my father, but what used to be my father. Just a husk. Dead at seventy-one. It means I'm probably already over halfway through my allotted span. Even more strangely, the thought in that most incongruous of places and contexts was even more painful than when I looked at his corpse lying on the bed or the box containing what used to be him being lowered into the 'hole', as my mother referred to the grave. It was all the more painful because I lost him long before he died. No, don't go there! Life is short, yes. Cruelly, pathetically, tragically short. Strike a light! Sic transit gloria mundi! So of course I had to agree with Geoff. My mate, Rob, got it right. 'You only get one bite of the cherry. We only pass this way once.' He's a non-believer like myself, despite our common Irish-Catholic background and seminary experience. Seems as if my colleague, Carol Osbourne, must be too, even though she's married to a vicar. What was it she said to me in our staffroom the other day? 'It's astonishing that we can't answer the most important question of all: Where do we come from?' Indeed. It's like not knowing how or where we were born, who our parents were. Of course, there are people in that position, I suppose. Orphans, for example. Lovely lady, Carol. I could almost fancy her! Except she's married to a vicar. And there's too much foreign 'crumpet' around, as Mark would say. Randy bastard. Even randier than me. He's a real hard case. The least sentimental person I've ever met. 'Love is just mutual need fulfilment.' What was it Margo, my American colleague, said about him? 'A brilliant man, but egotistic. Neurotic. Needs analysis himself. No compassion.' A pretty devastating summation of his personality. We're very different, but I like him. There's a refreshing, even bracing, honesty about him. I wonder what he'd say about Ana? He'd probably say something like, 'All she needs is a good shagging.' Margo again: 'He'd be good at stripping people down, but no good at putting them back together again.' I suspect you might be right, Margo. Oh, Ana! I wish you could just somehow let yourself go, let go of yourself, give yourself, trust me. I love you. You're the one I should be with, not the one I'm with! I can save you! I can repair you! You can save me too! We can save each other! I haven't given up on you yet. You've done a good job of trying to push me away, but I'm not going anywhere. Not yet. Wow, that Guinness is good! I wouldn't mind another one. No, better not. Had four. That's enough. Gotta work again tomorrow. Closing time anyway. Better go home and face the music. God, what a depressing thought! Why have I got myself into this situation? Depressed by the thought of going home to see my own wife! How sad is that? Oh, well. I've made my bed. Huh. Spare me the clichés. Better go. Can't sit here any longer without drinking. Had a few funny glances already. I don't really fit in here, I suppose. Workingman's pub. They probably see me as a bit of an oddity. An interloper. An outsider. Not unfriendly though. Better give the barman a wave as I go. Not waving but drowning ha.

When he opened the front door, Rania was in the hall, staring like a frightened rabbit. 'There's some dinner for you if you want. I'm sorry.'

'I don't want any dinner and I don't want any sorrow,' he replied brusquely, pushing past her and stumbling upstairs.

He crashed into his study, locked the door, plonked himself at his desk, poured himself a large Jameson's from the bottle he kept hidden in one of the drawers, though he was sure she knew about it, and took a first generous slug. It raced down his throat like liquid fire, igniting his innards, joined his bloodstream and slammed into his brain with an explosive force, blasting away the black thoughts, turning them into fireworks, lifting him up and away like a rocket from the real world towards that otherworld of blessed oblivion that he so desperately needed.

She followed him and tried to open the door, but couldn't. 'We shouldn't quarrel,' she said through the door, plaintively.

That's right, he thought, sitting and drinking the whiskey in the darkness. We shouldn't. So go away. And stay away. Leave me alone. Alone again, naturally. Thanks, Gilbert.

CHAPTER EIGHTEEN

London in the merry month of May

Mon 4.5.87

Met my friend and colleague, Roger, in Lloyd Park, where a May Day Festival was being held. Luckily it was dry, though with an ashen-grey sky overhead and a chilly wind blowing, despite the cherry trees being caked in pink-white blossom and the flowerbeds blooming prettily. Roger had tramped all the way from Epping Forest, which is a few miles north-east, in his sandals, T-shirt and cords, with his bulging, battered duffel bag over his shoulder as always (his belly bulged too, he having a ploughman's appetite) and with his long, unkempt, grey hair almost down to his fleshy shoulders. I use the word 'tramped', because there is something of the tramp or vagrant about him, though 'bohemian' is probably a more apt description. It's not that he's unclean or even scruffy, but he suffers from both body odour (sudoriferous I suspect) and bad breath, bad breath probably because, judging by the catastrophic state of his teeth, he has never been to a dentist in his life, maybe never even brushed his teeth in his life. It's a matter I've always felt I should broach with him, but never quite been able to summon up the courage. I was once on the brink of doing so, when he said something in the course of conversation about the superficiality and shallowness of judging people by appearances and that stopped me in my tracks. It's a shame because, as well as being extremely intelligent, he is a charming, sweet-natured man and would look fine if he spruced himself up. He likes both Epping Forest and Walthamstow mainly because of their associations with the writers Edward Thomas and William Morris. He's a writer himself and has written several books and articles in learned journals, mostly about obscure or at least lesser-known writers like those above, one or two of whom even I, with an honours degree in English Literature, had never heard of before I met him, for example, Richard Le Gallienne, who as it happens died at the age of eighty-one only two weeks after I myself was born, which I find a strangely moving thought and which gives me a feeling of spiritual connection with him, irrational and fanciful though that might be. Roger and I have become good friends, as well as colleagues, and I enjoy meeting him, because he is so erudite and interesting to talk to, or should I say listen to, though his seemingly boundless zest can become tiring after a while. On this occasion, though, our conversation was not about matters literary or intellectual, but his impending divorce from his Japanese wife, Yoko. We talked for two hours, wandering around the various stalls and stages or over tea and cake in the community café. I felt rather uncomfortable finding myself in the position of 'marriage counsellor', but did my best. I told him he needed to set up home properly with Yoko to give it a chance, instead of living in two separate bedsitters in the same building, as they do now. If only it were so simple though! He said (he speaks with a rather plummy Oxford accent, since he studied there, though he's a Brummy, an accent which reminds me of my old English teacher, Father Haynes, who also studied at Oxford, though he was Scottish) there were other problems, viz. that she was 'mentally unstable', was susceptible to 'black moods and irrational rages'. This shocked me, even though the signs were all there. He said that, partly because of her 'mental issues', she can't hold down a job and wants to be a kept woman, live an idle life, which further shocked me. He went on to say she'd 'despise' him for accepting a gift if she bought a place for them, which she (or her wealthy father) could apparently afford to do. 'It would be a relief if she left,' he said, giving me an even greater shock. 'But what would become of her if she went back to Japan?' he added anxiously. 'Nobody there wants to employ a woman over thirty. She has irrational hatreds for people. When she came to Ireland to see me after my accident, in tears actually, I opened a joint bank account with her, but changed it quick. She was dipping into it all the time. I couldn't afford a mortgage anyway. I have even fewer hours than you and there's no security of tenure now, thanks to Mrs Thatcher.' (Roger is a socialist like myself, though I think a somewhat disillusioned one after his experiences living and teaching in Eastern Europe. He speaks of socialism in those countries, e.g. Poland and Hungary, as being too 'Soviet'. I'd say he's a socialist in the Orwellian mould, like myself. He certainly admires Orwell the writer, as I do myself.) We ended up in front of a stage where some young colleens in green and gold costumes were doing Irish dancing to the music of a céilí band and I was glad of the light relief. Roger was enchanted by the dancers. 'What splendid little girls!' he exclaimed and I couldn't help feeling extra proud of my Irish heritage. When I eventually dropped him at Walthamstow Central tube station, he thanked me in his usual effusive way for my advice, though I didn't really feel I'd been able to impart much wisdom, despite having a failed marriage behind me myself, not to mention my present parlous one with Rania. After leaving him, I went for a pint in the Rose and Crown on Hoe Street and wrote to Ana, whom I'm missing. I felt guiltily relieved to get away from Roger, though being alone again and writing to Ana only reminded me of my own unhappy situation. Still, as always, a couple of pints soon helped to assuage that feeling. God, why does life have to be so complicated, so damned difficult? Well, there's no use asking *him* of course. He designed it this way!

Sun. 10.5.87
Had a big row with Rania about what should happen with my house if we broke up. She seems to think she'd be entitled to it and would throw me out! Yet legally it's my house and she's only lived with me for a couple of years and then only because I took her in, gave her refuge, when she ran away from her bullying family. What an insolent hussy! I stormed out of the aforementioned house, slamming the front door, jumped in my car and drove to the Marshes, my usual bolthole when I need some peace, respite, solitude or just fresh air. The Marshes are part of Lea Valley Park, a several-mile long slice of virtual countryside stretching out along the River Lea all the way from the Thames through East London into rural Hertfordshire. Having it on my doorstep is a real godsend, for which I'm eternally grateful, even if I have no god to be grateful to, other than the gods of chance or fate. And indeed the successive governments that have preserved this almost bucolic idyll from greedy developers for ordinary people such as me – though only a few years ago I was part of a protest to stop them being allowed to quarry for shale and even now I'm involved in another protest to stop them building on some disused filter beds instead of turning them into a nature reserve. I parked in one of the Victorian terraced side streets and walked down Coppermill Lane, past the waterworks and the reservoirs with their island heronries and flocks of Canada geese, towards the river, immediately in a different world, a world of space, sky, verdure, water, wildflowers, wildfowl, boats and best of

all, fresh air, fresh air scented with sweet perfumes wafting from the numerous blossom-laden hawthorn and elderberry, laburnum and lilac bushes. I crossed the railway line via the level crossing – ultra-cautiously having seen a woman almost killed there recently – and made my way towards the marina, with its congregation of colourful rivercraft, turned left and walked along the towpath downriver towards Latham's timber sheds at Lea Bridge Road. The greenery – mostly grass and nettles interspersed with clumps of reeds – on both sides of the towpath was waist-high in places, embroidered with white parsley and yellowy dandelions, while the meadows to my left were equally high grassy green prairies dotted with blue, white and yellow wildflowers, where bees buzzed busily and butter-flies flittered about prettily. On this side of the river there were no buildings almost as far as the eye could see, or even man-made objects, apart from pylons, the railway viaduct and the waterworks. On the other side, along this section at least, a luxuriantly wooded park rose up steeply from the poplar-lined riverbank, so that the surrounding streets, though not far away, were out of sight, contributing to the illusion that you were in some rustic, almost Constable-like, landscape rather than a suburb of London less than ten miles from Piccadilly Circus. On the river itself boats were moored or occasionally chugged past, most of them gaily painted narrowboats, and as always I was reminded that, according to the history I'd read, twelve hundred years ago Vikings sailed up this very river in their longboats on their way to a hard day's raping and pillaging. As always also Cat Stevens started playing 'Longer Boats' inside my head. The usual waterfowl – ducks, geese, swans, moor-hens, coots – paddled about busily (except the supercilious swans, who never look busy) on the oil-black water or foraged or relaxed on the banks, while occasionally a fish jumped to catch a midge or other unlucky insect, a fish that might be unlucky itself if it got hooked by one of the anglers sitting like garden gnomes by the riverside – not that I ever see them catch anything. Most of them are probably there just to escape from their wives, as I am myself, I reflected wryly. I walked as far as the hangar-like timber sheds, crossed the metal footbridge there and doubled back along the other bank of the river, lined here by grim-looking, barrack-like blocks of council flats, similar to the one I lived in myself once, and assorted industrial buildings. Soon I passed the Anchor and Hope, a scruffy though friendly little Victorian pub on the corner of a steep cobbled sidestreet that fell down to the riverside. I was tempted to stop for a pint of their excellent London Pride, but all the riverside tables were occupied by the usual bohemian-looking, chattering, fag-puffing crowd and I didn't fancy sitting inside, since it was claustrophobically small, especially on such a warm spring day, so moved on to my preferred watering-hole, the Robin Hood, just a block or two farther along. I prefer the Robin Hood because, apart from its name (Robin Hood having been a childhood hero of mine), though it's also a bit scruffy, it's much roomier inside, with lots of nautical paraphernalia and with a large patio outside, from where you get a panoramic view of the river and meadows. Best of all, the Irish landlord serves a very professional, properly topped-off pint of Guinness, in several of which I drowned my sorrows or attempted to while sitting at one of the tables on the patio and gazing out over the river at the bucolic scene in front of me – the bushy green grasslands and the gunmetal-surfaced, lakelike reservoir with its little wooded isle in the middle that always reminds me, incongruously perhaps, of the Yeats poem. (Though not necessarily incongruous, since apparently he was inspired to write it while walking along Fleet Street here in London town.) As well as gazing through a blur of alcohol-induced euphoria at the view, which always arouses in me nostalgic memories of both the Lake District and County Cavan, I wrote to Ana, telling her that whatever love I had for Rania had completely evaporated and I was going to ask her to leave, that I loved her, Ana, whatever her problems, and wanted her to come to London and marry me and live with me as my wife and my soulmate, to have and to hold, for better, for worse, for richer, for poorer (probably poorer, I jokingly added in parenthesis), in sickness and in health, till death did us part …

Sat. 16.5.87

Went for a drink with my colleague/friend, Ed, with whom I have quite a bit in common i.e. we are not only both of Irish descent and Catholic (or in my case ex-Catholic) but he's an ex-monk, while I'm an ex-seminarian. (Apparently he used to be called Brother Michael in the monastery.) As always he was dressed like a teacher from central casting, from the 1950s or even '20s or '30s perhaps: tweed jacket with regulation leather elbow patches, wool tie, check shirt, baggy cord trousers, leather brogues. I'm sure he could have walked straight onto the set of 'To Serve Them All My Days'! In spite of still being very much a practising Catholic, as far as I can tell, and an ex-monk, he has a good stock of risqué jokes, though he won't tolerate anti-Irish jokes, as he once made a point of telling me, before he knew I was Irish myself. We went to Minogue's on Caledonian Road, to hear some live traditional Irish music, though he's not as keen on it as I am, despite his Irishness. Before becoming a lecturer at the college, he worked for MI5 (about which he is forced to be secretive, but lets out little snippets now and again) and then a teacher in a rough, inner-city school, where the kids were routinely armed with knives and airguns, as he recounts amusingly. 'Sounds more like a jungle than a school!' I commented in horror, to which he replied philosophically, 'It was a living.' Somewhat to my surprise, he confessed that he had no 'intellectual pretensions', as he put it, and added, to my further surprise, that he got all his 'intellectual satisfaction' at home from reading French novels (he speaks good French) and biblical exegesis. Biblical exegesis! I was shocked and somewhat dismayed, realised that despite having apparently so much in common, at least in the matter of religion we were poles apart, not that I will let that spoil any friendship we have. He also told me tonight that the 'cops' were 'gearing up for revenge' for the murder of PC Keith Blakelock a year or so ago. PC Keith Blakelock was a policeman who was attacked and killed during a riot on the Broadwater Farm council estate in Tottenham. He claimed that, horrifically, the policeman had not only been slashed and stabbed to death with machetes and knives, but had had both his hands chopped off, a fact that was somehow kept out of the media. He seems to have access to classified or secret information about such matters, maybe from ex-security service contacts. I don't probe. He's a very good conversationalist and raconteur, I have to admit, so I enjoy his company, though there's something vaguely depressive about him, apart from his religiosity, that puts me off. Well, apparently he did have some sort of 'nervous breakdown' before he left the monastery. When he left or was forced to leave the secret service, he told me he had to go into hiding in a French monastery for a while, a monastery where he still spends most of his holidays, perhaps doing biblical exegesis. It all sounds a bit John le Carré crossed with Graham Greene, but he doesn't seem like the kind of bloke to make things up, so I go along with it. It has a certain vicarious excitement for me anyway, I must admit, since the world of espionage is one that fascinates me. He's also very lonely, I suspect, having no wife or girlfriend, partly I also suspect because he looks like Boris Karloff (the kids at the school where he used to teach called him Frankenstein, he laughingly informs me) and partly, I suspect, because of his monkish personality. He seems to be one of those who have left the religious life physically, but not quite mentally or spiritually, unlike myself. I have rejected that world and its belief system totally, regard it now as a world of illusion and delusion.

Mon. 25th May 87
Letter from Ana at last. I read it in privacy over my morning coffee in my staffroom/office, which I share with five other lecturers, but I'm always first in.

Madrid, 20th May '87

Dear Francis,

Can you forgive me my not writing for such a long time please? And also could you forgive my possible mistakes (language mistakes) in this letter? I didn't write to you before because I've been working and studying very much. Since you left me in Madrid, I handed in two 30-page papers (History and Middle English), prepared an exam that I will have tomorrow and preparing another paper for an American Literature subject and there are lots of things left for the next month. This week I finish my classes and next month until 30th June I will have some examinations. However, I don't want you to think I didn't remember you, exactly the opposite is true.

As today morning I have a free hour until American Literature class, I've made up my mind to write to you a short letter. I mean a short letter because I hope I will manage to write a long one – though not as long as your last one – in a short time telling you what you asked me to find out about what would be involved in opening a school in Spain and about my assistantship in England and consequently if I'm going to London in July or not. If I were going to live in England for one year, I wouldn't go in July but I would go in September. On Wednesday I want to go to the Ministry because I know the places for the assistantships have already been given out, not in an official way. Can you understand me? (I have my doubts about the words I must use.) *

Thank you very much for your last three letters. I couldn't choose which one was the nicest for me! It's a pity I haven't got them all here to re-read them and answer some or a few points I'd like to I hope. I beg you can understand me and you don't think I'm only a selfish girl who only wants to be admired by letter and doesn't know how to response to those wheedlings, cajoleries … (I haven't got an English dictionary handy.)

*I usually write your letter twice so that I can express myself better and you can understand me better too.

What about your book? Is it going to be published? The first thing I'm going to do when I become a bachelor (it sounds very well doesn't it?) is to read your book thoroughly and completely even if it weren't to be published. (Do you understand, my dear?)

By the way, I'm remembering you told me in one of your letters that you rang me up and I wasn't in, or smth like that. I'm afraid you misdialed (can you say it? or it's a false inference from my poor German?), because that day I didn't go out and I was at home on my own during the whole day. So, the key point is, are you going to telephone me again? It's May, do you remember? And you told me you probably will telephone me this month!

I hope you will be O.K. I'll try my best to write again as soon as possible, maybe I'll be more relaxed and in this way I'll be able to write a nicer letter but at the moment I send you my love and many kisses and a command: Remember me at least two minutes a day, please.

Te quiero,
Ana (xxxxx)

P.D. Don't worry about anything concerning me. If you have any doubts, ask and you shall receive. Don't worry if I didn't write more or less a month ago, I couldn't, believe me.

BESOS

Did you begin your Spanish classes with Aurora?

It was a 'nice' letter as usual, but I felt disappointed by it. She didn't reply to what I wrote in my last letter, telling her it was over with Rania and I wanted to marry her. She seemed to be more interested in her 'assistantship' in England than my proposal of marriage. In a way, it was typical of her to be so evasive. It was a bit like the way she tried to avoid sex. Was it her way of saying no? I started to regret having proposed to her. Of course, I'd been drunk when I did so. Maybe the moral of the story is, don't write anything important while you're drunk! Oh well, I thought, folding the letter up and slipping it back into my jacket pocket. Maybe I won't mention marriage again. Maybe I'll pretend I never said anything about it. Play her at her own game. I shouldn't think like that, I know, but sometimes I feel as if I'm banging my head on a brick wall. Flogging a dead horse. Wrestling with the wind. Chasing a will o' the wisp, a dream. Maybe it was all just a dream, a fantasy. Anyway, stop thinking about her, I told myself. I had an Advanced class to teach in a few minutes. Back to reality! I'd use one or two of those idioms though, I decided. They like their idioms. I'll have to think of a different context though. Not my lovelife …

Sat. 30.5.87

To Gatwick to meet my mother, who is on her way to visit my sister in America. It wasn't a meeting I looked forward to, because relations between my mother and me have been strained ever since I left the seminary, but are made far worse by me 'losing my faith'. I was once the apple of her eye, she used to idolise me as I used to idolise her, but now I suppose she sees me as a lost soul. Meeting her is almost like meeting a woman I used to love – an ex-wife perhaps – but only because I'm forced to. I'm forced to because, unlike an ex-wife, she is my mother and I am her son and I'd like to build bridges, but she, like my father before, makes it extremely difficult. That's because she clearly regards me as a 'sinner', an apostate and renegade who has turned his back on Holy Mother Church and is living a dissolute life, living 'in sin' with a woman he isn't married to. This is why neither she nor my father have ever visited me in London. This is why I have to go to Gatwick to meet my mother in an airport lounge on her way to America, rather than her staying overnight with me, which would be the normal, natural, logical thing for a mother to do. Everything has always had to be on their terms. They wouldn't bend an inch. They refused to come to my first wedding, even though it was to a Catholic girl in Catholic rites in a Catholic church! When I demanded to know why, they said it was because I didn't really believe in it, I was only pretending. My father used the word 'sham', which really hurt. Against that kind of bigotry you can't win. It makes me angry and depressed and those were the feelings that kept bubbling up on the train to the airport. But at least I had another letter from Ana, received this morning, to distract me, though it didn't give me all the consolation I'd hoped for.

Madrid, 25th May 87

Dear Francis,

Here it is. My second promised letter. I have two different types of tidings for you: a good one and a bad one. Firstly, the bad one: I'm sorry but I can't go to London in July, because (a long, long silence which surely will make you feel nervous, impatient, thoughtful and so on and so forth …) because I'm arriving in September. I mean, I got the assistantship in England. The academic year goes from 1st September up to 31st July, I think. So I will be there near you one year. I don't know the place yet, probably – using the civil servant's words – London, but I must wait for the British authorities' letter.

I can hardly believe it. I don't know if I'm happy or not. It's horrible. What am I going to do? I've never lived on my own before. I need as much help as you can give me. Francis, where am I going to live? What am I going to eat? Who will take care of me? Is it cold in England in Winter? Which type of clothes should I bring? How can I manage to give a lesson in Spanish if I've never done such a thing before? My great problems are: Where am I going to live? And, is living in London too much expensive? Oh, by the way, the second choice where I can be sent to – just like a letter or a thing – is Lincoln. I asked the second question because I'm afraid my salary won't be high enough.

Of course, I'd like to study smth there – maybe a literature course and, without any doubt, I'll try my best to pass the Proficiency exam. My "tesina", maybe, should be postponed – now I must arrange an appointment with my literature teacher.

Terrible. The first time I'm going to work and to live on my own and both things must be in a foreign country. I'm so frightened. I need you. I'm so childish and need your help – you're the only person who can take care of me there. To say so makes me feel selfish. I hope you'll be able to forgive my selfishness, won't you?

When I receive the letter from the British authorities I'll write to you again. Of course also I will before if their letter takes a long time, saying to you the place. Perhaps I must go to England before the 1st Sept. When do you come back from Ireland? Will you be waiting for me at the airport? I'm frightened of airports, planes. Maybe, I can't be sure now, you will have to look for some accommodation for me if I'm coming to London. Will you be so kind?

Again, it's a short letter. After writing it I'll continue

with my paper on Am. Lit. about Male Sexuality in Twain, Crane, Anderson and Hemingway (Huck. Finn, short stories such as: Crane, "The Bride Comes to Yellow Sky", Anderson, "I'm a Fool", "I Want to Know Why" and "In Our Time"). Do you have any suggestion to do?

All my love for my good friend, Francisco. Many kisses. I hope you will feel as happy as I am.

Te quiero,

Ana (xxxxxx)

P.S. Do you think I'll be able to speak English very well after a whole year in England?

I read the letter several times as the train zipped through the vernal West Sussex countryside. Despite the pastoral prettiness of the scenery and the warmth of the letter, my spirits struggled. Neither were quite enough to completely dispel the gloom I felt at the prospect of meeting my mother. Apart from anything else, conversation with her was always so difficult, since my life in London, my 'wife', my doings, were out of bounds and she never inquired about them. I knew she wouldn't even ask me how I was. The conversation would be all one way, from me to her, and so it proved. There were moments when I felt so sad and so angry that I thought of not getting off the train and later making some excuse for not meeting her. I couldn't do that though. My sense of filial duty prevented me. Besides, it would have been cowardly and I would have despised myself afterwards. After their refusal to come to my wedding, I had had fits of anger in which I resolved never to speak to them again, to disown them, as they had, I felt, to an extent disowned me or at least rejected me. I didn't do that though. It would have meant the forces of evil, of religious bigotry, had won and I wouldn't let that happen. I have continued to visit them, even though they have never visited me and they make me feel like a black sheep or prodigal son or at least that's always how I feel when I visit them, though they are never less than kind to me. I kept trying to suppress all these dark thoughts as the train raced towards Gatwick, kept rereading Ana's letter, finding some crumbs of comfort and consolation there, even if not quite the words I hoped for, no matter how hard I read between the lines: 'Yes, I will marry you.' Wasn't it funny, I reflected wryly, how it was all the women in my life who were giving me grief? I tried to stop thinking and distract myself by gazing out of the train window at the chocolate-box English villages with their church steeples, surrounded by fields full of ruminating cows and gambolling lambs, all illuminated by spring sunshine splashing down from a brilliant blue sky. It was the kind of scenery that would normally make me feel euphoric, fill me with the joys of spring, but by the time the train slid to a standstill in the station at Gatwick, I felt almost ill with anxiety. Maybe I was suffering from an illness, a 'terminal' illness, I joked morosely to myself, as I alighted onto the platform and headed with a heavy heart towards arrivals, to meet the woman who had brought me into this vale of tears.

CHAPTER NINETEEN

In Dublin's Fair City

Her name was Marie-Hélène. She was French, mid-twenties, with what Charles, his friend and the summer school course director, called an 'eighteenth-century face'. He wasn't quite sure what Charles meant by that, unless he meant she had an aristocratic look, perhaps because of her Roman nose or her lily-white skin, usually with minimal make-up. Anyway, appropriate perhaps, since they were in Trinity College, which also had an eighteenth-century air about it, with its cobbled quadrangles bound by Georgian buildings, not to mention its cricket and rugby fields.

She was slim, verging on skinny, with smallish breasts, a bump in her nose and a squint in one of her pale blue eyes. She wasn't the prettiest or sexiest-looking girl on the course, but he found her attractive. Perhaps because she looked a bit fragile. There was something sylph-like about her. She had wavy, auburn, shoulder-length hair and dressed rather plainly in sleeveless blouses or woollen sweaters with long summery skirts or jeans, wore very little makeup or jewellery – all of which were attractive to him. Maybe she would be the one, he speculated. The one he was searching for. His own get-out-of-jail card. Since neither Rania nor Ana were playing ball.

After class one day he invited her for a drink in Foleys on

Merrion Row. 'I don't like pubs,' she said, to his dismay. *Not a good start!* 'Why not?' he laughed. 'They're full of depressing people,' she said. 'Have you actually been in a pub here?' he asked. 'No,' she admitted. 'There you are then,' he laughed. 'You've been in Dublin for a week and you haven't been to a pub! So you don't know! You need to be educated! It's disgraceful! It's scandalous!'

'I will allow you to educate me then,' she smiled, to his relief.

'Slainte. So, what do you think of life so far?' he asked her, when he had found a perch in Foleys and come back with a pint of Guinness for himself and a glass of the same for her.

'Merde,' she said, which made him splutter into his stout.

'Come on, it's not that bad!' he laughed, though on reflection, he thought, she might be right. *'History is a nightmare from which I am trying to awake.'*

'Comment?'

'It's a quotation from *Ulysses* by James Joyce.'

'I don't read.'

'I haven't read,' he corrected. 'Present Perfect tense.'

'I haven't read,' she repeated dutifully, though dropping her aitch French-style as usual.

'Actually,' he pursued, though she didn't seem very interested – unlike Ana – 'it comes originally from a French writer called Jules Laforgue, who also wrote, 'La vie est trop triste, trop sale'.' He had taught the passage, from Nestor, to his Advanced class that very morning and checked it in his Gifford, so he knew. It seemed to be wasted on her though. A wasted pearl! Ana would have had her notebook out and be inscribing it studiously now, he reflected with a pang.

'C'est ma vie,' she commented, with a Gallic shrug.

'Well, let's see if we can make your life better,' he grinned, and proceeded to give her the third degree. She was going to be quite a challenge, he was starting to realise.

She told him she lived in a small flat in Paris with no TV and hardly any furniture and was a qualified accountant, but worked as a secretary, though she found the job boring and didn't get on with her colleagues, regarded it as 'slavery' and 'exploitation'. Her parents divorced when she was a child. She had fallen out with her mother, so hardly saw her. She had fallen out with her father too, because he had once hit her on the side of her face with his fist when she was a teenager. (He shook his head in horrified disbelief at this.) She had tried to forgive him, but couldn't. She had no boyfriend now, but had had boyfriends when she was at university. That was the best time of her life. She had worked in both Germany and America as an au pair.

She went on a Dale Carnegie course last year, she told him, and enjoyed it. He was surprised and amused by this, but kept his amusement hidden. She told him she was into astrology too, to his even greater surprise and amusement, but again kept his amusement well hidden. She surprised him even more by telling him she went to see a psychiatrist every Saturday morning.

'Why?' he wanted to know.

'It helps,' she said vaguely. *Eet 'elps.*

'Helps with what?'

'It helps me to make sense of myself. Though it's difficult to reveal everything.'

'I see,' he said sympathetically, though he didn't quite.

He was starting to realise that she was somewhat 'damaged', or at least 'neurotic', like a lot of Parisian women, according to Charles, who lived there, but that only made her more attractive to him, brought out his white knight.

'It helps me not to feel so lonely,' she added.

'You're lonely? You live in Paris, but you're lonely?' he asked, as if shocked, but he wasn't really – he knew big cities could be the loneliest places on earth, had experienced it himself in London. Sometimes he even felt lonely here in Dublin, despite being surrounded by friends and colleagues and students ...

'Paris is full of lonely people,' she said. 'Especially women.'

He nodded sagely. 'Haven't you got any friends?'

'I 'ave no family and I 'ave no friends,' she said with another Gallic shrug. 'I'm alone.'

God, her French accent was so sexy! Even her shrugs were sexy. Which was why he refrained from correcting her pronunciation. It reminded him with a mixture of pleasure and pain of Danielle, his former French girlfriend. *Plaisir d'amour!*

'I'll be your friend, if you want,' he said, genuinely moved, and reached for her hand with its twig-thin fingers, on only one of which there was a cheap-looking ring, but she pulled it away.

'No,' she said. 'I'm afraid. I don't want that. I don't want to go to bed with you. Though I do.'

'I wasn't suggesting going to bed,' he protested, taking a swig of Guinness. God, she really was damaged! But that just made the challenge even more interesting. At least she had admitted she wanted to go to bed with him, so that was something.

Later that evening, having kissed her chastely goodnight at her house on campus, he consoled himself in his own flat for a rather unsatisfactory assignation by reading one of Ana's letters, accompanied by a tumbler of Jameson's:

Madrid, 29th July '87

Dear Francis,

How're things? It seems a long time since I wrote the last letter. I've been busy as a bee studying and writing papers but all is finished. After the pressure of these last days at university, I feel completely relaxed, enjoying the leisure.

Maybe you're asking yourself how I got on with my exams. I can only say that all the exams were all right – I don't know any result yet – except English language – I found it quite difficult, short time to do it and it didn't measure what you'd been studying through the year, but what you should have known/learnt by "experience" – can you understand me?

Thanks a lot for sending the photos, they are really nice. It doesn't matter if they are technically perfect or not, I only care whether they can bring back some kind of memories to me or not and I can promise you they can. Your comments on their back are very interesting and no one has done such a thing for me before. I'm glad you wrote them. You make me feel proud – "proud" is not the right word but it'll do, I mean, a photograph is somehow impersonal, even though it's a picture of you. But the fact of writing something on their backs makes them special for me. I think when you say I'm a type of "goddess" you're referring to this. Some persons are very special and you're one of those for me. So I insist that "proud" is not a suitable word, can we say "unique"?

I haven't received any news from your authorities yet, concerning the assistantship. By the way, MJ didn't get the grant to EEUU, she's really upset.

I'd like to know where you'll be spending your holidays and where I ought to write so as to continue our letter contact for these last two months. I'm going to my village tomorrow. I'll be there until the middle of August as I hope my family and I will be able to make a 10-day journey to Asturias (North Spain). Later we'll return to Soto. I think you'd better write to Madrid, although I won't stay there, otherwise I'm afraid letters would take at least ten days

– remember our first letters – and we usually go back to Madrid to visit my grandmother.

Are you thinking that my letter is rather cold? Maybe. Don't be disappointed or something. Maybe the reason is either that I've lost my little fluency to write English or rather the streak of tranquillity that has filled my mind/soul/interior. Don't be upset. "Don't be anything." It's only a feeling. It's neither important nor definite.

Something more positive/optimistic: A smile is on my lips when I'm writing to you. My love and friendship are in my spirit at this very moment.

With affection and love,

Ana (xxxx)

P.D. WRITE SOON!

What happens with your book?

As usual her letter didn't give him the consolation he wanted or rather only gave him a mixture of consolation and disappointment. Yes, it was a bit 'cold', as she acknowledged herself, but there were flashes of warmth mixed in. 'My smile on my lips when I'm writing to you. My love and friendship in my spirit at this very moment. With affection and love.' If only she could be more like that, instead of blowing hot and cold! And yet he still loved her. In spite of himself, he still loved her. Little did he think he'd fall so deeply in love with her when he met her here in Dublin exactly a year ago! She'd well and truly ensnared him. Maybe not on Raglan Road exactly and maybe not in autumn, as Luke Kelly suddenly started singing on the Dubliners cassette he had put on, but certainly with her dark hair and pretty face. Hoist with his own petard indeed! Maybe it was because she *was* so complicated, so elusive, so mixed-up, so difficult, so frustrating. Maybe that was why he'd fallen for her. Because she was such a challenge. But no, there was more to it than that. There was something inside her – in her spirit as she called it – that melted his heart. Maybe it was because she was damaged goods, as he was himself perhaps. Maybe it was just because she was Spanish and reminded him of that legendary waitress in San Sebastian all those years ago. Or maybe it was just because she was pretty. Oh, she was pretty all right. As pretty as a doll. How he missed her now! All the more so because Marie-Hélène had been such a let-down. There was only one way to assuage the pain and that was to write to her. Even if he decided not to send it when he read it over in the cold light of morning. He had to release his feelings somehow. He grabbed his pad and pen from the table, took another slug of Jameson's and started writing:

Dearest Ana …

He invited Marie-Hélène out several times, stubbornly determined to crack her code. She was almost comically negative, pessimistic, downbeat, about the course, about Dublin, about Ireland, about life in general. She told him she felt 'dépaysée' here in Dublin, wanted to go home early. That almost made him throw in the towel, but didn't, made him all the more determined.

He invited her to a performance of *The Importance of Being Earnest* (which they had read in class) with a few other students and she went along, but to his annoyance declined to join them for a drink in Mooney's afterwards, instead went straight back to the college. To his further annoyance, she opted out of the customary coach trip to Glendalough completely, saying she preferred to spend the day on her own. She usually turned up late for their dates and once she failed to turn up at all, leaving him to drink the evening away alone in the Sean O'Casey. There were worse fates, he consoled himself, but he was not best pleased.

In spite of which, he decided to give her one more chance and invited her to a céilí with a group of other students the following Friday evening, which to his surprise she accepted. He had forgiven her for standing him up, reluctantly accepting her excuse that her period had suddenly come and she felt sick. To his further surprise, she actually seemed to enjoy the céilí, dancing enthusiastically the whole evening with a young, ginger-haired, ginger-bearded Dubliner, who looked not totally unlike Luke Kelly, while he sat supping Guinness and watching her with a mixture of possessive pride and, absurdly, jealousy – absurd because he had made it clear he didn't want to dance, hated dancing, was only there for the beer ha ha.

Towards the end of the evening she came and sat beside him and to his delight rested her head on his shoulder. He was tempted to put an arm around her, to show the ginger man she was his, but felt too annoyed with her to do so, even though he knew he was being petty, cutting off his nose to spite his face.

'Are you upset?' she asked, taking a drink of the mineral water he had bought her.

'No,' he protested, taking a swig of Guinness. 'Why should I be upset?'

'You seem displeased.'

'I'm fine,' he insisted, taking another swig of Guinness to emphasise it. 'I'm glad you're enjoying yourself.'

He was far from fine, but he wasn't going to admit that to her. He had no right to feel upset with her though. He had brought her here, he had declined to dance with her, she was obviously enjoying herself for once.

'He's asked me to go for a drink with him afterwards,' she said. 'Would you mind?'

'No,' he said, through gritted teeth. 'Do what you want. You're free.'

'You won't be upset? Sure?'

'Of course I'm sure!' he said impatiently, despite himself. He didn't want her to think he cared. Why was she even asking him? She could go to hell for all he cared!

The ginger man had started hovering nearby, to his further annoyance. *Fuck off, you ginger cunt!* 'Go on, go and enjoy yourself,' he said, giving the ginger man a cold smile and her a nudge with his shoulder, taking another swig of the excellent stout, even though he knew after three pints he was getting drunk. Using the 'c' word, if only to himself, was a sure sign, since he would never dream of using such a word when sober.

Later, at the end of the evening, he gave a lift to a few of the other students back to the college, deliberately avoiding her. *Let her go off with her ginger man!* But the thought that she might go to bed with him made him feel almost physically sick. That was it, he told himself. He'd just ignore her from now on. Give her the cold shoulder. She'd had her chance and she'd blown it.

'Attention!' one of his French passengers shouted as he almost collided with another car.

'N'avez pas peur!' he laughed back, swerving clear, but realising he was hardly fit to drive, not just because of the alcohol in his bloodstream, but because of *her*.

He had to stop thinking about her, he told himself, had to get her out of his system, forget about her. The four girls in the car, French and Spanish, were still a bit high, obviously up for more fun, plus one or two of them were very fanciable. He'd invite them back to his flat for a drink when they arrived, he thought. Put some music on. Have a party. Maybe even get off with one of them. And if MH saw, whenever she came back – if she came back tonight – all to the good. She'd made her bed, so she could lie in it with her ginger man!

He deliberately ignored her for the rest of the weekend. He certainly didn't want to hear about how she got on with her ginger man. To his delight he received a letter from Ana on Saturday morning, which helped to reinforce his decision to avoid her. He felt like a break from the students anyway, fancied a bit of 'me time', so decided to spend the weekend on his own.

On Saturday afternoon he took a train out to one of his favourite places, Sandycove, to visit the James Joyce Martello Tower Museum and go for a walk on the promenade, breathe in some fresh sea air. He felt guilty sneaking off on his own, because a few of the students asked him where he was going, what he was doing, and he gave vague, evasive answers, whereas normally he would be happy to invite them along. He felt guilty because, although he wasn't strictly on duty so was free to do what he liked, he regarded the students not just as students, but as friends.

That evening Charles invited him for a drink in Neary's off Grafton Street, which he gladly accepted, feeling the need of some company after spending most of the day on his own. As usual over several pints of stout they gassed about their seminary days, about life, about death, even more importantly (à la Bill Shankly) about football and about women, including the women on the course, a few of whom Charles rated as 'very fuckable'.

He told Charles about Marie-Hélène and Charles confirmed his suspicion, said she was a typically 'neurotic' Parisienne. Then Charles told him something that shocked him. Apparently that very morning Marie-Hélène had come to his office to *complain* about the course. Even worse, she had complained about *him*, though mostly about the teacher he shared the class with – who happened to be another personal friend of Charles.

'What did she complain about exactly,' he asked,

indignant – he considered himself a star in the classroom, took great pride in his professionalism and his mastery of his subject. No student had *ever* complained about him before, as far as he knew! Quite the reverse …

'Oh, she said you did too much grammar, didn't do enough conversation,' Charles said scornfully.

'Well, of course, we've based the programme on the survey of what the class wanted at the start, so …'

'Yes, yes, I know, don't worry,' Charles interrupted. 'I told her that. Gave her short shrift. Showed her the door. She's a malcontent. I know the type. The British Institute in Paris is full of them. It's part of neurotic woman syndrome. They just need a good shag.'

He laughed and took a slug of stout, but secretly he was furious. That was it – she was dead to him now. Thank God for Ana and the letter nestling in his jacket pocket. As for Marie-Hélène – she was a loser. He almost felt sorry for her. But by going behind his back and complaining about his teaching, she had committed just about the worst crime possible against him. That was a crime he couldn't and wouldn't forgive. A capital offence. She went straight onto the blacklist.

CHAPTER TWENTY

Where the Girls Are So Pretty

The following afternoon, Sunday, he sneaked off alone again and took a train to Malahide, another seaside, north of the city. Unusually for Dublin, it was a hot, sunny day, so after a short stroll along the beach – which was fairly empty despite the weather – he sat on his jacket on the silk-smooth sand, read the Sunday papers, ate the sandwiches and drank the bottle of Guinness he had brought with him for lunch, gazed out at the rare sight of the Irish Sea shimmering in a heat haze beneath a fiery sun, a view that included the islands of Ireland's Eye and Lambay, which seemed to be floating in the haze above the water, started to feel sleepy, rolled up his jacket as a pillow, lay back and fell into a semi-sleep. Anything to avoid thinking about her …

When he came to an hour or so later, he sat up sharply, realising that to his annoyance he had been dreaming about her, dreaming she was with him, and suddenly he felt lonely, missed her, wished she *was* with him, regretted coming here on his own. But then he remembered what Charles had told him yesterday evening and a wave of anger at her swept over him again. He could forgive her almost anything, but not that. She had betrayed him in the worst possible way. Stabbed him in the back. After all the affection and friendship he had shown her! *That* he could neither forgive nor forget.

To make matters worse, his face was burning. He had to get out of the sun, which was still fierce though it was five o'clock, or he'd look like a lobster in class tomorrow! It was a bit too early to return to the college though. He didn't want to meet anyone, certainly didn't want to meet *her*, didn't want to have to socialise, even though he felt lonely. He just wasn't in the mood to socialise, as he did every evening here in Dublin. There was only one thing to do, he decided, standing up stiffly, groggily. Go and have a few pints in Malahide. Hide in Malahide ha ha. Read Ana's letter again and reply. He'd brought paper and pen with him for the purpose. Thank God for Ana, whatever her limitations, he thought fondly, setting off in search of a suitable watering-hole with his jacket slung over his shoulder.

This being civilised Ireland, a suitable watering-hole didn't take long to find. He ordered himself a pint of stout, found a suitable nook, sat down and took out Ana's letter to read again before replying:

Soto, July 29th 87

Dear Francis,

How's tricks? How's Dublin? I miss it!

I'm not exactly a lucky person. Have I told you it before? Firstly, on July 16th I was writing a letter for you just as my daddy brought your letter from Madrid. After reading it, I tore mine. Secondly, I was planning a travel to Benidorm with some friends – Benidorm is the place where Maria José is spending her holidays – during the same week as you were "toying" with the possibility of coming to Spain. Therefore, I didn't encourage you to come. But, what happened? The week before the last week in July the car we were going to travel by broke down. The travel was cancelled.

And thirdly (advice: Keep cool please!) I've been sent to neither London nor to Lincoln, but to … Liverpool. Write everything you're thinking and send it to me please. Have you ever been there? What does the city look like? Can you describe it for me? Honestly, is it a good city to live in? I heard there's a high level of crime there. Is it true? Important: Can you help me to find a place to live? Do you know anybody there? Seriously, I need help. I'm terrified. Anyway, tomorrow I'm going to the British Embassy to find out any thing that can interest me regarding Liverpool.

If you received the letter late, would you mind telephoning me – better in the afternoon, to say to me if you can help me with the accommodation, if I will see you before Sep 7th – i.e. I must be in Liverpool that date, and if possible I will try to go there directly from Madrid. Of course, I admit any kind of suggestion.

I'm enclosing what I know about the schools:

The Blue Coat School (Boys)
Address: Church Road, L15 9EE
Headmaster: Mr. H. Arnold-Craft

New Heys Community Comprehensive School (Mixed)
Address: Heath Road, L19 4TN
Headmaster: Mr. A. McLelland

A good piece of news about this theme: My father wants me to study something while I'm living there and he's going to pay for it. Is it possible to study/read a literature course on smth at Liverpool University?

By the way, what can you tell me about the accent? Is English understandable there?

When you receive this letter you'll be in Dublin. I met you there a year ago. I can't imagine you there on your own.

I know it's a silly thought, even sillier if we consider how often you've been there on your own. Moreover, I can't imagine Ireland without Francis. Maybe you feel the same for Madrid. Do you? Don't feel more "lovesick" when you visit the places we were together, please. Don't gossip about me with your old friend, Rob. I don't mean old in age, of course. Say hello to him and that I haven't received any lines dropped by him yet. I miss Dublin. Can you imagine why? Despite the climate, Dublin was funny, enjoyable, unforgettable.

No more girls, Francis!

I passed all the exams. I got 10 over 10 in Middle English. Thank you for your help. I've just finished my studies at uni. I'm waiting for your advice and help and missing you very much,

Ana (love and kisses xxx)

P.D. 1. I'm very serious when I say – NO GIRLS! (xx)

P.D. 2. I haven't got any kind of information about Liverpool in the British Embassy. (FRUSTRATING).

Of course, you were there. Can you remember it?

Impossible to travel directly to Liverpool. Two possibilities:

i. Going to London and then by train or bus to Liverpool.

ii. Travelling by plane to Manchester and then I haven't found out yet how one can get to Liverpool. From Manchester to Liverpool: about 50 Kms. You can take the ferry from Dublin to Liverpool. Do you have any other suggestion? (Besos)

What a charming letter, he thought, taking a swig of stout. Even though she still wasn't saying what he wanted to hear. *Te quiero. Yes, I'll marry you. I want to spend the rest of my life with you* ... Ah, well, mustn't expect too much. He still had hopes though. Hopes of making her his. Liverpool. What a coincidence! He knew Liverpool well. He had attended the university there for a year to do his postgraduate teacher training fifteen years ago. *Fifteen* years already! He had fond memories of it, felt a certain affection for it, heretical though that might be for a Mancunian such as himself to admit. Of all the places in Britain for her to be sent! It was uncanny. If he was superstitious, he'd suspect there was something fatalistic going on. Maybe there was something going on. *There are more things in Heaven and Earth, Horatio* ...

He took out his paper and pen, eager to reply, to put her right about Liverpool, about their relationship, about love, about life, eager to make arrangements for her journey. He'd meet her at Heathrow, he thought, and drive her to Liverpool himself, spend a few days and nights with her, sort everything out with her. He'd enjoy revisiting Liverpool too and showing her the sights, the university, his digs, the pubs, the docks ...

It was all falling into place nicely. Serendipitously. They were being pulled back together, whether by the stars or pure chance it didn't matter. There was a poem in there somewhere too, he smiled to himself, taking another sup of stout and putting pen to paper:

Dearest Ana ...

He continued to avoid Marie-Hélène for the next few days, apart from speaking to her in class, though even there he adopted a cool, courteous, professional tone with her. Then, during the coffee break on Friday morning, she approached him and told him she had changed her flight from the evening to the early morning on Monday, which was the final day of the course, and asked him if he would give her a lift to the airport. But even if he had wanted to, it was out of the question, since he had to teach at nine o' clock, as he pointed out to her.

'If you liked me, you would,' she said, coquettishly.

'If you change it back, I will,' he said as a sop, feeling sorry for her, feeling guilty about blanking her despite what she had done.

'I'll try,' she said and to his relief moved away.

The following day she came and sat beside him at lunch in the refectory. 'I've changed my ticket,' she informed him.

'Oh, good,' he said, but didn't offer to give her a lift. She'd have to beg if she wanted one! And even then …

'You will give me a lift?' she asked.

'I said I would, so I will,' he shrugged, finishing his lunch. He didn't want to have conversation with her or give her the impression he was 'friends' with her again, things were as they had been.

'What do you do this afternoon?' she inquired.

'You mean, *What are you doing?*' he couldn't resist correcting her. It was a classic French mistake. 'Present continuous for future arrangement, not present simple. We did it in class the other day, remember?' He couldn't resist adding that little dig too, since she had complained about doing too much grammar. Ah, revenge was sweet!

'What are you doing?' she repeated dutifully and he was glad to hear she got the inversion correct.

'I'm playing tennis, actually,' he said.

'I hope you will enjoy,' she said, obviously disappointed.

'Thank you, I will,' he said, standing up and leaving the refectory, feeling guilty but unable to forgive her, wishing he didn't still find her so attractive …

'Thank you for getting your revenge,' she said, sitting beside him.

'Revenge? For what?' he asked, refusing to look at her.

They were at the leaving party, held in one of the university's grand function rooms, with lots of ornate plasterwork, oak flooring and chandeliers. Most of the students were dancing to the disco, with the usual throbbing beat and flashing lights, but he was keeping well away from the dance floor as usual. He had been observing her dancing though, trying not to feel either jealous or guilty, wondering if he was overreacting and being too hard on her.

'What's wrong?' she asked.

'What's wrong?' he repeated sarcastically, taking a swig from his bottle of Guinness and still refusing to look at her. 'I just don't understand you.'

'Why? Because I wouldn't go to bed with you?'

'I don't care about that!' he retorted, though he realised that subconsciously he probably did, it was probably part of the reason for his anger.

'So what I 'ave done wrong?' she asked meekly.

'Charles told me you complained about the class,' he accused, turning and glaring at her. 'Is that true?'

'Yes,' she admitted, bowing her head. 'I'm sorry.'

'You're sorry?' he said scornfully. 'It's too late to be sorry! Do you realise how embarrassing it was for me? I think you're the first student on this course who's ever complained about me! You of all people, after I'd been so friendly to you. Why didn't you speak to me first, if you were unhappy about something?' He really felt like putting the boot in, was even starting to enjoy it.

'I'm sorry,' she said again, head bowed. 'I was wrong. I should 'ave spoken wiz you. It was tactless for me.'

'Oh, it was tactless all right!' he agreed. 'That's putting it nicely. I just don't understand why you did that. You know, you are your own worst enemy. You make problems for yourself. You make trouble for yourself, as well as other people. Charles considers you a troublemaker.' He took a sadistic delight in adding the last remark.

'It's true,' she confessed, head still bowed. 'Sometimes I like to make trouble. I'm silly.'

'I just don't understand,' he said, shaking his head and turning away from her. 'Why? *Why?* That's not how to win friends and influence people!' He couldn't resist adding that little dig too.

'So, you're getting your revenge,' she said, looking up.

'It's not about revenge,' he insisted, though it partly was. 'I'm telling you this for your own good. Because I like you. Or I did like you. That was my bad luck, to like you. I'm telling you in a spirit of friendship. You're too – negative. You alienate people. You push people away with this behaviour. You've alienated *me*.'

'I'm sorry,' she said again, penitent. 'I know you're right. I'll try to change. Can you forgive me? Can we be friends again?'

He took a swig of Guinness from his bottle and paused before answering. 'I suppose so,' he said, his anger suddenly dissipating, perhaps because of the alcohol, perhaps because in spite of everything he still found her annoyingly attractive and not just physically. Also, he realised, he now had power over her and power was always an effective aphrodisiac.

'Thank you,' she said, to his amusement offering him her hand, which he shook, feeling a frisson of erotic pleasure as he did so.

'You don't want to dance?' she inquired.

'I can't – I've got a bad knee,' he said, clutching it. 'You go and dance if you want to.' Thank goodness the ginger man wasn't around, he thought. The party was limited to students, but inevitably there were a few gatecrashers, he had noticed.

'Can I ask you anuzzer favour?'

'What?'

'Will you take me 'ome later?'

'Yes, I suppose so,' he shrugged, taking a swig from his bottle.

He watched her covertly, desirously, as she went back to the dance floor. She was wearing a sexy short-sleeved, yellow blouse and long, flared, white skirt, had her brown hair held back with a silver Alice band, looked like a girl out of an American 50s musical – a type that had always appealed to him, maybe because it suggested a certain old-fashioned, wholesome, apple-pie innocence.

He was surprised she had asked him to take her home, though also secretly pleased, wondered if she was going to ask him to spend the night with her. The thought excited him. But it was too late, he told himself. It was the last night. There was no point. And there was Ana to think of. He didn't want to be unfaithful to Ana. *No more girls, Francis!*

Observing her twirling sexily on the dance floor, he wasn't sure if he'd be able to resist though …

After the party had finished and he had helped to clear up and said goodnight to everyone, he walked her back to her house as promised. He was tempted to put his arm around her, especially as she was bare-armed and there was a cool night breeze blowing across the cobbled courtyards, but he didn't. He was afraid of becoming too excited, didn't want to go to bed with her, didn't want to be unfaithful to Ana, who's admonition, '*No more girls, Francis!*', kept ringing in his head. So instead he offered her his jacket and to his relief she let him drape it around her shoulders, then leaned in to him shoulder to shoulder as they walked across the cobbles, which was about as much physical contact as he could endure.

When they reached her house – the 'houses' were just great, eighteenth-century, almost soot-black, granite blocks divided into somewhat spartan student flats – they stopped and he waited while she fished her key from her bag and opened the heavy front door, then turned to him.

'Would you like to 'ave some coffee?' she invited.

No more girls, Francis! No more girls!

'I'd better not,' he forced himself to say, with every ounce of willpower he could muster, after a few moments' hesitation. 'It's late and I have to teach tomorrow. Thanks.'

'Eh bien, bon nuit,' she said, not seeming too disappointed. 'Merci.'

'Bon nuit,' he said, leaning forward and kissing her on both cheeks, then hurrying away before she could ask again or he could change his mind. *No more girls, Francis!*

He didn't go straight back to his own house though. Instead he went for a walk around the cricket field, enjoying the cool night air and, apart from the occasional muffled sound of traffic on Nassau Street behind the high perimeter wall, the silence. He needed a few minutes of solitude to come back down to earth, try to regain some equilibrium, try to put her out of his mind, he told himself.

He couldn't get her out of his mind though. He couldn't help wondering if he'd regret turning her down. He was even tempted to go back to her house and knock on the window before it was too late, before she had fallen asleep. She'd probably already be in bed though. It was already too late. Anyway, Ana kept appearing in front of him like a hologram, smiling in that mischievous way of hers, wagging her finger and silently mouthing her refrain: *No more girls, Francis!*

The following afternoon, as promised, he gave her a lift to the airport, along with two other French students, having carried her suitcase to the car for her, then into departures. There, while waiting to check in, she showed him her passport. He took it and looked at the photo.

'It's terrible,' she observed, in her morose way. 'The reality is even worse though.'

'It's not,' he laughed, handing the passport back to her. God, she was so negative!

She stayed close to him until it was time to go through the departure gate. When the time came, he gave her a hug and kissed her on the cheeks.

'Au revoir,' she said. 'Thank you for everything. I won't forget you.'

'Au revoir,' he smiled, touched, but shocked to see tears in those crossed, pale-blue eyes.

CHAPTER TWENTY-ONE

It's not the leaving of Liverpool

A few days after returning to London from Dublin, he met Ana at Gatwick. He almost didn't recognise her, she had changed her appearance so much: green overalls, green and white striped shirt, canvas shoes, bangles and beads and, most surprising of all, a new, spiky, punkish hairstyle. She looked like a pixie.

He kissed her on the cheeks and hugged her, resisting the impulse to comment on her new image and glad she didn't ask him to, because he wasn't sure he liked it, preferred the old Ana. Anyway, he'd get used to it, he supposed.

That night they stayed in a bed and breakfast within easy reach of the M1, the plan being to drive to Liverpool the next day. To his annoyance, their room was twin-bedded, even though he had booked a double.

'I will sleep here,' she said, pointing to one of the beds. 'Ju will sleep there.'

He laughed, hoping she wasn't serious, and to his relief, after they returned from a meal and a drink in a nearby pub, she let him join the beds together. However, she wouldn't let him touch her, saying she was tired and wanted to sleep, which he reluctantly accepted. She even insisted they change into their nightclothes separately in the bath-room, which for him meant just stripping to his underwear.

'Please knock before you come back in,' she told him, which he obediently did, irritated but amused.

She then went into the bathroom herself and re-entered the room in a rather sexy pink nightdress. It didn't make sleeping beside her without touching her any easier for him. She got into bed and fell asleep quickly – or pretended to. He pretended to sleep himself, but lay awake for a while, wondering what he was doing here, why he was lying in a strange bed in a strange room on the outskirts of London next to this strange Spanish girl who wouldn't let him touch her, whom he hardly recognised any more from the girl he had met in Dublin just over a year ago.

There was something dreamlike about it. It couldn't be a dream though, because he wasn't asleep yet. But maybe it *was* a dream. Maybe *life* was a dream. Maybe he wasn't who he thought he was. Maybe he was asleep somewhere else, dreaming that he was awake, dreaming that he was dreaming.

He turned his head to look at her. She was asleep or seemed to be, on her front as usual. His heart went out to her. She looked so pretty, so sweet, so innocent, so fragile. He wanted to put an arm around her, but didn't dare, turned away again.

This was a form of torture. How on earth had he landed here? But he had made his bed himself so had to lie in it. Or did he? The bizarre thought suddenly flicked through his mind: he wasn't a prisoner, he could just get up, get dressed, sneak out of the room, out of the house, get in his car and drive away, drive home, back to reality, abandon her here.

He turned to look at her again and felt a stab of guilt that he could have had such a cruel thought. He couldn't do that to her! In spite of everything, he loved her, could never deliberately hurt her. God, it was ironic – he had set out to seduce her, but *she* had seduced *him*!

No, sleep was the only solution. If only he could sleep. Ah, yes, to sleep, perchance to dream …

The next day, after breakfast, he drove her to Liverpool, chatting and listening to some of his favourite Irish music on the car stereo: the Fureys, Moving Hearts, the Dubliners, Paul Brady, Christy Moore, Luka Bloom, the Wolfe Tones … Fortunately, she liked Irish music, which he always made a point of introducing to the students in Dublin, talking about it, taking them to concerts and gigs in pubs, playing songs in class as teaching aids or – especially in the case of the Wolfe Tones – using them to illustrate Irish history.

He enjoyed the journey, because she seemed more friendly than the evening before, chatting and joking with him, even allowing him to put an arm around her or hold hands with her occasionally, even letting him kiss her on the lips once. However, when they went into their room in their hotel – the Lord Nelson behind Lime Street station – and she saw a double bed, she suddenly froze.

'What's wrong?' he asked, though he had an intimation.

'I don't want to sleep with ju,' she said. 'Ju should look for another room.'

'I'm not going to look for another room,' he laughed emptily and put his bag down to emphasise it. 'You can look for another room if you want.'

Seeing the look on her face – a mixture of fury, terror and desperation – he regretted his last remark and suddenly felt sorry for her. But there was absolutely no way he was going to look for another room! Apart from anything else, he didn't want to pay for *two* rooms. So if she wanted to walk out, she could, though if she did he would be crushed with guilt, would have to follow her, couldn't leave her to her own devices on her very first day in this strange, foreign city.

'Look,' he said, sitting on one side of the bed and patting it. 'There's no problem. I'll sleep this side, you sleep that side. There's plenty of room for us both.'

For a few moments she continued to stand there, just inside the open door, her bag in her hand, looking both terrified and furious. He was afraid she really might turn and walk out. But suddenly he felt angry himself. This was ridiculous! Why had she asked him to take her to Liverpool, if she didn't want him to sleep with her? She was making him feel like some sort of pervert or predator! If she did leave, he wasn't sure he *would* follow her.

'Don't worry, I won't rape you,' he joked, though as soon as he said it he regretted it, especially as she didn't laugh or even crack a smile.

To his relief, she came in, shut the door, put her bag on the chair and lay down on 'her' side of the bed, curled up, facing away from him.

'What do you want to do?' he asked, lying on 'his' side of the bed, but leaving a clear distance between them.

'I need to rest,' she said. 'If ju don't mind.'

'OK,' he agreed, turning towards her and resting on his elbow. 'Me too. Later we can go out for a drink and something to eat if you like. Have a look around.' *He* would definitely want a drink later!

'Ju are in charge,' she said.

Was that a joke, he wondered with a half-smile? If only it were true! He didn't feel as if he were in charge. Quite the opposite. He felt like putty in her hands. Or a puppet. Somehow she seemed to have acquired power over him. How had that happened? Well, he knew how. He was in love with her. And he couldn't fall out of love with her, no matter how hard he tried, no matter how much she pushed him away.

If he was in any doubt, he only had to look at her back as

she lay breathing softly, almost inaudibly, beside him – so slim, so slender, so small, so childlike – and he felt a rush of protective love for her. How could he ever have thought of abandoning her? Never. He could never hurt her!

Suddenly, he felt an overwhelming desire to touch her. Hesitantly, he laid a hand very lightly on her back. To his relief, she didn't wake up or object. Slowly, he moved his hand up and down and round and round, caressing her back lightly. She didn't move. Whatever happened, he decided, he would look after her, take care of her, protect her. It didn't matter if she didn't want to be his lover or have sex with him. He had brought her here. He was responsible for her. She had been given to him. He would do what he had to do.

As if to seal the thought, he bent down and brushed her ear, in which she wore a tiny, diamond-like stud, with his lips, as lightly as a butterfly's wings might do, catching an erotic whiff of her scent, and whispered as he did so, 'Te quiero'.

Then he lay back on the pillow, closed his eyes and tried to sleep.

To sleep, perchance to dream …

The next day he went with her to visit the Blue Coat School, one of the schools she would be teaching at. It was a boys' only grammar school and he couldn't help thinking what lucky boys they were to have such a pretty young Spanish teacher! There had certainly been no pretty young female teachers at the seminary, where all women were regarded as agents of the devil. It brought home to him what a different world that had been, what a weird, warped, otherworldly world.

NON SIBI SED OMNIBUS

That was the motto on the school sign at the entrance.

'Can you translate?' he asked, stopping the car in the gateway.

'Can ju?' she returned the ball to him.

'It means, *Not for oneself, but for all.*'

'Ju are clever.'

'I have my moments,' he laughed. 'It's a good motto, I suppose.'

The seminary may have been a world apart, but it had got him a top grade in A-level Latin, he reflected wryly, driving in and parking. Not that he had ever expected to use it to impress a pretty young Spanish girl!

The main school building was impressive, looked to him more like a public school than a state school, or even a 'great house' or stately home, built in an ornate Victorian – or was it Edwardian? – style with an imposing clock tower in the middle. They stopped to admire it before going in. It reminded him of the school in *To Serve Them All My Days*, one of his favourite books and television programmes, which he had told her about. He could tell she was impressed, but intimidated too, having become more and more tense all morning. The fact that there were no pupils about somehow made it seem all the more imposing. He would have been slightly intimidated going in there for an interview himself, he thought, but didn't want to give her any hint of that.

'Vamos,' he said jauntily, ushering her in.

Afterwards he took her to her lodgings in a large, Victorian, six-bedroom house on Queens Drive. The landlord and landlady, Dennis and Gladys, gave them tea and biscuits, then offered her a choice of two rooms. He advised her to choose the bigger one, even though it would cost a bit more, so she did. It had everything she needed: a bed (a double bed he noticed, not that he'd ever be able to share it with her, sadly, even if she would let him), wardrobe, dressing-table, bookcase, desk, armchair and, he was glad to see, an electric kettle.

He helped her to move in, then took her to a nearby supermarket to buy some groceries, some of which she was allowed by Gladys to put in the American-size fridge in the large kitchen. It all reminded him of his own days as a student, including here in Liverpool, evoking the mixed emotions of excitement and loneliness he remembered feeling at being out in the big bad world on his own. It made him feel even more protective towards her, a foreigner and female, even though she was making it so difficult for him to show.

After moving her in, he drove her to his favourite part of the city, the docks, which were in the process of being redeveloped, and they went for a walkabout. He told her how the docks evoked in him happy childhood memories, because it was where they used to sail from for summer holidays in Ireland as kids. That was probably why he liked places like this, why he liked ships and boats and the sea so much, he told her, even though he was very much a 'landlubber' who almost felt seasick just looking at the sea.

He had to explain the expression 'landlubber' to her and, like the good student she was, she took a notebook out of her bag and wrote it in. By now they were sitting on a bench overlooking the water, even though there was a chilly breeze blowing and she was wearing only a light white mac. He had offered her the sports jacket he was wearing, but she had declined. He wanted to put his arm around her, but didn't dare.

She asked him what 'lubber' meant and for a moment he was stumped. 'Good question,' he laughed, to give himself thinking time.

'Ju don't know?' she said, eyebrows raised.

'I'm not sure,' he admitted, racking his brains. 'Maybe you should do it for homework!' That was always a good teacher's get-out-of-jail card when you didn't know the answer to a question.

'I catch you out,' she smiled impishly.

Good use of phrasal verb there, he thought – well, she was about to become an English teacher.

'Hm, at a guess I'd say it means something like "clumsy" or "awkward" person,' he offered, hating to be defeated on matters linguistic. 'It sounds like Old English or Middle English. Though I'm just wondering if it could have some affiliation with "lover", perhaps be a corruption of "lover". "Lubber", "lover". In which case, it would mean something like "land lover". I'll have to check it in my Oxford Dictionary when I get home.'

'Gracias, profesor,' she said, with another impish smile.

'De nada,' he laughed.

They were both silent, a silence broken only by the squealing and screeching of a few gulls and the muffled hum of distant traffic. He wanted to talk to her about sleeping arrangements tonight, but was afraid of upsetting her and spoiling the good atmosphere between them. But it was something that had to be broached sooner or later …

'About tonight,' he said eventually, steeling himself and turning towards her. 'Are you going to stay in the hotel with me?'

She said nothing, continued to gaze straight ahead. Again the demon appeared on his shoulder and whispered in his ear: If she refuses, just get up and leave her here. Walk away. Go back to London. It'll serve her right. She's just using you. Making a fool of you. Playing with you. *No! No, I can't do that! No, no, no! Go away!*

'Do ju want me to?' she asked, finally turning to look at him, so that their eyes met.

'Of course I do,' he smiled. 'I love you.' *Though I wish I didn't.* 'If you don't want to, I'll just go back to London tonight.' *And that will be it. I'll never see you again. Finito.*

Immediately, he saw that familiar look of terror in her eyes and he regretted his last remark. But he meant it. The thought of staying the night in the hotel on his own, while she was just a mile or so away, sent a shot of poison through his system.

'Can ju give me some time to decide?' she asked. It wasn't the answer he wanted.

You see! She's just using you. Messing you about! Wasting your time! Toying with you! She's a cockteaser! There's no future with her. She says she loves you, but she doesn't really. If she did, she'd be mad keen to stay with you. Begging to stay with you! Cut your losses and leave her. Dump her. Do it now. Just get up and walk away. Save yourself a whole lot of grief.

'You need to decide now,' he said sternly.

She glared at him with a mixture of fear and fury in her eyes, so that he felt himself starting to soften, was tempted to tell her to ignore what he had said about going back to London, she could go back to her house if she wanted and he'd stay alone in the hotel, see her in the morning. But that would be a mistake, he knew, the easy way out, like running away. This needed to be resolved *now*. It was now or never, to quote Elvis. Either she wanted to be with him or she didn't. Either she loved him or she didn't.

He locked onto her eyes with a stare of his own in an ocular duel, a battle of wills, one he was determined to win, though all he really wanted to do was throw his arms around her and hug her. Which of them would blink first, he wondered, almost as if he were a spectator on the sidelines, as if it were just a game, though it was deadly serious, could spell the end of their relationship?

'OK,' she said eventually. 'I'll stay with ju.'

'Speak. Say anything.'

They were having a drink in the Adelphi Hotel, another grand, even palatial, Edwardian building in the city centre. It wasn't the sort of place he usually liked to drink in, preferring proper pubs, but she had expressed a wish to go in, so he had humoured her. The external architecture was mightily impressive, but inside, as well as being cavernous, it was a case of faded glory – all slightly shabby furnishings and dim lighting. He didn't mind too much though, because they served a good pint of Guinness, a first sup of which he had just imbibed with a gasp of pleasure. She was drinking coffee.

'How's your mum?' he asked, taking his cue from her.

'She's worried about me,' she said.

'I'm sure she is,' he said. 'Does she know I'm with you?'

'Si. She knows, even though I didn't tell her.'

'Mother's intuition,' he laughed.

'She told me on the phone, "Don't sleep with him!".'

'Ah, I see,' he smiled. 'That's why you don't want to sleep with me. Because Mama said so!'

'No. Ju know why.'

'Why?'

'I'm scared.'

'You're repressed.'

'Si. I know.'

He was surprised to hear her agree, though she had admitted it before.

'You know you will always have problems with men, if you won't have sex. I mean, even when you're married. Or are you saving yourself for marriage?'

'I'm not saving myself for marriage,' she blushed. 'I'm just scared.'

'We don't have to have sex tonight,' he said. 'We can just sleep together.' He could see she was anxious about it – but then she was always anxious – so he wanted to reassure her. The Guinness was helping him to feel mellow.

'Maybe I'll never be married,' she said, ignoring what he had said.

'Why not?' he asked, shocked and saddened, though he knew there was no reason to be really.

'I think I'll be a career woman.'

'So you're going to climb up the greasy pole?' he laughed, then had to explain the expression. He was amused because she was so utterly unlike his image of a 'career woman'. He certainly couldn't imagine her in a power suit, bossing people around. She was so quiet, so shy, so nervous, so timid, so diffident, so *small*!

'Anyway,' he said, after she had finished studiously writing the expression in her notebook, 'even if you don't get married, you'll want a boyfriend, won't you?'

'Maybe, but it's OK if I don't.'

'What about Chema?' He had been wondering whether to ask her this since meeting her at the airport, but held back, not sure he wanted to know.

'It's finished.'

'Oh? Why?' He was pleased, but tried not to show it.

'He told me he wasn't in love with me.'

'Oh.'

'My friends think he just wants to have sex with me.'

He's barking up the wrong tree there!

'I see. So how do you feel about it?'

'I'm hurt, naturally.'

That wasn't quite the answer he wanted. 'I don't care about him,' would have been better. But hey, it was progress of sorts. It left the door open for him. Did it? He was kidding himself! She was still shutting him out. She wasn't exactly flinging the door open to him, anyway.

'MJ has a new boyfriend,' she informed him, somewhat irrelevantly.

'Oh, really? What's he like?'

'He's fat and ugly.'

'Oh, dear!' he laughed. 'So why …?'

'He's well off.'

'Oh, I see!' he shook his head and laughed again.

'She's started wearing provocative clothes.'

'Really? So she doesn't look like a librarian any more?' A mental image of the new, sexy MJ popped into his mind's eye, but he dismissed it guiltily.

'I'm jealous of her,' she said, ignoring his little joke.

I'm a tiny bit jealous of her new boyfriend. No I'm not. Stop it! Behave!

'Why?'

'She's so free.'

'You're not free?'

'My parents make me like a prisoner. My father especially. They try to give me a 2 am curfew. They locked me in the flat once when I wanted to go out with friends, because it was nearly midnight.'

'Midnight is quite late,' he grinned, teasing her. 'Though not in Spain, I know. So what did you do?'

'I was hysterical with rage.'

'Oh, dear. I'm sorry. I didn't realise it was that bad.'

'Nobody can tell me what to do!' she declared suddenly. 'Nobody is my boss!' Her eyes blazed.

God, maybe she wasn't as timid or docile as he thought! Not such a church mouse. She had a feisty side to her. He was realising that more and more. He wasn't sure he liked it. On the other hand, it did add a certain spice to her personality. And it meant she could stand up for herself when necessary perhaps. Which had to be a good thing.

'I'll try to remember that,' he laughed, draining his glass.

'Do ju want another drink?' she asked.

'Yes, but I think you're tired, aren't you?' he said.

'Si. But if ju want …'

'It's OK,' he said.

'Ju are sure?'

'I'm sure. Vamos.'

That night she slept in her shirt and knickers, not having her nightdress with her. As soon as she got into bed beside him, she turned away, curled up and went to sleep. He wanted to spoon up to her, but didn't dare. It was torture, just like last night. And the night before. And the night before that. Why was he doing this to himself, he wondered? Putting himself in this stupid situation time and time again? She wouldn't even let him touch her! He had to end it. He loved her, but he had to end it. He'd write to her and tell her when he got home. It would be better for them both. In the end.

Then, to his amazement, he woke up early in the morning to find her asleep in his arms. She must have snuggled up to him for warmth – or comfort – during the night. A surge of joy went through him. He pulled her closer to him and kissed her forehead lightly, then the rest of her face, including her closed eyelids. To his relief, she didn't object or resist. Encouraged, he slipped his hand under her shirt and slowly let it travel up to her breasts, started to squeeze one of them gently.

'Ju are hurting me,' she murmured sleepily.

'Oh, I'm sorry,' he said, removing his hand quickly.

'I think my menstruation has just begun,' she said.

'Oh, I'm sorry,' he said again, letting go of her.

'Let me check,' she said, sitting up and pulling down the covers. There were some specks of blood on the sheet. 'I will need some things,' she said.

For a moment he didn't know what she meant.

'Shall I go and try to get something?' he offered, though he knew the shops probably wouldn't be open yet, especially as it was Sunday morning, and he felt embarrassed at the very thought of having to buy such things, had never had to do so before as far as he could remember.

To his relief, though, she said she could wait, would go for a shower, which she did. While she was in the bathroom, he lay in bed, trying not to sink into a slough of despond. It was hopeless though, he thought gloomily. It was as if there was a conspiracy against him! A conspiracy by the forces of evil. It was time to admit defeat. It just wasn't meant to be. Leave her. Leave her here in Liverpool. *It's not the leaving of Liverpool, my darling, but when I think of thee.* Ah, yes, that would give the song a new twist, if he left her here, if this was the final curtain, the parting of the ways …

When they were both ready, he took her to a supermarket where she found what she needed, then to her house. He went to the front door with her and started to say his good-byes. She asked him in for a cup of tea, but he declined, said he wanted to get on the road, had stuff to do for work tomorrow and so on. Secretly though he just wanted to go, leave, end it, get back to his real life.

'Thank you for the present,' she said. He had given her a Christy Moore LP – *Ride On*, one of his favourites – before they left the hotel. 'Thank you for everything.'

'Look after yourself,' he said, tight-throated.

'What will I do without my mama to look after me?' she said.

'You're a big girl now,' he laughed. 'You have to look after yourself. Good luck with the teaching. Hasta luego.'

To his own surprise, he was having to fight back tears. He just wanted to go, though it broke his heart to leave her, because what he really wanted to do was stay with her, look after her, take care of her, protect her, keep her safe.

'I better go,' he said.

'Will ju come and visit me?' she asked.

For a moment he wasn't sure what she meant. 'You mean here, in Liverpool?'

'Si. Soon.'

'Sure,' he shrugged, tears pricking his eyes, though he knew he wouldn't, couldn't …

'In a couple of weeks?'

'I'll try. I better go.'

He wondered if he should give her a hug, decided it would be ridiculous not to, so put his arms around her, pulled her towards him and kissed her on the cheeks. Were those tears in her eyes, too?

'Te quiero,' he said, and it was true, he told himself, as he hurried back to his car, even though it might be the last time he said it to her. *This could be the last time. It would be the last time. It had to be the last time.*

When he got back into his car, he gave her a smile, blew her a kiss and signalled her to go in. She blew him a tentative kiss back and went in, closing the door behind her. Closing a door in his heart too.

He slipped a Clancys cassette into the stereo and drove away quickly, blinking back tears.

So fare thee well, my own true love,
For when I return, united we will be;
It's not the leaving of Liverpool that grieves me
But my darling when I think of thee.

CHAPTER TWENTY-TWO

London Town

Days pass. Back to reality. Back to Rania. Back to work. New term. New year. Liverpool seems like a dream. A dream within a dream. The strangest, most confusing of dreams. I try to put it out of my mind. I try to forget. But I can't. I start a letter to her, telling her I can't continue. But I don't post it. I can't bring myself to. I almost drop it in the postbox at college one day, but stop myself at the last moment. Signed, sealed, but not delivered. What's wrong with me? Why am I so weak-willed, so lily-livered, so soft? Why can't I stop loving her? Ray Charles knows all about it! Or whoever wrote the song. Maybe I won't write to her. Maybe just let it die a natural death. Maybe that's the best way. The least cruel way. Or is it just a coward's way? I don't know. I can't win.

At home we have a new lodger. His name is Farouq. He's thirty years old, black-haired, hirsute, swarthy and stocky. He's always in T-shirt, jeans and trainers. He's an Afghan refugee. He's also a pious Muslim and prays five times a day on his prayer mat. He says he was a lecturer in physics at Kabul University. Claims he had a house with eighteen rooms in Kabul and a Mercedes car, but his house was destroyed by Russian bombs. He lost everything. His brother and brother-in-law were killed. He escaped to the mountains and was with the mujahideen for five years. His main work was helping to disarm chemical weapons. But he was arrested by the Russians and tortured. As a result he has heart and kidney problems.

'If I won a fortune, I'd buy a missile for the Kremlin,' he says with a grin.

I laugh, but somewhat nervously. I quite like him, but I'm a bit wary of him. He has a glint in his eyes that I don't like so much. He tells me Rania isn't a good Muslim, because she doesn't pray five times a day like him. He hasn't yet realised that Rania is not your typical, subdued, submissive Muslim girl, but someone who'd argue with the prophet himself if he suddenly appeared in our living room, as I often tell her. To which she usually retorts something like, 'Yes, I would! Nobody tells me what to think or what to believe! I believe what I want to believe!' Fair play to her, I suppose. Though it makes it almost impossible to live with her.

Occasionally Farouq tries to engage me in theological debate, knowing I'm an atheist. I try to avoid these conversations, having learned that you can't argue with people who believe in gods or ghosts or fairies, since such beliefs in my view are *irrational*, but sometimes I can't escape. Sometimes I can't resist.

'You can prove the existence of god by looking at molecular structure,' he proclaims one day. 'Nucleus, protons and neutrons. Movement, force, energy.'

I'm immediately on the back foot because my science education consisted of one year at grammar school before I went to the seminary and I remember almost nothing. Maybe that's because I wasn't interested in science then or because the physics teacher was a sadistic bully straight out of the Pink Floyd songbook. Maybe that's why I wasn't interested. No, even at that early age my mind was on supposedly 'higher' things.

'But that's just electrical,' I protest, not really knowing what I'm talking about.

All I know is I can't believe some super-scientist called God designed it all. And electricity is just a force of nature as I understand it. There's nothing supernatural about it. Quite the opposite in fact. Which I put to him.

'You are a materialist!' he declares triumphantly, as if that's checkmate, end of argument, game over.

'And you're a fantasist!' I'm tempted to shoot back but think better of it. 'I suppose so,' I laugh nervously instead and make my escape.

Back to college. Mixed feelings about it as always. On the one hand, the long summer holiday is over (though I work in Dublin during some of it) and it's back to work, back to the daily grind. On the other hand, there's a certain buzz about meeting up with colleagues again, getting organised for the year ahead and meeting students old and new. We male teachers particularly look forward to meeting the female students old and new. At least Geoff, Mark and I do. We have a good chat while we're testing new students, during which process we also secretly grade the girls, not just on their English, but also their looks, marking them out of ten. It's naughty, but just a bit of harmless lad fun and helps to pass the time, relieve the tedium.

I tell Geoff a little bit about Ana and he tells me he's still with his French girlfriend, Corinne. 'It's nice,' he says, 'but I'd be glad if it finished tomorrow.' He's obviously fed up with her and is looking for a replacement. Or an addition to his harem. I know he's been after Bea, who's one of my students and who I fancy myself, so I put a marker down by telling him I saw her earlier and invited her for a drink, which she accepted. I also make a point of informing him she told me she'd been accepted in some ballet school *and* was modelling for the fashion department. Well, she is Spanish. And she is gorgeous.

If I'm honest, I don't really fancy her any more, partly because she's made it clear she doesn't want a 'relationship' with me and partly because of Ana, whom I love, or think I love, and whom I haven't completely given up on, despite the letter I've written telling her it's over hidden in my brief-case. I don't want Geoff to get off with Bea though, that would kill me, so I suppose it's a case of sour grapes on my part. Not for the first time I reflect to myself how sex makes us behave so out of character, so *venally*. I must admit when sex is involved I become uncharacteristically ruthless and all my innate niceness goes out the window. *All is fair in love and war.* I feel somewhat the same about Ana. I may have decided I don't want her or can't have her, but the thought of another man having her brings out an almost patholog-ical jealousy in me. Which is one reason I may yet fight to keep her.

One of the new female students is a Norwegian girl, to whom we both award a nine out of ten for looks. 'She's defi-nitely going in my Advanced class, even if she's a beginner!' Geoff jokes and I laugh, thinking I'll encourage him just to keep him away from Bea. Not that either of us would ever actually misplace a student just because we fancied them – we're far too professional for that, even though we joke about it. 'She probably is advanced, being Scandinavian,' I suggest, hoping I'm right. 'You know, I've never had a Scandinavian,' I add. 'I mean, in bed, not in class.' 'I've had a few,' Geoff reveals. 'Including a couple of Norwegians, as it happens. And I can tell you, Norwegian women are very animal!' 'Really?' I say, genuinely surprised. 'I probably shouldn't tell you that!' he laughed. 'Now you'll make a play for her.' 'No, she's all yours,' I laugh and add pointedly: 'I'll stick with the Latins.'

Not that I limit myself to Latins. I quite like German women, too, for example, whereas I know Geoff doesn't. He doesn't like 'Krauts', as he calls them, male or female. Whereas I like all women. I like Oriental women even more than Latins. It's probably got something to do with my past life. But then again, I don't think I'm any randier than the average red-blooded male. I reckon both Geoff and Mark, my South African colleague, are even randier than I am. As is Andy Jones, a new member of staff and another 'player', as he refers to both himself and me, though it's not an expression I'd apply to myself.

It's always interesting to find out what colleagues have done during the summer. You see another side of them, as they do of you, though most colleagues know now that I work in Dublin every summer, have done so for more than ten years, so they don't ask me what I've done, just 'How was Dublin?' or 'Did you do your Dublin thing again this year?'. Sometimes I think it must sound boring, I ought to do something entirely different, just to give them a surprise, even make something up, a trip to Timbuktu perhaps, but of course I don't, because I enjoy Dublin so much, in fact it's the highlight of my year. Six weeks of wine, women and song! Well, stout rather than wine, not that I'm averse to a glass of wine. Or should I say averse 'from'? I suppose I should, since that's what I told one of the students in Dublin this year, a pedantic, punctilious, generously-bosomed, middle-aged French teacher of English whom we dubbed Madame Moot Point, that being her favourite expression.

But I digress. I don't need to ask Big Ed where he has been, because like me he does the same thing every summer, goes on a retreat in his French monastery, the one where he claims he went into hiding after absconding from MI5. But I ask him anyway. Not that his retreat sounds like any retreat I was ever on – and I've been on a few in my time.

From what he says, his French monastery sounds like a lot more fun! Except I suppose for the absence of women. Unless he's not confessing all …

Margo, my American colleague, tells me she has been to America to see her mother *and* taught on a creativity course in Spain, where apparently a lot of 'screwing' went on. Keith Johnson tells me he went to Turkey for three weeks, staying in a village by the sea, and says it was 'very good. Better than Greece because better scenery. The people were very nice too.' I dare say he was with a woman and did a lot of 'screwing', too, since he's a jungly, macho sort of bloke, but I don't ask him and he doesn't vouchsafe. He's not a 'player', as far as I know. Even Grey Ken, the head of department and candidate for most boring man in the world, whom I bump into in the General Education office, has been somewhere exotic, namely Iceland. Or does he say Greenland? He starts chunnering on about geysers anyway. I don't really listen because I'm desperate to get away from him before he asks me about Dublin and then about my writing, as he inevitably does, so I have to toss him my stock replies.

It doesn't take long for me to have a run-in with Bertha, our 'Section Leader', as apparently we are supposed to call her now. She's large, she's Jewish, she's bossy. I negotiate a reasonably good timetable with her and the very next day I find a memo in my pigeonhole telling me she wants to take two hours of my very best class off me and give them to Roy Seaman. WHO ISN'T EVEN AN ENGLISH TEACHER! He teaches drama. And he's GAY! Well, being gay doesn't matter. I quite like him actually, in a purely platonic way. But he's not having two hours of my afternoon Proficiency class!

I tell Mark in the staffroom and he gives me his usual hardnosed reaction: 'Just tell her to fuck off.' (He has a pathological hatred for her.) Well, I don't tell her that, but

I do tell her I'm very, very, very unhappy. What really gets under my skin is that I know she's only trying to do this for some ulterior, self-serving motive of her own. Anyway, eventually, when she sees how dischuffed I am, she relents, though probably only because she knows I'm one of her strongest teachers and is afraid of alienating me.

When I tell Geoff during enrolments later, in between chatting about our usual topics, women and football, I have to laugh at his response: 'Well done, mate! That's how you have to deal with Bertha. Stand up to her. She's a bully. I'm starting as I mean to go on. In fact, I feel rather aggressive towards people like Bertha and Harriet Jenkins. They're too big for their boots.' Harriet Jenkins is 'deputy section leader' and backed Bertha up in her attempt to swipe two hours of my best class off me, to my great annoyance. I don't mind Harriet too much, but she's now blotted her copybook. She's a bit of a bossyboots too, and, according to Geoff anyway, a 'stirrer'. I'm a bit shocked, because she's usually very supportive of me. I suspect she likes to assert her power now and again, just to put me in my place – especially as I'm a man. Like Bertha though, she knows I'm one of the strongest members of staff, so she daren't upset me too much.

Rania remains as difficult as ever. I'm really starting to think there's something mentally or psychologically wrong with her. She has wild mood swings and flies into violent rages over the most trivial things – sometimes literally violent, because she will fling whatever's to hand at me, a shoe, a cup, a telephone. She's even tried to attack me with a carving knife and a pair of dressmaking scissors! One minute she's an angel, all sweetness and light, five minutes later she's a demon, screaming a torrent of abuse at me. It's some sort of personality disorder, if not an actual mental illness.

I don't think I can live with it much longer. I have to get

away from her. Yet I just can't bring myself to leave her or ask her to leave. I can't send her back to her bullying family. God knows what they'd do to her to punish her for running away from them in the first place. They'd make her life absolute hell. They might even do something terrible to her. Or drive her to do something terrible to herself. She might do it to herself anyway, if I chuck her out. I couldn't live with that on my conscience. So I really am well and truly trapped.

Her family are all a bit mad. They go from one crisis, one melodrama, to another, as if in their very own soap opera. One Saturday evening Rania gets a phone call from her mother saying her younger sister Karidah has been missing since Thursday. Mumkin, as they call her – or the begum as I call her – is wailing and weeping on the phone, begging Rania to come. That means I have to drive Rania there, so bang goes my Saturday evening in the Victoria having a few pints and listening to some Irish music with my students. I'm not happy, but I am genuinely worried that something really bad might have happened to Karidah, so I bite the bullet and go.

When we get there, the begum is in hysterics. It's emerged that Karidah has been staying at her elder brother Rafiq's house, because she's had a big row with the begum. The begum, instead of being relieved she's safe and well, is angrily accusing Karidah of having an affair with her own brother, even though he's married, denouncing her as a 'scamp'. The brother and his wife are even bigger 'scamps'. They're all in it together.

'I'm fed up with this family!' she wails, running into her bedroom. 'I can't take it any more! I'm going back to Guyana!'

I can't help being secretly amused, because this is what she always threatens whenever she feels wronged. Rania, her sisters and I follow her into the bedroom, where she has started pulling her clothes out of the wardrobe and throwing them on the bed as if to pack. Rania and her sisters stop her, lie her on the bed and manage to calm her down. I take it as my cue to escape to the Black Boy. I'm desperate for a pint and to get away from the histrionics for a while.

'I'm just going to pop out,' I say, when the begum seems to have calmed down enough.

'Where are you going?' Rania's youngest sister asks innocently.

'He's going to see a man about a dog,' another sister laughs. It's my usual code for a visit to the pub.

'He's going to the pub,' Rania blurts out, to my annoyance.

'To the temple, you mean,' the other sister laughs.

It's another of my little jokes, referring to the pub as my temple. I try to be a bit subtle about my pubbing out of respect, because they are Muslim and don't drink. Well, I know one or two of the brothers do secretly, but that's another story and I'm not going to tell tales.

'Let him go!' the begum declares to my surprise from her bed, where she's lying with the girls beside her. 'Mister Francis, I thank you for coming here. You are good man! I thank Allah for sending you to me. You are better than all my children. They are all scamps. Go to your temple and enjoy yourself. You deserve to relax. I'm sorry this family is so wicked. I'll go back to Guyana and leave them!'

'Thanks, Mumkin,' I grin, taken aback by her indulgent attitude. Then I jokingly add for the benefit of the sisters, 'Don't worry, I'll be back by midnight,' give them a wave and make a beeline for the front door.

In the pub I take a first sup of my Guinness with a gasp of relief to be away from the amateur dramatics and take out the letter from Ana that arrived this morning to read it again.

Liverpool, Sun. 13th, Mon. 14th Sept. 87

Dear Francis,

Do you want me to tell you everything? Here you are. It's 10 p.m. I'm sitting on a comfortable armchair in my bedroom thinking of you. How am I feeling? Up and down.

Let me explain. I sometimes feel as jumping into the next plane to Spain, as being fed up with being on my own. I've just discovered what I hate most in this world, that is making decisions. I like the easy life, I mean I'd like to be a child who goes to school every day and that's all: Dad will take care of you and nothing will happen to you. I know what you're thinking: "You're very childish, my dear." And it's true, but I can't help it. I feel defenceless. Would you mind being the person who looks after me?

As for my new dilema, I think English people are very different from Spanish ones. Nerys thinks I'd better live in her friend's house because I will be more independent and in contact with young English people. But I'm sure some of the teachers will be shocked if I tell them that I'm living on and with my family in Spain – today I told it to the art teacher at the Blue Coat and he couldn't believe it. I'm worried because I know that my family would never approve of my sharing a house with other young people. I'm worried about the idea as long as my family don't approve of it. I'd like to live there if the house suited me and the environment as well. My family are so far and so near at the same time. It's funny, isn't it?

I feel as living too quick. There have been many changes in my life for such a short time. I'm jumping from one step to another step of an unreal ladder that will be my living in England on my own. (¿comprendes?). This fast living also includes you in some way. You amused and frightened me in the Albert Dock. And I'm also referring to my new experience with you at the hotel. You're right when saying that I'm cold and warm at the same time. The fact is that I'm always confused. I'm always struggling inside my mind – that's why I'm so nervous, because I don't know what I should do and shouldn't do. I hate making decisions. They're so strict, when you've made one you can't go back over it and change it if you were wrong. (I don't know if you can understand this sentence, can you?)

Now it's Monday evening and I'm going to finish this short letter up. A curious thing that will probably make/drive you to be jealous: I've just found a second teacher of English language, I mean, apart from you a second teacher who teaches me English free. His name is Richard and he's just like you. He hasn't told me yet that I'm murdering the English language but he will, I'm sure. Today he asked me: "Ana, would you mind my correcting your mistakes?" (Of course, when I'm speaking English.) I answered: "Not at all. But don't correct me too much, please. Otherwise I'll get frustrated." His answer was: "O.K. Then I'll correct you about nine mistakes and won't pay any attention to the other ten" (or something like that). DON'T LAUGH AT ME.

And that's not all. He gave me some homeworks. I'm supposed to hand in a composition on <u>The most edifying thing that has happened to me since arriving at Liverpool</u> tomorrow. And a note under the title says: Marks will be given for sophisticated sentence constructions, vocabulary and PICTURES. Roughly one page. What do you think?

Anyway, I hope I'll see you soon. Forgive me for not posting the letter today as I promised. (Can you forgive me if I give you a kiss when I see you again?)_

Hasta pronto,

With love and affection,

Ana (xxx)

P.S. Nerys is a Welsh teacher in Blue Coat. She went to the police station with me to register and invited me to her house for tea.

P.P.S. Tomorrow I have to talk about energy in class.

P.P.P.S. The boys in Blue Coat are not bad. They call me Miss Rojo. It's funny!

Like most of her letters, like Ana herself, it evokes a mixture of feelings in me, confuses me. 'Would you mind being the person who looks after me?' Yes, I'll look after you! I want to look after you! I don't just want to be your surrogate dad though. 'You amused and frightened me in the Albert Dock?' What does she mean by that? How did I frighten her? Because I asked her to stay in the hotel with me? Because I threatened to leave if she didn't? But I didn't threaten to do that, did I? She must have been reading my mind. 'I'm also referring to my new experience with you at the hotel.' What does she mean by that? I suppose she means I frightened her because I insisted on sleeping with her, tried to have sex with her. I didn't force myself on her though. I would never do that. God, she's so afraid of sex! Talk about Fear of Flying. 'You're right when saying that I'm cold and warm at the same time.' I don't remember saying that, but I suppose I must have done. It sums her up perfectly anyway. She's confused all right. And confusing. But I could deal with that if she'd just let me in, lower the wall a bit …

'His name is Richard and he's just like you.' That's really bad news. I don't like the sound of that at all. I'm jealous all right. It's inevitable that some bloke would latch onto her sooner or later, I suppose. I didn't think it would happen so fast though. Damn him! Why did she have to tell me? It's almost as if she wants to push me even further away. Yet at the same time she's asking me to look after her and go and see her. She's confused all right! Maybe she's just naïve? No, she knows it's likely to make me jealous. She says so herself. She's got me in knots too. God, I wish I could just forget her. But I can't. I love her. I want her. I'm not going to let Dastardly Dick have her. If necessary I'll fight for her!

I knock back the last of my pint with a gasp of satisfaction and replace the froth-laced pint glass on the battered wooden table, but don't let go of it. It's a scruffy old pub in rough and ready Tottenham, with hardly any other customers apart from myself, just a couple of old geezers staring emptily at their pints and puffing on fags, looking as if they gave up on life long ago. Looking like lost souls. Well, aren't we all lost souls, swimming in a fish bowl?

I sit there for a few minutes, debating with myself whether to have another one. The world already seems a kinder place, its hard edges and angles blurred ever so slightly by the alcohol percolating through my system. Another one would really put it into soft focus. I reluctantly decide not to though. I always try to limit myself to one when I'm visiting the begum, because I don't want to appear even slightly drunk in front of her and the family. Besides which, I have to drive Rania home, not that another pint would impair my driving. But I know if I have a second pint, I'll want a third, so very reluctantly I let go of the glass, stand up and hurry out, giving a wave to the landlord and the two old geezers waiting for Godot, though I'm not sure they even notice.

CHAPTER TWENTY-THREE

So fare thee well my own true love

When he arrived at Lime Street station, Ana was waiting for him with her spiky hair, wearing a short red jacket over a white shirt with a brooch at the neck, tight jeans and spherical earrings, which she informed him later were a leaving present from MJ. Why had he come? He had been wondering all the way up on the train. She had implored him to. He felt responsible for her. He didn't want to let Dastardly Dick or any other man have her. He felt sorry for her. He loved her.

They went to his hotel and checked in. In the room, she suddenly told him her new friend Nerys had invited them to stay at her house and suggested they did. Here we go again, he thought – anything to avoid sleeping with him, even though she had promised she would stay with him as a condition of his coming. He didn't suppose Nerys would let them sleep together. Or would she? He couldn't be sure. Anyway, he didn't want to be under the surveillance of Nerys or anyone else who knew them.

'I don't want to stay at Nerys's,' he said, exasperated. 'I've booked this place and we're here now. I can't just walk out.'

Admittedly, the place was a bit shabby, with a fat, frumpy, grey-haired Scottish landlady, but he knew that wasn't why she didn't want to stay. She didn't want to stay because there was only a double bed. This was ridiculous, he thought. He should just leave now, except that it was nine o'clock in the evening and he didn't know if there would be a train to London. Besides which, how could he turn up back at home when he'd told Rania he was meeting an old school friend in Liverpool?

'I need a drink,' he said, biting his tongue. 'Vamos.'

In the pub she said she wanted to speak 'seriously', which immediately put him on guard.

'Go on,' he said, taking a first sup of Guinness to fortify himself.

'I want only friendship with ju,' she said.

For a moment he was too shocked to say anything. 'I can't accept that,' he replied finally, taking an even bigger sup of Guinness.

'Por qué?'

'Because I love you,' he shrugged. 'And I'm in love with you. So it's love or nothing.' *Good title for a novel there maybe. Or a short story.* 'You don't love me? I thought you did. In your letters you say you do.'

'I love you in a special way.'

She might as well have stuck a dagger in his belly. He took a slug of Guinness to kill the pain. *I love you in a special way.* The last words he wanted to hear! Especially as Buddy Holly was crooning 'Words of Love' on the jukebox.

'My mother loves me in a special way,' he replied sarcastically. 'Or used to.'

'Are ju angry?' she asked.

'Disappointed,' he said. He wasn't going to give her the gratification of saying he was *angry,* though he was angry. He was *very* angry. He was angry with her, but even more angry with himself. How had he allowed himself to be lured into the same trap yet again? What a fool he was!

'I'm sorry,' she said.

'I may as well go back to London,' he said, shocked by how cool and calm she seemed. There were no tears in her eyes as far as he could see. She'd certainly led him a merry dance!

'Ju want to go now?' she asked and he could see that look of alarm in her eyes that he was so familiar with, that always got to him, weakened him, made him crumple.

'I can't go now because it's too late,' he said.

He wasn't sure he could have gone even if it wasn't too late. She had dealt him a killer blow, but he still couldn't bear to abandon her, still clung to some forlorn hope that this was all a mistake, a misunderstanding, something was being lost in translation.

'Is this all because of "Richard"?' he asked sarcastically.

'Rick is just a friend,' she said. Was there the glimmer of a smile on her lips as she said it, he thought? Thank goodness she didn't say, 'Like ju'.

'Oh, it's "Rick" now, is it?'

'He prefers that,' she informed him, as if he wanted to know.

'So,' he said, taking a swig of stout. 'Tell me about "Rick".' At least it wasn't 'Dick'.

'He's a maths teacher.'

'Is that it? What does he look like?'

'Everyone says he looks like a famous musician. I forget the name. He plays the violin. Nigel?'

'Nigel Kennedy?'

'Si. Except I think he looks better. Even though he wears glasses.'

'Don't tell me he plays the violin too.'

'He plays the cello.' *Damn!*

'He's very amusing.' *Damn! I don't want to know!*

'Have you been out with him?'

'We went for a drink in the Adelphi.'

'I see,' he smiled, though he felt jealousy seeping through his system like poison. It seemed as if Dick – sorry, Rick – was going to step nimbly into his shoes. *Would he jump into my grave so quickly, I wonder?*

'But Rick couldn't drink anything.'

'Oh. Why not?' Not that he wanted to know. He had heard enough of Rick. Dick. Ricky Tricky Dicky.

'He lost his licence for drink driving, so he's trying to stop drinking.'

'I see.' He didn't want to know any more about Rick. 'What else have you been doing?'

She started to prattle on about how she had been to Nerys's house for dinner and other doings, but he hardly listened. He couldn't get Rick out of his mind. He couldn't decide whether he loved her or hated her. Every time he decided he loved her, an image of Nigel Kennedy, alias Rick, popped up in front of him, sawing flamboyantly on his fiddle and gurning at him ...

When they got back to the hotel, she said she wanted to go home, but he insisted she came in. 'I'll come in for a few minutes,' she reluctantly agreed, sensing how angry he was.

In the dimly-lit room he sat on the bed and invited her to sit beside him, which to his surprise she did. To his even greater surprise, she let him put an arm around her and kiss her on the lips. He took his jacket and shoes off, lay back on the bed and invited her to join him. Instead, though, she stood up and declared, 'I have to go.'

'OK,' he said, as if he didn't care whether she went or stayed, though inside he was seething. This was the last straw!

'What time shall I see ju tomorrow?'

'You won't see me tomorrow.'

He could see she was shocked, as he had intended, and a stab of remorse went through him.

'Are ju angry? Do ju hate me?'

It was time for a home truth or two, he decided, turning to stare at her, standing there in her white mac, looking so sweet, so innocent, yet so …

'I will be angry and I will hate you if you leave,' he said sternly. 'I haven't come all the way to Liverpool for a second time to spend the night on my own in this crummy hotel. I've told you, I don't want just friendship with you. I've got enough friends already. I love you and if I love someone, it's one hundred per cent and I give one hundred per cent. If I hate someone, it's one hundred per cent too. And hate is the other side of the coin. It's your choice. It's up to you.'

She looked even more shellshocked, but didn't move. He felt another even sharper stab of remorse. He loved her and wanted her, hated hurting her, but if she left now. the love he felt would turn immediately to hate, as if by the flip of a coin. This was it. This was the crunch. It was the end of the road. He couldn't do this any more. It was up to her.

'Will ju still write to me?' she asked quietly, her voice and her eyes full of anxiety.

'I don't know,' he said, though he did know.

For a while their eyes were locked in a silent duel again, but she must have seen the fury in his, because she was the first to blink and back down. 'All right, I'll stay,' she said, taking off her coat and starting to undress.

He knew she was shy about undressing in front of him, so he quickly stood up and left the room to go to the loo. When he came back, she was in bed and her coat, shirt, jeans and bra were on the rickety rattan armchair. He undressed to his underpants, got into bed beside her and took her in her arms, as much for an exchange of warmth as anything else.

'Te quiero,' he whispered and to his relief she let him kiss her, caress her freely and even fondle her breasts.

She didn't say anything, didn't do anything, was as unresponsive as a rubber doll, lay there lifelessly with her eyes shut, but he didn't care – this was progress. He'd try to make her come, he decided after a while, thinking that if she could just have an orgasm, it would break the damn wall of her inhibitions and release all her suppressed, locked-up, frozen emotions. He let his hand travel down her body, kissing and caressing it tenderly with his fingertips as he went, and slowly, hesitantly, started to ease her knickers down. To his relief she let him take them completely off and, after some gentle preparation, slip a finger inside her …

He tried his best to make her come, but got no response, apart from a spasm or two, which could have been pain or pleasure. Eventually he stopped, tired, and held her in his arms, defeated.

'You hurt me,' she said, opening her eyes. 'I can't. I don't know what to do. It's silly.'

'Sex is silly, when you think about it,' he smiled, feeling sorry for her, trying to cover up his own sense of failure. 'You don't have to do anything. Just relax.'

'I can't relax.'

'Try. Shall I try again?'

'If ju want.'

He tried again, but it was no good, so he gave up. It really was like making love with a doll. Or a mannequin. Or a dummy. Or worse.

'Never mind,' he said, holding her in his arms again and kissing her on the forehead. 'Sex isn't everything. We can try again another time.' His words sounded hollow even in his own ears though, and he felt an emptiness deep inside, an emptiness that threatened to spread and swallow all hope, all optimism.

'I rarely feel any desire for sex,' she said.

'It doesn't matter,' he said, caressing her stomach with his fingertips, trying to reassure himself as much as her. 'It's enough that you're here, that we're together.'

'It's wrong,' she said. 'I shouldn't be here. Why am I here? Let's sleep. Don't touch me. I can't sleep if ju touch me.'

For a while he kept hold of her, shocked, offended, defeated, then gently released her and lay on his back away from her, staring into the darkness. 'It's wrong. I shouldn't be here. Why am I here?' Her words detonated like bombs inside his head, sending shockwaves to his heart. They might just as easily apply to him. What a stupid situation! He would never let this happen again, he resolved. Lying in a strange bed, in a strange hotel, in a strange city, beside someone who didn't want to be here. He didn't want to be here. Ironically, Pink Floyd suddenly started playing 'Wish You Were Here' inside his head. Lost souls, yes, but not in a fish bowl. In space. Drifting away from each other, into the darkness, into the vacuum …

The following morning they had breakfast in the hotel and chatted about the Advanced English exam she wanted to take, schools, teaching, Liverpool, Dublin, family, friends … All sorts of things except what had happened the night before, the elephant in the hotel room. It was as if both of them knew. He just wanted to go home, but his train wasn't until 5 pm.

They walked around the city for a while, sightseeing as if they were tourists, then went for lunch in a pub called the Poste House. A loquacious Scouser sitting next to them told them it had been Adolf Hitler's favourite pub when he briefly lived in Liverpool in his early twenties, before World War One, and insisted on telling them the story. How Adolf had fled to Liverpool from Vienna to avoid military service and stayed in a flat with his married brother, Alois, for several months.

Normally he might have given the Scouser short shrift, but the story was fascinating – even if it was mythological – and he was glad of the excuse to avoid making more small talk with her, so he led him on with questions. It turned out, according to the Scouse historian, that Alois was married to an Irishwoman called Bridget Dowling, who had met him while he was working as a waiter in Dublin and who had written an unpublished book about her experience. Apparently she eloped with Alois from Dublin to London, where they were married before settling in a flat in Liverpool, which is where the army-shy Adolf went to live with them for several months, before Alois packed him off back to Vienna, considering him to be a lazy, shiftless scrounger. The connection with both Liverpool and Dublin gave the story an extra fascination for him, which the resident Poste House historian was only too happy to satisfy.

'So where is this flat exactly?' he asked his informant, who told him it was in Toxteth, not far away.

'Can you go and see it?' he inquired, thinking it might kill another hour or so.

'I'm sorry, whack, you can't any more,' the Scouser said sadly.

'Oh. Why not?'

'It was blown to smithereens by the Luftwaffe in World War Two.'

'I see,' he laughed. 'Poetic justice, eh?' He didn't really believe it though. It was too good a story to be true somehow.

When he had heard all he wanted to hear and exchanged a few more friendly words, he managed to politely deflect the Scouser's attention and return to Ana. 'It's a good story,' he told her, 'but I'm not sure I can believe it. I bet the pub pay him to sit here all day! Or the Liverpool Tourist Board.'

'Do ju think I'm spoilt?' she asked, ignoring or not getting his little joke.

'Spoilt?' he said. 'I don't think so. Why?'

'Everyone here says I am. How can they know after two weeks?'

'They can't,' he assured her. 'They don't know you. Don't take any notice. It's just Liverpudlians being a bit sour.' He was going to say 'astringent' but decided she might not know the word, though her English was very good, as it should be, since she was an aspiring English teacher. 'They're famous for it,' he added. 'As are Mancunians, for that matter. They're very similar in many ways, which is why they don't like each other. Or aren't supposed to.' He might as well give her a bit of cultural history since he was here, he thought.

'I like Liverpool,' she said.

'I do too – but don't tell any of my Mancunian friends,' he laughed, taking a swig of Guinness.

'I like the people. They like me. I feel well here.'

'That's good. I'm glad.'

'I wouldn't be here if not for you.'

'I wouldn't be here if not for *you*!'

There was a short silence between them. He glanced surreptitiously at his watch as he took another swig of Guinness. It was too early to go for his train.

'Am I a bad girl?'

'A bad girl? Why?'

'Because I have boyfriends and boys like me?'

He had hoped to avoid any serious conversation, but since she broached the matter, he decided it was time to give her another home truth or two. It would be his parting gift to her, perhaps, he thought sadly.

'There's nothing wrong with boys liking you or having boyfriends,' he said, suddenly feeling avuncular, though the last thing he wanted to be was her uncle. He wanted to be her boyfriend, not her uncle! Even now, as he glanced at her, he felt a pang of love and longing for her. 'But what is wrong, what you shouldn't do,' he continued, 'is to lead men on and then shut the door in their faces.'

He deliberately looked her in the eye as he said it and saw that hurt look he knew so well, immediately regretted saying it. It was true, though, he told himself, and he hoped he was doing her a favour by telling her, even though he felt an undercurrent of vindictive pleasure in doing so too.

'Do I do that?'

'Yes, you do.'

He looked away, unable to bear the hurt in her eyes, feeling guilty. It was too late to backtrack now though. Or was it? 'I'm not saying you do it deliberately,' he added, by way of mitigation, 'but that's what you do.'

She sat there stock-still, saying nothing, looking wounded, so that his heart went out to her. There was nothing he wanted to do more than put an arm around her, pull her close and tell her, 'Te quiero', but those days were gone.

'That's what you did to me,' he said, taking another swig of Guinness. *Sometimes you have to be cruel to be kind.*

'I'm sorry,' she said.

'It's OK,' he smiled. 'I still love you.'

'We can be friends?'

If only she knew how much those words hurt him! Like a dagger in his guts.

'If that's what you want,' he shrugged.

'Will ju help me with my tesina?'

'*Women in James Joyce*? Sure. I said I would, so I will.'

'Gracias.'

'You know I always keep my promises.' *Well, nearly always.*

'Will ju come to see me again?'

'When?'

'At half term?'

'I don't know. Maybe. If our half-terms are at the same time. I usually go somewhere though.' Probably not, he thought. He couldn't go through all this again. It was psychological torture.

'My parents are coming to see me. Ju can meet them.'

That definitely put the kibosh on it, he thought. Why would he want to meet her parents? It wasn't as if they were his prospective parents-in-law!

'We'll see,' he said, finishing his Guinness. 'I think it's time to go.' It wasn't quite time, but he couldn't endure the torture any longer. 'Do you want to walk to the station with me?'

He half-hoped she would decline, say she just wanted to go straight home, but she agreed. He was pleased, but it only delayed the pain of parting a bit longer. A parting that would be all the more painful for him, because in his mind at least it would be the final one. He loved her, but he just couldn't go through this torture again.

'Ta-ra,' the Scouse historian said as they left.

'Heil Hitler!' he replied, giving him a Nazi salute.

'What are you going to do this evening?' he inquired, as they waited on the concourse for his train. He was smiling wryly to himself, because he had read about so many such scenes in novels, had always wanted to be in one for real, and here he was …

The train was standing by the platform, but the gate wasn't open yet and there was a short queue. Talk about prolonging the torture! He was desperate to go now. To leave Liverpool. To leave her. To go back to his real life. Even though his real life was so unsatisfactory. Even though at the same time he wanted nothing more than to stay with her.

Before she could answer his inquiry, the gate opened and passengers started shuffling through. He was about to give her a hug and say, 'Te quiero', when she replied.

'I might call Rick and ask him to go for a drink. I feel lonely at home.'

He felt an almost physical pain in his guts, another twist of the knife. Not that he wanted her to be lonely, but …

'Good idea!' he declared breezily, giving her half a hug and a quick kiss on each cheek, hurrying to the gate, calling back, 'Hasta luego!'

He passed through the gate, showing his ticket – his ticket to ride – and hurried along the platform without looking back. Don't look back, he told himself. Don't look back! He didn't want her to see the tears in his eyes. He didn't want to see the tears in her eyes, if there were any.

He stopped at the first empty-looking carriage he could find, yanked open the door and stepped up. As he did so, he paused, unable to resist a quick backward glance, thinking he'd give her a farewell wave, maybe even blow her a kiss, but she wasn't there any more.

CHAPTER TWENTY-FOUR

London

When he arrived at Euston he called Rania, who told him to hurry up home because Farouq was cooking dinner for him. He was a bit put out, though he knew he shouldn't be, because he wanted to go for a pint. He was gasping for one, so he would anyway, he decided – it just meant he'd have to rush it, which he didn't like doing.

'What's he cooking?' he teased Rania. 'Not one of his mountain-goat stews, I hope. Has he been to the forest today? Or just the park?'

It was a running joke between them that Farouq went hunting in nearby Epping Forest or in the even nearer Lloyd Park, where there were ducks, geese, swans, squirrels and such like. Not to mention rats. And not that Rania found the jokes all that funny, being Muslim herself, and somewhat defensive of Farouq, though even she found him a bit over the top, while he considered her 'not a good Muslim' because she didn't pray five times a day like him or go to the mosque every Friday.

'Don't be so ungrateful,' she scolded him and he laughed.

Farouq was no vegetarian and was always trying to persuade him to partake of the various animals – wild or otherwise – he cooked up in a huge pot in the kitchen, enough to last a week and enough to pong the whole neighbourhood out. But at least he didn't bring the poor animals home alive and slit their throats in the backyard, he had observed pointedly to Rania. He would definitely have drawn a line at that.

'I've got something to tell you,' she added.

'Yes?' he said, an alarm bell ringing.

'I'll tell you at home. Later.'

'I'll be home in about an hour,' he said, hanging up, worried.

The shadows were lengthening ...

Later he forced himself to chat genially with Farouq over dinner – which to his relief contained no dead animals. He didn't feel very sociable, because he was both physically and emotionally tired, as well as worried about what Rania had to tell him, though he had a strong suspicion. She had refused to tell him in front of Farouq, said she would do so in bed, which only reinforced his suspicion.

A glass of rioja on top of the excellent pint of Guinness he had imbibed in the Royal Standard down the road helped to loosen him up and relax him. It was also making a point to both Rania and Farouq that he was free to do what he liked in his own home and that he made the rules, not they, or at least not Farouq. Besides, didn't Mohamed himself enjoy the occasional bottle of vino? And wasn't Paradise supposed to be running with rivers of wine? Not to mention the houris keen to minister to your every need. The Muslim Paradise sounded a lot more fun than the Catholic one, he had to privately admit.

To make conversation, he asked Farouq about his life in Afghanistan and Farouq was only too eager to oblige. At least it distracted him from thoughts of Ana, he reflected, only half listening as Farouq regaled him with tales of his student days in Kharkov, though his ears did prick up when he started talking about the many Ukrainian girls there were at the university, how beautiful they were, how sexy they were, how one once knocked on his door in the student hostel where they were living, asked him for a cigarette and ended up in bed with him ...

Oddly enough, according to Farouq, most of the girls on the course were women, even though it was physics. They were all very bright too, he said, though he also couldn't resist bragging that that didn't stop him coming top of the class in the final examinations and being awarded a gold medal. He would have liked to ask Farouq more about those sexy Ukrainian girls, but couldn't in front of Rania. It was probably just as well, he supposed, since talk of sex only reminded him of Ana and lengthened the shadow that already lay over him.

'So tell me,' he said, when they were in bed.

'I think I'm pregnant.' They were the words he had been dreading.

'Why do you think that?' he murmured sleepily, keeping his eyes closed.

'I did a test.'

'Are you sure you're not just constipated again?'

Last year she thought she was pregnant, but after lots of tears, sickness, doctors' appointments and tests and investigations in hospital, it turned out she was just constipated. He sometimes teased her about it, but she didn't like to be reminded.

'Don't be horrible,' she said. 'Aren't you happy if I'm pregnant? Don't you want a little Francis?'

'It could be a little Rania,' he grinned. 'That would really be a disaster.'

'You're horrible' she pouted, though she knew he was only joking and he knew she was too excited to be really upset.

'I know,' he murmured. 'It's better you should find out now, before we go any further.' It was another of his little jokes. *Many a true word.*

'Seriously, darling, will you be happy if I am pregnant?'

'Yes, I suppose so.'

'I know you'll be a good father.'

'Mm. Maybe.'

'You will. I know.'

'How do you know?'

'Because you're a good man. And a good husband.'

'Am I?' He tried to be both, but sometimes he wondered.

'Yes, even though you're always chasing other women.'

'That's not a very nice thing to say.'

'It's OK, as long as you don't do anything with them.'

'So I can chase them, but not catch them. Is that it?'

'You know what I mean.'

'Can I sleep now?'

The conversation was starting to become surreal, as if in a dream. He was starting to wonder if he wasn't already asleep and having a weird dream. If she really was pregnant, he would be well and truly trapped. Trapped for life with somebody he didn't love. He could insist on an abortion, he supposed, but he would never do that. If unlike Farouq he was unwilling to kill a rabbit or a duck, he wasn't going to kill a child, no matter how embryonic. Especially his own child.

'Do you want to sleep?' she asked.

'I am very tired,' he murmured drowsily.

He could tell she was in an amorous as well as a talkative mood, but that was the last thing he wanted.

'All right, darling,' she said. 'I'm so glad you're home. I miss you when you go away. I wish you wouldn't go away and leave me. I love you.'

'Mm. Thanks.'

'Just tell me one thing before you sleep.'

'Hm?'

'Do you love me?'

'I suppose so,' he mumbled. 'Goodnight.'

He felt himself slipping under the waves and he knew that when he woke up in the morning he really would wonder if all this was just a bad dream …

CHAPTER TWENTY-FIVE

London

Liverpool, Wedn. 30th Sept. 87

Dear Francis,

I tried to write on Sunday evening as I promised, but I was so tired that I fell asleep after writing a couple of sentences. (Before going to bed I had a wonderful bath. I think that's why I relaxed so much.) First of all, I would like to say thanks a lot for being so sympathetic with me, I mean sympathetic, helpful, loving, flexible, nice … I admire you because it seems to me that you can understand me (although you don't understand why I behave in that way, you accept it – maybe saying that the only reason is that she is Ana).

I'm terribly sorry if I've hurt you. I know I've hurt you and I'd like to be forgiven. I can't stand the thought of having another enemy. Even if you don't want to be, you are a special friend of mine, never an enemy. Do you hate me? I can't imagine you hating me, nor do I want to feel your hatred if you do.

I'm thinking that maybe you're expecting some explanation about what happened last Saturday. I'd rather not to explain anything, as just thinking of it hurts me and probably it may hurt you as well. However, if you want me to explain, I will. If so, let me know it, please.

How do you feel? I'm in a down moment. I feel as the moment just after suffering from an attack of nerves. I don't feel like doing anything. I'm thoughtful, relaxed, worried, sad, sleepy, confused, tired, homesick … And frustrated.

Let me explain (a note of humour to this boring letter): This morning I began to do the exercises of the Proficiency book you recommended me and when I finished the first one and wanted to know how many were wrong, then I discovered that the answers weren't in this book. I stopped working on that and got angry. Now after writing to you, I'm going to go on reading J. Joyce's biography. Studying helps me not to think (it seems a contradiction, isn't it?).

Anyway, (word used by you when you wanted to finish something, e.g. a conversation on the phone) I'm looking forward to receiving any news from you. I'll write again soon and post my fortnightly composition to you.

With love and affection,

Ana (xxx)

P.D. Nothing happens with Rick on Sunday evening.
Today I've received my first wage in all my life.
I'm very glad!

He folded the letter into its envelope, slipped the envelope back into his inside jacket pocket and took a first sup of the Guinness he had just carried from the bar of the Lord Palmerston to a table in the corner. He waited for a few minutes, enjoying the first hit of the alcohol and mulling over the contents of the letter. Then he picked up his pen and notepad and started to reply. It was going to be one of the most difficult letters he had ever written.

The letter he received back from her shocked him. It shocked him so much he had to read it several times, even though each time it only deepened the shock and widened the wound:

Liverpool, 11th Oct. 87

Dear Francis,

1. First of all: CONGRATULATIONS! My best wishes to the mother and child.

2. Of course, I was very shocked when I received your letter, but by the time I'm answering it I've almost come through the surprise. Now I'm completely satisfied with the decision I made that weekend. This fact reaffirmed my suspicion, namely you would never have left R. I know that you admitted it in one of your last letters.

3. To be honest I feel cheated by you. You should have said to me that your girlfriend might be/was pregnant. I also feel guilty – both of us must have hurt her very much. I'm very sorry. In fact, if you had said it to me before I would have made the same decision. You might have known it and that's why you didn't say a single word about the subject.

4. There are two questions in my mind. Did you know she was pregnant before you came to Liverpool? And would you have given me the news before I went to London or not? I think fate protects me against MEN. I am very glad not to have gone to London then.

5. Let me try to explain why I changed so quickly: Female intuition? Destiny? Fate? When I took the decision, I could only give you one reason: I couldn't give myself up to you. Why? Today I may say that there are three different reasons. Firstly, my feelings as for sleeping with you were very negative. We behaved immorally – to understand "immorally" you should think about your child's mother and forget about my religion. The

fact is that neither of us were free. Secondly, something inside me prevented me sleeping with you. I didn't feel so attached to you as to sleep with you, at least by the end of our relations. (Triangles don't work!) And thirdly, the difference of ages. I am very young and I didn't want to waste my youth with feelings of guilt. Sorry, I don't want to hurt you by saying it. As you can see, I'm in one of my "UP" moments, e.g. I like living.

6. Regarding the half-term/weekend I tried to telephone you from North Wales on Wednesday evening, but nobody answered the phone. I couldn't telephone you by 3.30 because you were driving. On Thursday/ Saturday evening I tried to telephone you again but all the telephone boxes near home were vandalised so that I was waiting for your calling me at home. Anyway, it's fair for you to know that I wouldn't have gone. I wasn't in the right mood. (I never lie. Forgive me.) Too soon to see you again.

7. Life in Liverpool: Very enjoyable. I'm very glad to be living here. Rick has introduced some friends to me and we usually go out together. Work is O.K. And my "tesina" goes ahead. I finished reading Ulysses and now I'm reading some books on it (including The Bloomsday Book by Harry Blamires that you recommended).

8. You were right when you said that I was going to leave England from London. If you still want to see me answer this letter and I'll tell you the dates of my departure and return. If I'm not saying them to you now is because I don't want you to feel "used" by Ana. (A wink: of course, I need somebody in London to help me.)

Love,
Ana

He decided to reply immediately, though he knew he should probably wait twenty-four hours, as was his rule, until the shock had lessened. As for the hurt, that would take more than twenty-four hours! He would write it now, but not post it till tomorrow, he decided. And he would type it rather than handwrite it as he had always done. That would be an instant indication to her that things had changed, changed dramatically.

London, 13th Oct. 87

Dear Ana,

Thank you for your letter, though it has shocked and hurt me deeply. I should warn you that I'm going to write some things here that may shock and hurt <u>you</u> deeply, so feel free to throw this letter away unread if you wish. I warn you it's going to be a long (though I hope not too prolix – there's a new word for your vocabulary perhaps) letter too. However, if you do choose to read it, please don't bother to reply. I think there's nothing to be gained by engaging in a 'war of words'. You have given your side of the story and I will have given mine. I hope we can end it here and remember each other without too much bitterness in time to come perhaps, when time has done its healing work, even with some fondness.

I was about to say I don't write what I'm going to write out of revenge, but I dare say there is an undercurrent of subconscious revenge in my words, whether I like it or not. (I'm not a saint yet.) I feel I have to say what I'm going to say though, because you have made some comments about me that I find deeply offensive and that I also consider to be *untrue* or at least only partially true. (No, I know I'm not perfect either.) Moreover, I think your letter portrays a distorted version of what has happened between us, because you have a distorted view, so I want to give you *my* version of events, just for historical accuracy. Not that our relationship matters to anyone else except us. Let me also say, before I begin, that I find the *tone* of your letter offensive. I'll try not to adopt a similar tone, but please forgive me (to echo you) if I fail. Forgive us our trespasses, as we forgive others.

I'm going to go through your letter paragraph by paragraph and make my own comments and observations on some of the things you've written. As I said at the start, you may find my comments and observations hurtful, but you have been warned. You always say how much you value honesty and you're always claiming to be truthful: "I never lie. Forgive me." There seems to be an implication in your words that I am less than honest and truthful. But I like to think I am honest and truthful too, so I'm going to give you my 'truth'. Remember, truth is usually a many-sided or multifaceted thing. One man's truth is another man's falsehood. It's what lawyers all over the land are paid to argue about in courts every day. It's rarely if ever simple or one-dimensional. Indeed, a famous person apparently once asked his accusers, when he was on trial for his life, "What is truth?"

Yes, I mention a famous trial and I have to say your letter – both tone and content – have made me feel as if I have been on trial, with *you* as prosecutor, judge, jury and executioner. And you have found me guilty! But I reject your guilty verdict. While I may not be completely innocent in this matter (or in my other daily doings), I don't consider myself to be guilty. In fact, I consider myself to be a pretty upright, honest and decent person, perhaps even exceptionally so, though that may not be for me to judge. Having said that, I do realise that my behaviour may not always appear that way to others, but I always have my own good reasons and motives for my actions. I certainly never set out to deliberately cheat, harm or injure anyone in any way.

I try to live by the maxim, "Do unto others as you would be done by", and I'd like to think that most of the time I succeed. I'd also like to think that my general behaviour is why I am highly respected (and sometimes even liked) by all who know me, both personally and professionally.

I suppose I should say thank you for your 'congratulations' and your 'best wishes to the mother and child'. But if I were to do so, it would only be out of false politeness and neither sincere nor heartfelt. To be honest – since you're so big on honesty – your 'congratulations' and 'best wishes' don't ring true with me. In fact – and forgive me if I'm misconstruing – do I detect a note of irony, even sarcasm, in your words? I have noticed a sarcastic edge to your sense of humour, but until recent events, looking through the prism of love, I chose to interpret it as 'mischievous' or 'impish' rather than sarcastic. Please don't be too offended by this observation – I confess to having a sarcastic side myself, though I do try to tone it down. As Oscar Wilde quipped, it is the lowest form of wit.

In your second paragraph, you say you were 'very shocked' by my letter, so that makes two of us and the score is even. I'm sure you didn't set out to deliberately shock or upset me and I hope you will believe the same is true for me here. Let's at least grant each other that grace. In the same paragraph, you write, 'Now I am completely satisfied with the decision I made that weekend'. I'm afraid I find this remark shocking, because it is so pompous and crassly *self-centred*. (I notice you are very fond of the first-person singular pronoun. You did ask me once if I thought you were 'spoilt' and I've now realised I probably gave you the wrong answer, because the scales have fallen from my eyes.)

Anyway, I presume by this 'decision' you mean the decision not to sleep with me or have a romantic relationship with me. Yes, you told me several times you wanted only 'friendship', but you know I never accepted this, you knew I wanted a physical relationship with you, you knew I was 'in love' with you. Yet by your actions you let me go on believing you might want more than a platonic relationship too. You continued to write what can only be described as 'romantic' letters to me (including those kisses in brackets – maybe the brackets should have been a warning bell for me), letters that led me to believe you might have romantic feelings for me. You invited me to Madrid under this impression. You invited me to Liverpool. You led me on. Then you shut the door in my face. (And I don't think I'm the first man you've done it to.)

Looking back, I feel foolish now. I know I should have seen through you much earlier, but I was blinded by love. There is a very vulgar expression in English for women who do this to men (lead them on, but then refuse to have sex) but I won't lower myself to using it about you. Besides, if I'm honest, it doesn't really apply to you, because I don't believe you do it deliberately. I think you do it without realising you're doing it, because there is something psychologically wrong with you – as I have discussed with you. So I'll give you that much benefit of the doubt.

In the same paragraph, you say: 'This fact reaffirmed my suspicion, namely you would never have left R. I know that you admitted it in one of your last letters.' That word 'suspicion' is toxic, but also revealing, because it tells me so much about you that I hadn't fully realised or had subconsciously hidden from myself. Looking back now, I remember how I always felt strangely uncomfortable with you, but couldn't quite work out why. Now I think I know why. The clue is that nasty little word, 'suspicion'. I think you were always looking at me with suspicion in your mind and heart. Because of your suspicious nature, you never believed or trusted me fully. For the same reason, I think you won't ever be able to trust any man. No wonder our relationship has failed! It was poisoned from the very start. (By the way, there's a song entitled 'Suspicious Minds' made popular in the sixties by Elvis Presley – you might want to listen to it, especially the first verse.)

'To be honest I feel cheated by you.' When I first read those words, I didn't know whether to burst into laughter or tears. I couldn't believe you had written them. Then I felt angry. Now they just make me feel a profound disappointment, disillusionment and disgust. There are probably few worse insults you could throw at me than to call me a 'cheat'. After all the love, affection and kindness I've shown you, you dare to tell me I'm a cheat! It negates everything. It reduces everything to a lie. And what sublime irony, in the light of what I've said here previously, about how you led me on! About how you lead other men on. I hope you're not doing the same to 'Rick'. I feel sorry for him. I almost wish I could speak to him to warn him about you. I feel sorry for Chema too. And José. But believe it or not, the one I feel most sorry for is *you*.

You say to me I should have told you my 'girlfriend' might be pregnant. But why should I tell you something that might or might not be the case? You knew I was living with her and in a relationship with her, so you knew it might be a possibility. I didn't hide it from you. I was very open and honest about it with you. I laid all my cards on the table. Maybe next time I should be more 'economical with the truth'. You go on to ask me if I knew she was pregnant when I visited you in Liverpool and if I would have given you 'the news' before you came to London. I'm not going to dignify these questions with a direct answer, because I find the insinuation behind them deeply insulting.

Ah, suddenly you feel 'guilty' and 'very sorry' for hurting her. (As far as hurting her goes, speak for yourself, don't accuse me.) I'm afraid I find this very hypocritical of you. You knew from the start I was in a relationship with her, because I told you, yet you engaged willingly in a romantic relationship with me. You accuse me of cheating *you*, but you were quite willing to cheat *her*! Maybe you only changed your mind when you decided I was never going to leave her for you. Maybe that's when you suddenly became all moral and self-righteous and holier-than-thou again. And by the way, just for the record, you were wrong to think I'd never leave her. You knew how deeply unhappy and dysfunctional our relationship is, especially on my part, because I spelled it out to you, and I was one hundred per cent serious about leaving her for you. But you never gave me any encouragement or very little. You put a wall up and built it higher and higher. I tried my best to pull the wall down, but you just kept replacing the bricks and building it higher. Always 'another brick in the wall', as the song says.

'I think fate protects me against MEN.' I'm sorry to say that statement says so much about you, especially your use of the upper case for the word 'men'. A psychiatrist would have a field day with it. I'm no psychiatrist, but it seems to me you have a serious problem. And I think that problem is at least partly caused by Catholicism. I'm not telling you anything new here. We've spoken about it and you have acknowledged it. I wanted to help you and I tried to help you, but you kept me out. I'm not blaming you. I see it as a kind of illness, a mental illness, I suppose. I'm sorry if this sounds cruel or insulting. I don't wish to be. In fact, I say it out of some residual concern for you. I think you need or at least could benefit from some professional help. Otherwise, I fear you're going to have an unhappy life and I don't wish that on you. Quite the reverse – I wish you all the best and for once hope I'm wrong.

'Let me try to explain why I changed so quickly,' you write. 'Female intuition? Destiny? Fate?' You changed quickly all right. In fact, you changed so quickly and so often I never knew where I was up to. Sometimes I felt as if you were just playing with me, like a puppet on a string. (There's another song in there.) 'I couldn't give myself up to you,' you write. How clearly I can see that now! I only wish I could have seen it so clearly then. Maybe I would have been able to save myself and you this pain, by ending our relationship sooner. Ah, well, hindsight is a great thing! 'My feelings as for sleeping with you were very negative … I didn't feel so attached to you as to sleep with you, at least by the end of our relations …' And yet you continued to write romantic letters to me, told me you enjoyed my romantic letters to you, encouraged me to write them, invited me to visit you in Madrid and in Liverpool. Oh, you really led me up the garden path! And you presume to say, 'We behaved immorally'! Again, speak for yourself. Don't dare to accuse me. I find it very insulting as well as presumptuous of you.

You tell me to think about my 'child's mother' and forget about your religion. Thank you, but I assure you, I don't need any advice from you about my responsibilities in that department. If and when I become a father, I will take full responsibility for both mother and child. My child's welfare and happiness will assume paramount importance. As for forgetting about your religion, I'm afraid I'd find that impossible. As I've told you, I believe your religion, Catholicism, is at least in part responsible for your 'difficulties' with the emotional and sexual side of life. As indeed it is responsible for some of my own difficulties. I think we have both been damaged by it to some degree, perhaps I even more than you. The difference is that I consciously strive, with some success I like to think, to repair the damage and liberate myself, whereas it seems you are still a prisoner, a willing prisoner. In which case, I feel truly sorry for you, because as I've intimated earlier, I fear it means you will never be free or happy. Which adds a certain piquant irony to your statement that 'neither of us were free'.

Now I come to what I find possibly the most shocking and offensive reason you give for not wanting a relationship with me, 'the difference of ages'. I find this shocking, first, because you never once mentioned it as being a problem or as far as I remember even referred to it, second, because I thought your feelings for me were so strong and deep that it didn't matter to you. How wrong I was in retrospect! Or perhaps it really didn't bother you until now, until you needed a further excuse to run away. I'm sorry if that sounds cynical of me, but you will understand that your letter and your behaviour have made me feel somewhat cynical. 'I didn't want to waste my youth with feelings of guilt,' you say, and add, 'Sorry, I don't want to hurt you by saying it'. If you really didn't want to hurt me, you wouldn't have said it. Or you would have said it sooner, so that we could both perhaps have avoided this unpleasantness. So I'm afraid your apology has a very hollow ring to it. All the same, I'm glad you've said it, because if we had got together, I certainly wouldn't have wanted you to feel you were 'wasting your youth' with me. That would certainly have ended in tears.

I'm glad you're enjoying life in Liverpool and work and studies are going well. I wish you all the best, not just for this year, but for all the years to come. I hope that, in spite of all that's happened and all I've said here, you will have a long, happy, fulfilling life. You once asked me if I hate you. I don't hate you. I'm not even really angry with you. I say goodbye more in sorrow than anger. I'm very sorry we couldn't make it work. I'm sure there has been some fault on both sides. Or maybe it's entirely the fault of Fate for throwing us together, when we didn't really belong together. Anyway, as I said at the start, I'll try to remember you with fondness rather than bitterness.

'Too soon to see you again.' Yes, I agree, it's too soon to see each other again. To be honest, I think it's better if we *never* see each other again. I would find it difficult and I think it would only cause both of us more pain. I'm sorry. (You see, I never lie.) However, if you are ever in desperate need of help while you are in the UK, or indeed wherever you are in the world, I will be here for you.

Good luck with your tesina and have a good life.

Francis (x)

CHAPTER TWENTY-SIX

London

'This is going to feel cold,' the midwife said and proceeded to smear what looked like Vaseline all over Rania's ballooning belly. Then she moved the instrument back and forth over her belly, almost as if it were a magic wand, while they watched the pictures on the screen next to the bed.

There *was* something magical about it, he thought, not just the technology, but the fact of the new life taking form before their very eyes. New life that *he* had created! For a moment he couldn't help feeling an almost godlike sense of power. Yet it was only what billions of men – and women – had done for aeons, what millions were probably doing at this very moment. There was nothing special about it. And yet …

'It's having a good wriggle,' the midwife said. 'It looks fine. It looks beautiful!'

A ripple of pride went through him. He looked more closely at the screen, trying to make out the features of a baby human being. Apart from what looked like a skull – the bulbous, Mekon-like skull of what might have been an alien life form attached to a strangely small, wriggling body – he could make out a tiny hand with five little digits.

'That's unusual,' the midwife observed, noticing too, but he didn't bother to ask why – he was too enthralled, didn't want the spell of wonder to be broken.

'Look,' the midwife said, pointing at the screen. 'There's its little heart beating away.'

He gazed in awe at what looked to him like a tiny blob of matter pulsating rapidly, regularly, rhythmically, awed to think this was the organ that everything else depended on, the organ that would – he hoped – beat many more millions of times, would still be beating in forty or fifty years' time when his own had stopped, like the ticking of a clock. No wonder they called it a 'ticker'.

'And there's its little bladder,' the midwife pointed out, somewhat anticlimactically.

It amused him, as it amused him the way she referred to the life form as 'it'. It didn't seem right somehow. Even if it did look like something from another planet. Suddenly he decided he wanted to know.

'Can you tell if it's a boy or a girl?' he asked.

'It looks like a boy,' she said, pointing again. 'That could be a little penis.'

He couldn't see anything that looked like the organ she referred to, but he was happy to believe her. Somehow, giving the life form a gender – whether male or female – made it seem more human, less alien. Not that he would love it any more or less whatever gender it was. Not that he would love it any less even if it was an alien. It was alive. It was living. It was a miracle. That was all that mattered.

'How old would you say it is?' he asked.

The midwife proceeded to measure the baby's cranium with a clear plastic ruler and did some sort of calculation. It was twenty centimetres, she announced. That meant it – he – was approximately twenty-two weeks old, she informed them. Which meant it would still be legal to kill it, he thought, with a shudder of horror. It also meant that conception happened just before he went to Liverpool, he did his own secret calculation. Which meant it was just as well his relationship with Ana had run into a wall.

Some walls had silver linings, he reflected wryly to himself. It was a mixed metaphor, but it made perfect sense. No doubt walls like clouds cast shadows too. But now, suddenly, at last, the shadows were gone, at least for the time being.

'Are you happy, darling?' Rania asked, when the midwife had cleaned her up and gone for a while. 'Happy to have a little boy?'

'I was half hoping it was a little girl actually.'

Why did he say that, he wondered? Well, it was true. Or half true. And partly to upset her preconceptions. Preconceptions hah!

'Maybe we'll have a little girl next time.'

'We're not actually sure it is a boy. The midwife didn't seem too sure. It looks more like a little alien at the moment.'

'Don't be horrible! It is a little boy. I can tell.'

'Yes? How can you tell?'

'He never stops kicking me!'

'Well, maybe he'll be a footballer when he grows up.'

'I hope he'll be better than that.'

'Such as what?'

'A lecturer like you. Or a doctor. Or a lawyer. Something professional anyway.'

'You're so stereotypically Asian!' he laughed.

'I'm not Asian,' she objected. 'I'm South American.'

'Yes, OK, it was just a joke.'

'I don't like your jokes sometimes.'

'Well, you better get used to them. It looks as though we're stuck with each other for the next eighteen years or so at least.'

'I want us to be stuck together for ever.'

'Hm.'

'Don't you?'

'We'll see. Let's concentrate on the here and now, shall we?'

What an unromantic reply! He wished he could make a declaration of everlasting love to her. This was the moment if ever there was a moment, with their half-formed child inches away inside her, his little heart beating helplessly but hopefully, his blind little eyes unseeing, his tiny hand as if waving hello and reaching out to them to be brought safely into the world, this world of wonder and beauty and joy, but a world also of peril, of pain, of sadness and suffering. But he couldn't bring himself to do so and for a fleeting moment he wondered if he had committed a terrible wrong in bringing a new life into such a world, a world where love was the only saving grace, a world which only love made meaningful or bearable ...

'I just hope I'll die before you,' she said.

'I don't think we should be talking about death here in a maternity ward with you pregnant,' he laughed. 'Anyway, why do you say that? I think I'm likely to go before you, since I'm fifteen years older.'

'I don't think I could live without you beside me.'

'Well, you'll probably have this little feller to look after you if necessary,' he laughed, putting a hand on her belly.

'Can you feel him kicking?'

'God, yes. He can't wait to get out!'

'He can't yet.'

'I know. He's not fully baked yet.'

'You're funny.'

'I have my moments.'

'I'm scared though.'

'Scared?'

'Scared of giving birth.'

'It's nothing to be scared of it. I went through it myself forty years ago.'

'Funny.'

'As I said …'

'You will stay with me, won't you?'

'Stay with you?' Did she mean for ever or …?

'During the birth.'

'Oh. Of course.'

'You do love me, don't you?'

'Is that a statement or a question?'

'It's a statement and a question.'

Just then the midwife returned to do some more checks. It meant he didn't have to answer the question – the million-dollar question. He was relieved, because he didn't know the honest answer. *I never lie. Forgive me.* He wasn't sure if he loved her. One thing he did know for sure, though, was that he loved the little alien kicking and wriggling a few inches away inside her. And he knew, knew deep, deep down in his guts, this was one love affair that would last for life.

He was in his office at college, preparing for his evening class, when the call came. Her labour pains had started. He told Geoff, who he knew would take care of his class for him, and rushed home. To his relief Rania's sisters were there ministering to her. The pains were getting stronger all the time, Rania said. This was it, it seemed.

They helped her have a shower and then he drove her to the hospital, where they made her change into a flowery operation gown and gave her a bed, hooking her up to drips and monitors. They also gave her a triangular rubber cushion, which they said would help with the pain. After a while, when the pains were getting so bad she was in tears, they gave her an injection of pethidine.

Later, a West Indian midwife in a white coat came, pulled the curtains round her bed, donned latex gloves and examined her. The cervix was only dilated three to four centimetres, she said, but it needed to be seven to ten. So it was a waiting game. When the midwife examined her again at three in the morning, there had been no improvement and by now Rania was crying like a baby herself. 'I want it out! Take it out! I don't want it inside me any more,' she wept and wailed, whereupon the midwife jokingly told her off. 'Hush, there, don't be silly! Baby will come out when he's good and ready!'

'Can't you give her something stronger?' he asked, holding her hand, but otherwise feeling useless and wondering why nature had designed the process to be so traumatic. To his relief, the midwife said she would see if she could find a doctor to give her something stronger and disappeared.

Well, it couldn't be God who had designed it like this, could it, he reflected while waiting? He wouldn't have designed possibly the most important process in any human life to be so gruellingly painful, would he? There was something sadistic about it! No, it couldn't be God, unless he had a very twisted, sick sense of humour or was some sort of psychopath.

Eventually, the midwife came back and said they would give her an epidural. After another wait, a young doctor in a green surgical gown came to administer it. They sat Rania on the edge of the bed with a pillow on her lap, bent her over and spread a surgical drape on her back. 'Is there any risk to this?' he asked the doctor – it looked very invasive. 'There's no risk to the baby,' the doctor assured him. 'Or the mother, except for a one in two hundred chance of a severe headache. She won't be paralysed, no. She has to keep still though. That's the important thing.'

Rania was rocking backwards and forwards, crying

hysterically, so that he and the midwife had to hold her by the arms while the doctor slipped the needle into her spine, making her scream as if she was being stabbed with a stiletto – which in a way she was, he supposed, hardly daring to look, wishing he could take some of the pain for her. So this was the price of a few minutes of pleasure!

Afterwards, her contractions continued, but she calmed down, said her legs felt heavy, numb. He catnapped in the armchair. One of the midwives came in every fifteen minutes to take her blood pressure and temperature. At 7 am the West Indian midwife examined her again and said she still wasn't sufficiently dilated. Rania had started crying again, because the epidural had worn off. He asked if she could have another one, but the midwife said no, the contractions were getting stronger and she wouldn't be able to 'push properly' if she had a top-up.

At 8 am the West Indian midwife went off shift and a Scottish midwife came on, wearing a pale blue uniform. Rania's contractions were getting more and more frequent and stronger and stronger. 'No more pain, please!' she was wailing. 'Stop it, please!' However, the new midwife wouldn't let her have any more anaesthetic either. 'Push!' she ordered. 'Push with the pain. Use that pain. Don't waste it. Long ones. Now short ones.'

At 10.30 the top of the baby's head appeared. The midwife tried to pull it out further, but it seemed to be stuck, as if it didn't want to come into the world after all. He was in an agony of frustration and terrified that something would go wrong, the baby would die even before it was born or be damaged by the process. Why, oh why, did it have to be like this, he wondered? Not just for mother and baby, but for father too.

After trying for a while in vain to release the baby's head, the midwife said they would have to do an episiotomy.

When she explained what this was, a wave of panic swept over him. It sounded like an emergency measure and he was sure the baby was in serious trouble. What should be a joyous, natural event was turning into a nightmare! He started to feel an irrational anger, anger with the medical people, with Rania, with himself, with God if there was a God, even with the baby itself …

After some further, nerve-racking delay, a female Asian doctor appeared, gowned in green, spread a surgical drape over Rania's lower half, injected her with a local anaesthetic and picked up what looked like a huge pair of scissors from the trolley. He looked away, felt like running away, rushing out of the hospital as far away as possible, but of course couldn't, was trapped as if in a horrible dream, had to hold the screaming, struggling Rania down on the bed with the aid of a nurse while the doctor cut her.

A minute or so later, the baby suddenly shot out with a brief cry and the midwife plonked it on Rania's belly. It was long, bluish-pink and bloodied, but seemed to be alive and undamaged. Rania smiled weakly at it. He was so drunk with relief, he felt like laughing, but limited himself to what probably looked like a dopey grin. The grisly part of the business wasn't quite over yet though. For one thing, Rania had to be 'sutured', but they'd do that later, they said. No hurry.

The midwife cut the baby's umbilical cord and pegged the end at the baby's navel. She then pulled out the placenta, which looked like a big lump of liver, and deposited it in a bowl that quickly filled with blood. In fact, there seemed to be blood everywhere, including on his own shirt. It looked like a crime scene, he smiled to himself, where somebody had been murdered rather than born. And even funnier, he was the chief suspect ha ha. He thought of saying all this to the midwife and nurses present, but refrained, deciding it probably wasn't the time for facetiousness. They'd probably heard all the jokes before anyway.

By now the midwife had removed the baby to a plastic cot by the side of the bed and was busy sucking the mucus out of its mouth and nose with a pump. He gazed at it with an overwhelming feeling of paternal pride. It looked more like a baby human now, rather than an alien, because its body had turned pink, though its tiny hands were still a bit blue and wrinkly, its eyes had opened and it was blinking, as if surprised at finding itself on this strange new planet called Earth, surrounded by these strange creatures who were apparently called 'humans'.

'You've got a lovely boy,' the midwife commented, as if reading his thoughts. 'He looks in very good nick.'

By way of reply he couldn't help laughing, almost giddy with a mixture of happiness and pride. He didn't know what else to say or do. He was literally speechless. It was a kind of miracle. Or at least magic. And *he* was responsible for it! That was the most amazing thing of all. *He* had created this new life, this new being, and brought it into the world, almost without trying. Without really intending to. He could hardly believe his luck. It was something that at one time he had feared would never happen. And now it had happened. He was a father!

Shortly afterwards, the baby was examined by a paediatrician, weighed and declared OK, to his further relief. Later, another doctor came, an Indian lady, to suture Rania, for which they first put her feet in stirrups and a surgical drape in place. When the doctor explained that she was going to give her two injections of local anaesthetic, Rania, who was childishly scared of needles, started crying again, 'No! No! Please no! I don't want it!' As a result, he and a nurse had to hold her down as before while the doctor, having told her off, proceeded with the operation, during which Rania cried and screamed as if she were giving birth all over again.

The operation took quite a few minutes, because as the doctor explained, the stitches had to be inserted 'in layers', which was a detail he didn't really want to know. Both he and the nurse laughed at Rania, bawling like a baby, as they held her by the arms, but he couldn't help wondering darkly again why something so natural had to be so traumatic, so painful, so stressful, so messy. Whoever designed the process had a very sick sense of humour indeed, he decided, if this was the price you had to pay for a few minutes of pleasure and bringing a new life into the world. Still, he thought, glancing at the new life in the cot beside him, if that was the prize, maybe it was worth all the suffering. He was glad he wasn't a woman though.

'I bet you is glad you is not a woman,' the West Indian nurse joked, reading his mind again.

He left the hospital at 2.30 pm and arrived home at 3. As soon as he went through the front door, he picked up the mail from the mat and to his surprise noticed a letter from Liverpool, immediately recognising her schoolgirlish, unjoined-up, vertical handwriting. He decided not to open it until he had had a nap before going back to the hospital, so left it on the desk in his study. He was too emotionally drained and sleepy to process whatever it contained. He'd open it when he woke up, he decided, collapsing into bed and sinking into a deep, dreamy sleep.

When the alarm woke him three hours later, he had a bath, made himself a cup of tea, went into his study and sat down at the desk. He looked at the envelope lying on the desk without picking it up, wondering why she had written after all these months, wondering what might be in it, wondering whether it would be hostile or friendly, wondering if it might be a letter of apology or even a letter beseeching him to come back to her, all was forgiven. He picked it up with one hand and with his other hand the letter opener.

He turned the envelope over and over in his hand a few times, looking for clues, but there was nothing on the back, on the front only a postmarked postage stamp with the queen's head and his name and address written in royal blue ink. Judging by the thickness and weight of the envelope, there was only one page inside. He started to insert the letter opener into one of the corners, where there was the slightest of gaps, but then stopped, and replaced both letter and opener on the desk. He suddenly realised he didn't want to know what was inside. Whatever it was, good or bad, it didn't matter. It was over.

He unlocked his desk, pulled out a drawer, picked up the envelope, hid it at the bottom of the drawer and relocked the desk. Then he put the key back in its hiding place. Tomorrow, he thought, he'd either hide the letter better or just destroy it – tear it up into tiny pieces and bin it or even burn it in the garden. The love he had felt for her was dead. It seemed like a dream now. But the dream had died. Turned to dust. Roy Orbison was singing 'It's Over' on the bedroom radio next door. That seemed to confirm it. Thank you, Roy.

Yes, it was over.

ABOUT THE AUTHOR

Eugene Vesey was born and brought up in Manchester, where he attended Xaverian College, a Roman Catholic grammar school, until the age of eleven. He continued his education at Roman Catholic seminaries in the English Lake District and English Midlands, where he also studied philosophy and theology. He graduated with an honours degree in English Language and Literature from the University of Manchester and obtained a PGCE (postgraduate certificate in education) from the University of Liverpool. He lives and works in London, where he has taught English as a Foreign Language in colleges for many years. Apart from writing, he enjoys reading, listening to music, studying classical languages, gardening, walking and watching Manchester United. As well as *The Spanish Girl*, he has published four other novels and two volumes of poetry. You can contact Eugene at eugenekvesey@gmail.com or find him on Facebook or his Amazon Author Central page. Eugene is also on Twitter: @VeseyEugene. Over the page you can see some information about Eugene's other books, including some reviews.

GHOSTERS

Ghosters is the prequel to *Opposite Worlds, Italian Girls, Hearts and Crosses* and *The Spanish Girl*. At the age of twelve, Frank Walsh leaves home in Manchester and enters a Roman Catholic seminary in the English Lake District to fulfil his dream of becoming a missionary priest. At twenty-one, having lost his faith, he makes an unsuccessful attempt to commit suicide, leaves the seminary and returns home. With the help of Sally, the girl next door, he slowly manages to recover from depression and starts to feel 'normal' again. After finishing university, he leaves home yet again – and Sally – to live in London. There he tries to escape the ghosts of the past and fulfil his dream of being a writer, while teaching English to foreign students in a private school in Soho. He has a passionate love affair with one of his students, Marina, a vibrant, eighteen-year-old Yugoslav girl. They plan to marry, but a chance meeting with a ghost from the past threatens to destroy this dream too. Yet Frank refuses to be beaten, because he still has one dream left …

'I like it … imaginatively strong … I was riveted … sensitively worked out … intelligently written … powerfully presented … this heart-felt painful re-creation of a central hidden part of our culture.'

Kate Cruise O'Brien, Poolbeg Press Ltd., Dublin

'An impressive and skilfully crafted novel by an author with an equally impressive flair for originality and narrative-driven storytelling, Eugene Vesey's "Ghosters" is an inherently compelling read from beginning to end. Especially and unreservedly recommended for community library Contemporary General Fiction collections.'

Midwest Book Review, Dec. 2018

'A must read for both believers and non-believers! Extremely well written and moves at a pace that keeps you captivated. Crucially, it deals with the disturbing subject of child abuse in the Catholic church in a revealing, but sensitive, way, without pulling any punches, drawing on the author's own first-hand experiences … provides a graphic and disturbing insight into the emotional traumas suffered by both the victims and ironically the perpetrators … an informative and thought-provoking book that could and should be adapted into a television drama.'

John Vesey, Amazon*****

'This novel deals with some very sensitive and difficult issues in a very interesting, serious, intelligent way. It's very well written. It's obviously autobiographical but that in no way invalidates it. The story really carried me along and I couldn't wait to find out whether Frank would be able to turn his life around or not. I won't give the game away by saying whether he does or not! The writing style is unshowy, verging perhaps on plain, but that for me gives the story an extra patina of truth. The story is so engaging that it doesn't need any embellishments of any kind in my view. I'd recommend this book to anyone who is interested in a very good human story, well told, and who is interested in such issues as child abuse, religious indoctrination, love and self-fulfilment. It is a bit slow at the start, but I found it difficult to put down once I got into it.'

Orinoco, Amazon*****

'Wow! Brilliant! Especially if you're Polish and Catholic like me. Well, I should say 'lapsed Catholic'. This story reminded me why I no longer believe. Every Catholic bishop and priest should read it. So should every parent who tries to indoctrinate their children with any strange, supernatural beliefs – in the end it's likely to be counter-productive. I could identify so closely with Frank even though I'm not a man. My own story is almost parallel. When I was reading this book, I felt as if I was looking in a mirror! I actually understand myself better now! That's what good literature should do, isn't it?'

Polish, Anonymous

'An inspiring read, *Ghosters* has a really powerful emotive effect as it charts Frank's life throughout his childhood and as a young adult in a very truthful and honest way … It deals with faith, religion and love and most of all identity. It is an empowering story that allows the reader to connect to Frank, the main character. This is a thoroughly enjoyable read that grips the reader throughout.'

Miss A. M. Kearney, Amazon*****

'Christian romance is a bit misleading perhaps, but this book does deal with the question of religious faith – specifically the Catholic faith and theology – in a very intelligent, dramatic and moving way. More accurately, it deals with the loss of faith. The main drama is about how Frank Walsh manages to recover from his drastic loss of faith, reinvent himself and forge a new life, in effect a new identity. But the story also encompasses other themes, such as child abuse (very topical)] and romantic love both homosexual and heterosexual. I found the story of Frank's progression from despair at losing his faith (and therefore his vocation to the priesthood) to relative happiness as a young, carefree teacher in London to be completely engrossing. The author deals with all these themes very honestly – sometimes pain-fully honestly – so for me this was a riveting read.'

Nena, Amazon*****

'I especially liked the first two chapters. The thoughts Fran had in the train to St. Mary's, about venial and mortal sins – I understand that culture since we, in Spain, are Catholic by tradition. It seemed to me like I had been watching a film of those young lads passing through the gates of St Mary's college. At the end of chapter three it seemed to me the school/castle had more than a couple of ghosts! After reading chapter six, I think how easy it is to manipulate young minds. I like the way the author has introduced the story between Fran and Father Director. It has made me see very clearly how things like that can happen. I am really enjoying it.'

Maria-Angeles Sanchez Soto, Madrid

'I have just finished reading Eugene Vesey's trilogy of novels, *Ghosters*, *Opposite Worlds* and *Italian Girls*, and have been thoroughly moved by their content. The three books are exceptionally well written, as you would expect from a scholar of English, and I would advise any reader with an interest in the problem of clerical abuse and the detritus it leaves behind to get the three.'

Paul Malpas, Boyle, Co. Roscommon, Ireland

'I'm messaging because I just read your novel, *Ghosters*. Read it in 2 days! I wouldn't have done that if the prose had been full of what Amis refers to as 'barked shins' and 'stubbed toes'. What I liked about your writing was the choice to write sincerely, avoiding flamboyance or rhetorical flourishes. It made it a page-turner because it seemed so genuine. You have clearly worked hard on your craft. What resonated with me most was the account of your loss of faith. Altogether, an enjoyable read. Glad you wrote it.'

Alan Berreta 16.12.21

Amazon Average Customer Review *****

OPPOSITE WORLDS

Opposite Worlds is the follow-up to *Ghosters*. It finds Frank alone and lonely in London, having been jilted by his Yugoslav girlfriend, Marina, on their wedding day. On the rebound from this, he has a passionate affair with Kalli, a gorgeous Greek singer and belly-dancer, who is a student in his class at the school in Soho where he teaches English to foreign students. When Kalli leaves him, Frank finds himself alone again. Then one evening, in a folk club in an Irish pub, he hears a young Irish girl singing and falls instantly in love with her. Her name is Mary, he contrives to meet her and Mary falls in love with him. Love leads to marriage – reluctantly at first on Frank's part – but their marriage proves to be a collision of two very different, indeed opposite, worlds …

'Leading on from *Ghosters*, *Opposite Worlds* provides a graphic, courageous and honest account of the damaging effects of institutional abuse – physical, emotional and sexual – which Frank endured during his seminary years. He enables the reader to walk with him as he slowly reveals his hurt hidden soul. The struggles facing Frank adjusting from his years of incarceration in such a repressive regime are similar to cult survivors and service personnel adjusting to civilian life. This is further compounded by the guilt Frank experienced leaving the seminary and in particular his mother's negative reaction and later rejection due to his changed attitude to religion and relationships. In addition, the teachings of the Catholic Faith in terms of its dogmatic negative view of women/sexuality/same sex relationships create further struggles for Frank. The author brings to life the relationships Frank has with some of his students and wife because of his descriptive ability, which enables you to get to know the characters as well as have a deeper sense of his inner turmoil – you can feel his turmoil. Frank's return to the junior seminary with his wife is cathartic for him in the sense he is free from the Ghosters – they no longer control him and his wife has a greater understanding of him. Significantly, in the book Frank recognises the damaging effects of a system that denies normal human affection and contact, which is opposite of the unconditional love essential for human growth and development. Frank expresses guilt about the Director of the junior seminary's suicide because he threatened to expose his paedophile activities, but his action was courageous and prevented the abuse of others. Similarly, he was not responsible for his friend's death, though he feels guilt about this. Whilst we are now supposed to be knowledgeable and more enlightened about the sexual and physical abuse of children, with its damaging consequences, this is not necessarily the case. *Opposite Worlds* provides this enlightenment and knowledge, because Frank's experiences are the testimony of a survivor. It is a book that would be helpful for Social Workers, Mental Health Professionals and Counsellors to read.'

Tony Pritchard, ex-Social Worker and Counsellor

'I have just finished reading Eugene Vesey's trilogy of novels, *Ghosters*, *Opposite Worlds* and *Italian Girls*, and have been thoroughly moved by their content. The three books are exceptionally well written, as you would expect from a scholar of English, and I would advise any reader with an interest in the problem of clerical abuse and the detritus it leaves behind to get the three.'

Paul Malpas, Boyle, Co. Roscommon, Ireland

'Opposite Worlds is an extremely well written book – thoughtful, descriptive and emotive. The journey of exploration and discovery for Frank Walsh enables the reader to identify with him on a deep emotional level. As you read, you feel how Frank is thinking and feeling as if you're in that moment with him. Overall, it's a great read as it explores identity, relationships and belonging. It gives a clear insight into the life of Frank Walsh and touches the reader on a deeper level. A definite recommendation!'

Miss A. M. Kearney, Amazon*****

'I read it with great enjoyment. Couldn't put it down.'

John Barber, Paris

ITALIAN GIRLS

At the end of *Opposite Worlds,* the prequel to *Italian Girls,* Mary, Frank Walsh's wife, has left him, frustrated by both his infidelity and infertility. Unlike Mary, Frank does not believe in marriage, nor does he believe in God any more, though like her he was brought up as a Catholic. He even spent nine years training to be a priest, an experience described in *Ghosters,* the first book in Frank's saga, and an experience that still haunts him. The beginning of *Italian Girls* finds Frank feeling liberated but lonely, as well as guilty about the break-up of his marriage. He tries to find solace in love affairs with his international students at the colleges in London and Dublin where he teaches English. Ironically, though, these affairs make him realise what he really wants is a wife and children after all. He has always had a thing for Italian girls, ever since a boyhood crush on the actress Gina Lollobrigida, so when he falls in love with Cinzia, an Italian student, he thinks he has found the love of his life and the wife of his dreams. But has he? Or will his quest lead him to a different continent entirely?

'Italian Girls is a very well-written, intelligent and techni-cally adept, well-structured novel, just like Ghosters and Opposite Worlds. Eugene Vesey is obviously an excellent writer. He especially expresses the characters' emotions very well. The story takes you on a journey, the journey of Frank Walsh's search for lasting love. It explores themes of love, loss, sex and self-discovery, as well as giving an insight into the world of a college of further education. I found it very moving – in fact, it brought tears to my eyes! I was gripped from the first to the last page. It's a very good read and I really enjoyed it even though it made me cry. What a great writer! He deserves to be much better known. I can't wait for his next novel, which I hope will continue Frank's story.'

Miss A. M. Kearney, Amazon*****

'I have just finished reading Eugene Vesey's trilogy of novels, Ghosters, Opposite Worlds and Italian Girls, and have been thoroughly moved by their content. The three books are exceptionally well written, as you would expect from a scholar of English, and I would advise any reader with an interest in the problem of clerical abuse and the detritus it leaves behind to get the three.'

Paul Malpas, Boyle, Co. Roscommon, Ireland

'I finished your book yesterday and let me tell you I have enjoyed it very much, especially the second half of the book getting more and more involved with Frank, alias "The au pairs' delight". Well, well, well, I didn't expect Frank to be such a "Casanova" and in some passages I even felt quite embarrassed (I couldn't help it). But you can feel very proud of your novel!!! It's well written, easy to read and interesting. I had to look up the dictionary several times, but consider-ing that it's not my mother tongue, that is "Pecata Minuta". All my respect to you as a writer, because you had all my respect as a teacher already.'

Olga Miguel Menoyo, Bilbao

HEARTS AND CROSSES

Hearts and Crosses continues the story of Frank Walsh as recounted in *Ghosters*, *Opposite Worlds* and *Italian Girls*. Frank is a young teacher of English to foreign students. While teaching on a summer school in Dublin, he falls in love with one of his students, a French girl called Danielle, and they embark on a passionate affair. Frank lives in London with Rania, a Guyanese girl who was also one of his students in the college where he teaches. They are married, but only in Muslim rites, as she is from a Muslim family. Frank is not religious, though he was once training to be a Catholic missionary priest, and agreed to this only out of love for Rania, just as he agreed to marry his first wife, Mary, in a Catholic wedding ceremony. Now though, he realises it was a big mistake, because Rania is not the girl he thought she was and their relationship is strained to breaking point. He sees Danielle as his escape until he meets Cinzia, his Italian ex, again and the flame is rekindled. He can't quite bring himself to leave Rania and can't decide between Danielle and Cinzia. Then one morning a letter arrives from France, which solves his dilemma …

'Excellent Read – I Cross My Heart:
This is the first of Eugene's novels that I have read so far. Let me tell you, it did not disappoint. Part romance, part literary fiction, part observational comedy, the story is set in the mid-1980s and focuses on Frank Walsh, a teacher of English as a Foreign Language (EFL). There are essentially

three women in Frank's life, and the story is ultimately about which of these three women, who all love Frank, he will choose.

The story takes place across London, Dublin and Paris. The characters are wonderfully drawn and really come to life on the page, being believable, realistic human beings.

The mid-Eighties were an interesting time in British history, with Thatcherism at its peak, and perhaps a more romantic era, before the internet and mobile phones, where people had to communicate by the written letter and rely on the postal service.

Eugene is an excellent writer with an authentic voice. Clearly, he is not shy of several interesting life experiences himself, and this really comes through in his writing.

Through Frank's analysis of the students he teaches, we as the reader are treated to an education in English grammar ourselves. I particularly enjoyed the acute observations of the most common faux-pas the French make when using English.

Whilst being an easy-to-read novel, with a story and plot that zips along with humour and wit, there are also serious moments in Frank's sometimes torrid relationships that make us dwell on the human condition. The way in which Frank expresses incredulity when dealing with difficult situations highlights the fact that we use humour to deal with things that we fear, or do not understand.

Although the novel is not the first in the Frank Walsh series, it provides the first-time reader with an interesting and provocative introduction to his character, and once you reach the end of Hearts and Crosses, you do feel compelled to want to read Eugene's other novels to find out more about Frank's earlier life.

As a once EFL teacher myself, to students in South Korea, and having had many foreign friends at university, I can relate to and even find some semblance of nostalgia in Eugene's story.

This story is real. It's about real life, about real people. It's gritty, it's witty, and it digests like an Irish coffee, leaving you with a feeling of warmth. Superb.'

Mr M. L. Hollin, Amazon, *****

'Good romance novel with excellent cultural characterisations:

There is a lot to like in this romance novel which is also sprinkled with humorous aspects which reflect the nuances of people from different cultures.

When a foreign language teacher falls in love with three very different women, he is faced with the dilemma of having to choose between them. Whom will he choose?

The characterisation is excellent, and the story takes us from England to Ireland and to France. You can really identify with the real-life characters and their experiences.

Recommended!'

Worldly Traveller, Amazon, *****

'A Beautiful Love Story.

This book is a great book to read, it's exciting and descriptive and holds your attention meaning you never want to leave it down.'

Geraldine McLoughlin, Amazon, *****

VENICE AND OTHER POEMS

Venice and Other Poems is Eugene's first book of poetry. It includes poems written when he was a teenager to poems written recently. In other words, it covers a span of nearly fifty years, from his schooldays in the sixties to 2014. However, the poems are in alphabetical not chronological order. Each poem expresses a state of mind or emotion at the time, an observation of a scene or a reflection upon some experience. So in a sense the poems are autobiographical, though not necessarily an exact mirror of the author's life – there may be some 'poetic licence' here and there. Perhaps it would be better to describe each poem as a prism. As well as reflecting his own life-experience though, the author hopes that in at least some of these poems readers may catch a glimpse of their own lives, past, present or even future.

'This is a very appealing collection of poems. They are well constructed with lots of descriptive, emotive language. The writer explores deep subjects such as Love, Identity and Loss. I would recommend this collection as it has a lovely selection of poems that touch you with many emotions.'

Miss A. M. Kearney, Amazon

THIRTY-NINE POEMS

Thirty-Nine Poems is Eugene's second book of poetry after *Venice and Other Poems*, which he published in 2011. Unlike the poems in that collection though, it contains mostly poems written in more recent years. As in that collection, the poems are in simple alphabetical order rather than chronological order. Like the poems in that collection, each poem expresses a state of mind or emotion, an observation of a scene or a reflection on some experience. So these poems also are autobiographical, without necessarily being an exact mirror of the author's own life. And he still hopes that, as with the poems in his first collection, in some of them at least readers may catch glimpses of their own lives, past, present or future.

'Thank you so much for your "Thirty-nine Poems". I immediately read the first one and I have cried … cried with a hope. Then I have just read the back cover and I've found it very interesting and emotional. I will read it with much interest after I have cried for some things I need to cry for. Perhaps doing it liberates me a bit from my sorrow.'

Maria-Angeles Sanchez Soto, Madrid

*All Eugene's books are available from
Amazon and other major online retailers
such as Foyles and Waterstones.*

Eugene is on Facebook
and you can contact Eugene at
eugenekvesey@gmail.com
or on Twitter
@VeseyEugene